Killing the Unicorn

LIZELLA PRESCOTT

TO MY LOVELY READERS ON MEDIUM

This novel started as a serial on my Medium blog. Thank you to everyone who read it, poked it, prodded it, and encouraged me to turn it into a book. I deeply appreciate your getting to know the characters, even (especially?) when they misbehaved.

Extra special thanks to A. Maguire for her most excellent editorial insights and Danna Colman for buffing the rough edges (and spiky typos) from the final copy.

CONTENTS

ACKNOWLEDGMENTS

Editor : Danna Colman
Photography: Zohre Nemati via Unsplash

1 FAKE IT UNTIL YOU FEEL IT

I smelled his musky aftershave before I felt his embrace. His arms wrapped around me, and his lips found the soft, tender skin on my neck. Out of habit, I leaned into his hard, sculpted chest. At six-feet and change, he was nearly a foot taller than me. Once upon a time, his muscular frame had made me hot and wet with liquid joy.

"The kids are finally asleep," he rumbled, nuzzling my ear. "Let's have some grown-up time." His hands roamed from my bulky waist to my overstuffed thighs.

I closed my eyes and pictured my husband Mann just a few weeks past his thirty-ninth birthday. He might have been a movie star or a model if he hadn't fallen for technology first. His hair was a deep chestnut, subtly salted with gray. His eyes were a warm, thoughtful brown. His nose, broken in a lacrosse accident many years ago, was a few endearing millimeters away from perfection.

He was the father of my adorable, two-year-old twins, and he still wanted me, with all my lumps and flaws. I should have melted into him. I should have burned with longing. I should have desperately wanted to shuck off my clothes, to be vulnerable and intimate and *seen*.

But I felt nothing but a bone-deep exhaustion, lightly tinged with irritation. I had just finished putting our two cherubs to bed after a grueling day of attachment parenting. All I wanted was to savor the quiet of the house. Besides, sex in its most traditional form was painful for me, a side effect of an unspeakably difficult pregnancy.

"C'mon, honey," he whispered, pressing himself into me. "We don't have to do anything that will hurt. I just want to be close to you. It's been so long."

He was right. It had been a long time, longer than I care to say. I decided I had to try. I had been a half-assed sort of wife since the girls were born, and he deserved more. *We* deserved more. I half-moaned, half-sighed as his hands found my round, flaccid belly. I would fake it until I felt it, or something like that.

But the shock of his hungry hands slipping under my bra band made me cringe. I imagined how my droopy, blue-veined breasts and crenelated belly would look in the bright, unforgiving light of our white-walled living space. And I flinched.

A less attentive man wouldn't have noticed. A more selfish man wouldn't have cared. But Mann, exquisitely attuned to my needs, stopped. He put his hands on my shoulders and turned me around, so I was gazing into his kind, brown eyes. He pressed his lips gently against mine.

"I'm sorry. You must be exhausted. The girls were wild today, and I had to take that stupid investor call. Let's order some sushi and open a bottle of something. Would you like that?"

I smiled and nodded guiltily. I didn't deserve a husband like him. I wasn't nearly grateful enough.

***

The plastic takeout containers and half-empty bottle of cabernet on the coffee table told the story of a peaceful evening. I rested in the crook of Mann's arm while we watched a reality show about pudgy bankers trying to survive in the Australian Outback. Of course, if they got into trouble, their guardian-angel producers were waiting in the wings.

As the credits rolled, Mann kissed me goodnight. "I'm going up to my office and read a few startup proposals. I have a huge, ridiculous backlog."

I smiled. Despite his discreet, carefully invested billion or so dollars, Mann was a disciplined worker. He drove himself as hard as he drove his employees. Harder even. I was the slacker in our relationship, drifting aimlessly in a job I despised.

"Don't work too hard," I said, kissing him back. "I love you."

He smiled. I scanned his face for signs of disappointment that we had spent the evening on the couch and not in the bed. All I saw—all I wanted to see—was his open, guileless face.

"Love you, too. Get some sleep."

As soon as Mann disappeared up the stairs, I poured myself another glass of wine. I pressed a few buttons to bring up our home entertainment network and conjured the video feed from our baby monitor. My two daughters, Briar and Rose, one light and one dark, curled in their cribs like quotation marks. Their faces were calm, their breathing even.

I exhaled a long sigh of maternal relief, minimized my children, and switched to a biker drama. It was stupid and soapy, but it reminded me of the feral, jagged-edged woman I used to be. I remembered one of the last times I rode my old bike—a light vintage Harley I named Lucy—down route 1.

It was a beautiful weekend ride that cleaved open my soul. My fears dissolved in the roar of the road. Flying around the curves and looking into the endless ocean, I believed I was free. In my mind, I was leaving my tedious job, my tiny apartment, and my thrillingly awful boyfriend Karl. It was a glorious illusion until I heard a loud hiss, and my bike sputtered and lost power.

I pulled off the road and onto the shoulder, muttering curses. It had to be a flat. I removed my helmet and fished my toolkit from the saddlebag. I lay the bike gently on the ground and inspected the tires. The culprit was obvious. A rusty screw poked from the rear tire, accompanied by the soft whistle of leaking air.

Satisfied I had found the problem, I paused to savor the moment. I looked over the guard rail, towards a rocky bluff that melted into clear blue water. The air was fresh and salty. A light breeze ruffled my hair. I felt like floating. The braying honk of a pickup truck brought me back to Earth and my quotidian task.

I fashioned a tire plug with a small knife. It took me a few tries, but I wedged the plug into the space the nail used to be. The telltale whistling stopped. I was about to retrieve my collapsible pump, the gadget Karl was always telling me was useless weight, when a red car pulled in behind me.

Its tires scraped against the sandy asphalt, but the engine was silent. I know now it was a Tesla, one of the new breed of quiet, electric cars. A man got of the car. He was tall, model-handsome, and dressed like a haute geek in a blue button-down and khakis.

"Hello there," he said, struggling to speak over the traffic. "Do you need some help?"

***

I smiled at this pretty, clean cut man. Although he was the polar opposite of the rangy, scruffy types I thought of as my type, something about him drew me. His posture was casual but confident. Even from a distance I could tell he didn't have the soft body and slumped posture of an office drone.

"Nope," I said, holding up my pump. "Thanks, but I've got it covered."

The man blinked, as if he couldn't believe a woman could cope with a simple flat tire. "Are you sure? I'd hate to leave you stranded. It would haunt me for the rest of my days."

I laughed at the formal and yet overdramatic way he spoke. Every syllable was clearly enunciated. "Yeah," I replied, letting my voice lapse into an inland drawl. "It's just a flat. No big deal."

I knelt beside my hog and filled the tire while my heart flopped and revved. I reminded myself I had a boyfriend waiting for me at home, no doubt sprawled on my double bed, smoking something or other. Karl was kind of an asshole. And maybe he drank a little too much and our fights got a little too violent. But he was unpredictable and exciting. He distracted me from the future we didn't have. He tugged on the worst and most familiar parts of my soul.

I waited for the Tesla and its strangely attractive owner to slip away. But they didn't. When I finished testing the tire, he was still there. Smiling like the sun. "It's nice to meet you," he said. "I'm Mann Gottlieb." He paused as if I was supposed to recognize his name. When I gave him a blank look, he shrugged and added, "You know, I've always wanted to date a woman who could fix a flat."

I grinned. "And I've always wanted to date a huge nerd." It was my turn to pause. I have a self-destructive streak, nurtured since birth, and it

4

told me Mann was too good to be true. 'Go home to Karl,' it whispered. 'That's where you belong.' I winked at Mann and hauled my bike off the ground.

"But I'm not going to," I said. "I have a boyfriend." I started my Harley and drove away, both disappointed that I would probably never see Mann again and weirdly excited that I had rejected him. That I had the upper hand.

I smiled at the memory and poured myself a little more wine and told myself I had changed. The bikers onscreen had their sordid little affairs and love triangles. But that wasn't me anymore. I was a mom. A good, normal person. I pressed another button so my sleeping daughters and the biker drama appeared side by side.

Present and past. Good and bad. I closed my eyes for a moment. I told myself I should go upstairs, so I would be in bed, keeping it warm for Mann. But I didn't. I remained on the couch and fell into a deep and selfish sleep.

***

My eyes were sticky and hard to open when I heard the babble of my children and the subtle sounds of someone cleaning quietly, so he wouldn't wake me up. I realized I was lying on my side, on a smoother than usual surface.

Oh no, I had passed out on the couch.

Rose, my explorer, hauled herself onto me as if I were an especially intriguing mountaintop. "Mommy, get up! Get up!"

Briar put her hands on my face as I blinked the world into existence. "Mommy feel OK?" she queried, her golden head cocked to the side.

They were adorable, the apogee of my existence, and yet I wanted to steal another five minutes of sleep. I yawned and stretched, careful not to unbalance Rose. "Let Mommy sleep another minute," I sighed, allowing my eyes to flutter close.

"No!" howled Rose in protest. "Mommy get up now! Now!"

I could feel Rose reaching her hand into my tangled nest of hair when, suddenly, her weight was gone. I opened my eyes, and Mann was holding our squirming child in his arms.

"Let Mommy rest, Rosie," he said, carrying her into the kitchen and tempting her with a snack.

Briar stayed by my side, stroking my hair and looking concerned. "Mommy get up?" she asked quietly. "Please?"

I levered myself into a sitting position and hugged my small, fearful girl. Rose romped around the kitchen, opening and closing cabinet doors under her father's watchful eye. I had lingered in sleep for too long.

I picked up Briar and padded into the kitchen. Rose detached from her collection of pots and threw her arms around my knees. Mann threw his arms around me, and we spent a blissful moment, suspended in loving togetherness. Rose was the first to squirm away. Mann, ever the doting father, followed her.

I gently placed Briar on the floor. "Who wants pancakes?" I asked in what I hoped was a suitably cheerful voice.

"Me! Me me me me me!" chirped the girls.

Mann stroked my arm. His face creased with concern. "Are you sure? I could make breakfast."

I remembered the last time Mann tried to cook and the charred, tragic remnants of a grass-fed steak. "Oh yes," I said, smiling wryly as he scooped up the children.

As I mixed the pancake batter, I thought about my father, who never once tried to cook, and my mother's elaborate culinary offerings, all calculated to impress him. I was so lucky to have Mann, who would try anything, do anything, to make me happy.

Somehow after we had met on the road, he found me. He texted exactly one day later.

I still want to date a woman who can fix a flat.

I've never been the cheating type. But he caught me at a weak moment. Karl and I had fought the night before. We got too drunk and shared too much. We drifted into a confused, inchoate violence. Me reaching for him. Him shrugging me off. Me clutching at his chest. Him pushing me onto the floor, kicking at my thighs. Me finally staying down.

The next morning, I was tender all over. I had resolved to leave, but I wasn't sure how. Mann's text was a lifeline. Karl was still snoring when I texted back:

I still want to date a massive geek.

***

I watched Briar and Rose eat their blueberry pancakes slathered in organic syrup. Mann drank a revolting concoction of coffee, clarified butter, and vitamin supplements—he believed food was purely fuel—and I downed a low-fat protein shake.

My girls were happy and imaginative. Rose pretended to be a blueberry pirate, and Briar was a fairy, turning rocks into blue fruit. While Rose was fiery and Briar was cautious, neither one trembled with fear. I was proud that both girls expected safety and kindness from their world. I was thrilled that they might someday look back upon their childhood with fond memories instead of anger and fear.

My childhood was the opposite of what I want for my girls. My father was a wrathful, Old Testament god; my mother and I were his reluctant acolytes. Even now, I remember cowering in my room, listening for sounds of my father stomping through his domain, looking for someone to sop up his rage.

He was just a computer hardware salesman with an anger problem, frustrated by the limits of his life. But, to my younger self, he was the ultimate judge. And he always found me wanting.

"Helen, is that pancake burning?"

I snapped out of my trance and noticed the blackening disk on the griddle. Yes, it was starting to hiss and smoke. "Sorry," I said, transferring the crispy mess to the sink.

The girls giggled. Mann hugged me and kissed my mouth. "Don't worry about it. I'm sure I would have burned all of them."

I brushed Mann's cheek with my lips and poured another cup of batter onto the griddle. He was the opposite of my father. An angel. A benevolent spirit. I resolved to be more grateful for him, my children, and my calm, peaceful life.

***

Arranging an outing to the park with two two-year-olds was as fraught as planning a military invasion. I gathered snacks, toys, pacifiers, diapers, extra clothes and special plastic bags for diaper disposal. Mann chased the girls and wrestled them into shirts, pants, socks, and shoes. Together we strapped them into car seats.

As we closed the rear doors to my trusty white minivan, Mann and I shared a look. It was a wistful thing, a nostalgia for the silence we used to share. A wry smile crept across his face. I smiled back and then looked away. I cursed myself for not holding his gaze a few moments longer.

I drove us to the park while Mann kept up a steady patter with the twins. My hands were sweaty. My heart fluttered in my chest like a sick bird. I was sure something terrible was going to happen. Maybe I would have a stroke and collapse behind the wheel. Maybe a truck, driven by an aging alcoholic, would jump lanes, and kill us all.

I took long, slow breaths, trying to focus on the traffic and not on my telltale heart. I've had occasional panicky episodes since I gave birth to my girls. I'm not sure if the cause was the sudden realization of my children's utter vulnerability or plain old hormones. Either way, I was glad that Mann was here.

He gently squeezed my arm. "I know you, Helen," he murmured. "You're stronger than this You're better than this."

As I brought myself back under control, he pointed out cars for Briar and made fart noises for Rose. His posture was relaxed and his smile effortless. He loved his children in an artless way I couldn't, despite my best efforts, replicate.

Yes, I envied him even as I loved him. He gave our girls emotional as well as financial stability. He was the embodiment of the secure attachment style: a man who loved and accepted love as if it were water. He was the fun one and the stable one. I was the mercurial one, at once anxious and avoidant. I enforced bedtimes and evening routines.

When we arrived at the park, the girls cheered, and I wiped the sweat from my hands. As I freed my children from their car seat prisons, my eyes kept drifting to the dent on the door. It was a long depression with scrape lines like claw marks. Briar followed my eyes with concern. "Car have an owie?"

I kissed the top of her head, and a disloyal thought flew through my brain. Mann and I kept our finances rigorously segregated. We each spent our money in separate domains. I took care of the children and their daycare, my minivan, and all our meals. Mann paid for everything else. And yet, because everything in Palo Alto was insanely expensive, I was too broke to fix the damned dent. Mann literally had millions at his disposal. Why couldn't he help? Why couldn't he see that I needed his help?

"Mommy!" yelled Rose, pulling my hand as I shrugged the diaper bag over my shoulder. I scooped up Briar with the other arm, and we all converged upon Mann, who greeted us with a grin.

I shook my head, willing my ungrateful thoughts to float away. No relationship was perfect. I certainly wasn't perfect. Why should I expect Mann to be perfect? I watched him lift Rose on his shoulders, and the hard knot in my head softened. He loved us. I just needed to let him.

LIZELLA PRESCOTT

2 YOU SHOULD SEE A PSYCHIATRIST

I sat in an undersized hospital gown at the edge of an exam table, feeling like a fat, unhealthy loser. Dr. Marla Yu, my gynecologist, read my chart with a small frown on her exquisite face.

"Helen, I'm concerned about you," she said in her brusque, tough-loving voice. "You've gained fifteen pounds since your last appointment. Your blood pressure is higher than ever. And you wrote on the intake form that you're still having panic attacks. Is that true?"

I nodded, feeling the shame course through my veins. I knew I was overweight. I had never quite lost the baby weight that had piled on during the last few months of my nightmarish pregnancy. Even the meds I was taking for my blood pressure and panic attacks—two beta blockers, an ACE inhibitor, a diuretic, and Xanax—seemed to pack on the weight.

Dr. Yu sighed. She was a brilliant doctor as well as distressingly lovely, with a tiny waist and swan-like neck. I was sure she was weary of lumpy, frumpy women and their excuses. I remained silent, giving her nothing new to judge.

"Helen, I'm not going to sugar coat it. The preeclampsia you had with your twins is a risk factor for high blood pressure and heart disease. Based on your readings today, you have second stage hypertension. Plus, you're gaining weight and apparently under a lot of stress. You're a ticking bomb."

I shrugged. She wasn't telling me anything I hadn't already suspected. Since my near-death experience during the twins' delivery, I was certain my life was fragile and likely to fray. Dr. Yu clicked her tongue and graced me with an intense, angry stare.

"Helen, you need to take me seriously. You have two young children. I don't want anything to happen to you. Are you hearing me?"

"Yes, doctor," I said in a sulky voice.

"You need to start eating better and commit to losing weight. I'd also like you to see a cardiologist and a psychiatrist. Who knows, you might have some lingering PTSD from the twins' delivery. I'm going to renew your prescriptions and email you a list of referrals."

"Uh huh," I said, eager to get dressed and leave. I respected her. She had saved my life and my children's lives. But I needed to get away. I could not listen to one more minute of her well-meaning judgment.

"And Helen?"

"Yes?"

"Start taking care of yourself, and that's an order. Next time, I want to see a lot less of you."

***

The parking lot outside Dr. Yu's office was painfully bright. I squinted as I hurried to my van, certain the sunlight was exposing every last bulge and ripple in my slightly-too-tight pants. I scowled at the dented door and climbed inside. My heart was revving. Dr. Yu's words echoed through my head.

Overweight

Second stage hypertension

Ticking bomb

Glare was shining from the rear bumper of a sleek Porsche. I looked away, closed my eyes, and fell into the past. Its hungry, sharp-toothed mouth swallowed me up. I imagined myself in the hospital, my veins filling with magnesium sulfate, my frog-pale legs resting in stirrups.

My head felt huge and hot, like an overfilled balloon straining to float away. My thoughts were sluggish and repetitive. *Am I going to die? Will my babies be OK? How will Mann raise the girls alone?*

Mann sat silently with me the entire time. He was too honest to tell me everything was going to be OK. I wouldn't have believed him if he had. But his presence was comforting. He was a quiet oasis in a cacophony of beeping medical devices, barked commands, and harsh whispers.

Dr. Yu, perhaps frustrated by the severity of my condition, would periodically scowl at my vitals and tell me to "calm down." My vision was browning out around the edges when someone yelled, "They're crashing!" The oxygen mask clamped down on my face.

No, not again.

I took quick, sharp breaths to blow the panic away. My hands shook and perspiration dripped down my neck. My lips were numb. I could not imagine facing my supervisor, a hard-edged twentysomething, at WorldFeed. And yet I knew I should pull myself together and drive to work. My mother had been so frightened of poverty that she endured my father's casual violence rather than leave. She preferred a daily beating to the daily grind. I was not going to be like her. I was not.

I started the van and began driving with every intention of driving to the office. But I didn't. The entrance to the freeway slid by in a bright, blue-skied blur. Instead, I drove to the tidy pink bungalow that was my children's in-home daycare. The white trim around the windows made me think of icing, sticky and sweet. I suppose that's why my daughters called it the cake house.

As I plodded up the walkway, Poppy, the babysitter, opened the door and waved at me. She was Bay Area beautiful in plain clothes that accentuated her Snow White coloring and slender build. Her face was fresh, but her eyes, camouflaged behind chunky frames, looked tired.

Along with her day care business, she ran some sort of education-centered startup on the side. She had already pitched her idea to Mann several times; he said it was intriguing but underdeveloped. He also jokingly called her one of his groupies, but I wasn't fazed. All she wanted from my husband was his venture capital.

"Hi Helen. Picking up the girls early?"

"Yes," I said, smiling. "I'm going to skip work and take them to the library. It's sort of naughty and wholesome at the same time."

Poppy frowned. "You should probably text Mann. He said he'd come by after work to look at my new business plan and pick up the kids."

I sighed inwardly. Mann had pulled strings to get me the job at WorldFeed, and he wouldn't like me skipping out. I knew he would be unhappy with me, but I couldn't—wouldn't—change my mind.

"Yes, I'll let him know," I said fake-smiling.

Poppy flashed me a harried half grin. "Let me get your girls."

As I waited, I let everything go. My appointment with Dr. Yu. The mediocrity of my career. My endless guilt about not doing enough, being enough, for Mann. I slipped on the mantle of motherhood like it was a comfortable sweatshirt and greeted my girls with a true, genuine smile.

I sent my husband a guilty, emoji-laden text.

Ditching work and taking the girls with me. No need to pick them up. CU 2nite for dinner.

***

The sign for Izy's Ice Cream was bright and shiny. Both of my girls waved at it with manic glee. A closer inspection revealed the words "homemade" and "organic," a sop to overindulgent parents like me.

Mann would have passed this gaudy purveyor of fat and sugar without a second glance. He would have distracted the girls with a funny song or a silly face. He would have brought them home ravenous and primed to devour their vegetables.

Not me. I had much less resistance to my daughters' innocent wiles. I wondered if it was some kind of character flaw. I didn't have Mann's natural ease with our daughters, so I overcompensated for my awkwardness with toys and treats.

We paused outside the ice cream shop, watching people line up at the counter and walk away with brightly colored cups and cones. The girls scented their sugary prey and squeezed my hands. "Ice ice, please please," they chirped.

I considered resisting for no more than a nanosecond.

"Would you like some ice cream?" I asked.

The girls cheered and lisped, and we all tumbled into the shop. Rose put her hands on the glass counter housing more than forty different colorful flavors, while Briar pointed shyly at the broad, tattooed woman handing out samples. I enjoyed the girls' happiness. A crackle of naughty excitement was followed by a twinge of guilt. It was all too familiar.

Mann and I started dating when I was still with Karl, the last of several boyfriends who tore off their masks to reveal my father. After Karl and I had our epic fight, I didn't do the hard thing, the right thing, and leave him. Instead, I embraced sneaking around. Of course, I didn't fool Mann for even a second.

Karl and I are just roommates. It's over except for the Facebook status update.

Oh Helen, I know you're still with him. And I don't care. When you're ready, you'll leave him and come to me.

Mann was so confident in himself—and in us—that he actually didn't care I was with another man. He never talked about Karl or asked about him. The most he ever did was stroke the skin around my fading bruises and sadly shake his head. I should have ditched Karl and never looked back. Instead, I stuck around for the petty revenge.

I took money from his bank account and then put it back in. I hid the remote control. I watered down his expensive alcohols. I stopped cleaning, cooking, and shopping. And, through it all, I watched him struggle and fume and explode with a childish sort of glee. I didn't need Karl anymore, I was free, but I was going to make him suffer.

"Green one? Green one?"

"Choc'late cone?"

I shook my head and returned to my girls, who had made their selections: a cup of lime sherbet for Rose and a traditional chocolate sugar cone for Briar. I gathered paper napkins and plastic spoons. As I helped the girls spoon ice cream into their greedy mouths, I told myself I was no longer the same woman who delighted in secret, passive revenge.

And yet there I was, sharing gooey desserts with my girls when I should have been at my desk. I knew I was doing wrong. I couldn't stop smiling.

As I wiped Briar's messy, softly giggling mouth, it occurred to me that I wasn't nearly as evolved as I wanted to be.

***

The girls tore into the house high on sugar. Mann was waiting at our dining room table. He gathered their supple, squealing forms into his arms and corralled them into their high chairs. On their trays sat perfectly balanced little meals of roast turkey, sweet potatoes, a green salad, and sliced pears. Their sippy cups were filled with water.

Yes, my wonderful husband had made my children dinner while I was avoiding the perfectly respectable job he had found for me. Guilt crashed over me like an icy wave. He really was the better person in our relationship by far.

"Thank you," I said quietly. "Those girls don't know how lucky they are."

He smiled wryly. "You took them for ice cream, didn't you?"

I nodded sheepishly. "But they're still eating dinner."

Rose, despite her belly full of sherbet, devoured her sweet potatoes. Briar, as always, tore her turkey into small pieces and daintily picked at her food. It was actually an impressive display, considering the amount of ice cream they had stuffed into their flexible little bellies.

I joined Mann at the table, which, except for an extra plate for fruit for the girls, was empty. Without food, its glossy, white surface looked sterile. I supposed I should begin preparing some sort of dinner for me and Mann. I wasn't then, nor have I ever been, an enthusiastic cook.

"Would you like me to warm up some leftovers? Or call in takeout?" I asked.

Mann shook his head. "You didn't go back to work today. Your boss called me. She was concerned. She's wondering if you're OK. So am I," he said quietly. "You're not overdoing the Xanax, are you?"

"No," I snapped. "I didn't overdo the Xanax. I just had a doctor's appointment in the afternoon. It was stressful." I didn't elaborate. I had no interest in talking about Dr. Yu's medical opinions. Just thinking about the exam made my heart quiver and jump.

He frowned. "You told me your mother stayed with your father for his money, so she wouldn't have to work. Could you be repeating this pattern subconsciously?"

I shook my head. "No, that's not exactly right. My mother stayed with my father because she didn't want to be poor. And she didn't want me to be poor."

"Listen, Helen. I love you. Deeply. And I don't want our relationship to be transactional. I want you to have your own money and your own career. I want us to be equal partners."

I barely stifled a snort. "Equal partners? You have a billion dollars, so much money I can't even conceptualize it. I earn sixty thousand dollars a year, which would be plenty if we didn't live in Silicon Valley. But we do, so almost all of my income is going to Poppy and Whole Foods. I don't even have enough money to fix the dent in my van."

Mann sighed. "How many times do I have to tell you? If you need money for something, all you have to do is ask."

I sighed, too. This was not a new fight. We had gone round and round on this issue more times than I could remember. "I don't want to ask you for money. I want us to share our money. All our money."

Mann looked desolate. His brown eyes took on a gray cast. His handsome features settled into a neutral mask. "Would you even be with me if I wasn't successful? Am I just a bank account and an investment portfolio to you? You don't ever want me to touch you…"

I opened my mouth to answer when the doorbell rang. "Are you expecting anyone?" I asked.

"It's Poppy. She's going to watch the kids while we go out to dinner. It was supposed to be a fun surprise."

***

When we arrived at the restaurant, the first thing I did was to order a bottle of wine. The second was to excuse myself to the Ladies room where I popped a single, holy Xanax. Mann vaguely disapproved of all drugs beyond Scotch and fine wine. He thought they were for the weak. But I wasn't as strong as Mann, no matter what he thought. I needed the extra help, especially when we were fighting.

After I swallowed the pill, I checked myself in the bathroom mirror. I was ten years and thirty pounds away from the woman I was when Mann and I met. My hair was dull and thin. My face was round and creased. Pregnancy and motherhood had ravaged me. Somehow, fatherhood had barely grazed Mann.

I frowned at my weary reflection. Dinner in the company of another adult was a rare luxury. When eating with my girls, I focused on getting precious bites into their tiny mouths and avoiding the waste that Mann hated so much. Probably half my daily caloric intake came from bread crusts and half eaten cheese sticks.

I forced my lips into a smile. I wished Mann and I hadn't been fighting. I almost-but-not-quite wished I had driven back to work after my doctor's appointment. But this dinner was an opportunity for us to relax and reconnect, and I resolved not to spoil it.

I returned to our table mellow from the Xanax and my tenuous resolution. I kissed Mann's cheek before I sat down. His face was nervous, as if he didn't trust my affection. I worried that he was going to be cold and aloof all night. I shouldn't have. He held my hand and asked if he could order for me.

"I love you," I said. "That's all that matters. I don't want to fight."

Mann's face relaxed. "Me neither. And I want to apologize. I haven't been fair to you. I have been expecting you to meet all my needs and all our children's needs, and that's just not reasonable."

I shrugged. "I shouldn't have skipped work today. And I want us to be intimate again. Really, I do. I need to get in shape. Be more focused. Really sort myself out."

Mann shook his head. "Helen, I want you to do all those things, too. But I want you to do them for yourself, not for me. I don't want you to feel pressured."

"Maybe I need some pressure."

"No, you need to be yourself. And I haven't been letting you do that."

I shook my head. I didn't know what Mann was getting at, but it sounded suspiciously like a prelude to a breakup. *It's not you, it's me. I'm just not good for you.* I was about to ask a dangerous question when the waitress, an immaculate, vaguely young woman, delivered our salads. We attacked our greens, and our conversation faded away. I was, for the moment, relieved.

All too soon, the young—she was definitely young—waitress retrieved our oily plates, and Mann spoke again. "Did you know Micah and Jessie have an open marriage?" he whispered in a low, conspiratorial voice.

"What?" I exhaled, thankful he wasn't going to keep poking at our relationship. "Your CFO is poly? When did he tell you?" It wasn't quite as shocking as my reaction suggested. We lived in a pocket of Silicon Valley where polyamory is almost as common as giving up meat.

"When we got drinks after work last week. He said it saved their marriage. They're really communicating for the first time in years."

I whistled. I hadn't known Micah and Jessie's marriage had needed saving. In our small, insular circle, they were lifestyle icons. Poster children for gilded coupledom. Their Instagram feed was full of mannerly children, rugged triathlons, enriching vacations, and enviably flat abs. I was friends with both of them but hid their feed. It made me painfully aware of my loose belly and near-feral toddlers.

"Good for them," I said, coloring my voice with a heartiness I did not feel. What I really felt was a squirmy sensation in my stomach, a physical prescience.

Mann kissed my hand, his lips grazing the knuckles. "Is that something you would consider?"

My gut spasmed. I forgot to breathe. "What?" I squeaked. "An open marriage?"

He nodded and pressed his lips against mine for the first time in months. "Yes."

I looked at his hopeful, wary face. He was my husband. My best friend. The father of my children. Like the captain of a wind-battered ship, he had seen me through ten weeks of strict bedrest. He fed me, washed me, and changed my bedpan (oh, the shame!). After my C-section, he cleaned my incision and shuttled babies to and from my swollen, aching breasts. He stood by me when my libido dwindled while my waistline remained stubbornly the same.

If any man deserved a fulfilling sex life, he did. But did I have the courage to let him find it with someone else? Was I capable of allowing him to enjoy someone else without finding a way to make him pay?

I wasn't sure. When I stubbornly clung to Karl, Mann never asked me to give him up. He loved me without condition or reservation. Could I do the same without making him pay? "Why?" I asked, stalling for time.

He sighed. "I've been pushing you to be everything to me. Sex partner. Lover. Co-parent. Roommate. Confidant. Best friend. Everything, really. And I was serious when I said it wasn't fair."

I nodded, then frowned. "And you think the answer is sleeping with other women?"

"Y-y-yes," said Mann, nearly choking on his wine. "I mean, sort of. You're clearly not feeling very sexual right now. And I hate pestering you for sex and then resenting you for saying no.

"Traditional monogamy says it has to be that way. But what if I could get my needs for sex met elsewhere? Wouldn't we both be happier? Wouldn't it take a huge weight off our marriage?"

I sighed. I had to agree that his logic was sound. And yet my emotions were anything but logical. "I'll think about it," I said. And I did. Even as Mann and I skimmed the surface, talking about the children and all the movies we wanted to see, I thought and obsessed and agonized for the rest of the night.

3 MY ANSWER

The next morning, Mann turned off my alarm after I hit snooze for the fifth time. I was groggy and gritty-eyed, wholly unprepared for another work day. The twins had been restless all night, escaping from their cribs and marauding through the house. I found them jumping on the couch at three a.m.

When I rolled over, gathering the strength to emerge from my blanket cocoon, Mann kissed me. "Why don't you stay in bed a little longer? The twins are asleep. I'll make you some coffee."

For a few glorious moments, I reveled in guiltless lounging, stretching my limbs and reaching for the threads of a floaty dream. Sleep and freedom from the constant vigilance that children demand was my newest, most precious vice. Sex was an awkward obligation, a reminder of my increasing weight and age.

I closed my eyes and let myself drift. Then I remembered last night's conversation and Mann's simple, eminently reasonable request. My heart rate surged, flooding my body with adrenaline and jangling my nerves. The peaceful interlude was broken.

When Mann arrived with my coffee—hot, steaming, and perfectly adulterated with cream and sugar—I knew it was an offering. He didn't say anything, but I could see the fragile hope in his smile. It tugged at my heart.

Throughout our hurried morning, he was even more attentive than usual. He made the twins' sandwiches, helped Rose pull on her shoes, and made Briar put down the iPad and eat her eggs. Instead of rushing to work, he took a conference call at home, muting his Bluetooth and helping me wrestle the girls into the car. He waved as we sped away, a broad, toothy grin splitting his face.

Despite the bright California sun, a cloud of guilt followed me all the way to Poppy's house. How could I deny my husband when he was so good to me and our children?

***

I stopped in front of Poppy's house. As my daughters squirmed and cooed, I freed them from their car seats and walked them to the door. Rose, my brave one, the one who takes after Mann, rang the bell. Timid Briar, my childish familiar, clung to my leg.

The door opened. Poppy beamed at the girls. Her multi-colored adult braces gleamed like jewels. She looked fresh and casual in a Stanford T-shirt and torn jeans, and young enough to be my daughter. I felt instantly old.

"Good morning, Helen," she chirped. "You're a few minutes early, but that's OK. I'm always happy to see Briar and Rose."

The girls giggled and surged into the house, Briar's blond head bobbing after Rose's brown one. I blushed, my pale skin turning a blotchy fuchsia. Leaving one's children at daycare early is a major faux pas. It's the kind of thing only a mother who is in a hurry to abandon her offspring for the company of grownups would do.

Once the girls scrambled inside, Poppy inspected me, frowning as if I were a bruised fruit. "You look like you've had a rough morning. Want to come in for a quick cup of coffee? The other kids won't be here for at least half an hour."

I hesitated. I should have gotten back in my car and headed to work, where I was chronically behind on my daily quota of tweets and posts. But I desperately needed to talk about Mann's request. And Poppy was uniquely situated to advise me. According to her Facebook relationship status, she was part of a polyamorous triad with a married couple in San Francisco.

"That would be nice," I said, following her inside and trying not to simper with gratitude. As always, I admired the simplicity and cleanliness of her space. She gave Rose a tambourine and Briar a coloring book, and put on a pot of free trade dark roast.

While the children colored and the coffee brewed, Poppy settled me at the kitchen table. I glanced shyly at her, working up the nerve to expose my shriveled, ungenerous soul.

"Um, can I ask you a personal question?"

Poppy grinned, exposing a row of chiclet-colored adult braces. "It depends on how personal it is."

"I've seen your posts on Facebook about being poly. Um, how is that working for you?"

Poppy fell silent. Her expression was thoughtful. "I'm not sure I can say it's working for me or not. It's not something I chose, it's something I am. Like having dark hair and brown eyes."

Dark hair, brown eyes, perfect legs. Plus, she was hardworking, bright, and ambitious. I almost sighed. If I agreed to open my marriage, this was the kind of woman my husband would be dating. If I chained him to a sexless marriage, I would lose him. But if I set him free in the Bay Area's garden of twentysomething butterflies, I would also lose him. There was no way to win.

I tried to keep my face neutral, but my expression must have been alarming. She scooted her chair until she was next to me and started rubbing my shoulders. "Mann told me he was going to ask you about opening up your marriage," she said. "I've been poly for *years*. I'd be glad to answer your questions."

"Does Mann want to date *you*?" I blurted, bringing my hand to my mouth.

"Absolutely not! That would be a huge conflict of interest if he invests in my startup. No offense, Mann is a great guy, but I'd much rather have him on my board of directors than in my bedroom."

I sighed heavily, relieved she wasn't fazed by my awkward outburst. I glanced at the Hello Kitty clock on the wall. Its tail swung like a metronome. Tick tock, tick tock. My heart revved in a way it hadn't since the terror of my pregnancy. I told it to be quiet. I was sitting across from a bona fide poly expert. I was going to ignore my fear and get some answers.

I took a deep breath and asked, "Have you seen open marriages work? Or is it just something people try before they get divorced?"

She stood and walked to the coffee pot, pouring two large mugs. Her voice was studiously mild. Cautious. "I've see it work when partners communicate well. Would you like soy or almond milk?"

"Soy," I said meekly. Poppy was a committed and vociferous vegan. "But does it work when one person isn't, um, very interested in sex?"

Poppy placed the steaming mug in front of me, her mouth stretching into a Technicolor grin. "It's perfect for that kind of situation. I think monogamy forces people to expect too much from one person. Your partner has to provide friendship, love, sex, cooking...even technical support."

I giggled for half a breath and then frowned. I knew sex was important to men in general and to Mann in particular. Wouldn't he leave me for a woman who provided excellent sex? Wasn't that a bug in the system? A fatal error?

"Um, Poppy? Don't take this the wrong way, but, do you ever want to be with just one of your partners? Would you ever consider it if the husband offered to leave his wife for you?"

Poppy's face contorted and coffee spewed out of her nose. "Fuck no. Stephen would be a morose son-of-a-bitch without Laura to lighten him up. Look, if anyone's going to steal your husband, it's going to be a mono woman. Poly people don't *want* exclusivity. The biggest problem with triads I see is couples treating their third like crap. Couple privilege, you know?"

I didn't know, not at all, but I thought I was starting to. For the rest of my time with Poppy, she referred me to a long list of books and websites. When I kissed my daughters goodbye, I was feeling more confident. Perhaps an open marriage was something I could research. Dissect. Contain.

Besides, Mann had once shared me with Karl without a word of complaint. Couldn't I do the same thing?

***

The main parking area at WorldFeed was full, so I found a space in the overflow lot with the contractors and other untouchables. The sun shone down, snickering that I would spend the next nine hours in an artificially lit cage, experiencing the so-called fulfillment of a career.

As I quick-stepped across the asphalt, I recalled the conversation I'd had with Mann before my maternity leave ended.

"I'm exhausted," I said, lying with my head on my daughters' special breast-feeding pillow. "I need more time at home with the girls. I'm just getting the hang of this motherhood thing."

He looked at me with heavy, disappointed eyes. "You'll be happier if you're independent. I know you. You'll get bored sitting at home all day. And then you'll start resenting me. If you don't already. I miss your wit. I even miss your sarcasm."

I shook my head. "I don't resent you. I'm just so tired I can barely think. Besides, almost dying kind of puts things into perspective. I can't even pretend to care about my job anymore. But I do care about out girls. And it's not like we need the money." Mann had just sold one of his startups for an infinity of dollars.

His face shifted from disappointed to a cool neutrality I knew hid deep hurt. "I want you to be with me because you love *me*, not my money or our lifestyle or our kids."

"I love you, Mann. *You*. I wouldn't have had children with anyone else. *I love you.*"

He kissed my lips. They tasted like sadness. "You've barely touched me since the children were born. And now you want to stop working. What am I supposed to think?"

I didn't know what to say, how to make him believe I really did care. I had transformed from a flawed woman into a deeply flawed mother. I was no longer the woman who rode her motorcycle down the freeway, convinced she was immortal. And I was no longer the woman who refused to sign a prenuptial agreement, passionately arguing I would always work for a wage and never be dependent like my mother.

I sighed. Mann was right. I had promised one thing, and then delivered another. And I could no longer prove my love with passionate sex. It was just too painful. The only thing I could offer—the only action I could take—was going back to work. So I did. I sucked it up, tucked it in, and returned to a job I despised.

My pace slowed as I approached the front doors of WorldFeed. Reluctantly, I stepped inside, dreading the coming day. My vision blurred and dimmed as my eyes adjusted to the vaguely greenish artificial light. I moved slowly, like a salmon struggling against the tide, as my younger, childless coworkers whizzed by me, clutching mammoth mugs of caffeine. My heart revved and jumped.

I followed a labyrinth to my desk and turned on my venerable PC. As the hourglass whirred, I took a deep breath and willed my blood pressure to settle. After the preeclampsia, it remained stubbornly high. My little plastic pillbox, which I filled every Sunday night, made me feel old. And now Dr. Yu wanted me to see a cardiologist.

Ticking bomb.

I put on my noise-canceling headphones in a futile attempt to mute the sales staff chattering around me like macaws. Then I got to work, parsing bone-dry press releases into tweets, blog posts, and news articles. Our commandment was quantity over all. Every press release begat ten units of content and one hundred shares. I cut, pasted, and tried to lose myself in corporate mundanity.

But I couldn't quell the anxiety fizzing in my brain. I imagined telling Mann that yes, I agreed to an open marriage. I could see his face flushing with joy...as he opened an OKCupid account. Ugh. My gut churned. I tasted bile. I envisioned saying no instead, watching his face crumble with disappointment. No, no, no. Guilt clawed inside my skull.

I tried another deep breath, but my chest was tight. I could only take small sips of air. Automated messages from the content submission system strobed across my monitor. *Work faster*, they blinked. *Produce more.* I gasped, struggling to open my lungs. I felt suddenly off balance, as if the earth had shifted on its axis. My heart thudded against my sternum. Sweat trickled from my hairline.

I did the easy thing, the cowardly thing. I ran away from my desk and through a labyrinth of hallways, skittering back into the sunshine. Outside of the office, breathing unprocessed air, I was both relieved and ashamed. I was a terrible employee. If Mann weren't on the WorldFeed board, I would have been fired by now.

I sighed. I wanted to be brave. I really did. Did I have the courage to open my marriage, to save my family? Honestly, I didn't know. But was I ready for the cataclysm of divorce? Although we didn't have a prenuptial agreement, I didn't have access to any of our theoretically joint assets. And Mann was so touchy about money and so well connected.

No. I didn't want to think about the bloody mechanics of divorce. I loved Mann. I wasn't going to lose him and my life, imperfect as it was, without a fight.

***

Mann walked through the front door, his nose twitching from unfamiliar smells. I was cooking a complete meal: fajitas with homemade tortillas and grass-fed beef, guacamole, *pico de gallo*, big salads. Of course, I had burned the first batch of fajitas and disabled our smoke detection system. But I persevered, ready and hopefully able to save my marriage.

The twins were playing on the floor, Briar building block towers and Rose knocking them down. Mann dropped his computer bag on the breakfast bar and greeted the girls. Rose threw herself into a crazed hug-and-tickle combo, squealing with glee. Briar took a hesitant step forward, her pale eyebrows flying together like arctic birds.

"What's the occasion?" asked Mann, giving Briar a more restrained paternal squeeze.

I filled my lungs with oxygen. I'd had a nap and a much needed Xanax. I was ready to take a baby step outside the bounds of convention. I opened my mouth to speak. My voice only shook a little.

"I thought about what you said last night. I agree. I think we should try an open marriage."

Mann's face bloomed like a flower in the springtime sun. The furrows between his brows smoothed. His lips curled into a heartfelt smile. "Wow, that's wonderful. I knew you were strong enough to trust our love. Thank you."

My traitorous mind tried to conjure a vision of his future polyamorous dating profile, but I quashed it. Instead, I locked onto his bright, eager eyes. I congratulated myself for my open mindedness. "You're welcome. But don't get too excited. There will be rules, you know."

"Oh yes," he said, smiling. "Of course. I want you to feel comfortable."

I filled a small tortilla, smiling at the girls, who were too blessedly young to understand. "How about don't ask-don't tell? It's classic."

Mann smiled wryly. "I could do 'don't' tell.' But do you really think you could handle 'don't ask?'"

I thought about it for a moment, and he was right. Every time he left the house, I would have wondered whom he was seeing and what they were doing. The constant doubt would have eaten me alive. "OK, you're right.

Would you be comfortable seeing other women just for sex? Could you keep your other relationships compartmentalized?"

Mann chuckled. "Do you think I'm that kind of guy?"

I thought about it. When we first started dating, we didn't sleep together at all. We rode my bike up and down the peninsula. Went to concerts. Slept under the stars. We made out a lot, but the sex came later. It was part of a beautiful, loving package.

I sighed. "I guess not."

He nodded. "I want a real relationship, not just a few disconnected parts. I want the thrill of getting to know someone at all levels. And I want to share it with you."

Yes, Mann was a whole package kind of guy. But was I ready to cheer him on as he dated other women, bedded them, and maybe even fell in love? I didn't want sex—it was painful, both emotionally and physically—but I wanted to want it.

Mann wiped a glob of salsa from Briar's chin and continued. "In a perfect world, you'd be friends with whoever I end up dating. I know you've lost touch with people. Maybe our open marriage could fill a gap for you, too."

I nodded. When I had preeclampsia, I was tough to be around. I whined too much. Complained too much. Wasn't grateful enough for my happy ending and continued life. My friends faded away into a sea of Facebook and Instagram updates. I was still skeptical, but I wanted to try. I was *going* to try.

We ate. We talked. We put the children to bed, and we talked some more. We talked through his needs and my fears. And we talked ourselves into a fragile, new life.

4 THE SELECTION

Mann shuffled papers around his desk, his movements taut with atypical anxious energy. I hadn't ever seen him this nervous and uncertain, even during his first startup. From our wild beginning to my nightmare pregnancy, he was always confident. Calm. Comforting.

But today he was twitchy with anticipation. He had spent his afternoon texting with Micah and obsessively straightening his home office. I didn't like it.

"Do you think we should give Emma a tour of the house?" he asked. "It's a little messy. You can definitely tell we have kids."

If I hadn't already taken two Xanax, I would have snapped at him. Since I dropped the kids at Poppy's, I had spent *my* afternoon retrieving fermenting juice cups, double-bagging diaper trash, and scrubbing the floors around our many guest toilets. Did I miss a few stray pacifiers? Maybe, but the house was cleaner than it had been in weeks.

"You know," I said, "if the house isn't up to your lofty standards, let's meet her at Java Bean. Isn't meeting in a public place standard operating procedure for Internet dates?"

Mann pursed his lips, turning them thin and white. "I thought of that, too. But I'm not comfortable meeting her in public, where anyone could overhear us. Even Micah and Jessie aren't completely out. Lucky for us, Emma is happy to come here. She's going to make a safe call."

A safe call. I supposed that meant she would phone a friend to confirm she had arrived and departed unscathed. Very modern. Very sensible.

"OK, fine. If you're worried that the house is too messy, we can have drinks by the pool. We've got plenty of wine and cheese."

Mann was about to say something else when the doorbell rang. I smiled wryly. "Showtime!"

***

Emma, a handsome, broad-shouldered blonde, stood on our front porch, smiling awkwardly. She looked uncomfortable in a sundress with spaghetti straps that didn't quite match her long, angular frame. Her sharp cheekbones and hooded eyes reminded me of Greta Garbo, hinting at strength and mystery. She carried a bottle of wine like a shield.

"You must be Helen," she said in a husky, Australian lilt. "I'm Emma. It's wonderful to meet you. Your husband says such lovely things about you."

I blushed furiously and bit my lip. I instinctively hated the idea of Mann discussing me with other women. I took a long, deep breath and tried to smile. I told myself my discomfort was a relic of monogamous conditioning, one more thing I would need to overcome.

I must have paused a little too long, because Emma asked, "Excuse me, you are Helen, right?"

"Yes, I'm Helen. Sorry, I'm just a little nervous. Please come in."

"Absolutely, I'm just going to make a quick call." Emma fished her phone out of a large, canvas bag and pressed a button.

Yes, I'm here. Everything is fine. The wife is gorgeous. I'll touch base in about an hour.

I blushed again, this time from the unexpected praise. When I met Emma, I was thirty pounds overweight. Without clothes, I looked like one of those ancient fertility figurines, all breasts and belly and butt. I would have looked ridiculous on a motorcycle, entirely unlike the modestly curvy-yet-strong version of myself who had flirted with Mann on the side of the road.

"Everything OK?" I asked, acknowledging the call but not the compliment.

"Everything's perfect," she said, flashing a too-bright smile. I grinned back and leaned hard into my Xanax buzz, leading her into our over-sized house. She craned her head and spun around, taking the whole thing in.

"Your home is stunning," she gasped.

I shrugged. "It's big, maybe a little too big." To be honest, I had stopped noticing the dimensions of our house years ago. The massive open spaces were Mann's vision, not mine. I prefer cozy corners and dimly lit nooks. Places that are shadowy. Places where our worst selves can hide.

As Emma continued to gape at the arched ceilings and pricey fixtures, I wondered if she ascribed all sorts of unearned virtues to the rich. Perhaps she had read about the last company Mann had sold. Perhaps her agenda extended beyond mere dating to a more disciplined sort of greed.

I took another deep breath and reminded myself to think positive, to give her a chance. It was too soon to start resenting her. All she had done was say something nice about our house. She was probably just being polite.

I was about to shoo her onto the patio when Mann appeared at the foot of the stairs, looking coolly casual in a vintage shirt and subtly tailored khaki pants. His voice was small and questioning, but the acoustics of the room gave it resonance and depth. "Emma?" he asked. "Is that you?"

My throat constricted when she ran across the bamboo floor and flung herself into his arms.

***

I sipped from a large tumbler of wine, swaddling my emotions. Emma and Mann slathered each other in mutual admiration.

"I'm sorry if my greeting was a little effusive. It's just that I'm a software developer, and you're my hero. The Kudzu Framework is so perfect for rapid development. I wasn't surprised at all when Excedra bought you out. I guess I've always worshipped you from afar," she gushed.

Mann smiled the distant, satisfied smile of a man who is accustomed to being told he is wonderful many times a day. "I didn't know I had such a lovely acolyte. But let's not bore my wife with tech talk. I want to know how you stay in shape." He slowly traced an invisible line down her tanned arm. "Your deltoids are a work of art."

My hand holding the wine glass shook slightly while Emma flushed, her tanned cheeks deepening to rosewood. "I work with a trainer. I also rock climb, both indoors and outdoors."

Mann nodded, grinning. "Rock climbing sounds stimulating. Maybe you can show us the ropes sometime. And you'll have to give Helen the name of your trainer," he said, playfully pinching the flesh on my upper arm. If it weren't for the sedating effects of the Xanax and the wine, I would have punched him.

"Sure, I'd be glad to," said Emma, giving me an appraising look. "And, Helen, since it wasn't clear from your husband's profile, I'd like to ask you a personal question. Do you mind?"

"N-no," I sputtered, still fuming.

"Are you bisexual?"

I shook my head, rushing to reassure her she wouldn't have to handle my excess flesh. "No, I'm not. Actually, I'm more like asexual. I have a medical issue that makes sex, er, challenging."

"Pity," she said quietly. "So what do you hope to accomplish by adding a third person to your marriage?"

I shrugged and took another large swallow of wine. I felt strangely disoriented as if a wall had fallen away to reveal an endless sea. I wanted to dive into the water and swim far away. But I could only do it if I set down all my burdens and left them on the beach.

"I want my husband to be happy. I want us both to be happy." I blinked my eyes. My head was swimming. Everything around me sparkled and quivered.

"I see," said Emma, her face smudged and solemn. But I didn't see. I was falling, slipping under the surface of consciousness and into the cool, comforting depths.

***

I heard the distant sounds of Mann returning with the children. He must have collected them from Poppy's. I was lying in bed with a dull, throbbing headache. I waited for him to come get me, but he didn't. He fed them, handled their baths, and put them to bed.

"Where's Mommy?" they asked from their room down the hall.

"Mommy isn't feeling well," he replied.

When the bedtime noises faded into silence, I emerged from under the covers, blinking my eyes like a mole. What Mann had said was true. I wasn't feeling well. Headache and humiliation do not pair well. I vowed never to combine Xanax and wine again. When I heard a soft knock at the door, I was prepared to be contrite.

"Can I come in?"

"Sure," I rasped.

Mann regarded me with the blank face he often used to cover strong emotions. Like rage. "Listen," I said, preempting whatever awful and perfectly justifiable thing he had come to say. "I fucked up. I combined wine and Xanax and ruined our date. I am unbelievable sorry. It will never happen again."

The corners of his mouth puckered into an almost-frown. He sat on the edge of the bed and took my hand the way he had when I was pregnant and sick. "I know this is hard on you. Poppy said that the transition to poly can be rough. It can bring out all kinds of insecurities. She really is quite wise for a Millennial."

I nodded. Poppy was right. Compared to Emma, I felt like something dull and stretched and worn. An old sock. An old woman. I sniffed. Mann squeezed my hand.

"Are you sure you want to do this? Are you really sure?" His voice was sad and raw. Worried and disappointed.

I exhaled a long, jagged breath. I was afraid he had come up here to suggest a divorce. But he had given me a reprieve instead. I would not waste this opportunity to be the wife he deserved. "I'm sure. I meant what I said. I really want you to be happy. I just shouldn't mix wine with a double dose of Xanax. I know I should cut back on the chemicals and work on my willpower."

Now it was his turn to exhale. He was relieved, too. "I'm glad to hear it," he said, kissing my forehead.

"I love you, Helen. We are perfect for each other, except for the sex. We have a bug in the system, and an open marriage is the most logical workaround. Once we have the hang of it, I'm sure our relationship will be better than ever. Better for both of us.

"Now get some rest. I talked to Emma. She's agreed to give us another chance."

***

Our Lyft barreled down the freeway towards a small, disreputable bar in East Palo Alto. Emma said it was a total dive. She was certain no one would recognize Mann. Despite his misgivings, he had agreed. It was a gesture of goodwill, to make up for my unfortunately timed collapse.

The silent glide of the Prius did nothing to distract me from my fears. I dreaded watching Emma beam her sexy happiness at Mann. As the car skimmed the road, my stomach squirmed. My heart flipped and rolled. A lump formed in my throat. I could feel my veins tightening and my blood pressure rising. I considered calling it off.

But I didn't. I couldn't. I knew there was no turning back. Mann was committed to opening our relationship, to beginning a new chapter in our lives. He was confidence personified. Hopeful. Optimistic. I was the opposite, a bundle of irresolute nerves and doubts.

We stopped in front of a dirty-looking storefront with tape on the window. A small, neon sign flashed the word *Bar*. Mann reached under my cotton wrap dress and squeezed my knee. "Are you going to behave?" he asked with a glint in his eye I hadn't seen for years.

I answered with the naked, dimpled truth. "I don't know."

***

Entering the bar was like visiting another country, someplace gritty and bracingly perilous. The lighting was dim, the furniture was battered, and the patrons were frayed around the edges. E-cigarettes glowed with the promise of a consequence-free nicotine high.

Mann took my hand as we crossed the threshold. I was glad to be walking beside a tall, muscular man. As my eyes adjusted to the low light, I noticed a handful of women by the bar. They wore torn jeans, thick belts, and tight tanks over dark, lacy bras. Long, curly hair cascaded down their backs. With my limp, mom's bob and worn, printed dress, I did not belong.

Mann and I circled the room, searching for Emma. We passed her twice before she waved us down with a crimson grim. When we met her before, in the safety of our white-walled home, she had seemed pleasantly pretty, athletic and vaguely masculine. But here she was an electric mixture of leather and lace and blood red lips. Sexy and mysterious. Beautiful and dangerous.

"Hello, you two!" she cried, holding a tumbler of something clear.

Mann dropped my hand like it was a dead fish and threw his arms around her. "Emma, dear. Thank you for giving us another chance."

When they parted, Mann caught my eye. His expression was both stern and pleading. *Do your part*, it seemed to say. *Make her feel comfortable.*

I pasted on what I hoped was a convincing smile. "I'm so sorry for the other day. My tolerance isn't what it used to be."

Emma turned to me, her smile a few watts dimmer. "Oh, don't worry about it. We all struggle with *compersion* from time to time."

My face must have gone blank, because she said, "*Compersion* is feeling genuinely happy when your partner meets a new love interest." Then my memory clicked. I had seen this word on Poppy's reading list.

I nodded and glanced longingly at the pool table. I am a surprisingly decent pool player. And I needed something to occupy me while Mann and Emma got to know each other. "Would you two like to play a game?" I asked.

Emma shook her head. "I don't play. I'm awful. But you go ahead. Maybe Mann will sit out with me?"

Mann pulled her in, so her head rested against his collarbone. She sighed and smiled. They seemed easy together. Connected. They must have been talking online without me. "Sure," he said, lightly kissing her lips. "That sounds delightful." Then he turned to me with a quick smile. "Helen, you have a blast."

I stood in the center of the bar like an orphan while Mann and Emma settled into a dark booth. I told myself to stop being a child and walked to the ancient pool table, where two older men were playing. I added my name to the list and waited. If I squinted, I could turn Mann and Emma into hazy, non-threatening blobs.

Soon enough, I was up. I played and won against a quiet, sixty-year-old man with a gray Fu Manchu mustache, a college boy from Stanford, and a hyperkinetic materials engineer. I was proud of myself for focusing on my game and not Mann and Emma's table. In fact, when I ran out of opponents, Emma was sitting by herself.

Instead of joining her, I kept to the shadows, observing. I watched her slender hands fiddle with her phone. Unconsciously, I mapped the motion of her long, elegant fingers to a series of digits. Effortlessly, I committed her password to memory. Like pool, it was another one of my useless talents.

I was about to announce myself when Mann returned. He towed Emma out of her seat and into a full-bodied embrace, his qualms about public exposure apparently gone. I watched them drink each other in. I guzzled oxygen until I felt weak and dizzy.

I coughed. They turned. Their lips were red and swollen. Their mirrored smiles were proud and bemused. Their fingers entwined. Mann looked at me with pleading eyes, a child asking permission for dessert. "I'd like to bring Emma home with us tonight. Can we? Please?"

I felt the way I used to when I roared downhill on Lucy. Terrified and exhilarated all at the same time. One small slip, and my life would be over.

"Yes," I whispered. "Yes."

***

Poppy, my savior, delivered the twins at exactly nine o' clock. We carefully removed their warm, sleepy forms from her car, carried them upstairs, and tucked them into bed. I turned on the video monitor and kissed them goodnight.

I tried to forget that Emma and Mann were in one of the downstairs guest rooms, consummating their relationship. As Poppy and I descended the stairs, I was certain I could hear soft, barely audible moans. A wave of nausea flowed through me as I imagined Emma's thick, golden curls brushing against Mann's shoulders. I told myself to get a grip, to stop being such a stereotypical jealous wife. Mann deserved a healthy sex life, and I wasn't going to stand in the way.

As the bumps grew louder and more emphatic, Poppy's espresso-colored eyebrows flew to her hairline. I wished she could stay for drinks and be my polyamory coach. I needed someone to guide me through this emotional gale.

"I'd ask about that noise," said Poppy, her mouth a perfect red bow, "but I'm late to a party in the city. We'll have to catch up on Monday."

My heart sank, but I forced a smile. I watched her white, thigh-high boots walk into the night. I was alone with my jealousy. My bed was full of Emma, and my stomach was full of bile. I decided I would keep a vigil, watching over the twins on the video monitor until I felt tired enough to crash in one of the guest rooms. I took one Xanax and then another.

Almost instantly, I felt calmer and pleasantly fuzzy. The inside of my mouth turned to felt. When I padded into the kitchen for some water, I saw Emma's black leather clutch sitting on the breakfast bar, stuffed with secrets. I knew it was wrong, but I helped myself. After all, she was helping herself to my husband. I almost giggled.

Its contents were initially disappointing. She apparently traveled light, with nothing but a wallet and her phone. The wallet was slim, containing a driver's license and a single credit card. I palmed the phone. Without thinking, I typed in her password. My head buzzed with a bitter kind of excitement.

At first, I sorted through ordinary stuff. Work correspondence. A GitHub project. Professional development. But as I peeled back layer after layer, I discovered something that transmuted my jealousy into something pure and righteous. Emma had a serious girlfriend named Luna, a burgundy-haired content marketer with a talent for creative profanity *who had no idea Emma was dating other people.*

Well, I hate betrayal. And dishonesty is even against the rules of polyamory. Magically, the right thing to do converged with what I wanted to do. I was the goddess of Karma, righting an obvious wrong. I found all of Emma's correspondence with Mann and several other men—including plenty of nude photos—and forwarded the whole steaming mess to Luna's Gmail account.

When it was done, the jealous demons left my body. I felt empty, but in a good way, as if I had just hiked ten miles. I dragged the baby monitor to the bedroom I usually shared with Mann, smiling and spent. The house was quiet now.

I thought about Mann and Emma in the guest room, who were no doubt sticky and entwined. Now that I had pawed through Emma's life, I no longer felt threatened by her. She was unworthy. She was temporary. She was my gift to Mann. And, just maybe, she was enough.

I hoped that Mann, now sated, would stop pushing so hard for openness. I was ready to look harder at our own relationship, to see if we could fix our problems without an Emma or two buzzing around the edges. Oh, it would be hard. But perhaps we could reconnect for ourselves and for our children.

I fell asleep in increments, listening to the twins shift in their beds and imagining myself back on Lucy, flying down the coast and listening to her comfortable roar.

5 THE UNICORN

I chopped vegetables while Briar and Rose tried to rouse Mann from his torpor. They brought him piles of books and begged him to "readme now."

"Again," they cried. "Again, Again." He read story after story with a soft, listless delivery. I noticed. The girls didn't. I flipped omelets and listened to him drone.

Just one week ago, Emma had told Mann her life was too complicated for a new relationship. She said her girlfriend wasn't ready to share. When he read extracts from her goodbye email, I clucked sympathetically. Inside, I was dancing to a wild, percussive beat. *I got away with it. I got away with it.* Emma had assumed she'd been hacked.

I felt guilty once the giddy relief had burned off. I had knowingly sabotaged our first potential third. And Mann was despondent. He had liked Emma more than I had thought possible, considering the fleeting nature of their connection. Or maybe he was simply inexperienced with rejection. Either way, he fell into a dull, pervasive melancholy.

I tried to help him heal. I treated him gently, plying him with wine and carefully prepared meals. I allowed myself to hope this setback would lead him to put our new, open arrangement on hold. Perhaps this bitter taste of no would discourage him from seeking new women while we worked on ourselves.

I vowed I would try harder to locate my libido and the source of my physical pain. I began searching for more specialists. I emailed Dr. Yu and steeled myself for another round of invasive exams. But I never made the appointments.

While we were eating leek and onion omelets and feeding bits to our reluctant progeny, Mann received a text. His face glowed. His lips twitched playfully. His eyes crackled with excitement. He looked alive for the first time in days.

"Helen," he said, shoveling a forkful of egg into Briar's pouty mouth. "I got a text from Micah. He and Jessie are having a party for all their poly friends on Saturday. And we're invited!"

***

Mann sailed through the week on a wave of anticipation. I paddled around a pool of uncertainty, making panicked circles. Even worse, it was a peculiar, demanding kind of anxiety. Only constant activity could keep it at bay. When I paused to rest, my heart would pound, and I would wonder about my blood pressure.

I harnessed my agitation for feats of motherly productivity. I woke up at three a.m. and sorted the girls' clothes into piles: too big, too small, and just right. I took them to the library on the way home from Poppy's, carrying shy Briar while keeping a hand on fearless Rose. We checked out fifteen books. I read them aloud while a chicken cacciatore simmered on the stove.

Every night I opened a fresh bottle of wine. I wanted to stay off the Xanax—I was on my last refill—so I drank a little more to compensate. And Mann was happy to join me. He wanted us to communicate more, which seemed to mean extolling the superiority of our new, poly way. He quoted evolutionary psychologists who opined that monogamy was unnatural. He urged me to talk through my jealousy.

Of course, Mann didn't understand jealousy. How could he? He always got everything he wanted. So I kept quiet, agreeing with him in a noncommittal sort of way. Pouring myself another glass. After we put the girls to bed, Mann would go back to his office, grinning like a satisfied cat. I would clean the kitchen until I quivered with exhaustion.

By the end of the week, I was a strung-out, sleep-deprived mess. I was also miraculously seven pounds lighter. This modest loss gave me just enough confidence to attend Micah and Jessie's party instead of faking a last-minute stomach bug. I slid into my standby black cocktail dress without the agony of Spanx.

I felt light, free, and only mildly terrified when I followed Mann to the car.

***

"Helen, it's so good to see you! You look ravishing!" Jessie, a muscular wraith with hungry eyes, hauled me into the party like the Ghost of Christmas Future. I glanced back at Mann, who had been captured by Micah. The two of them were chatting with a clutch of smooth-faced women who couldn't have been more than twenty-five.

"Interns from Micah's passion project," said Jessie, noticing my stare. "Don't worry, they're all legal."

I frowned. I could all too easily imagine Mann going for a girlfriend who was fresh out of the box, a babysitter with benefits. But I remained calm and allowed myself to float in Jessie's wake. She pulled me through a living area filled with beautiful people, taking me straight to the bar in the back yard.

"What would you like to drink? Vodka? Rum?" she asked, baring perfect teeth.

I was surprised she was suggesting the hard stuff. I must have looked a bit sharp around the edges, liable to cut her other, softer guests. "Chardonnay, please. Unoaked if you've got it."

Jessie filled two large glasses, one for her and one for me. "Cheers!" she said, taking a healthy sip.

I was about to turn away in search of a quiet corner where I could pretend to be reading a very important text, when Jessie threw her matchstick arms around me.

"Mann told me you're exploring poly," she said, her voice casually loud.

I nodded, cringing slightly. "I guess that's one way you could put it."

Jessie laughed. It was a bright and brittle sound that sliced through the ambient chatter. "The early days can be rough, especially when your partner is…extroverted like Mann is."

I flinched. By 'extroverted' she meant desirable, something Mann, a thirty-nine-year-old CEO with defined abs was, and I, a thirty-nine-year-old wage slave with a mommy pooch, was not. I'm sure Jessie had no idea what Mann saw in me. She hadn't known me when I was reckless and bold.

"It's not so bad," I said vaguely. Despite our issues, I would never have complained about Mann to Micah's wife, no matter how friendly or understanding she seemed. And, really, she seemed less friendly than famished for some indication Mann and I were failing.

"Well, just wait until your husband gets caught up in the NRE."

"NRE?" I asked, puzzled.

"New relationship energy. When he connects with someone new, he might forget about you for a little while. But don't worry. It's a natural part of the process."

I nodded as if she were imparting sage wisdom and not the most banal common sense. Everyone knows desire makes people selfish. I remembered how excited Mann had been about Emma, how he brought her to bed without even asking me. I wanted to harrumph that new relationship energy was obviously a hippie euphemism for instant lust.

Instead, I smiled. "I appreciate your insights."

Jessie cackled again and kissed my cheeks European style. "If you need to talk to someone, you know where to find me. Gotta go play hostess with the mostess." She swooped into the growing crowd.

I made a halfhearted attempt to look for Mann. I didn't find him, but the food table was adequate consolation. It was covered with ostentatiously healthy delights: kale chips, carob cookies, gluten-free pizzas.

As I went to fill up my plate, I didn't watch where I was going. There was a collision and lots of spilled wine.

***

The woman I doused with chardonnay could have been my twin if I were fifteen years younger, thirty pounds lighter, and still care- and child-free. She was exactly my height with long, dark blonde hair the same shade as mine, and a more delicate version of my face. We even wore similar dresses. Hers was the mirror image of mine, white chiffon instead of black cotton.

"Oh my God, you look just like my sister." Her voice was as sweet as concentrated stevia.

"Um, thank you. Older or younger?" Of course, she meant older. She was obviously still in her twenties.

"Older." She smiled and swayed on her high heels, leaning into me. "I miss her so much. She died in a car accident five years ago. It was a drunk driver."

Tears flowed down her face, carving trails of mascara. She was beautiful, but also drunk or close to it, and drowning in grief. I put an arm around her to keep her from falling. We walked to a couch in one of the less-trafficked rooms.

She sniffled while I awkwardly patted her back. Mann's eminently reasonable interest in finding another, more sexual partner had opened a bottomless well of insecurity inside me. I felt weak and out of control. But next to this gently sobbing woman, my nameless twin, I felt comparatively strong. I wasn't the pretty one, but I was the strong one. The good one.

When her tears slackened to a drizzle, I asked, "What's your name?"

"Julia," she said with a small hiccup. "And I'm sorry I broke down like that. It's been a tough year. A tough life, really."

"I'm Helen." I was about to say something along the lines of *I know what you mean* but stopped. Yes, I'd had a rough pregnancy and a delivery that left me with medical issues. And, yes, I was struggling to accept the change in my marriage. But no one had died. My children were healthy and safe. My husband was wealthy and handsome and generally kind.

I settled for asking, "Is there anything you'd like to talk about?"

She smiled in a way that conveyed bravery and extreme forbearance. "Oh, if I talk about it, I'll just cry some more. Can you tell me who you know at this party?"

For half a breath, I was let down. I had been hoping to hear something wild and garish that would distract me from my silly, first world troubles. "My husband knows the hosts, Micah and Jessie. I suppose I know them a little bit, but they're his friends."

Julia nodded. "Matt and Anna, the couple I'm living with, know Jessie. I was sort of invited by osmosis. They're having a date night, and I was feeling lonely. So I came here."

"Are you dating Matt and Anna?" I asked, fascinated. Julia was the embodiment of my worst fears, a beautiful, dewy-faced third. And yet, here she was, sad and lonely.

She shrugged elegantly. "We're going through some issues. I don't really want to talk about it."

I respected Julia's reticence. I wouldn't have wanted to share my relationship troubles with a stranger, either. I was beginning to feel mildly ashamed, as if I were an emotional vampire, hovering over Julia and scenting blood. I would have left her to enjoy the party on her own if Mann hadn't appeared.

"I see you've made a new friend," he said. "Helen, can you introduce me to this lovely young lady?"

***

We came together like magnets. Mann positioned himself on the couch between Julia and me. We each helped ourselves to one of his shoulders, resting against him as if he were an ancient oak. I felt it was a bit presumptuous for Julia to snuggle up to my husband but wrote it off to cultural differences. I assumed physical boundaries would be more porous and less fraught among the openly poly.

Mann, like the natural leader he was, took control of the conversation. We debated the merits of different natural foods stores, roundly abused the gelatinous texture of chia seeds, and compared the latest Apple and Android phones.

When Mann and Julia began an intense discussion of yoga positions and chakras, I slipped away to the food table. I piled a plate high with healthy pseudo junk food—dry kale pizzas and chewy carob bars. I prided myself on leaving Julia and Mann to converse unchaperoned. It was only for a few minutes, but I was sure it was an important step.

When I turned to go, I nearly ran into Jessie's bony clavicle. "Excuse me," I yelped.

"Oh good, I was looking for you," she said. "I see Mann is talking to Julia Weatherstone."

I shrugged with as much indifference as I could muster. "They seem to be getting along." I bit my tongue to avoid adding, *is that a problem?*

Jessie frowned. "She's having a rough time with poly. She moved in with two of my closest friends, and she's driving them crazy. A touch of toxic insecurity, you know?"

I nodded. I did know, being appallingly insecure myself. In fact, Julia's difficultly with the poly lifestyle made me predisposed to like her more. She seemed to have human feelings beyond simple, ecumenical lust.

I mustn't have seemed alarmed enough, because Jessie added, "Be careful with her, OK? She has some kind of Gothic backstory. Lots of tragedy and drama."

"Thanks, Jess," I said brushing by her. "I'll be sure to keep that in mind."

When I returned to the smaller, quieter end of the party, I found Julia leaning against Mann. He was stroking her hair. She was blinking back tears. Her white dress and casually curled hair exuded a bridal vibe. A jolt of insecurity zinged through me. *They look perfect together*, I thought, biting my lip.

"Helen!" called Mann, waving. I hurried across the room and placed my heaping plate on the coffee table, feeling like a servant or a fussing, bustling mother-in-law. They exchanged small, intimate smiles and turned to me.

"I have something to ask you," said Mann, his voice low and portentous. "Julia has been telling me a little more about her current situation. She's having some difficulties with Matt and Anna and needs someplace to stay. It would be just for tonight."

From the upright way Mann was sitting, I knew this was a test. I had already failed with Emma. But now I had another chance. I could pass with Julia. I could let her into our home under controlled circumstances. I could get used to her presence in the house without the immediate threat of hearing her bounce and howl in bed.

"Sure," I replied, smiling evenly. "We'd be glad to have you." Her eyes shone with relief and a reassuring gratitude.

***

After the party, I dropped Mann and Julia at the house. Julia's movements were choppy and tentative. She looked as unsure as I was. I forced my lips into a small smile.

"There are some spare T-shirts and yoga pants in the downstairs guest room at the end of the hall," I said, directing her to my old, pre-pregnancy skinny clothes. "Help yourself."

She nodded and hurried to catch Mann, who had already started walking towards the door. When she caught him, he took her arm. They crossed the threshold looking like a newly married couple. I blinked back tears as I drove to Poppy's house. I tried to ignore my insecurities as they yipped and growled.

Collecting the girls was a relief. Their warm, sleepy forms gave me focus. My childhood was a nightmare that had taken more than a decade to fully awaken from. I had followed in the footsteps of my mother, getting involved with cruel, violent men until I lucked into Mann. My girls had an idyllic home with a wonderful father and low-friction lives. They would grow into smart, stable, and loving people if I didn't fuck things up with a messy, unnecessary divorce.

I kissed Rose goodnight and then Briar. They stretched and sighed. I told myself I was doing the right thing.

After the children fell asleep, I stalked the house. Emma was fresh in my mind as I listened for quiet conversation or muffled cries of joy. Instead, I found Julia quietly reading a book in the far downstairs guest room and Mann taking a business call in his office.

Feeling a queasy mixture of shame and relief, I crawled into bed and tried to read a mystery about a small town weaver. But I could not lose myself in the warp and woof of the story. I found myself on high alert, listening for Mann's footsteps, wondering if he would go to Julia. Or when.

I finally took one of my precious Xanax. Like a computer that had run too long and too hard, I crashed into dreamless oblivion.

***

High-pitched screams and a sudden jolt of the bed tore me from sleep. I blinked open sticky eyes, expecting an earthquake in progress. Instead, I found Briar and Rose jumping on the pillows.

While the girls happily squirmed, Julia and Mann slowly entered the room. Their smiles seemed genuine if low key. They weren't touching. I sagged with guilty relief.

Mann balanced a tray holding eggs Florentine, toast, and coffee. "We decided to give Mommy the morning off," he said with a wink.

I wondered how much Julia had factored into this plan. Mann had always been good to me, but this felt forced. It felt like a consolation prize. Perhaps he and Julia had spent the night together, after all.

Julia nodded. "I was up early. I helped Mann with the Hollandaise sauce. I hope you like it." Her voice was small and shy, as if she wanted my approval.

When the girls calmed down, Mann put the tray on my lap, and I began eating. Rose stole my toast and Briar asked politely for my strawberries. Between the three of us, my breakfast quickly disappeared.

"Thank you, that was delicious. I should have lots of energy for this morning's cleaning party."

The girls giggled and Rose repeated the word 'party' several times. Cleaning on Saturday had become tradition for the girls and me. Unlike most of our neighbors, Mann didn't believe in spending money on house cleaners. Too self-indulgent, he said. And he never had time to do housework himself: too many important meetings and trips. He made a show of trying. But his spurts of effort were random and unreliable.

In theory, I could have hired a cleaner myself, like every other woman I knew. But I honestly couldn't afford it. Most of my salary went to Poppy and the girls' food and clothes. And asking Mann for money made us both horribly uncomfortable. So I gradually became our family's *de facto* maid. My daughters filled in as my somewhat willing assistants.

Mann and Julia exchanged a knowing glance. "What is it?" I asked, unhappy to be left out of their secret.

They both beamed. "We have a little surprise for you today," said Mann. "I'll be bringing the girls to the park while a lovely woman I found on Squeaky Clean dot-com does the house. Julia will take you shopping."

I stifled a sigh. Like it or not, I was going to have hours of time alone with Julia. Plenty of time to reveal my insecurities. Plenty of time to chase her away.

I told myself to think positive. I could control myself for a few hours. Heck, it might even be fun. After all, I'd even liked her before Mann started liking her, too.

6 GETTING TO KNOW HER

Julia and I coasted in Mann's Tesla. She gazed out the window. I drove. As we swooped along route 280, I felt oddly vulnerable. I was used to looking down at the traffic from my Honda Odyssey. I missed its loud, friendly rumble. The Tesla's quiet ride magnified the silence that sat between us like an invisible wall.

I glanced at Julia, but I couldn't gauge her thoughts. Her face was half-covered by huge sunglasses. Was this outing really her idea?

She and Mann had ambushed me. They pushed me into a potentially awkward social outing when I would have rather spent the day alone or with the girls. Besides, I loathed shopping. Mann and I kept our funds rigidly segregated. We lived in separate financial realities because we were both stubborn and willfully obtuse.

"Take the next exit," said Julia. "I'll guide you to the mall."

Her voice was higher and sweeter than Google Maps' and just as accurate. I pulled into the farthest parking spot from the main entrance. Proximity to Julia was making me feel fat. I felt the need to burn calories.

"Oh, this is going to be so fun," she chirped, showing off small, even teeth.

I grimaced. The last thing I wanted to do was watch Julia try on tiny little jeans and itty bitty yoga tops. I pasted on a small, artificial smile. "I hope so. Just so you know, I don't have much of a budget for shopping. But I'd be happy to keep you company," I lied.

Julia beamed and winked. "Mann said you refuse to spend money on yourself. That's why he gave us his card. He said we have to use it."

***

Inside the candy colored mall, I ceded control to Julia, following her in a sort of angry fugue. I had no idea what Mann was playing at, giving Julia his credit card. I wish he had given me a budget for anything other than this vapid outing.

After all, my wardrobe was perfectly serviceable, filled with stretch pants and comfy neutrals. When the twins arrived, my body became a machine, something to cover, fix, and fuel. My physical self was for function, not display. I was too old for leather pants and biker chic. I was, now and forever, a mom.

Julia's heels click-clacked along the faux marble floor, a forceful metronome. I shuffled along in tennis flats. She studiously ignored my glum expression, keeping up a steady stream of cheerful patter.

"I love this place. It's my favorite mall in the South Bay. It's so full of possibilities. Is there anywhere in particular you'd like to go?"

I shrugged. "No, I don't shop very often. Go wherever you want."

"I know just the place!" She grinned and picked up speed, the sound of her heels now the quick rat-tat-tat of machine gun fire.

Like a zombie, I trailed her into a department store packed with a dizzying array of merchandise. She studied me out of the corner of her eye, pulling items off the racks like an over-caffeinated magpie. I focused on my breathing amid the garish displays as she filled my arms with dresses, tops, and jeans.

I allowed myself of be herded into a dressing room while she waited outside like an especially charming prison matron. Sheep that I was, I dutifully tried on the outfits she suggested, my stomach squirming with resentment.

But as I slipped into one outfit and then another, something strange happened. I looked and felt...kind of good. Julia was obviously a fashion savant. Everything she had chosen for me fit perfectly. I twirled before her like a proud child, even smiling a little.

Indeed, one flowy sundress with a dark, indigo print had magical properties. It somehow turned my milk-worn breasts into perky cleavage and my wide hips into subtle curves. I felt younger. Prettier. As if I really were Julia's older sister.

Julia herself approved wholeheartedly, clapping her hands together with glee. "Oh, Helen, you look spectacular!"

"Thanks," I murmured.

"No, seriously, you should wear it home. We can put your T-shirt and jeans in a shopping bag."

I did as she said, walking out in the magical dress. I also selected a few more basics, another nice but lesser dress, and a pair of stretchy, forgiving jeans. Julia flagged down a gum-cracking cashier, and began our transaction.

I was thinking *hey, this isn't so bad,* when it hit the scanner. A second version of the dress I was wearing, but in a single-digit size. Perfect for Julia. My lips puckered into a frown. Now I couldn't wear it in front of Mann. Once he saw Julia in it, I would forever be the inferior copy.

"You got the blue dress, too?" I asked, my voice a low, scratchy whine.

"I couldn't resist. It's perfect with our dark blond hair. My sister and I wore the same clothes all the time." Her hand dabbed at her eye, as if to ward off tears.

Hot shame flooded through me. I was the harpy in this scenario, not Julia. She wasn't trying to upstage me; she was remembering her beloved sister. I followed her like a penitent. Once again, I had failed to look beyond myself and my claustrophobic little life.

We drifted to the makeup counter, where an older woman with powdered cheeks painted our faces to match. When it was done, Julia wheeled her chair next to mine for the big reveal. We looked shockingly alike, with my wrinkles and blemishes smoothed down and our eyes bracketed in matching shadows.

"We're practically twins," she said, her peach lips curving into a bittersweet smile.

***

Sitting at a restaurant without desperately trying to keep my children quiet felt like the height of refinement. As Julia sipped her water, the rim of her glass remained stainless, her lipstick in place. I left greasy half-moons.

After an over-long deliberation, we both ordered perfectly dull, healthy salads. The silence from the car descended again. This time, I vowed to break it. Julia was a good, well-meaning person. I had clearly misjudged her. And I reminded myself, she was a potential third. I owned it to Mann to get to know her.

"So what do you do when you're not saving the hopelessly unfashionable?"

Julia responded with the reflexive reassurance women always provide. "Oh, you're not unfashionable, you're a mom. You have more important things to think about."

She hadn't answered my question. I probed again. "That's very kind. But, seriously, what sorts of things do you like to do?"

She sighed gently. "I love Ashtanga yoga. I'm studying to be an instructor. Not to make money but to subsidize my habit, you know? I also do some freelance writing. Mostly ebooks about fitness, weight loss, stuff like that. Nothing special. "

I nodded. "I know what you mean. I write social media copy from press releases. It's basically corporate spam, but it pays the bills."

Julia's mouth dropped into a perfectly peachy 'o,' the universal expression of shock. "I can't believe you work if you're not absolutely in love with it. I know who your husband is. You could stay home with your two, beautiful children. That's what I would do, if I were you."

The salads arrived before I could howl, "How dare you?" And then I remembered my own impassioned arguments to Mann. I hadn't wanted to leave the twins to spend endless days in a glorified content mill. Why was I angry with her? She was agreeing with me.

Instead of snapping, I sighed. "Mann has strong feelings about women being independent. He wants his daughters to grow up with a working mother. But it's been hard. And I'm still not sure we're doing the right thing."

I smiled, so certain my reply had been a model of diplomacy. I was horrified when Julia started to cry.

***

"What's wrong?" I asked. Julia shook her head and made small, keening sounds. Tears flooded her face, reminding me of when we met. Heads swiveled. People stared, judging. My face flushed.

What could have set her off? I remembered Julia buying the matching dress, and it clicked. "Julia, are you thinking about your sister?"

She shook her head wildly, dislodging her bun. Her sculpted shoulders heaved. She shivered with rapid fire sobs. She dabbed at her face with her napkin, streaking eyeliner down her cheeks.

I was nonplussed. If she wasn't grieving for her sister, then what was it? I glanced down at my salad and then up at her sorrowful face that was somehow still pretty despite her pink nose and ruined makeup. I did my best to appear kind and trustworthy. "Do you want to talk about it?"

Julia shook her head again, but less violently this time. She stabbed her fork into a pile of lettuce and brought it to her mouth. I speared a cherry tomato. I nearly choked on it when she said, "I envy you so much it hurts."

Why in the world would someone like her envy someone like me? I guessed it was my marriage to Mann. He usually makes a flawless first impression. I suspected Julia's picture of him and our life together was somewhat idealized.

I was about to explain how Mann was just a normal, flawed human being like the rest of us, when she said, "Your twins are so precious. They remind me of my girls. Lily and Selena. They were twins."

My eyes widened. In many parts of the country, it's common to have children at a youngish age. But it's less so in the Bay Area, where one's twenties are for startups, roommates, and Tinder. I supposed she must have married impetuously and ended up on the wrong side of a custody battle. If so, she was living my worst fear.

"What happened?"

More tears sprung from her eyes. "They died with Malcom. My husband. Their father," she murmured. "A drunk driver merged into him. It happened two years ago."

I was wrong. A custody battle wasn't my worst nightmare. This was. Losing children to the grave. I found myself imagining how her twins might have died, the fear on their faces, their piteous screams. My hands began to shake. I blinked back a few tears of my own.

"I'm so sorry. I can't imagine."

"You're right. You can't."

We ate in silence for a few more minutes until she said, "Do you mind if we take our salads to go? I'm not really hungry anymore."

I nodded and put my salad in a to-go box. I had been meaning to ask her when she was going home, but I couldn't do that. Not now.

***

Thank goodness Mann and the girls were still out when we arrived. I didn't know how the sight of my children might have affected her.

Julia climbed out of the car in slow motion, struggling to stand under the weight of her grief. I walked her inside. She thanked me in soft mumbles. Then she carried her purchases to the guest room and closed the door.

I took a deep breath and texted Mann.

Hey, how are the girls?

He sent a video of Briar and Rose eating organic ice cream cones, their noses smeared with chocolate and pistachio.

Did you know about Julia's daughters?

He texted back after a long pause. *Yes, the poor thing. She told me last night. Did you two have a good time?*

Unable to think of exactly what to say, I took a picture of my shopping bags nestled on the foyer. He sent back a half-winking emoji.

I exhaled and collapsed on the couch. The house was quiet. I thought about making a cup of tea and downloading a book, or maybe soaking in the hot tub. But I couldn't stop thinking about Julia. First, her sister died in a car crash with a drunk driver, and then her husband and children died the same way. No wonder she was weepy and a bit unstable.

It was also a big, terrible coincidence: two accidents, two drunk drivers. It made me want to know more, to make sure she was telling the truth and not manufacturing drama. After all, Jessie had warned me about her. And Emma had proved that not every poly person was a paragon of honesty.

My heart fluttered as I scurried upstairs to my office and turned on my laptop. I Googled the name Julia Weatherstone and found nothing. Zero. Nada. I checked the Big Three—Facebook, Twitter, and Instagram. Still a void. More searches. More directories. More nothingness.

According to the Internet, she didn't exist. I re-ran my searches with other possible spellings of her name: Wetherstone, Whetherstone, Witherstone. I found a few matches—an eighty-year-old woman, a sixty-year-old woman, a forty-year-old transgender man. But no Julia.

I frowned. This complete absence of data felt false. No one her age eschewed social media. No one. She was hiding something. I could feel it.

But was it really something to worry about? I supposed she was probably hiding from the cruel attention social media can visit upon victims of tragedy. Maybe she wasn't trying to hide a dark stain on her character. Maybe she was just protecting herself.

And yet I craved the full story. She was staying, however temporarily, in my home, and with my children. She could grow closer to Mann and become our third. At a minimum, the bad luck she brought to the people closest to her was alarming.

I took a deep breath and remembered my blood pressure. I was spiraling into obsession. It was time to stop. Instead, I would do the sensible thing. The sane thing. I would talk to Mann.

***

Mann came home with the girls and cartons of Chinese takeout. The sweet ruckus they made summoned Julia, who appeared in her wrinkled shopping outfit like a tired ghost. The girls, instinctively sensing her distress, ran to her, throwing their arms around her thighs.

"Up! Up!" cried Rose. Julia scooped my dark-haired hellion into her arms. Briar, after a few discouraged whimpers, settled for me. Mann, unaccountably domestic, set the table with a mix of ceramic and plastic plates. He arranged cartons on the table, poured juice into sippy cups, and opened a bottle of wine.

Julia and I herded the girls to their seats and helped them nibble on sesame noodles. When they were sluggish and full, I took them to the bath. Julia came too. She fussed over the girls as they gurgled and cooed. They loved squealing her name, pronouncing it *Jooooooolia.*

Every so often I would notice an extra sparkle in Julia's eyes, perhaps tears waiting to be shed. I imagined grief circling in her mind like a hungry dog. I hoped she was finding more comfort than pain in my children.

After the girls fell asleep, we rejoined Mann, who was just finishing up a business call. We sat beside him, me on his left, and Julia on his right. He smiled and poured us each a glass of wine. "It sounds like they love you, Julia," he said.

She blushed and dropped her eyes to the table. I cringed but only for a moment.

"They're lovely girls," she whispered, sniffling lightly. She looked intently at me and then Mann. Her eyes still sparkled. She looked nervous. Or scared.

"I know this is going to be a little awkward," she said. "But I have something I'd like to share with you. About Matt and Anna, the couple I've been living with."

***

Mann and I listened silently as Julia became a dessert course Scheherazade.

"I met Matt and Anna right after I moved to the Bay Area. I came here for a fresh start. My old house in the Central Valley had become a mausoleum. I spent all day crying and looking at pictures. I was thinking about death, about…you know, joining my family."

Mann stroked her hair. I reached for her hand. I thought about my twins, safely sleeping upstairs.

"I had no real plan. I just stuffed my car with memories and drove north until the weather got cooler. I rented a storage unit for my things. I stayed at hotels, trying different places, seeing how they felt. I knew I should look for work, but I wasn't quite ready.

"I have a few friends—had a few friends?—in the area. People I knew from college. Couples. I tried staying with a few of them, trading house cleaning for a spare room. But they were all pregnant. Or trying to get pregnant. It was unbearable.

"I went back to my hotels and took a lot of yoga classes, but I was…lonely. I know, nobody says they're lonely these days. It's like a personal failing.

"At first, I thought dating was the answer. I tried Match and Tinder. But it didn't really work for me. I was emotionally drained. I didn't have the energy for one-on-one commitments, even short ones. That's when I got into poly. I thought people who were already in relationships wouldn't want so much from me."

Mann and I nodded, urging her on.

"I met Matt and Anna at a party. They were young—but not too young—pretty, and fun. They wanted to take care of me. And it was easy to let them. We spent so much time together that I ended up moving in. They even let me take my stuff out of storage and put it in their attic.

"Everything was easy and organic. I found myself smiling sometimes without trying. I was getting better. Stronger. Until Anna started trying to get pregnant."

I squeezed Julia's hand. She blinked away a tear.

"She ordered me to stop sleeping with Matt. And she wanted me to do all their cooking and cleaning so she could focus her energy on conception. Matt told me she was being crazy, that we could be together without her knowing. But I wasn't comfortable with that. He got angry. Crazy angry.

"Then things got really weird. They would take my cell phone if dinner wasn't ready on time or the bathroom wasn't clean enough. They forced me to watch them have sex. Not participate, just watch. And one time, when I said I was going out on a random Internet date, they locked me in my bedroom.

"I know the situation isn't healthy. I want to break up with them. But I'm afraid. My stuff is still in their house. It's all sentimental—photo albums, my daughters' clothes—and I don't know what they'll do if I tell them it's over.

"I know it's a big thing to ask, but I was wondering if I could stay here for another day or two. Maybe figure out how to get my stuff back from Matt and Anna.

"You're both so kind," she concluded, her gaze alternating between Mann and me. "So wonderful."

I looked at Julia, trying to reconcile her fresh-faced appearance to what she had just described. What she had been through sounded dark and terrible. Abusive and awful. I wondered if that sort of situation was a real risk of being poly. "I'm sorry you went through that. I know this might sound ignorant, but...does this sort of thing happen...often...in poly relationships?"

Julia shook her head vigorously. "Oh no. All of my other poly experiences have been great. Usually, the biggest problem is, you know, time management."

As I watched Julia, I wondered how she could have consciously chosen to stay with such a terrible, abusive couple. I silently asked, *Why didn't you leave?* But then I remembered Karl and the rest of my dark, twisted dating past, conveniently buried in the back of my mind. I inspected Julia's smooth, pensive face. What demons was it hiding?

Julia, as if she could hear my internal dialogue, tried to explain. "Look, I know there were red flags. But I wanted to believe in them so much. I'm still dealing with a lot of grief. I'm still processing a lot. I just....screwed up."

Mann answered without even glancing at me. His expression was intent. Intense. "We all screw up sometimes. You're only human. And, I think, very brave," he said, squeezing her hand. "Of course we'll help you. Anything you need."

I nodded in what I hoped was a supportive way, but I felt uneasy. Julia's story was sad but also unsettling. I recalled Jessie's warning. *Gothic backstory. Drama.* I would talk to Mann later. I would ask him to look into Julia's past. No, I would insist on it.

7 SUNDAY INTRIGUE

Cocooning in a warm duvet, still a half-baked caterpillar, I reached out my hand and found…nothing. The space beside me in bed was cool, the pillow unrumpled.

I sat up, panicked. Where was Mann? Adrenaline surged through me. Was he with Julia? Had they slept together? Where were the girls?

I inhaled, counted to five, and exhaled until my lungs were empty balloons. Mann and I had an open marriage. The rules were different now. He was entitled to sleep with her, whether I liked it or not. As long as he looked into her background. As long as she wasn't crazy. As long as she was safe.

I redirected the flow of my thoughts away from Mann and towards my children. I glanced at the monitor. It was six thirty a.m. Briar and Rose were still tightly curled commas. I picked up the screen and crept down the stairs in search of coffee.

But when I padded into the kitchen, coffee was already made. Mann was sitting at the table, sipping from a giant blue mug with a WorldFeed logo and pecking at his laptop.

"Good morning. You're up early," he said with an incredulous lilt to his voice that suggested I was a habitual slug-abed. Or maybe I was just being defensive.

"Any coffee left?"

"Help yourself, love."

I joined him at the table, holding my own steaming mug. My heart, that consistent betrayer, pulsed and quivered. I ignored it. I had to stay calm. This was my opportunity to ask about Julia.

"You know..." I said, groping for the right words. I was struggling for some way to raise my concerns without seeming jealous.

"What is it?" he asked, his voice on the edge of impatience. I frowned. He was definitely grumpy this morning. He was almost never short with me.

"It's Julia. Don't you think she's had a lot of drama in her life?"

Mann furrowed his brow. "She's lost children. I can't imagine how heart-wrenching that would be. You can't, either."

I nodded, fast-forwarding through my acknowledgment of her pain. "Yes, yes, that would be unthinkable. Did you know I searched for her online? I found nothing. Absolutely nothing. It's like Julia Weatherstone doesn't exist. I wonder if she's hiding something."

Mann sighed softly. "Weatherstone is her new name. She changed it about six months ago. Her old name, and the social media baggage that came with it, got too painful. Strangers were posting about her dead daughters. It was truly ugly. I don't blame her at all."

"What is her old name?" I asked, wanting to see the horror for myself.

Mann shook his head. "It's not my place to tell you. It's up to her if she wants to share."

A flash of anger burned through me. I might end up sharing my husband—hell, my life—with this woman.

"I think I deserve to know her name. It's beyond tragic that her children died, but she's staying in this house with our children. I want to know if she's a lunatic or a criminal."

Mann sighed, exasperated. "Yes, I checked her out. And, no, there is nothing to worry about."

"But..."

"Don't you trust me? Do you really think I would do anything to put this family at risk? I love you and our children. You're my first priority."

Before I could answer, the girls began to stir, twirling on their beds. The monitor crackled with life. I listened to their childish chirping with a dull, creeping disappointment. They were calling for Julia.

***

Julia made crepes while Mann pored over financial statements, and I wrangled the girls. I usually made pancakes on Sunday mornings. It was sort of a tradition. But Julia, bright-eyed and freshly showered, volunteered in such a sweetly humble way that even the gentlest refusal would have seemed cold. While she whisked the batter, Rose grabbed onto her legs.

"Me help! Me help!"

I went to extract my overly enthusiastic daughter, but Julia stopped me. "Oh no, don't be silly, she can help."

A portrait of motherly patience, Julia placed the bowl on the floor and handed Rose the whisk. Rose dipped it into the batter and waved it over her head, giggling wildly. Briar peeked out from behind the bar and smiled.

I wanted to smile, too, and get batter in my hair. But I knew how Mann hated messes. I intervened before he could yell at the girls and make us all feel horribly uncomfortable. Of course, Mann rarely raised his voice. He was nothing like Karl. Or my father.

"C'mon, Rose," I said, guiding her wrist. "You put the whisk inside the bowl, not over your head."

Rose howled in protest. "No, no! Not Mommy! Julia help me!"

Julia looked at me, her eyes as eager as a puppy's. Jealousy burned behind my temple, oh how it burned, but I wasn't hard enough to deny her. I quietly stepped aside. She showed my wild Rose how to mix the batter without creating an unholy spatter. I brought Briar to watch and then, through some strange alchemy, the girls began to take turns.

Mann, watching the scene unfold, grinned. "You're a miracle worker, Jules. You should teach Helen your trick. She's always shooing the girls out of the kitchen."

Julia glowed, and I smiled through gritted teeth. "It's nothing," she said, hugging Rose.

Then she dazzled us all, flipping perfectly round crepes on my smallest skillet. The girls sat silently, rapt with wonder, while I simmered in envy.

***

After breakfast, the girls showed Julia their dolls while I cleaned up. Julia was the star today. I was the crew. Mann, as always, was the producer.

When the dishes were loaded into the washer and the skillet was freshly oiled, I treated myself to a bonus cup of coffee. In theory, I was supposed to avoid caffeine because it could increase my blood pressure. In practice, coffee was my gasoline: corrosive but necessary.

While I sipped liquid energy, Julia exercised her powers of toddler whispering. Soon my girls were playing quietly together. Then she fixed her own cup of coffee and joined Mann and me at the kitchen table.

"I have something to tell you," she said. Mann's head snapped up and so did mine.

"Go ahead," I said in a saccharine voice that covered my dread. "We're listening."

"I'm so grateful to you for letting me stay here. I feel safe and comfortable for the first time in a long time."

Mann's hand flew to Julia's like a snake striking a mouse. "You're welcome to stay as long as you want."

I bit the inside of my cheek to keep from snapping. Mann and I were going to have a talk. Lovely and perfect as Julia was, I hadn't given my permission for an indefinite stay.

"Oh, that's so kind of you. I don't mean to impose again, but I…called Matt and Anna. We talked. We're over. It wasn't nearly as bad as I'd feared. They're not happy, but they seem to understand.

"I made arrangements to pick up my stuff from their place. Today. I would be so grateful if I could borrow one of your cars. Maybe the minivan? I sold my car when I moved in with them. I know…dumb, right?

"I would be even more grateful if one of you could come with me and hold my hand. And, you know, carry some heavy boxes."

Mann squeezed her hand. "We're here for you, Julia. I'm meeting a rep from a Bangkok incubator this afternoon—real edgy stuff—but I'm sure Helen would be glad to help."

I glared at Mann while he stared back at me, all wide-eyed innocence. Julia thanked me profusely.

***

I dropped the girls at Poppy's, then I picked up Julia for what I feared would be an ugly confrontation with Matt and Anna.

As we snaked through the placid streets of Palo Alto, I felt like a getaway driver on the way to a heist. My heart slammed itself into my rib cage, telling me in no uncertain terms what it thought of the idea. I ignored it and focused on driving below the speed limit, but not so slowly as to suggest guilt.

Julia was quiet, tapping her fingers against the cloth armrest. She was clearly nervous, as befitting a woman about to meet her recent exes. I couldn't believe that Mann had volunteered me for this mission. Or that I had resentfully accepted.

When we arrived at the designated address, a sweet little pastel bungalow that reminded me of Poppy's place, I parked several yards away from the driveway under a shady tree. I didn't want to make it too easy for Matt and Anna to read my license plate.

Julia sat silently, her face empty. I imagined she was corralling her dread, locking it away somewhere it couldn't interfere with what she had come here to do. Her fingers thrummed and tapped. Despite myself, I felt for her. I smiled as best I could and squeezed her hand.

"Julia, would you like me to come in with you?"

She shook her head. "Thank you. But I think I can handle it for now. I want to at least try to be brave. Understand?"

I didn't, I'm not brave, but I nodded. Julia slipped out of the car and marched to the front door. She knocked. A tall, dark-haired woman answered. This had to be Anna. She threw her long, finely muscled arms around Julia, who only softened a little bit.

I rolled down my window and turned on my camera, bearing indelible witness, just in case. Julia turned and waved to me, and disappeared inside.

About ten minutes later, Julia and probably-Anna began ferrying an array of bulky boxes and bags. I got out of the van and helped Julia, who was listing and struggling with her load. I watched Anna carry hers with sure, athletic grace. She didn't look like an abusive, controlling she-beast. But appearances lie.

Together, we filled the van with box after box, and bag after bag, as if we were completing a puzzle.

When we were done, all of us breathing heavily, Anna turned to me. Her eyes were red and swollen. "Don't let her fool you," she said. "She's tougher and meaner than she looks."

I almost stammered out a lame question, something along the lines of, 'What do you mean?' But Anna was already hurrying back to the house.

I herded Julia into the van and pulled into the street. "What was that all about?"

Julia shook her head and blinked her eyes. "She wanted me to stay. After everything they did to me. I couldn't believe it. She said she was heartbroken. I don't think she has a heart."

"Oh, everyone has a heart," I murmured. "Especially the crazy ones."

As I drove, it occurred to me that I might be one of the crazy ones. I stayed with Karl for months after I found Mann. My attachment to bad, old habits was too deeply ingrained. I might never have left them behind if fate hadn't done it for me.

As much as I didn't like imagining Mann with Julia, I reminded myself that I had put him through something similar. Worse, really, because of my lies.

***

"Chase! Chase!"

Mann was chasing Rose around the yard while Briar sat in the garden, smelling morning glories. I was pulling weeds. Julia was picking flowers to make bouquets for the girls. A bottle of wheat-colored wine sat on a table by the pool, along with two chilled glasses.

"Helen," Mann called. "That wine over there is for you and Jules. You two should have a drink. Try to relax."

When Julia grinned with unfeigned delight, Mann's eyes burned with more happiness than I'd seen from him in years. He chased Rose with renewed glee and roused a reluctant Briar from the flower beds.

I followed Julia to the table and poured us each a glass of wine. She raised her glass in a toast. "To endings and beginnings."

I clinked her glass and swallowed an oversized mouthful of chardonnay. I craved a Xanax to go with it. Julia was glowing, and my jealousy flourished like kudzu in the warmth of her joy. Mann was stealing worried glimpses of us. His face had a hopeful yet wary cast that I remembered from our ill-fated dates with Emma.

I stifled a gasp. It finally clicked. I knew why he had set up this tableau. I knew why I was nervous. And I knew what he wanted from me.

Emma, I was sure, had been unmitigated bad news. She worshipped Mann and his work. She never once asked about the girls. She claimed my husband like a lost piece of luggage. Who knows what she would have done if I hadn't taken action.

Julia, for all her issues and all my doubts, was trying. She talked to me. She was kind to the girls. And the girls liked her. More than liked her, which both comforted and needled me. I wished I knew her name, but I had no reason to doubt that Mann had thoroughly vetted her, that she was OK. And I had agreed to an open marriage. I had given my word.

Deep down, I supposed, I was selfish. If I had my way, Mann wouldn't have a girlfriend. And he wouldn't want one, either. But was Julia, all things considered, really so bad?

"I think my husband has a crush on you," I said.

Julia looked up. "What do mean?"

I almost groaned. She was going to play coy. I was going to be Mann's procuress, a role I preemptively despised. "He's interested in you. I think he would like to pursue you. And I want you to know that's OK with me."

Julia's face went blank again. Her pupils grew and her lips reddened. She was processing, maybe even fantasizing. Just when I thought I would have to say something again, perhaps something extolling Mann's virtues, she spoke. Her voice was a tiny squeak. "Do you really think he likes me?"

I stifled a roll of my eyes. "Yes, I do. And I think we should do something about it."

"What?" she asked, taking a large sip of wine.

"I have an idea."

And then I told her about the plan that would make me perhaps the most unselfish wife in the entire Western world.

***

"What time are our reservations?" Mann called from upstairs. His voice had the dull timbre of someone fulfilling an obligation.

"Seven twenty. You better hustle your butt," I yelled.

Julia giggled conspiratorially. I had cordoned the children into high chairs and, for once, they were eating. While I tended to the twins, wiping mouths and assisting with oddly sized bites, Julia waited, wearing her smaller copy of our twinned blue dress.

When Mann appeared in the kitchen, his expression was irritated. "Helen, what are you doing? Why are you feeding the kids when our reservation is in twenty minutes?"

Julia emerged from behind the staircase, her steps small and tentative. As she approached, her face wore a nervous half-smile. "Surprise?" Her voice was small and forlorn. "Helen and I worked it out. You're going to dinner with me tonight." She paused, plunging into uncertainty. "That is, if you want to."

Mann looked at her and then at me. He grinned and mouthed 'I love you, Helen,' and took Julia's hand. "Yes, of course I would."

He led her outside without even a goodbye to me and the children. Julia waved and flashed me a grateful, ecstatic smile. I continued feeding the girls, conscious that I was, at last, alone.

Alone in the house. Alone with all of Julia's bags filled with clothes and memories…and secrets.

***

After the girls went to bed, I popped a Xanax and headed straight for what was fast becoming Julia's room. A MacBook shrink-wrapped in a floral cover sat on the bed like an invitation. Perhaps it contained her real name or some other key to her past.

I ran my fingers over the machine. It was warm to the touch. It was also almost certainly password protected, and I am no hacker. To have even the smallest chance of cracking it, I would have to watch her type it in. And passwords are usually much longer and more complicated than simple, six-digit pin numbers.

I stared at it for a long while. I thought about all the things I should be grateful for. The twins. My health, which was suspect but could be so much worse. And Mann, who loved me in his own way and was trying to make things work. He had sacrificed his sexuality for *more than two years,* all to stay married to me. I owed him.

Julia was my gift to my husband. A gift and a reparation of sorts. I decided I wasn't going to look for reasons to take her away.

8 WHO'S REALLY IN CHARGE

After only a few weeks, Julia became a fixture in our lives. A new and unexpectedly pleasing routine emerged.

Every morning, I took a long shower. It was a guilty pleasure I hadn't indulged in since the girls were born. Sometimes I wonder if I sold my soul and risked my children for those extra fifteen minutes under the hot water.

Julia, my de facto sister wife, awakened the twins and made breakfast. She did it cheerfully, effortlessly coaxing the girls out of bed. They responded to her with smiles and tight hugs. I worried about how intensely the girls were bonding with her. But I let my unease go down the drain along with the warm, soapy water.

Mann either slept in or left for a meeting. He didn't figure into our mornings, which bothered me less than I thought it would. After all, with two wives, what is left for a husband to do?

When I was clean and dressed, I descended the stairs like a freshly crowned queen. I greeted the girls and Julia. And they greeted me back.

"Good morning, Mommy!"

"Good morning, Helen."

During breakfast, I returned emails while Julia entertained the girls. Afterwards, I whisked them to Poppy's and drove to work.

Julia remained at home, doing yoga in our upstairs studio and casting domestic spells. She cleaned the kitchen. Bought groceries. Prepped meals. Sorted the recyclables. And she did it all with the help of a second Tesla just like Mann's, another one of his many company cars.

She fit perfectly into a hole we never knew we had. She did all the wifely things I had once grumpily shoehorned around my ten-hour workdays. My schedule was unexpectedly spacious. I had time to breathe.

I started going to the gym during my lunch hour instead of chasing errands. I spent my time at home snuggling my children instead of shooing them away from the hot stove. And I had an invaluable extra hand during the slippery, pink-limbed insanity that was bath time with the twins.

For the first time in years, my numbers pointed towards a better future. My blood pressure and weight were down. My average speed on the treadmill was up. Perhaps I wouldn't need Dr. Yu's referrals after all. My daughters were thriving, eating and laughing more. It seemed that, contrary to expectation, sharing my husband was actually good for me.

And it was good for Mann. He came straight home after work, where he greeted his girls—all four of us—with disarming affection. He might pat me on the shoulder or swoop in to tickle the twins. More awkwardly, he would sometimes surprise Julia with a passionate kiss.

Those kisses were the only indication that he and Julia were physically involved. The rest of the time, they were admirably discreet. In fact, I believe the kisses embarrassed Julia almost as much as they did me. She always pulled away first, her eyes downcast and her cheeks hectic with color.

While I didn't exactly like Julia, the woman who was sleeping with my husband, I was coming to depend on her. And perhaps that was enough.

***

Of course, our equilibrium didn't last. It was our fourth Wednesday with Julia when things began to fall apart.

Briar and Rose were sleeping. Julia was hand-scrubbing a pan that had once cradled a vegan lasagna. I was sitting at the kitchen table, finishing the day's quota of tweets. Mann was in the screening room, watching a TED talk. Just another peaceful, poly day.

I was about to wander upstairs to read and give Mann and Julia some alone time, when Mann materialized in the kitchen like a self-satisfied genie.

"Girls!" he cried. Julia and I froze like gazelles in the presence of a lion. "I think it's time we had our first relationship summit. Join me in the movie room."

I groaned inwardly. Mann had been organizing summit talks with his various managers for the past several weeks. Now he was bringing his mania for meetings home.

Of course, Julia obeyed like a well-trained employee. Mildly disgruntled—I hate meetings of all kinds—I finished a handful of tweets before strolling into the screening room. I guess I should have moved faster. I found them on the couch, locked in a full-bodied embrace.

I coughed. "Shall I come back later?"

Julia gasped like a dying fish. "Oh my God, I'm so sorry."

Mann took her hand and gave it a firm squeeze. "There's nothing to be sorry about, Jules. Helen, did that make you uncomfortable?"

My first instinct was to say no. Like most people, I don't want to be the sensitive one, the delicate snowflake who spoils everyone's fun. But I had used some of my newfound free time to dive more deeply into polyamory. While philosophies varied, the one thing all the experts agreed upon was the importance of open and honest communication.

I took a deep breath and fully committed to being utterly lame. "Yes, it did make me uncomfortable."

Mann regarded me with hooded eyes. "Can you tell us why?"

I shuffled my feet. They were sitting together on the couch, lightly touching. I was standing in front of them like a naughty student.

"Mann, you know that I have medical issues, that I can't be, um, intimate the way we used to. But that doesn't mean I don't need affection. I feel hurt that you seem to be pouring all of your energy into your new relationship with Julia…who is, of course, perfectly wonderful."

I exhaled. I was proud of myself. I had used nonjudgmental "I statements" and framed my concerns without attacking Julia, who was nodding respectfully. But Mann looked troubled. Perhaps even offended. He put his arm around Julia, as though he was protecting her.

"Helen," he said, "thank you for being transparent. I know you're feeling a little jealous and left out, and a lot of that's my fault. But I also wish you could try to rely on yourself a little more when you feel a bit lonely.

"You used to be so independent and headstrong. I miss that part of you. You can trust in the strength of our relationship, the one between you and me, and allow it to ebb and flow naturally."

If I had been brave, I could have said so many things.

I support your relationship with Julia, but I'm not ready to watch you grinding on the couch.

I can be independent and still not like sharing so much so soon.

How can I trust our relationship when it's constantly changing?

Instead, I looked down at the floor and noticed my big toe poking out of a threadbare sock. My toenail was long and uneven. Gnarled. Then I glanced at Julia's bare feet. Her toenails were the delicate peach of a freshly caught clam. They were manicured. Glossy.

A wave of self-loathing washed through me. No wonder Mann preferred her. She was fresh and new and well maintained. Her baggage, as tragic as it was, remained lost in the past. It was not written on her body, inside and out. I inhaled, exhaled, and tried to be oh-so-mature.

"I'm happy for you and Julia, really I am," I said. "I guess I'll just have to work on, um, my jealousy issues. And being more self-sufficient."

Mann's face glowed with an unctuous smile. Had he always looked so smug and self-satisfied? Julia blushed. Perhaps she was embarrassed on my behalf.

"So, now that we're all here, are there any other issues you want to discuss? Helen? Jules?"

I sighed. Mann had been so patient—so inhumanly patient—when I lingered with Karl. Back then, I was wild and brittle. Mercurial and fragile. And yet Mann put up with me. He tolerated so much without displaying the slightest hint of jealousy. I told myself I owed him the same care and understanding now.

I smiled and shook my head. "Good," he said. "Our first successful relationship summit is complete. Helen, do you mind if Julia and I go out tomorrow night? Micah's band is playing in town."

"Nope," I said, heading back to the kitchen to finish Julia's scrubbing. With Mann, Julia and I formed a triangle. And Mann—at least, for now—was on top.

***

Although I stopped short of asking them to be more sensitive, Mann and Julia cut back on the PDA. I believed it was Julia's doing.

For days after our cringe-inducing relationship summit, she treated me like an unexploded bomb. She did my remaining chores. She made my favorite meals. She ran interference with Briar and Rose's tantrums. She put the girls to bed.

And I let her do it. I was strangely heartbroken. I felt as if I had lost Mann, even though he still loved me. Even though we lived in the same house. I nestled into my sadness and let Julia handle the girls, who were leaning hard into their terrible twos. I told myself she owed me for effectively stealing Mann.

One evening, I was working beside the pool. Mann and Julia were playing with the girls. Together, they made a pretty, sprightly family. Mann was the handsome father with just a touch of gray. Julia was a prettier, younger, and funnier version of me, a version that Briar and Rose increasingly seemed to prefer.

Motherhood had never come easily to me. I had to work at it every step of the way. I was too scared, too indulgent, too stiff. Julia, like Mann, was a natural with children. Just watching her made me depressed. I couldn't compete with her ease or bubbly personality. I knew my limits. And, really, I should have been thrilled my children had found such a wonderful, caring friend.

As I finished another vapid, keyword-laden post, Briar and Rose ran to me, smiling.

"Daddy dinner," chattered Rose. "Daddy dinner."

Briar hugged her sister.

Mann came over to collect them. "I'm going to bring the girls inside and make dinner. Julia deserves a night off."

"Sounds good," I said, conjuring a tepid smile. I waved to the girls who were already running for the house.

"Helen, do you have a minute?"

I turned my head. Julia was standing over me, her face tight and solemn. Just the sight of her made me queasy. She was eating my life, bite by delicate bite. I swallowed down a mouthful of bile. Julia was caring for my house and my children…and even for me. I had no right to resent her.

"Sure, Julia. I could use a break."

She slid into the chair across from me, and her lips curled into a tentative smile. Despite her obvious unease, she looked radiant. Her face was tanned. Her dark blond hair had lightened in the sun. Somehow, Julia had stepped into my dull, exhausting life and made it glamorous.

"I know this is going to be a little awkward, so I'm just going to say it." The words tumbled from Julia in a verbal waterfall. I braced myself for something awful. "I've been spending a lot of alone time with Mann lately. I don't feel like we're being fair to you."

I shrugged. I was well versed in how new relationship energy made poly people ignore their old partners for the new and the shiny. She and Mann were a textbook example.

"I'd like us to make a schedule. To make sure we both get enough quality time with Mann."

I sighed and looked down at my laptop, pretending to field an important email. I wanted no part of her schedule. If I agreed to it, any time I spent with Mann would be a gift from her.

"Thank you for thinking of me, Julia. But I don't think we need a formal schedule. Enjoy the new relationship energy while it lasts."

Her eyes flickered, and her mouth contracted. For a sliver of a second, her expression became something open and wild. "Oh Helen, it's not new relationship energy. It's love."

I inhaled and exhaled slowly. "Isn't that a little premature? You haven't known him all that long."

She smiled broadly. She looked like a perfect flower child, loving and careless and free. "I don't mean love in a possessive, let's-buy-property-together sense. I'm talking about love in the now. In the moment. Don't be so serious!"

I sighed. I was always serious now. I didn't used to be.

***

"Are you sure the volume on the monitor is turned up?"

"Yes, Helen,"

"Rose has night terrors. If you hear her screaming, you need to wake her up immediately."

"Yes, Helen."

"Briar sleepwalks. Be sure you put the gate up so she can't get onto the stairs."

"The gate's already up. You did it yourself a few minutes ago."

"Oh, yes, that's right."

"Stop worrying, Helen. I want you two to have a great time."

I smiled weakly. Julia had been with us for more than a month. Mann had vetted her thoroughly. He trusted her completely with our children. And yet the idea of leaving Julia alone with the twins made my guts writhe.

Mann kissed Julia and then took my hand. "C'mon Helen, you've been wanting to try the Greenhouse for ages."

He led me gently but firmly out the door while I called, "Text me if you need anything!"

Sending Mann and me on a date night was Julia's price for abandoning the formal schedule. It had seemed so reasonable at the time. And the idea of eating in a dimly restaurant, filled with quiet adult conversation, had been deeply alluring.

But now, sitting in the passenger seat of Mann's eerily quiet Tesla, I wished I was home, watching my children sleep.

I thought of Briar and Rose alone with a woman whose own, parallel twins had been marked for death. Yes, they died in a car accident with their father, at the hand of a drunk driver. But perhaps the vehicle wasn't properly maintained. Or the car seats weren't correctly installed.

Perhaps Julia was somehow to blame.

My heart fluttered, urging me to turn back. I could feel my veins constricting. I really should have taken a Xanax, but I was down to my last ten. For emergency use only.

I closed my eyes and took long, deep yoga breaths. I tried positive self-talk.

You're overreacting. You're blaming Julia for her children's accident simply because she was their mother and because you always blame yourself. Don't be judgmental. Don't make assumptions.

I kept telling myself that everything would be OK, but my heart wouldn't listen. It kept thumping away, tapping out its dire warning.

"Are you OK?" asked Mann. "You look sort of green."

I opened my eyes and repressed a groan. I couldn't tell him what I was thinking. All I would get was a lecture about not trusting him or Julia enough, even though Julia clearly didn't trust me enough to tell me her real, Google indexed name.

"I'm fine," I said more harshly than I'd intended.

"If you're not feeling well, we can go home. Do this another time." He sounded almost eager, as if he'd rather not do this at all. I was sure he'd rather be with Julia, doing whatever they do when I'm asleep.

For just a moment, my annoyance with Mann swept away irrational fears. I let my lips twist into a sardonic smile. "Oh no, honey. I want to do this now. Right now."

***

The restaurant was wonderful. At first. A waitress brought me a glass of pallid wine. I watched the people in the room, not even pretending to read the menu. Everyone looked young and happy. Freshly showered and child-free. Definitely unmarried.

The waitress arrives silently, as if on a cloud. Mann ordered for me. We made polite conversation about the news and the girls. I finished my first drink and ordered a Cabernet the color of spoiled blood. I felt calm and relaxed, as if I was floating above my real life. I was sure it was going to be a good night. Maybe even a great night.

And then Mann tearfully confessed that Julia was the best thing to ever happen to him. "She is a miracle. She is everything we were missing. I think we're falling in love. And I owe it all to you. My wonderful, open-minded wife."

I raised my glass and clinked it against his. I said nothing. I didn't want to plumb the depths of his feelings. I didn't want to hear more about how much he loved Julia, about how I paled and shriveled in comparison.

Mann, floating on the fumes of wine and infatuation, took my silence as license to declaim. "Darling, I've been meaning to ask you something. Why don't you leave the kids with Julia during the day instead of dragging them to daycare? They love her, and you could pay her what you're paying what's-her-name."

I bit the inside of my cheek. My anger tasted sour and coppery. I remembered pleading with Mann at the end of my maternity leave to stay home with the girls, and his unyielding resistance. Why was it now OK for Julia, a woman we'd known for a mere month, to spend all day with our children?

I wanted to snap, to yell, to slam something. I wanted to tell him that I would never—never—pay my money for his girlfriend to spend time with our children while I worked a job I hated.

But I couldn't. We were in a shrine to good food and polite discourse. A place where a loud woman is assumed to be unstable, or even insane. So I sipped my wine and pretended I was talking to my boss, a flighty dervish of a woman who has at least ten wildly impractical ideas every day.

"Wow," I said, feigning patient interest. "I never would have thought of that. Tell me more."

9 THE VOMITING VIGIL

The ride home from the restaurant was slow-motion torture. Mann made calm, reasoned arguments for allowing Julia to care for our kids. Quietly digging my nails into my palms, I made equally sedate rebuttals.

I took care not to criticize Julia or bring up the fact that she hadn't even told me her real name. Instead, I explained how the girls loved Poppy's house, and how spending time with other children was terribly enriching. By the time we pulled into our driveway, my right hand was bleeding. We had reached an achingly polite impasse.

When I stepped inside, the smell hit me like an overturned truck. It was the sweetly acrid bouquet of vomit. Wrinkling my nose, I followed it to the living room, while Mann lagged several steps behind. I soon found Julia, Briar, and Rose huddled on the couch, their bodies curled into postures of extreme distress.

My largest stockpots stood like reluctant soldiers on the floor in front of the coffee table. For a moment, I wondered why. Then Rose whimpered, and Julia seized her, holding her over the two-gallon soup pot. My beloved child unleashed a wave of lumpy, pink goo. And another. And another.

I wanted to run away from the evil-smelling horror like any sane person would. But I was a mother, so I did the opposite. I dropped my purse and hurried to Rose's side. When Briar started to moan, I aimed her over the smallest pot and let her dab her lips with my shirt.

After several long, gut-churning minutes, the girls stopped puking. Their heads drooped like wilting flowers. Julia and I nestled them into the couch, tucking them under washable chenille throws.

When the girls had settled, Julia parted her lips to speak, then snapped them shut. She covered her mouth and ran to the closest downstairs bathroom. I grimaced at the loud, liquid sounds.

Mann pinched his nose and sidled towards the staircase. He was a germophobe and an emetophobe. Of course, he would flee. "I have an all-hands meeting tomorrow," he said. "I can't afford to be sick."

When Julia returned, her face was chalky and her expression miserable. "It seems like we all have a stomach bug," she said wanly. "Why don't you go to bed and let me stay up with the girls? You have to work tomorrow."

For a brief, shameful moment, I considered taking her up on it. It was an opportunity to sleep uninterrupted in my clean, vomit-free room. But then I looked at my girls, at their sleepy, clammy faces. I wanted to care for them. I needed to. Besides, this was my chance to draw a boundary, to make it clear that the girls belonged to me.

"Oh, that's so kind of you, but you're sick. You need to rest. I'll stay up with Briar and Rose. You focus on getting well."

Julia's lips twitched into a thin-lipped, possibly insincere smile. "Alright. I suppose. If you're really sure…"

She let her voice trail off. A flash of anger surged through me. She sounded like she didn't trust me with my own children, as if she were their protector and not me. I smiled broadly. Maybe even cruelly. "Yes, I'm sure. Very sure."

After Julia left, I put grape-flavored Pedialyte with ice into two sippy cups and gave the girls small, metered sips. Briar fell into a fitful sleep. Rose asked to watch *Frozen*, which I reluctantly allowed. My nose itched, but I kept my hands by my sides. I knew better than to touch my face before scrubbing up.

When Rose's eyes finally closed, I decamped for my bathroom. As the hot, soapy water rinsed away a massive viral load, I remembered the last time I'd thrown up. I was in the hospital, thirty-eight weeks pregnant with the girls. My right side throbbed while my stomach churned. It was HELLP

Syndrome, a severe form of preeclampsia. The blank-faced OB suggested I make a will.

Watching myself in the mirror, I could easily imagine myself close to death. Dark pouches shadowed my eyes. Deep folds connected my nose to the corners of my mouth. I looked old. Finite.

I shook my head, returning to the present. I didn't have time to contemplate my mortality. I needed to be a calm, reassuring presence for my girls. I needed to be fucking serene. So I decided to take one—or two—of my last remaining Xanax.

I opened the cabinet and reached for the nearly empty bottle. I really didn't want to call Dr. Yu for a refill, especially since I hadn't followed up with any of the cardiologists or psychiatrists she recommended. When I placed the bottle back on the shelf, my stomach unclenched. A brand-new, full bottle sat at attention beside the ibuprofen.

I popped a pill, grateful for my newfound abundance, and padded downstairs. I made myself comfortable on a reclining chair, ready as I would ever be for the vomiting vigil.

***

I awakened the next morning to what sounded like a wounded mastodon. I looked around the living room. The girls were fitfully sleeping on the couch. Julia was, I hoped, still in her room.

I followed the moaning upstairs to the master bathroom, the one Mann and I shared. He was hunched over the toilet, expelling last night's free-range steak. His brow was slick with viral sweat. His face contorted with a mixture of rage and fear.

"You look awful," I said quietly, respecting the depths of his misery.

He groaned and rested his head against the toilet's cool, porcelain rim.

"The girls had a pretty rough night," I reported. "I'm going to run them into the doctor's office. I'm taking the day off from work."

He opened his eyes and looked at me, as if he were about to say something. I suspect he was going to suggest I let Julia handle the girls while I went to the office. But instead, he emptied more of his stomach into the bowl.

"Can I get you some water? Or some Pedialyte?"

He shook his head and grunted softly. It was my cue to exit. He didn't like company when he was sick. He didn't want anyone to see him as vulnerable or weak. It was, ironically, one of his only weaknesses.

***

Transporting sick children is always a perilous business. I lined the floor of the minivan with plastic tarp. Then I bundled the girls into makeshift ponchos made of garbage bags and strapped them in. And yet I was certain I would end up scrubbing vomit out of the car seats' many crenelated straps.

At the doctor's office, I carried the girls in, still swaddled in trash bags. I placed them on a couch, desperately hoping they wouldn't puke. The nurse at the front desk wore a wide smile sharply delineated by plum-colored lipstick.

"I have an eight o'clock appointment for Briar and Rose. The last name is Gottlieb."

"Can I see your insurance card?" Because Mann kept neglecting to fill out certain paperwork, the girls and I were on my crappy WorldFeed insurance plan. Although I hated my job, I was oddly proud to supply this one necessity for my girls.

But when I opened my wallet to produce the magic blue card, it was gone. I pulled out credit cards and store loyalty cards, scrutinizing each one, hoping I had missed something. But I hadn't. My insurance card had vanished.

How could that have happened? I wondered if Mann had borrowed the card for some reason, maybe to get information for a tax form. It was a stretch, but it was all I could think of.

The nurse regarded me with a tired, disapproving gaze, her smile turning into concertina wire. "Insurance card?" she asked in a sharp, resonant voice. Other mothers in the waiting area—there were no fathers that morning—turned to stare, perhaps suspecting me of poverty or disorganization.

"Look, I seem to have misplaced it. Can't you just pull the information from your computer files?"

The nurse huffed as if I were asking her to climb Mount Everest. "Fine. But you'll have to wait."

She found my insurance data, and the doctor eventually called us in. But not before Briar and Rose barfed all over the waiting room couch as I smiled apologetically while the other, waiting mothers grabbed their children and shrank away.

***

With the help of prescription nausea meds, the girls revived quickly. They ate two bananas and a handful of crackers. They even played a little before their nap. I placed them in their own beds and said another secular prayer.

Then I began the hunt for my insurance card. Sure, I could have gone online and printed another one, using the girls' safety scissors to cut along the dotted line. But I wanted my durable, plastic blue card back. It represented safety. Independence. Emergency service.

I went through my purse and my computer bag. Nothing and nothing. I checked the master bedroom. Mann was snoring lightly. He smelled sweet, sour, and earthy, like decomposing fruit. I let him rest and padded into his office. I found his wallet and looked inside. Nothing again.

For a moment, I wondered if one of the girls might have taken it. Rose had hidden my wallet once. But I couldn't imagine her stubby little fingers actually grasping and extracting the card. Still, I tossed the crib and found…nothing.

Finally, my thoughts turned to Julia. The second wife. The third. Our third. I couldn't imagine her actually reaching into my wallet and lifting my card. After all, what on earth could she do with someone else's insurance card?

Get healthcare, duh. Especially if she wasn't insured. After all, we were roughly the same height with similar features. She was the good copy, the pretty copy. I was the faded, swollen version.

I went back downstairs and rapped lightly on Julia's door. "Hello?"

When she didn't respond, I turned the knob and stepped inside, a preemptive apology in my throat. But I got lucky. She was sleeping on her back like a fallen angel, arms thrown over her head. Her purse and wallet sat on the dresser in plain view, along with keys to Mann's Tesla…and my bright blue card.

I was, frankly, elated. Julia had really stolen my insurance card. I had not suspected her unjustly! My doubts about her weren't entirely grounded in jealousy! I grabbed the card and shoved it into my pocket. I was thinking about going through her wallet and her purse when she stirred and blinked open her eyes.

"Helen?" she asked.

"Just checking on you. Do you need anything?"

"No, just rest."

"Of course," I said, closing the door. I would talk to her later. And Mann. Especially Mann.

***

The evening crawled by. The girls lolled in front of the television. I couldn't stop thinking about my discovery. Was stealing the insurance card a game changer? Would it convince Mann that my worries about Julia weren't a smokescreen for jealousy? I wasn't sure, but I hoped.

After dinner, Julia crept into the kitchen. She moved slowly like a convalescent, filling a red kettle with water and putting it on the stove. She made a face and smiled at me as if to say, *Everything's OK.*

"I'm going to make some tea and go sit with the girls. I'm glad to see they're looking so much better."

"Me too," I said, feeling a small pang of guilt. She had, after all, cared for my girls when they were sick. "I need to talk to you, just for a minute."

The twins were hypnotized by Daniel Tiger. It was my chance to talk to Julia, to get some answers.

"When I looked in on you today, I found my insurance card on the dresser. Can you tell me why you had it?"

Julia froze. Her face went slack and empty. I supposed her mind was working furiously. Nobody who transgresses ever plans to get caught. "I'm sorry," she said, her voice small and contrite. "This is really embarrassing."

I wanted to snap at her that getting caught for stealing is an intrinsically embarrassing experience. But I held my tongue. I wanted to know what had prompted her to look into my bag, open my wallet, and help herself. Perhaps she had helped herself to other things, too.

Julia's eyes dropped to the floor. "I had a UTI. It always happens when I have sex with a new partner. I don't have health insurance. After Malcom and my girls died, I just kind of forgot about it. It didn't seem important.

"I felt weird about asking you or Mann for money. I thought if I just borrowed your insurance card, I could get treated without bothering anyone. I went to the Whole Health clinic, over by the freeway. I was going to put it back, I swear. But then we all got sick, and…"

Julia trailed off. Her eyes swam with tears. I wanted to tell her to grow up, that it would have been perfectly reasonable to ask Mann for money, that I would have vastly preferred it to having this conversation. But she looked so sad, so lonely. She glanced at the girls, who glanced back, their faces frankly curious.

I shrugged. My time was up for now. "OK, Julia. Just please don't do that again. When I brought the kids to the doctor this morning, I didn't have my card because it was in your room. It was a problem."

Julia's hands flew to her mouth like doves. "I'm so sorry. You can't believe how sorry I am." She turned and fled to her room, like a startled nymph. I felt like an ogre: big and heavy and needlessly cruel.

And the whistle of Julia's abandoned red tea kettle felt like a warning.

At midnight, I warmed up some chicken soup. My stomach ached with a biting, angry pain. I hoped it was hunger. Mann shuffled into the kitchen and silently filled his bowl. He sat down across from me and took small, measured sips.

"How are you doing?" I asked, truly concerned.

He looked up at me and smiled, perhaps reacting to the warmth in my voice. His expression was softer than I'd seen it for weeks. A little of the tenderness he had been hoarding for Julia was trickling down to me. "I've been better. How about you?"

I smiled back. "I've been lucky. So far."

"And Julia?"

My heart leaped into my throat, and I swallowed it down. "Did you know she stole my insurance card?"

Mann choked on his soup. "What?"

"She took my card out of my wallet and used it at a clinic. She said she had a UTI and didn't have enough money for antibiotics. She pretended to be me. She committed fraud."

Mann's brow wrinkled. "Why didn't she ask me?"

I shrugged. "Maybe she doesn't want you to think she's a mess who needs someone to take care of her. And that's what she is, you know. A hot mess."

"That's not fair," said Mann, his face hardening into a stern mask. "She lost her family."

I shook my head. For a so-called genius entrepreneur, he could be awfully dense. "She's a mess *because* she lost her family. She's broke. She's confused. She's still grieving. Are we ready to take that on?"

Mann bristled. "Are you saying we just throw her out because she's going through a tough time? Because she's human? Do you remember what a wreck you were when your parents died?"

My eyes stung. My parents had passed away the year before I got pregnant, my father from a heart attack and my mother from cirrhosis brought on from too much drink. Mann had been immensely patient and kind.

"Yes, and I'm grateful. But we have children now. They come first, and I'm not sure she should be around them. I'm not sure being around Briar and Rose is good for *her*. At the very least, she needs a ton of therapy."

Mann stood up and shook his head, equal parts annoyed and disappointed. "Helen, please stop using the kids as an excuse. You're overreacting because you're feeling insecure. Stop judging Julia and focus on yourself. If anyone needs therapy, it's you."

With that, I was dismissed. He turned and walked away. I stayed in the kitchen, crying gently through a light Xanax fog. Perhaps he was right. Perhaps I needed therapy. Perhaps we all did.

My stomach growled and lurched. It had turned against me, too.

10 NO EXIT

I was still convalescing. Achy. Tender. Everyone else had bounced back. And yet Mann and Julia were sleeping in while I fed Briar and Rose. They must be catching up on sex, I thought bitterly. Mann refused to believe that Julia's taking my insurance card was a problem.

Would anything she did ever be a problem for him? What if she burned the house down? Or killed one of the children? I pinched the back of my hand. Even I knew that sort of thinking was the express bus to madness.

I forced myself to focus on solid, practical things. The remains of breakfast. The dishes. While I cleared the table, the girls banged pots and pans. They spotted Mann and Julia before I did.

"Daddy!" chirped Briar.

"Jooooooolia!" shrieked Rose.

The girls flung themselves into their arms, and I observed once again what a lovely family they made. Julia was an airbrushed version of me: younger, slimmer, and more energetic.

Mann murmured something, and Julia kissed each girl on the forehead. Then they turned to me shyly, like nervous school children. It was as if they had a plan.

"I'm going to take the girls to see their grandmother. We'll make it a sleepover," said Mann. "Give you and Julia some time to get to know each other."

The girls echoed, "Gramma! Gramma!"

I frowned. Mann's mother had Alzheimer's disease. She lived alone in a small house with two rotating, live-in care aides. We used to see her every other weekend until several months ago, when she began slapping and pinching the girls. Since then, Mann had visited alone.

"Are you sure that's a good idea?" I asked.

Mann clucked indulgently, casting me as a mother who worried excessively and irrationally. "Lydia, her nurse, says she's having a good day. And she has them so rarely now. Besides, I'll be with them the whole time, watching like a hawk."

I sighed. He was good with the girls. Despite his faults and his uncomfortable affection for Julia, he was a careful, responsible father. And the girls deserved a chance to know their grandmother, even fleetingly.

I did the only thing I could have. I let them go.

***

Julia and I had the house to ourselves. But that didn't mean I was going to spend my time with her, pouring out the dregs of my soul.

We moved about in awkward orbits, me trying to find some solitude and her trailing with offers to clean, make snacks, teach me yoga. Her mood was persistently apologetic. Tentatively friendly. Shyly victorious.

While she hand-washed the dishes in the kitchen, I slunk away to the patio with a book. I tried to put myself in her shoes. What would it be like to be so grief-stricken and alone? What would I do to fill the void? Would I steal someone else's family?

I had no idea. Yes, I lost my parents. It was terribly sad. It was also inevitable. The natural order of things. Honestly, it was even sort of a relief. My father and I were always separated by his rage and my fear. I missed the idea of having a father more than I missed the man. And my mother, free at last, was a disappointment.

And then there was Karl's disappearance.

But losing one's children is an affront to nature. It's freakish. Unspeakable. Perhaps a loss of that magnitude would make everything else seem small.

Yes, I was beginning to feel stirrings of sympathy for Julia. And yet I was increasingly loathe to share my life with her. I didn't trust her seemingly endless kindness and willingness to serve. I believed it concealed a raw, devouring need.

"Helen, would you like a glass of wine?"

I looked up and saw Julia standing beside me in a bikini and a filmy cover up. Her hair was loose and beachy. Her cheeks creased with a tentative smile. Her nose crinkled adorably.

For a moment, I wanted to strangle her. My face warmed with an anger so intense I nearly gasped. Was I really just jealous of her and Mann? Was that all it was? Or was I reacting to something else, something more sinister? I breathed slowly and managed a small smile. "Isn't it a little early?"

Julia grinned. "It's five o'clock somewhere." She took my silence as consent. She poured us both large glasses of chardonnay and sat down beside me. I eyed the wine with suspicion. My stomach was still uncertain.

"I just wanted to say how grateful I am," she said. "I mean, Mann told me, but I'm sure you made the decision together."

My heart paused. I held my breath, as if I had just boarded a roller coaster. To hell with my stomach. I took a long swallow of wine that burned my throat. "What, exactly, did Mann tell you?"

"He said that I could live here officially, really move in. He also bought me health insurance, so I'll never have to borrow your card again. He is so generous. You both are."

Julia's eyes grew big and moist. She beamed like everything was completely forgiven, like we were all one big, happy polyamorous triad. Her transparent joy was both touching and enraging. I wanted to slap her pretty, glowing face.

I had to get myself under control. I wasn't going to ruin our marriage. I wasn't going to say anything I might regret, at least not until I talked to Mann.

I took a long, deep breath and exhaled the anger. I look another gulp of wine and reminded myself whom I was really mad at: Mann. My man. Her man.

***

When Mann arrived the next morning, the children announced his return, flying through the house and flinging themselves onto Julia and me.

"Momeee! Jooolia!" they shrieked. I listened carefully to their voices, inspecting every syllable for evidence they were beginning to prefer her to me.

Mann stepped into the kitchen looking tired and under-caffeinated. Nearly twenty-four hours alone with the girls and his ailing mother had definitely taken a toll. Normally, I would have been sympathetic. But now I was glad to see his edges dulled and cracked.

"So, how did it go?" I asked in a brittle voice.

"Fun. Sad. Exhausting. I don't think my mother has much longer." Julia and I nodded while he paused, his eyes lingering on her lips and her smooth, finely muscled arms. "I'm going upstairs to shower and unpack. I'll see you in a little while."

Mann climbed the stairs with the gait of an old man. Julia tracked his movements and shifted her weight, as if to follow. No, she would not get to him first. Not today.

"Julia? Can you watch the kids for a second? I'm going upstairs. Just for a minute."

She smiled broadly like a second string player who has just been tapped for the big game. "Sure! Go! Take as long as you want!"

That was all I needed to hear. I hurried up the stairs and blew into the bedroom Mann and I shared less and less. He was unpacking his dull, meticulously constructed clothes. He loved subtle quality.

I pretended to cough. "Mann?" He turned to look at me. I could see the disappointment in his eyes. Perhaps I had let him down by simply being me and not Julia.

"Did you invite Julia to move in without asking me?"

Mann's face tightened. Small creases spread out around his eyes. "Oh Helen, I'm sorry. I thought we'd already talked about it. I was sure you said it was fine. Anyway, I'm not sure why you're so upset. She's been our guest for weeks."

I frowned and tried to remember when we had talked. Could I have possibly consumed too much wine and Xanax and simply forgotten? I didn't think so. But Mann sounded so calm, so reasonable. He wasn't perfect by any stretch—whoever is?—but he wasn't a liar. Was he?

I struggled to hang onto my anger. "You must have misunderstood. I don't remember telling you she could live here. I don't even remember us talking about it."

Mann sighed deeply. "It was late. I knew you were tired. I should have picked a different time. So, what do we do now? Julia is excited about living here. And the girls love her. Do you want me to tell her we need to take a step back?"

Now it was my turn to sigh. "I don't know. I just don't know."

Mann put his arm around me. "Do you think we could try it? Give it a chance for a few months, let her feel like she has a real home? If it makes you too uncomfortable, we can tell her it didn't work out."

My anger floated away like a lost balloon, leaving me uncertain and confused. I hated the idea of Julia moving in, but I also hated the idea of disappointing her and Mann. I was also concerned about the odd gap in my memory. Perhaps I needed to cut back on the wine and the Xanax.

"OK," I said, leaning into Mann. "We'll try. But no promises."

***

Monday was a relief. I loaded the girls into the car an hour early and drove to the Pancake Hut. The girls would enjoy a special breakfast, and I would enjoy not watching Mann squeeze Julia's thigh under the table.

The restaurant was blessedly quiet. We easily snagged a booth. I looked at the menus and ordered three small stacks of pancakes while the girls ripped their napkins into tiny pieces. When the food arrived, they dipped their fingers in syrup and munched in relative silence. I soaked in their presence, unmediated by Julia's grating good cheer.

Afterwards, I took the girls to daycare as usual. Today, Poppy looked eerily like Snow White. Her dark hair curled at the ends, and she wore a blue dress with red trim. I felt more like the wicked queen. I followed the girls inside, hoping Poppy would talk to me.

"How's the open marriage working out?" she asked, red lips curving into a half-smile.

I struggled to find the right words. My mind retraced the twisted path that had led me here. Just two months ago, I had been nervous but cautiously optimistic. Unselfish and brave. Ready to bend the rules of monogamy and make my husband's life better, more fulfilled.

Now I was bitter. Depressed. Jealous. I had somehow forgotten Mann's pain, the needs I hadn't, couldn't, fulfill.

Poppy cocked her head slightly to her left. "That bad?" she asked. "Want to come in for some coffee?"

"Yes," I said, gratefully following her inside. She put on the coffee and settled the girls with a family of multicolored, singing dolls. Weighed down with pancakes, they played quietly.

Poppy handed me a steaming mug with the manner of a nurse dispensing morphine. I took a sip. My eyes, both traitors, stung.

"What's wrong?" she asked in a quiet, inviting voice.

"Everything," I choked out, confessing my misdeeds with Emma, the rise of Julia, Julia's dark past, and Mann's burgeoning love. I told her about Mann and Julia's unstoppable new relationship energy and admitted to jealousy so thick and ever present I could barely breathe.

"When I agreed to an open marriage," I said, "I thought I could handle it. But it's just so hard."

I wiped at my eyes and sipped my coffee. Poppy regarded me with a furrowed brow. "How long have you known Julia?" she asked.

"Almost two months."

Poppy shook her head. "No, that is not OK. They're moving too fast for you. Too fast for most people. Sure, you're jealous. But they're throwing gas on the fire. You need to talk to your husband."

I sniffed. What did she think I was doing? "I tried talking to him, but he just keeps saying I'm insecure."

Poppy shook her head. "You have to make him listen. And talk to her, too. Be honest. Tell her you're uncomfortable."

She paused and added, "Look, I'll be talking to Mann later today about my startup proposal. Do you want me to say something?"

I was about to ask what she would say when the doorbell chimed. Poppy hopped up. Moments later, five two-year-olds, all part of the same Byzantine carpool, tumbled into the kitchen.

I dumped my coffee into the sink and waved goodbye to Poppy, who mouthed, "Talk more tomorrow."

I left for work tasting a small tang of hope. With Poppy to advise me, perhaps I could navigate the tangled mess I'd made of my home, heart, and mind.

***

The next day, I arrived at Poppy's brimming with cautious optimism. She waved us inside, but she seemed distracted. Somehow off. She gave Briar an extra hug along with her favorite bunny book, and kissed wiggly Rose on her forehead.

The Hello Kitty clock on the wall tick-tocked while Poppy poured our coffee. She sat across from me, spilling hot liquid from her mug. Her eyes were slightly swollen, as if she'd been crying.

Perhaps everything in her poly paradise wasn't as perfect as I'd thought it was. I was about to ask how she was when she said, "Fuck, Helen, I'm going to miss your kids. I wish I could have kept them through the end of the week. I'll refund you for Wednesday through Friday."

I stared at Poppy, the information floating through my mind, but not latching onto anything solid. "What are you talking about?"

Her dark eyebrows flew together. "Mann told me you were taking the kids out of daycare. He said you'd hired a private nanny."

I shook my head slowly. "No, that's news to me. Anyway, I pay their fees, not Mann. The girls are staying."

Poppy sighed heavily. "No, they can't. I'm sorry. Look, I know you and your husband are having problems. I don't want to get in the middle of anything. I'm sorry, but I still need my startup funding."

***

As I drove to work, I played Poppy's words over and over in my mind. She was deeply invested in her after-hours startup. Mann was a big deal in Silicon Valley, a well-connected investor. She hadn't wanted to cross him. I was disappointed but not surprised.

Since I married Mann, I had lived in his shadow. At first, I was a happy robin, nesting in a strong, sheltering tree. But now I was a bug caught under his boot. My anger, deprived of its rightful target, turned on me. My heart and head pounded as one awful, pulsing entity.

I walked to my desk through a cloud of rage and despair. People may have waved at me, or said hello. I may have nodded back. I logged onto my

PC and went through the motions of work. I fell into a trance, my thoughts looping through my conversation with Poppy and its implications.

After an hour or two, automated warnings began to strobe across my screen.

You missed your target.

Work differently.

Work smarter.

I forced myself to focus. I changed the settings on my headphones. I typed like the wind, producing tweets and posts without having a single, well-formed thought. I spent lunchtime at my desk, eating a tahini and watercress sandwich Julia had prepared for me.

I blinked back tears as I crunched down on the cress. I could no longer pretend that Julia was a harmless infatuation, something to be endured and eventually forgotten. She would, until I negotiated some other childcare option with Mann, be spending her days with Briar and Rose. And her nights with their father.

And I didn't even know her real name.

My heart echoed in my ears, refusing to calm. I put two fingers on my neck and felt my thumping pulse. The message quivering in my chest was clear, although I didn't want to hear it. Perhaps, instead of talking to Mann, I should divorce him.

11 A TERRIBLE MOTHER

At noon, I crept into a quiet part of the WorldFeed parking lot and made an appointment with a divorce lawyer. It felt like an irrevocable leap into an endless abyss. I almost canceled at least ten times.

I left work an hour early, hiding behind dark glasses. Brittany, my boss, beamed her disapproval from behind waist-high cubicle walls. "Later," muttered my nearest coworkers, who knew me as the old woman who was always complaining about the noise.

As I started my car, I felt vaguely guilty, faintly hopeful, and immensely frightened. Even my driving was conflicted. I accelerated too quickly and braked too much. I was relieved and terrified when I pulled into the office park where the lawyer's office hid among a dozen tech startups.

I parked at the edge of the lot and hurried into the office like a vampire running from the California sun. I was afraid I would run into my husband who meets with startups all the time. I hadn't made a decision yet. I wasn't ready to explain myself.

The lobby was painfully white and bright, dotted with narrow, minimalist chairs. The space was big and airy. I felt exposed, like a fly on a white tablecloth. Squashed into the widest chair I could find, I typed my biographical information into an iPad and swiped *submit*. My heart quivered. My hands were clammy. What was I doing here?

I wondered if I was making a giant, life-altering mistake. Perhaps the best next step was therapy. Or simply speaking to Mann in a louder voice and refusing to stop until he agreed to listen. I glanced at my phone. Less than one hour before I had to pick up the girls.

"Mrs. Gottlieb?" A woman in a blue pantsuit peered at me through silver-rimmed glasses. Her hair was frosted, and her face was hidden behind a wall of makeup.

"Yes, that's me." I stood up, lightheaded from fear. I wanted to leave, but I couldn't go back now. I was too much of a good girl to walk out the door without a long, simpering explanation.

The woman nodded, but didn't smile. "I'm Agnes Tremblay, and I specialize in high income divorce. Please come with me."

She motioned to her office, but she didn't offer to shake my hand. I cringed inside. My armpits were clammy. Sweat trickled down my sides. Perhaps she had scented me and decided I smelled like weakness. I followed her at a polite distance.

Her office was as spare and intimidating as the lobby. A smooth-faced man who couldn't have been older than twenty-five—an intern? a paralegal?—offered to get me water. I declined.

Agnes sipped from her bottle, watching me like a vulture inspecting a carcass. "Can you tell me a little more about your marriage? And why you want to leave?"

I took a deep, ragged breath and provided a quick synopsis of what I called the Julia situation. I talked about my unconventional arrangement with Mann. Her tragic past and theft of my insurance card. Mann's growing infatuation and refusal to tell me her real name. How he unilaterally changed the girls' childcare arrangement without consulting me.

Towards the end of my recitation, Agnes began tapping her manicured nails against the table. Her thin lips curved into a frown. I babbled faster and faster, like a teenager in the principal's office trying to talk my way out of detention.

"Let me get this straight," said Agnes in a voice that had picked up a slight East Coast edge. "You allowed your husband to move his flaky girlfriend into your home? Even when you believed she could be a threat to your children?"

I blushed and stammered, unable to formulate an answer beyond a spastic, "Y-yes. But it was c-complicated."

Agnes' eyes narrowed. She radiated contempt. "If that's true, you are a weak sister and a terrible mother. You should have come here when your husband got the girlfriend in the first place.

"I'm going to be honest with you. I prefer to represent clients I can respect or, at least, sympathize with. You don't tick either one of those boxes for me."

I didn't hear the rest of what she said. Of course, she was right. My open marriage had opened my girls up to danger. And now I was stuck, and they were stuck. "Excuse me," I said, holding back an ocean of tears. "I've got to pick up my kids from daycare."

I discovered I could leave, after all. I ignored her cries of "Wait! Wait just a minute, ma'am!" and threw myself back into the blinding sun.

***

At home, I popped a Xanax and settled on the couch like an ailing bird. The words *terrible mother* echoed in my head. Why hadn't I asked Julia to leave as soon as I decided she shouldn't be around the girls? Did I really believe she was a threat? Or was I just a jealous wife, afraid of losing her marriage and couples' privilege?

I remembered my own mother. How helpless she was before my father's rages. How weak and ineffectual she had seemed to me. How useless. Had I somehow become her when I wasn't looking? I thought choosing Mann—smart, responsible, level-headed Mann—instead of someone like Karl had saved me from that fate. But now I wasn't so sure. After all, I didn't really leave Karl, didn't make a true conscious choice. I just breathed a sigh of melancholy relief when he left me.

I pretended to work on my laptop, watching Julia prepare dinner and play with the girls. She was, I had to admit, a wonder. She chopped vegetables while Briar clung to her legs and Rose crashed a plastic truck into the wall. She dubbed the girls sous chefs and helped them place eggplants and mushrooms into a large casserole dish.

When the girls were playing quietly with blocks, Julia brought me a glass of wine. I took it, although I could barely face her solicitous eyes. "Tough day at work?"

"Yes," I whispered, taking one sip and then another. The wine buzz gave my Xanax high a happy little sheen. I told myself I could cut back tomorrow. As I drank, Julia taught the girls to count their blocks and kissed their small heads. It was all infinitely sweet and domestic. Maybe I was overreacting. Maybe leaving the girls with Julia in the day wasn't such a terrible idea.

I quickly compared the two of us the way a stranger might. Julia, as far as I knew, took no drugs. She was sober, sprightly, and actively engaged with the girls. She exercised. She cooked. She took care of herself and others.

Me? I was a lump on the couch. Overweight. Over-medicated. Mildly intoxicated. In no condition to handle an emergency.

The lawyer was right about me. I should have been a warrior mother, spiriting my girls out of their clutches entirely. I should have grown a spine. I should have taken an unambiguous stand. I should have been a strong, respectable woman any lawyer would be proud to represent.

Or maybe I should have unselfishly embraced poly and been grateful for Julia's help and Mann's happiness.

I was so confused and dejected my head ached. The room spun. I had drunk too much. I heard the soft, barely audible thud of Mann's car door. No, I couldn't face him yet. He couldn't see me like this.

"Julia," I called, levering myself into an uneasy standing position. "I'm going upstairs to lie down. You can start dinner without me."

***

My drugged dreams were thick and turgid. I found myself in a labyrinth, which I had to escape or die trying. I heard my girls' shrieking. I had to rescue them. But every path I took was wrong. Every route led to monsters. I narrowly escaped lantern-jawed predators bristling with teeth and claws. My heart hammered in my chest as if it was about to give up.

When I could smell the monsters' fetid breath, an angel of pure light set me free. I looked up, and…it was over. I breached the surface of consciousness with a dry mouth and sticky eyes. And I was not alone. Mann and Julia were looking down at me, their faces wearing twin expressions of concern.

"We put the girls to bed," said Julia softly. "They were asking for you."

"We're worried about you," added Mann. "We know that you're feeling jealous."

The moment he said 'jealous,' I struggled to sit up. Julia, who remained smoothly beautiful even after chasing the kids—my kids—all evening, stroked my shoulder as if I were a nervous dog.

"It's OK. Everyone gets jealous. And Mann and I think we've made things hard on you."

Mann sat down on the edge of the bed, leaning into me. He took my hand and squeezed. I squeezed back. It seemed like we hadn't touched for weeks, not since he fell in love with Julia.

"We're sorry," he said. "We know we've gotten a little carried away. We know you feel excluded. And we want that to change. We want to share our happiness with you."

Julia smiled and winked, rubbing my back while Mann held my hand. I nodded slowly, trying not to stiffen under their modest attentions. I told myself that they were trying to connect with me, that I should try to connect back.

But it felt like a trap. They sounded over rehearsed. They were offering me happiness, but not Julia's real name. They were apologizing for making me jealous, not taking my children out of daycare without even asking me.

"That sounds nice," I said, trying to keep my voice steady and stable. "But I also want to ask you, Mann, about the girls' daycare. Why did you pull them out without asking me?"

Julia's hand flew to her mouth. "Mann? I thought you and Helen had talked this over."

"Shit," he said, pushing hair out of his face. "I had been meaning to talk to Helen, and then I had that intense meeting where I had to fire the board and...oh God, Helen, I'm so sorry I totally forgot. That was unforgivable."

"We thought I could try watching the girls during the day so you wouldn't have to take them back and forth to daycare every day," added Julia. "But if you're not comfortable with the idea..."

Julia trailed off and stared at the snow-white duvet on the bed. Mann regarded me with a concentrated intensity I hadn't seen since before the children were born. I stifled a sigh. They seemed so sincere, so contrite. Was it all a misunderstanding?

"Julia," I said, my voice shaking. "If you'll be spending time alone with the children, I need to know who you really are. I need to know your name, the one you used before you came here. The one Google knows."

Julia flushed and then spoke with passion. "I'm sorry, but I don't want to tell you that. You'll search for me on Google, you'll read some shitty things, and then all I'll ever get from you is pity."

"Then why did you tell Mann?"

Her collarbone rose and fell. "He said he needed to know I would be safe around you and the kids. Because you're his first priority.

"Listen, your husband ran a background check. He dug into my hospital and school records, my Internet history. He talked to my old therapist. And all he discovered was that I'm fine. Well, not fine, but not a danger. I'm not going to hurt or kidnap your kids, okay?"

Mann put his arm around me. "I know we haven't handled this very well. It's been a steep learning curve for all of us, especially me. But I love you, and I want you to trust me. And Jules. OK?"

Resting against Mann's muscular bulk felt so good after what had felt like eons apart. And Julia, despite her faults, was so good with the girls. What they said sounded so reasonable.

Couldn't I be reasonable, too? Shouldn't I trust them? Shouldn't I try?

"OK," I said, releasing a heavy weight I hadn't even known I was carrying.

***

The next day was as fine and fragile as glass. I got up early and outfitted Julia's Tesla with the girls' favorite car seats.

Mann skipped a meeting to eat breakfast with Julia, the girls, and me. He touched me almost as often as he touched Julia. I could tell he was trying. When I told the girls they would be staying home with Julia, they whooped "Hooray!"

I played with them for the twenty minutes I would have spent driving them to daycare, then hugged them goodbye. Briar's fingers got caught in my hair. Rose tried to steal my phone. "Pictures?" she pleaded.

Driving to work without the girls was a strange experience. I missed their chattering presence, the sound of Rose's feet tapping against my seat. I told myself they were fine, that Mann had run a background check. I reminded myself to trust my husband. And maybe even Julia.

As I walked to my desk, my phone chirruped. It was a picture of the girls playing in their sandbox. Briar was making shapes with a stick. Rose was filling a little red bucket with a tiny garden shovel. I rubbed my eyes. This was going to be even more difficult than I had expected.

But I tried. I tried hard.

Julia sent me cute photos and messages throughout the day. The girls cycled through wholesome activities straight out of the Montessori playbook. I churned out a steady stream of content slurry and tried not to cry.

When the clock struck four, I was ready for the day to be over. I was collecting my things when Brittany appeared behind my desk like a jittery ghost.

"Oh, hey, Helen," she said in a casual drawl that belied her rapidly shifting focus. "I see you and Mann have a new nanny."

I blinked, wondering how she knew about Julia. Then I remembered Mann's Facebook page. He was always posting pictures of Julia, whom he called a "family friend." And he had half a million followers. My boss must have been one of them.

"Yes," I said, attempting a small, insincere smile. "She's great."

"Glad to hear it!" she said, clapping my shoulder with a limp, cold hand that made my skin crawl. I guessed she had read a blog post extolling the management virtues of casual touch.

"So how can I help you?" I asked, hoping she would take her hand away.

"Listen, I'm wondering if you can help me out with a little problem. We're behind on our net content flows, and Ashley and Melissa have maxed out their overtime."

I cursed Mann's compulsive need to share his life with strangers. I was sure Brittany wouldn't have asked me to stay late if she didn't know I had what appeared to be a goddamned live-in nanny.

"Sure, Brittany. I'd be glad to," I said as another picture from Julia rolled in. The girls were both eating from the same slice of watermelon.

Brittany, from her vantage point, could see the screen. "OMG, your kids are so insanely cute. I have no idea how you leave them for work every day."

Neither did I.

***

An incipient migraine shifted behind my temples as I walked through the front door. The house was dark and quiet. Only shadows greeted me. I tiptoed upstairs to check the girls' room and found them in bed. I kissed their sleepy foreheads. They did not stir.

I crept back downstairs and searched for Mann and Julia. They wouldn't have left the girls alone, even if they were asleep. Besides, Mann's car was in the driveway. I searched the top floor first and then the bottom. I moved slowly, methodically.

I finally found them by the patio. Julia was giggling softly at something Mann had said. He was stroking her hand. The baby monitor balanced against a bottle of red wine.

Julia noticed me first. "Hello, Helen! We're celebrating my first full day with the girls!" Her lips were the deep purple of Merlot. Mann kissed her hand. My stomach clenched.

Mann regarded me through hooded, half-drunk eyes. "Come, join us. Have a drink."

I pulled up a chair. The sky was the smudgy bluish-gray of twilight sliding into night. They hadn't thought to bring a third glass so I sipped from Mann's. The red liquid tasted of spoiled dreams.

"I tried to keep the girls awake until you got home," said Julia. "But they were completely exhausted. I might have overdone the activities just a little bit."

"Jules is building her own curriculum and tracking the girls' progress on video," Mann enthused. "How freakin' amazing is that?"

"Very," I said, wishing I hadn't agreed to work late. Maybe, if I was fired, I could stay home and Julia could show them the virtues of corporate servitude.

Mann took my hand and Julia's. "You know, Julia and I were thinking of heading inside for some adult playtime. Would you like to join us?"

I glanced at Julia, whose face was a frozen mask, and then at Mann, who had obviously passed from half-drunk to fully loaded. I supposed this was Mann's misguided attempt to make me feel included.

"No thanks," I said, to Julia's obvious relief. "You two enjoy yourselves." I reclaimed the baby monitor and gave Mann a quick and insincere kiss.

As I walked back to the house, I heard the sharp sounds of a burgeoning argument. God help me, I smiled.

12 PAST, PRESENT, AND FUTURE

I lingered in the shadows, just beside the door, listening to Mann and Julia clash. His voice was a placating rumble, full of gentle apology. Hers was a cry in the dark, piercing and hurt. I heard the words "cruelty" and "consent."

I strained to hear more of their discordant song, hope bubbling in my breast. I had agreed to tolerate Julia, but a big part of me still wanted her gone. Their fight, like an aria, reached a thrilling, howling crescendo.

I expected them to storm off. Perhaps Julia would leave for a hotel. Instead, to my disappointment, they stayed. Their voices grew lower and softer. They leaned towards each other. They shared a kiss. And more, sinking onto a chaise. It was after all, a warm, spring night.

I slipped inside and closed the door. I had heard enough. My heart ached with emptiness. I was losing Mann and my girls, and there was nothing I could do. I knew I should go to bed. Try not to dwell on something I couldn't change. But I was not, am not, nearly that evolved.

I shucked off my shoes and padded through the dark house, silent and insignificant as a shadow. I let my feet carry me to Julia's room. Perhaps a little rummaging could help me discover her real name. Or a soft spot in her armor. A fear or a debilitating doubt.

Without her password, her MacBook was useless to me. I opened her purse and then her wallet. The last name on her driver's license was

"Weatherstone." Same with her credit cards. She must have made the new name legal.

I moved onto her closet. It smelled like sandalwood. Diaphanous dresses floated from hangers alongside clingy pants and tops: the clothing of a woman who believes in her own beauty. I pulled at the waistband of my sensible black pants, the work equivalent to mom jeans. They were loose, resting on my hips.

I wondered how much weight I had lost, worrying about Julia. I wanted to try on her clothes, to see how tight they were, if they could change me. I took a dress from the rack and held it against me. I breathed in its sweet, musky smell.

And then I put it back. I couldn't actually wear her clothes. It was too intimate, too much of a violation. I went to her bathroom instead, remembering her adventure with my insurance card. Maybe she had gotten herself some prescription drugs.

With a malicious sort of glee, I opened her medicine cabinet. I groaned with disappointment. At first glance, there was nothing to see. No Advil. No prescription meds. No birth control pills. Just an electric toothbrush, organic toothpaste, acetaminophen, and vitamins.

I took a closer look at the vitamin bottle's pink, flowery label. "Prenatal vitamins," it read. And she wasn't on the pill. I put it back in her medicine cabinet, took a picture on my phone, and closed the door.

Shaking, I hurried out of her bathroom and into the kitchen. I poured myself an overlarge glass of wine. Was Julia pregnant? Or trying to get pregnant? And did Mann know?

***

I spent the next day obsessing over Julia's phantom pregnancy. As I drove to work, I imagined her hosting a warm little embryo, or maybe two. When traffic slowed, I could see her face flicker between caution and joy.

I walked slowly to my cubicle, visualizing her big announcement to Mann. It began with an apology and ended with a triumph. I could practically feel Mann's joy. I could see him turning to me and saying, "Aren't you excited our daughters are going to have a sister...or brother?"

After the nausea of the first trimester, Julia would swell prettily, more like a blooming flower than a stuffed sausage. I was sure she would sail through pregnancy without illness or effort. I logged onto my computer and banged on the keys, channeling my preemptive rage into my work.

And yet, despite my anger-fueled efforts, I fell behind. Julia flooded my phone with pictures of my girls. I looked at my children's toothy smiles, and my stomach ached. Would Julia lay claim to my children as part of her new family? Or would she push Mann into giving them to me as part of some just-barely-enough settlement? I did not, could not, know.

My mind churned like a dust storm, inventing new, terrible scenarios and then blowing them away. I started at the same arid press release for twenty minutes, writing and deleting Twitter copy. A blinking notice appeared on my screen, telling me the leader board had been updated. It was Brittany's latest attempt to "gamify" management with an app that ranked all her team members by hourly output. I was, of course, dead last.

If my name hadn't been Gottlieb, I probably would have been fired. I was sure Brittany and my young, single coworkers were laughing at me. *Look at Mann's slow, stupid wife.*

Perhaps I should have done something so outrageous they would have had to fire me. Like drinking openly at work or hijacking a client's Twitter account. Who knows how my life and my marriage might have gone?

With this thought in mind, I left at the stroke of four. Brittany fumed, and my coworkers muttered resentful goodbyes. When I arrived home, I found Mann and the girls sprawled in the movie room, possessed by cartoons. Briar and Rose were so enraptured they didn't even look at me.

"Where's Julia?" I asked, hating the belligerent tone of my voice.

"At a yoga class," he murmured.

I sat down next to him and watched talking mice fly through space and invade a planet full of cats. Rose laughed loudly. Briar simply stared.

I took a deep breath and thought through several different ways I could broach the delicate subject with Mann. Then my heart began flopping like a freshly caught fish and I blurted, "Is Julia pregnant? Are you and Julia trying to get pregnant?"

"What!?" yelped Mann as if he'd been stung by a bee. "No, she's not. We're not. Whatever gave you that idea?"

My heart pounded. I gasped for air. "I looked in her bathroom. I didn't see any birth control pills. But I did see prenatal vitamins."

Mann quickly recovered his composure. "Julia has an IUD. She's not ready for another child, not after what she's been through." He paused, his face darkening. "Next time you want to know something like this, ask me and Julia. Together. We're trying to make this work. You need to try, too."

I frowned. "We should have had a conversation about birth control and family planning up front. Let's say that Julia has a good year or two with us and decides she wants a baby. What then?"

Mann sighed. "We'll talk about it. We'll figure it out."

"If she said she wanted to have a baby today, would you say yes? Would you?" I held my breath, waiting for his answer.

"Of course not. She's still grieving, and we haven't been together long enough to know if having a child with her would be wise."

I exhaled. He sounded sensible. Sane.

I watched the mice swallow blue pills and hallucinate a distorted world. Rose guffawed, and Briar giggled softly. I was reminded of the last hours of my pregnancy. The magnesium sulfate burned through my brain and turned my thoughts to ash. The world winked from at the end of a long tunnel. I was receding. Dying.

Yes, I could understand why Julia wasn't ready to try again. But I couldn't quite let it go. "If Julia isn't planning on getting pregnant, why is she taking prenatals?"

"She has anemia. She takes prenatal vitamins for the extra iron. Like I said, next time, ask her."

***

Knowing that Julia wasn't pregnant, I focused once again on making our trio work. I got up earlier so I could wake the girls each morning and spend quality time with them before Julia took over. I started making breakfast again. I stretched my patience with a little extra Xanax here and there.

The week ended without incident. Julia and I were coming to understand each other. It felt like we were cordial exes, reluctant friends and co-parents coming together for a common good.

The new stability soothed me. I felt rooted enough to take care of trivial items like refilling my blood pressure pills and bringing my pants to the tailor. The panic that had jolted my heart faded away. I considered making those follow up appointments suggested by Dr. Yu.

On Saturday, I decided I was ready for a big, scary step. After breakfast, I announced, "Julia, I'm going to take the girls to the park. Would you like to come along?"

The girls jumped up and down, cooing, "Joooolia, please."

I controlled my breathing. I was afraid she would say no. I was afraid she would say yes. At first she looked as wary as I felt, her eyes flickering between the girls and me. Then her face bloomed into a smile. She said, "Yes, I'd love to come. Have you packed their snacks?"

"N-n-n-not yet," I stammered. I was the sort of parent who routinely left the house with nothing but my children and a single water bottle. Apparently, Julia had been the kind who left nothing to chance, a dedicated curator of her children's comfort.

"I'll do it!" she chirped, directing the girls to collect backpacks I didn't recognize. Briar's was pink. Rose's was red. Julia must have bought them while I was at the office, I thought with a pang.

She moved efficiently, making sandwiches and passing zip locked bags and juice boxes to tiny little hands. She made the process of getting the girls ready for an excursion seem brisk but orderly. For me it, was always a howling swirl of chaos.

"Helen, are you ready?"

The girls held Julia's hands, Briar on the left and Rose on the right. I had to admit they looked perfect together. A lovely familial portrait. I felt sad and vestigial, like an infected appendix. Stop it, I told myself, just stop it.

"Yes, I'm ready," I said cheerily, vowing solemnly to enjoy the day.

If only vows weren't so easily broken.

***

The outing to Magical Park was promising enough, at first. We trooped out of the van and allowed the girls to lead the way. Briar, spotting a garden of colorful flowers, stepped out of character and pulled her sister by the hand.

"Briar is so sweet," said Julia, watching the girls. "She is gentle and artistic, just like my Serena. Lily was the sporty one."

An invisible band squeezed around my chest, just from hearing my daughter's name alongside the dead girl's. I took a deep breath and tried to say something human. Something not cruel. "Briar really cares for you. You must miss your girls terribly."

Julia sniffed. Her eyes watered. I was going to ask if she was OK, but even I knew how foolish that would be. Of course she wasn't.

I kept my eyes on the children. They had reached the garden and were smelling the flowers. Rose was naming their colors in a loud, ringing voice. I steered Julia to a nearby bench.

"I can't imagine how you must feel. Take all the time you need. I'll keep an eye on the girls."

Julia nodded, wiping at her eyes. "Thanks," she murmured.

I turned back towards the garden where the girls were playing and...*shit*. Briar was still smelling the flowers, but Rose was gone. I ran to my daughter, as ungainly as an ox. "Where's your sister?"

Briar pointed to a plastic climbing structure covered in nubby footholds. It was about twenty feet away. Rose, the child we used to call 'Monkey,' was scaling to a dangerous height. Galvanized by fear, I scooped up Briar who made a small grunt of protest but otherwise allowed it. I ran again, huffing and puffing, Briar bouncing uncomfortably against my hip.

When I reached Rose, I set Briar on the ground. "You're climbing too high," I called in a treacly voice that didn't fool my daughter one bit. "It's not safe." I plucked her from her perch, thankful for my lunchtime work outs.

Rose, her will thwarted, released an anguished howl. "Nooooo! Nooooo!" she cried, thrashing in my arms. "Put me down!"

I did my best to hold onto my squirming daughter while heads swiveled to watch and judge. Some eyes were sympathetic. Others were narrow with suspicion, perhaps wondering why my daughter was trying to get away.

I stroked Rose's hair and tried to redirect her to the flowers, but she only yelled louder and wiggled more. I smiled weakly at the bystanders. Briar, upset by Rose's screams, started to sob quietly. It was every mother's nightmare. We were causing a scene.

Into this cacophony of childish chaos strode Julia, recovered from her attack of grief. Her blond hair hung loose at her shoulders and shone in the sun. Her white sundress swirled around her legs. She looked like a worried, maternal angel. When Rose saw her, she stopped sniffling and squirming. I set her gently on the ground.

Rose ran as fast as her stubby little legs could carry her, while Briar clung uncertainly to my leg. "Joooolia," cried Rose. "Mommeee!" Julia swept her up. Then Briar broke free and joined her sister in Julia's arms.

The girls, pulling at Julia's hair, kept cooing "Jooolia Mommeee. Julia Mommy." I watched them silently and gathered up the bloody fragments of my heart.

***

The motion of the van lulled the girls to sleep. Briar's pale eyelashes fluttered. Rose's mouth pouched into a small, red bow. I drove slowly, carefully. Julia in the passenger seat was tense and alert, her posture upright and stiff.

"I'm so sorry," said Julia. "I didn't know the girls were going to do that."

I shook my head. "They're children. They're still learning to talk. These things happen."

And I believed it, too. The girls hadn't rejected me. They had simply expressed their affection for Julia, the woman who cared for them all day while I Facebooked and Twittered on behalf of faceless corporations. No, the girls were not to blame.

Julia's shoulders relaxed. Her mouth curved into a small smile, almost a smirk. She looked like someone who had gotten away with something. I frowned. She wasn't encouraging them to call her Mommy, was she? "Do the girls do that during the day?"

"Do what?" she asked, her posture once again rigid.

"Call you Mommy."

"Every once in a while. Honestly, I sort of like it. It helps me remember the good times with my daughters, Lily and Serena. But I'll tell them to stop if you want me to."

I stifled what would have been a long, groaning sigh. I didn't want my girls to call Julia "Mommy," to think of her as their mother. And yet I quailed before Julia's grief. I steeled myself to set what I hoped was a gentle yet firm limit.

"It doesn't have to be a big deal." I said. "Just let them know you're Julia, not Mommy."

***

The rest of the weekend passed in a haze of anxiety. I watched Julia and the girls for signs of excessive attachment. And I found them. The girls called Julia "Julia Mommy" and Julia corrected them halfheartedly. 'Just plain Julia,' she'd say with a rueful grin.

I was losing my girls, and I didn't know what to do. Of course, Mann was no help at all. He told me not to overreact. He said I should be happy the girls cared about Julia so much. He said they had plenty of love to go around.

And, yes, he was right. In theory. But I still hurt. Julia, at home all day with no obligations except to care for our children, was winning the battle for their little hearts and minds. It was as if I had died, Mann had remarried Julia, and I was haunting my own life as a ghost.

13 CONSIDER IT FORGOTTEN

The next morning, a saggy gray Monday, I awakened with an amazing idea. It was simple, straightforward, and easy to implement. It would help me get over my anxiety about Julia spending so much time with my girls. It was also illegal as hell.

I spent the drive into work trying to talk myself into it. It wasn't *that* illegal, I told myself. And, if I did it right, there was no way I would get caught.

As I made my way through the poorly lit cubicle farm clutching a cup of lukewarm coffee, I watched my soft, Millennial colleagues with a speculative eye. Had any of them knowingly broken the law? And had they regretted it? I suddenly felt daring and dangerous, an echo of riding Lucy through the fog.

I settled at my desk, vibrating with excitement and nervousness. I worked with damp, shaky hands, making even more mistakes than usual. Red performance warnings floated across my desktop. I clicked them away like so many mosquitoes.

"How's your Monday?"

I jumped at the sound of Brittany's voice and came dangerously close to spilling my coffee. I had no idea how long she had been standing behind me, watching me screw up.

"Fine. Just great," I said with an insincere smile.

Brittany peered through stylized reading glasses she was too young to really need. "You seem distracted, like you don't want to be here. Are you sure everything's OK?"

"Everything's wonderful," I said, grinning like a loon. And then I decided. It was time to execute my plan. I got up and squeezed by Brittany, whose lips puckered like she just bit into a lemon.

"By the way, I have to step out for a doctor's appointment. I'll be back at noon." I almost felt sorry for Brittany, a dedicated manager stuck with a devious slacker like me.

***

I drove to Gadget Town and bought myself a top-of-the-line nanny cam and a GPS tracker for Julia's car.

I paid in cash.

I texted Julia and found out she and the girls were at the park.

And then I went home.

***

The house was quiet. Too quiet, as if it was watching me and silently disapproving. My heart hitched and fluttered as I installed the nanny cam and matching mic in the living area.

I felt like a criminal. According to California law, I was one. I was going to record Julia without her consent, an actual, get-caught-and-go-to-jail crime.

As my tell-tale-heart echoed in my ears, I wondered if I was inching my way closer to a stroke. I took a deep breath and vowed to make a doctor's appointment soon. My heart pounded unabated, refusing to trust in my good intentions.

Once the cam was hidden where the twins wouldn't find it, I took a deep breath and waited for my panic to subside. But it wouldn't. I kept wondering what I might discover. Julia telling the girls that she is their real mother? Julia whispering that I leave for work every day because I don't love them?

I checked my phone. My heart flipped and flopped. I was running out of time. Julia would be back soon. I unpacked the GPS tracker and put it in my purse. I'd install it at night when Julia was with Mann. Then I brought all the packaging materials outside and tossed them in my van. I'd leave them in a dumpster at the office.

I went to turn the ignition, but I couldn't. I was overwhelmed with panic. The beige walls of the Odyssey were closing in. Trapped in an airless box, I imagined what would happen to me if I were caught. Julia confronting me in tears, Mann leaving me and taking the girls.

My breath came in small, panicked sips. I was too spooked to drive. I had to calm down. *Fuck.* I ran back into the house and up to my bedroom. I opened the medicine cabinet and reached for relief. My nervous hands fumbled and knocked three bottles of Xanax to the floor. Damn it.

I scooped them up and popped a pill. And, because I didn't trust myself, I grabbed one of the bottles and stashed it in my purse for work. As the pill dissolved in my stomach, nothing seemed all that important anymore.

***

One day passed and then another. I felt calmer than usual. More centered. It was partly because I had started taking Xanax at work. But it was also because I knew footage of Julia was accumulating, hour by hour. I knew I would have my answers soon.

The next night, while Julia and Mann were eating dinner at a new, upscale Indian place and the girls were asleep, I had a viewing. I even made it an occasion, popping a Xanax and pouring myself a glass of wine.

I watched as my worst fears unfurled. Whether she knew it or not, Julia was stealing my girls, letting them know that she loved them more. But she was doing it in a subtle way that Mann wouldn't recognize. I listened to the crackling audio and let myself cry.

Your mommy is your mommy. And I am Julia Mommy. We both love you very much.

Your mommy's at work so she can earn money. I'm here because I love you.

I know your mommy doesn't let you have cookies before noon. It will be our little secret.

A secret is something special you keep to yourself. Something you guard. Something you never tell.

I wished I could run to Mann, ask him to watch the recordings with me. I desperately craved his support. But I knew I wasn't going to get it. It was too easy to imagine him rolling his eyes and telling me to work on my jealousy issues. He might even tell Julia that I recorded her without her knowledge. She could go to the police or even hire a lawyer.

And maybe, just maybe, Mann would help her do it.

I had no idea what to do. Until I had a plan, I would have to be constantly vigilant. I would monitor Julia at all times, and in real time. I would do it at work, and I would dare Brittany to fire me.

I tiptoed downstairs and quietly reconfigured the nanny cam for live streaming. Then, heart still quivering, I connected the GPS tracker to Julia's car, the one Mann was letting her use.

The divorce lawyer had been right. I was a terribly inadequate mother. But I was becoming a half-decent spy.

***

The next morning, Mann left me. Actually, he left all of us.

I was flailing through a dark, unsettling dream, running from something that moved like liquid fire, when I felt a sharp tap against my shoulder. I gasped and blinked like a mole. My eyes adjusted to the darkness. For once, I wasn't alone.

A soft-focus vision of my husband gazed down at me, smiling softly. The expression on his face was sweetly patient. It was the one he usually showed to Briar and Rose. And Julia. "Good morning," I rasped.

He stroked my cheek. "I totally forgot MobilityCon is this week. I'm leaving for Boston this morning. I'm giving the keynote tonight."

Still groggy, I stared blankly. He kissed me lightly on the brow. "Take care of Julia and the girls. Don't let me down."

He hurried out the door, but lingered in the hallway, watching me like a guardian angel. "I love you," he said, smiling as he turned away.

I lay in bed and stared at the ceiling, trying to decide what I was feeling. I slowly realized I was pleased. He hadn't said I love you since Julia moved in.

***

Without Mann, Julia was lost in a way that made me darkly happy. Instead of waking the girls, she wandered through the house, opening doors with nervous hands. I suppose I could have stopped her and told her that Mann had left for a conference. But she didn't ask, and I didn't tell.

While she searched, I got the girls out of bed and herded them downstairs. I made them a casual breakfast of cereal, which they consumed with a surprising degree of joy. Julia wandered in circles, opening doors and periodically checking her phone.

I guessed that Mann had neglected to text her a goodbye message, or even reply to what I imagined were her increasingly agitated texts. It wasn't a big surprise, at least, not to me. Mann often forgot the rest of the world when he was working.

Eventually, Julia poured herself a cup of coffee and sat down beside me. She gripped the mug with pale knuckles. The tension around her mouth finally broke. "Helen, do you know where Mann is? When I woke up this morning, he was gone. I can't find him anywhere."

I shrugged and repressed a mean-spirited giggle. "Mann is at a conference. He probably didn't remember it until he got a last-minute text from his assistant," I said calmly.

"How long will he be gone?"

Her voice was tinged with whiny sadness. Schadenfreude crackled through me. "Who knows? A day? A week? A month?"

Her face crumpled, and my glee curdled into guilt and worry. Did I really want a distraught woman watching the twins?

I forced my lips into a reassuring smile. "I don't think he'll be gone more than a few days. He'll miss the girls too much."

When Julia perked up slightly, I kissed Briar and Rose goodbye. Briar cooed, and Rose hooted. Julia began cleaning up the breakfast dishes like a good wife.

On my way out, I paused in the garage, and my false smile became real. I remembered the GPS chip affixed to her car.

***

My workday was surprisingly effortless, even under Brittany's impatient gaze.

Being able to watch Julia and the girls at all times and track their movements kept my anxiety tolerably low. Oh, I felt a surge of anger every time I heard a stray 'Julia Mommy' or my girls threw their arms around her. But I was mostly OK.

If I couldn't make her leave without Mann's consent, I could at least minimize the damage. I had a plan to turn 'Julia Mommy' into the much less concerning 'Aunt Julia.' Even better, it was entirely reasonable and sane. It was as if Mann's departure had somehow cleared my head. Where before I saw problems, I now saw solutions.

I even managed to focus on my screen and meet every last content quota. My name climbed the performance leader board. I remembered I wasn't really dumb or slow. I was capable of doing this awful job; I simply didn't want to.

At home, I found Julia in the kitchen, Briar jumping on the couch, and Rose ripping pages from old used up books. Julia looked paler than usual. Purple smudges shadowed her eyes. I supposed she was still off balance from Mann's sudden departure.

Waving off her feeble objections, I helped chop salad greens and convinced her to make turkey sandwiches instead of a multi-course meal. After a quick dinner, I told the girls I would put them to bed tonight. Julia nodded blankly. Briar and Rose gave her quick squeezes but didn't balk when I led them upstairs without her.

***

The girls were sleeping. The baby monitor was silent. I watched Julia sip her chamomile tea, her mouth curled into a frown. I remembered how sad she had looked when I first met her at Jessie's party. I sat down beside her and allowed myself to empathize. "Are you OK?"

She shrugged. "I have good days and bad days. Today is a bad one."

I considered waiting, putting off my plan. I didn't want her usurping my place with my children, but I didn't want to hurt her, either. I reminded myself she was good with Briar and Rose. As kind, patient, and understanding as she was presumptuous. I took one nervous, halting breath and then another.

No, I was going to talk to her, anyway. I had to assert myself.

"Julia," I said in what I hoped was a soft, gentle tone. "Sometimes I hear you talking to the girls on the baby monitor. It sounds like you're encouraging them to call you Mommy." I was proud of myself; the baby monitor was a good cover for the nanny cam.

Julia blanched. Her pupils leaked into pools, as if I had caught her doing something wrong. "They like to call me Julia Mommy," she said in an empty, faraway voice. "It makes me feel better. Less alone."

"I know," I said, trying not to let my anger leak into my voice, "but I think it could be confusing them."

Julia nodded, still sipping her tea. "What should they call me then? Just Julia?"

I smiled at my nemesis, my younger, more attractive mirror. Yes, I felt threatened, but I could rise above it. I could be benevolent. I could be good. "How about Aunt Julia?"

"Yes. Let's give that a try."

***

When I returned from work on Friday, Mann was still gone. Childish shouting and a loud, continuous whine echoed through the house. I found Julia pulling Briar off of a howling, spitting Rose while a pot of brown rice burned beside Julia's whistling red kettle.

I quickly turned off the stove and sent the girls to their time out chairs, where Briar sulked and Rose sniffled. Then I walked Julia to the dining table where her MacBook sat.

"I'll take care of dinner," I said, while she nodded and pulled up her screen, which was locked. She would have to enter her password to use it. My heart leaped with guilty joy. It was finally going to happen. I was going to learn her password and find out who she really was.

I fussed with a heavy vase in the center of the table. Then I moved oh-so-slowly away. Still, she paused. Did she somehow know about my odd ability? Was she waiting for me to leave?

She didn't. She wasn't. Julia coughed. Her hands fluttered like birds. I committed their movements to memory.

***

Even after the girls had gone to bed, I was practically vibrating with excitement. Julia's password was my Rosetta stone. I would use it to understand this woman who had grafted herself to my life like a barnacle, and perhaps even detach her.

Yes, Mann would be sad. Even heartbroken. After a suitable mourning period, we could revisit the rules of our open marriage. I would allow him to acquire mistresses in the usual way, and keep them mercifully secret.

I opened a bottle of wine and poured myself a generous drink. I was ready for my victory lap. Julia was still on her computer, tap-tap-tapping away, her face tired and grim. "Can I get you a drink?" I asked.

She shook her head. "No thanks."

I put the wine into the fridge and wandered back to the table, hoping to start a conversation. I was desperate to celebrate, and perversely, Julia was the closest thing I had to a friend.

Oh, I had hundreds of social connections who broadcast their lives on Facebook and sent me emoji-laden birthday greetings. But since my pregnancy and dramatic, near-fatal illness, my friends had quietly fallen away.

I wasn't positive enough, said one. Insufficiently grateful for my wonderful life, said another. Unwilling to lean in, said a third. By the time I climbed out of my depression and warmed to motherhood, I was alone, except for Mann and the children.

I took a large sip of my wine and, perhaps foolishly, perhaps cruelly, attempted to engage Julia. "How are you doing? You seem down this week."

She looked up at me. Her eyes were damp and focused on something invisible in the distance. "I miss my girls. Oh, yours are lovely. A marvelous consolation. But, as you have so often reminded me, they aren't mine."

I choked on my wine. I knew then that talking to Julia was a self-indulgent mistake. "I'm sorry. I can only imagine how you feel."

She sighed. "I'm not looking for pity. I know how grief stinks, how it makes people shrink away. Just like you're doing now."

Yes, she had me. I had shifted my chair away from her without being fully aware, putting distance between me and her fate. "I'm sorry."

She shook her head. Her hair, more lank than bouncy, drooped around her shoulders. "It's not your fault. It's nobody's fault. I just want to hope again. I want to think about the future and smile. I want what you have. A husband. And a baby."

I gasped. It was as if she had looked inside my chest, reached inside, and tore out my greatest fears, bloody and beating for me to see. "Mann said you weren't ready yet. For a baby."

"Mann's not ready," she snapped. "He thinks I would be sick like you were. He's afraid of being overwhelmed. He says you and the twins sucked him dry."

My throat burned with the injustice of her words. Of Mann's words. I took a large gulp of wine and blurted, "I had preeclampsia. My delivery was a nightmare. I almost died."

And then she wilted. "Jesus, I'm sorry. Sometimes I get locked into my grief. Forget everything I said."

I nodded. She looked so sad and so lost that, if I were a different sort of person, I would have hugged her. Instead, I lied.

"Consider it forgotten."

I waited for her to go to bed, I hoped she would leave her computer on the table. But she didn't. She took it to her room, mouthing a silent goodnight. But that was OK. I had time. I wouldn't forget a thing.

14 PANDORA'S BOX

On Saturday morning, Mann swept into the house like a tornado. He dropped his bags and his jacket on the floor. He scooped up Briar and Rose, who greeted him with happy whoops. Holding onto the girls with one arm, he threw his other arm around Julia.

I was left alone at the kitchen table, chewing my oatmeal. I'd weighed myself that morning, and I was a mere eight pounds away from my goal weight. I should have been happy. And yet my mouth tasted like ash.

Mann, his arms full of wiggling female, smiled at me. "Come here, Helen, my love. I missed you, too."

I put down my spoon and slowly approached my family. I attached myself awkwardly to the group hug, a fifth wheel. We were saved by Rose, who began thrashing and begging to go outside.

"'Side, 'side," she whined.

Julia, her cheeks once again a beautifully modulated pink, grinned. "I'll take them," she said, ushering the girls into the yard.

Alone together, Mann and I were lost. We stared and shuffled. "Would you like something to eat?" I asked. "We have muffins. " I didn't have to add that Julia, and not me, had made them.

"Sure," he said, sitting down at the table. "And some orange juice."

I served Mann his makeshift breakfast and returned to my gruel. "Did you have a good time at the conference?"

He shrugged. "I met a few new hires, found a few interesting startups. Nothing too exciting."

When he bit into the muffin, he smiled. "Did Jules make this?"

"Yes, she and the girls made them this morning."

"Good, I'm glad she's feeling better. I think she had some separation anxiety while I was gone."

I shrugged and stifled a grin. "Maybe a little."

He took my hand and brought it to his lips. "I'm glad you were there for her. I'm sure it wasn't easy." I shrugged again, but this time I smiled. Was the new relationship energy dying down? Could he once again care for me?

"Listen," he said, still beaming. "I have an idea."

"What kind of idea?"

"I know you want to spend more time with the kids. And Jules is hurting right now, even if she's too proud to say so. I was thinking I'd take her for a weekend in Napa while you stay here with the girls. I reconnect with her while you reconnect with them. Does that sound good?"

After a reflexive stab of disappointment, I slapped a grateful smile onto my face. Wasn't he right? Wasn't more Julia-free time with the girls what I really wanted? And wasn't there something involving Julia's computer I desperately wanted to do?

"That sounds great! Let's tell her the good news."

***

When Mann and Julia left, each clutching a haphazardly packed day bag, they took the sunshine with them. By noon, it was raining.

My girls, solar powered little animals, grew peevish and slow. They fought over dolls, ate too many grapes, and watched movies. I cleaned the house. Julia, during her week of pining after Mann, had let things slide.

Wiping down surfaces and reorganizing kitchen cabinets, I felt strangely content. Yes, I was annoyed that Mann had chosen Julia once again. I hated that my husband was falling in love with another woman, and that I was obliged to watch. And yet it was good to bring the girls snacks and tickle their soft little feet.

When nap time rolled around, they were genuinely sleepy. They surrendered to their cribs without even a token protest. I made myself a cup of tea and listened to the raindrops hitting the patio.

The gloomy weather suited my mood. I was tired after a long week of work and Julia-related upheaval. I enjoyed sitting quietly without the guilt induced by a bright, industrious sun.

When I finished my tea, I took a slow walk around the house. I scanned the floors for unmatched socks, headless dolls, and other childish effluvia. I deliberately made my way to Julia's room, savoring the anticipation. The door was only halfheartedly shut. I nudged it open.

Probably because she and Mann had left abruptly, the space was a swirl of chaos. Clothes lined the floor. Toiletries sprawled across the dresser. In the middle of the bed lay a sleek, silvery MacBook lay tethered to a white charging cable. The Rosetta stone. Julia's password waited in my memory like a bomb about to go off.

I paused for a long second, watching the machine as if it were a sleeping snake. Was I really going to spy on her innermost thoughts? Was I going to rifle through her darkest secrets? Was I going to spy on my husband's cherished girlfriend, my children's surrogate aunt?

Yes, I was. I grabbed my own personal Pandora's Box and opened it wide.

***

Abetted by the cloudy skies, the girls would nap for two or more hours. I had plenty of time to rummage and ransack.

I typed in Julia's password and got it right on the first try, congratulating myself for my normally useless talent. If I were a criminal—a real criminal—I would be in great demand.

Her desktop opened like a blooming rose. A full-screen picture of Briar and Rose at the park gazed out at me. Suddenly queasy, I swallowed a mouthful of spit. I breathed deeply and nosed around until I located a folder labeled "personal records."

Discovering her true identify took a mere five clicks. It was easy. Almost too easy. Before she was Julia Weatherstone, she was Julia Campbell Logan or Julia C. Logan or plain old Julie Logan. She had been a real person with a real name. A real Google trail. A real history. One that Mann knew and was hiding from me.

I wasted no time. Fingers flying, I sifted through the Internet, collecting pieces of her life like a magpie. A post here, a picture there. I pieced it together like a collage. The more I added, the more it took shape. A narrative began to emerge.

Julia had been born under a dark star. Everything I found on social media suggested she was an only child. Her older sister, the one who died, was a negative space. A void.

According to an old local news story, Julia's young parents committed suicide when she was four. Together. On the marital bed. They dressed themselves in elegant clothes and, in an anachronistic touch, mailed notes to their parents, timed to arrive just slightly posthumously. Someone, after all, needed to look after baby Julia.

But the postal service was unspeakably slow. Four days later, a neighbor found Julia hiding in her bedroom, almost dead from dehydration. Her eyes were red, sore, and completely drained of tears.

She went to live with her mother's parents and became a shockingly directed young person, as driven as her parents were flighty. As she grew, she became an obsessive achiever, winning accolades and scholarships and acceptance to UC Davis. She blogged about her parents' overly choreographed deaths. She became a modest Internet celebrity.

She wrote nothing about her sister.

Then, one by one, her grandparents died. She met Michael Logan at the fourth and final funeral. It was the purest coincidence. He was there to pitch his latest doomed project—Deadpool, a new app for comparing casket and burial prices—to the mortician. And he pursued Julia with same hopeless fervor he applied to his failed ventures.

To his amazement, this one succeeded. Exhausted from years of dogged achievement, Julia was ready to coast. The fledgling couple eloped and got pregnant weeks later. They produced twins Lily and Serena. Julia brought the babies to play on their great-grandparents' graves and shared the pictures far and wide.

Obsessed with recapturing her pre-baby figure, Julia became a hard-core yogini. She taught her own home-brewed brand of yoga and posted adorable pictures of her children on Instagram. She was, once again, creeping up on social celebrity.

That's when it happened.

"Mommy!"

I blinked. Rose was standing in front of me, clutching her favorite blanket. *Shit.* She had climbed out of her crib. I must have somehow missed the action on the monitor. I looked down at the screen. Briar's escape was in progress. I picked up Rose and clambered up the stairs.

Julia's past would have to wait.

***

I did my best to stay present with the girls. But it wasn't easy. I had a visceral need to read the rest of Julia's story. I was desperate to connect her past trauma to her presence in my life.

I was so unsettled and eager to know more that I had to quash my curiosity with a Xanax. The girls followed me into the bathroom, pulling at my legs. I opened the bottle, swallowed the pill, and plunged myself into a guilty fog.

We drifted through the rest of the day. I could not stop eyeing Julia's computer, which I'd left on the kitchen table. We watched the rain together. We made cookies and burnt them. We read story after story until my voice grew hoarse.

When the sky cleared, we went outside. The girls jumped in the puddles that had formed on the pool cover. They ran through the grass. Rose clambered onto a patio table while I showed Briar a slug.

"Look, Mommy!" called Rose. "Look!"

And I did, just as she slid from table to chair, and from chair to concrete slab. Rose howled and I, the distracted mother high on Xanax, rushed to her side, leaving Briar with the slug.

My heart quivered as I checked a sobbing Rose for injuries. There was no blood. But I did see a small scratch worryingly close to her right eye and the puffy beginnings of an ugly bruise.

I hugged Rose and stroked her back as guilt thickened in my throat. I was a bad mother. Inattentive. Chemically compromised. I could imagine Mann pointing to Rose's bruise, wondering why I was so worried about Julia when the kids only got hurt with me.

Once Rose stopped crying, I brought her and Briar, who I'd just barely stopped from licking the slug, inside. Pandora's box kept whispering. I pretended I didn't hear.

***

Both girls kissed me goodnight, smiling. Rose's eye was swollen and dusky, foreshadowing the shiner to come.

"Goodnight. Love you both," I murmured, both guilty and eager.

Downstairs, I watched the girls on the monitor, as they began to doze. Briar silently squirmed, curling onto her side. Rose chattered, sprawling on her back like a queen.

When I was sure they were out, I seized Julia's computer. The screen was full of Google entries, shared photographs, and social media timelines. I fast-forwarded to the day it happened, the day her twins and her husband died. She'd told me it was a car crash. A freak accident. An echo of her sister's death.

But the story I pieced together was something different entirely.

After the twins came, Julia and her family moved into an improbable Victorian house in the fancy part of Davis, California. They had a pool, a small patch of garden, and a half-acre strip of drought-friendly Astro-Turf.

Their house stood out from its pastel neighbors. Its gaudy, orange-yellow paint job and narrow, two-story design set it apart. Despite myself, I approved of its shameless cheek.

Their final night together was windy, dry, and perfectly combustible. Neighbors from miles away saw the flames and recorded them on their phones. Smoke flooded the bedrooms on the second floor. Malcom, Lily, and Selena suffocated and slipped from this world. The firemen found a single survivor: a woman sleeping on the sunporch, unconscious from alcohol and smoke.

Julia, once revived, was distraught. She had fought with her husband. One of their usual fights about money and regret. He claimed she was disappointed in him. Biding her time until she found a better, richer man. She reassured him while he accused her of lying and stomped off to bed.

Afterwards, she had a shot of vodka, or two, or four. Just enough to blur the edges of a bad night. Just enough to wrap a comforting haze around her world. I could understand. Truly, I could.

But instead of going to sleep, she made a cup of mint tea, to wash the taste of alcohol from her mouth. She boiled the water on the gas stove, in her favorite red kettle, a replica of the one that now sat on our stove. She poured hot water into a chipped mug. She stuffed tea leaves into a silver ball. She watched the tea brew in a trance.

Somehow, she turned the burner to low, not to off. And didn't notice. She sipped her tea on the porch and collapsed into sleep. Her singular mistake lit the house and her very existence on fire.

She begged for punishment, to live out her remaining days behind thick, impenetrable walls. She scratched her face and tried to tear out her own eyes. The local paper said she attempted *enucleation*. She was, of course, hospitalized.

Investigators confirmed Julia's story while she recovered in the psychiatric ward. The local prosecutor did not press charges. It was a tragic accident, he said, not a criminal matter.

But the Internet felt differently. A group calling themselves the Angels of Vengeance thirsted to avenge her children. They stalked Julia as she sifted through the wreckage of her home. They tracked her across Facebook and Instagram to the various rentals she passed through like a ghost forever trapped outside the afterlife.

Strange men wearing masks visited her lonely rooms. They left Post-Its on her windshield, calling her a murderous bitch. Once they slashed her tires. Another time, they left dead mice bearing the labels Lily and Serena. Her guilt would not permit her to ask the police, or anyone, for help.

When they set her car on fire, she changed her name and left for good. Julia Campbell Logan died, and Julia Weatherstone was born.

***

I blinked my eyes at the screen, struggling to process all I had learned. In a way, Julia was responsible for her children's deaths. She put her own pain over their safety for a single night and paid the ultimate price.

And yet what she did wasn't so different from the moments of inattention that parents experience all the time. I remembered Rose's fall this afternoon. And I thought uncomfortably about the Xanax I'd taken. Was I any better than she was?

I closed my eyes and tried to put myself in her place. Julia had been through enough tragedy to break most people. Perhaps her life would have broken me. I opened my eyes again, grateful for my living children and sheltered, if imperfect, life.

And then I considered her sister, the one who supposedly had looked just like me. Had she ever existed? And, if so, what had happened to her? Maybe nothing. If she was ten or fifteen years older than Julia, perhaps she had lived an undocumented life. Millions of people aren't on Facebook. Perhaps she had been one of them.

Her parents could have let her slip into foster care a year or more before Julia was born. It was as plausible as anything else.

I almost walked away.

I almost closed the open files, cleared the browser cache, and closed the computer.

I almost decided that I had learned enough.

But I didn't. Something dark and hungry inside me had to know more. I wanted to get deeper into her head. Not to protect my children, but to feed my ravenous curiosity. So I went through her folders, searching and scanning, until I found a document named *The True Story of My Life*.

The timestamp was yesterday.

***

My heart thrummed like a hummingbird's wings as I opened the file. It was set up like an old fashioned diary with dates followed by observations. The story began six months ago, when she met Matt and Anna at a party, soon after she moved to the Bay Area:

I am watching the most beautiful couple in the world. He is smooth and tanned with a face like a troubled hawk. He dances like a wet dream. The woman with him is tall and slender like a willow. She twirls with reckless, thoughtless abandon. She is everything I will never be.

They are older than I am. Wealthier. More established. Most of the people at this party are. Single women get in for free. Couples pay a little. Single men pay a lot. It's the polyamorous social economy in its most brutal form. It's also one of the only places where a broken creature like me holds any real value. Which is why I'm here.

I can barely pass through a day without sobbing over my lost ones. I cannot sit still for more than an hour at a time. I have to keep moving, feeling my muscles contract to be sure I'm alive. I'm a zombie. A cipher. A wraith. And now I'm going to be what Malcolm always said I was: a gold-digging whore. You see, I need someone, or maybe two someones, to take care of me.

It's either that, or die.

15 SUCKING THEM DRY

I opened a bottle of wine and poured myself an obscenely large glass. I knew I shouldn't mix it with Xanax, but I needed something to neutralize the adrenaline pouring through my veins like an invading army.

Memoir-Julia was nothing like the fragile, desperate woman who maybe loved my husband and children just a little too much. The tone of the writing was arch. Sorrowful. Dark. Even slightly menacing. I had to read more:

I slither onto what passes for a dance floor and start moving with the willow wand. She smiles nervously. She's not entirely sure she wants to be here. I take her hands and focus my energy on her scared, brown eyes. Because my biology is mostly hetero, I am more physically attracted to the man she's here with. But if I give my attention to her, I know his will follow.

Soon enough, she's twirling me to a driving beat. We're swaying and pumping our hips like raw sex. As the tempo slows and shifts into something softer and more sensual. I lean into her, and she does not object. The tall, dark man with narrow, mobile hips, the one I believe should take care of me, puts his arms around us. The willow stiffens and then relaxes. Hands travel. Sighs are emitted. We drift from the dance floor to the stairs.

There are rooms on the second floor for exigencies like this. Soft places for lust to fall. But I wasn't ready for that. Not yet. I needed to establish a connection. I needed to learn if

this couple would be my golden ticket, if I would be their unicorn. "Want to get a drink?"
I whisper.

"Yes, yes, yes," they murmur.

***

We sit on an oversized couch. I am in the middle, already wanted. I can feel the warmth radiating from both sides. They tell me their life stories without compunction or hesitation. I am already becoming their perfect accessory.

The woman is Anna, a wistful architect, who wishes we still built cathedrals. The man is Matt, her husband, a software developer who recently won the startup lottery. His company was acquired and his options are worth more than his house. Yes, I think, they can afford me.

"What is your passion?" asks Matt.

"I teach yoga to beautiful people," I say, stroking Anna's face. Her cheeks turn pink under my touch.

Matt smiles and leans into me. I can feel his breath on my ear. "How did you get into poly?"

"I don't believe in possession. I believe that we have as much love as we want to give."

It was even sort of true. Malcolm tried to do everything for me, to be everything. But his price was endless, slavish, groveling devotion. In my darkest moments, I considered killing him. Maybe I should have done it. If I had, my children would be alive today.

Matt and Anna liked my answer. They pressed themselves against me. And then Matt leaned over and whispered something in Anna's ear. She giggled. "Would you like to come home with us? See our house?" she asked in a suggestive, breathy voice."

"Absolutely," I said, letting them lead me into the night.

***

The house is modest by Central Valley standards. But in Palo Alto, it must be worth a few million. I follow them into the dimly lit bungalow. I can tell they don't have children. The space is too neat and artfully arranged. There are too many breakable vases and finicky digital toys.

The conversational portion of the evening is clearly over. Matt takes the lead, pulling Anna and me to the bedroom. Then he motions to their pristine, impeccably made bed. I take my cue and sit down on the edge, both feet on the floor. He looks at Anna with hot, hooded eyes. She smiles with abandon, pleased with her own daring. "Would you like to unwrap our present?" he asks.

Anna giggles again. This time it's a high, nervous sound. "Is that OK?" she asks gazing at me like a frightened deer. "Would you like that?"

"Yes," I say demurely. "But only if you would."

Anna's hands are cold as she unties my halter and struggles to pull it over my head. Matt extends his hand, helping me to my feet. Anna fumbles with the button on my jeans and pulls them down. I kick off my heels and step out of the puddled denim. They watch me as if I were a statue.

"You are beautiful. So beautiful," they murmur.

Matt takes Anna's hand and places it on my neck and then my waist. Her hands are now cool, but bearable. Matt's warm hands slide over me. They are rubbing me as if I were a lamp, a magical vessel with a genie inside. But all I have inside is sorrow, grief, and an immense thirst for care.

***

Anna and Matt are sleeping, twining around each other like cucumber vines. I dress by the moonlight while they sigh in their dreams.

With my help, they've had a magical night, every married couple's fantasy. For them, I am a unicorn, a selfless woman who brings happiness and joy without making any emotional demands.

Not yet, anyway.

I order an Uber on my phone and wait in the kitchen where I can see the street. Their refrigerator has a little clipboard on it, where they keep their grocery list. A red pen topped by a cheerful stuffed ladybug hangs from a plastic leash.

I write my new name—Julia Weatherstone—on their list, along with a quantity of "one, while supplies last."

***

I have become a fixture at Matt and Anna's house. Oh, I still return to my grim little room at the motel, but not nearly as much as I used to. I enjoy being part of a family again, even if it isn't really mine. I am steadily inching closer to my goal, worming my way into the center of the apple. My next objective is to move in.

Tonight, I am cooking dinner while Anna and Matt drink wine and complain about spending long hours in their open plan offices, drinking free trade coffee and petting their colleagues' dogs. I focus on the tofu-tamari stir fry in the wok while they babble. As far as they know, I'm a freely traveling yoga spirit, their very own beam of light. A creature of the moment. They've never asked about my family, my past, or if I have children.

They wouldn't believe the darkness inside me, the grief that strains its leash, the sour restlessness that won't let me become a happy little corporate drone. I let them see what they want to see. Their domestic little unicorn. Their hippy happy yoga sprite. In a way, their selfishness makes me feel better about using them. By not learning more about me, they are being negligent. And negligence always has a price.

"Oh shit," mutters Matt.

"What is it?" asks Anna, all loving and concerned.

"I have to run into the office and reset the server cluster. It might take a few hours."

Anna frowns, all sad-faced to be left alone with me. "Should we hold dinner?"

"No, go ahead, I'll be back as soon as I can."

I make up plates filled with stir fry and brown rice, being careful to serve myself less food. I am not overweight. But I am curvy, and lying naked next to Anna's spare lines has made me want to occupy less space. Anna smiles at me shyly. "Thank you for making dinner. This is wonderful."

"You're very welcome," I reply, taking a small sip of Merlot. And now it is time for me to ask a sharp question that could cut us both. "You and Matt seem happy. Have you ever considered having children?"

Her eyes widen and cheeks turn pink. Something akin to anger flickers across her face. "We have! We do! We're trying. It's just that it hasn't worked. Yet."

I mold my expression into something like sympathy. "Oh no! That's terrible! Are you looking into IVF? Or maybe a surrogate?"

She shakes her head. "We're not that far along yet. I want to see a fertility specialist, but Matt is against it. He doesn't want to do anything unnatural."

"How about adoption? How would you feel about raising someone else's child? You know, biologically speaking?"

She shrugs and her thickly lashed eyes narrow in a way that tells me that the subject is closed. After a moment of awkward silence, we start talking about movies, yoga, and herbal tea.

Anything but what matters.

***

We huddle around the monitor together. The results are in. I am oddly nervous, although I have no reason to worry. Matt types in the URL to the STD testing site and Anna squeezes my hand.

"Negative," he says cheerfully. "We're all negative."

Anna exhales. "Well, that's a relief."

My smile is hard and bright. Not offended at all. "I wasn't worried one bit."

Matt looks at Anna and then at me. He reminds me of a hawk gazing down at a mouse. Focused. Predatory. Single-minded. "I think we should celebrate," he says, rubbing the small of my back with his big, warm hand.

Anna's face stiffens slightly. Her lips twitch into an artificial smile. Since we talked about her desire to have children—and her barren womb—she's been cooler to me. Distant. Breezy.

She doesn't know I've had children—she still hasn't asked—but perhaps she can smell my fertility. Perhaps it threatens her. And perhaps it should.

Matt and I have started sleeping together without her. It's relaxing. I don't have to constantly compare my body to a willow wand. And I don't have to force myself to touch her soft, milky skin.

It has become clear that Anna and I would rather not sleep together. But we want to please Matt, so we perform what has become a choreographed routine. Clothing is shucked. Skin is pressed. We sigh loudly and moan ostentatiously. There are swellings and emanations.

When everything is done, I get up to shower and give Matt and Anna some post-coital couple time. As I walk to the bathroom, Anna stirs. "Oh God, I'm sorry. We were so excited about the STD results that we forgot to talk about birth control. You're on the pill, right?"

"Yes," I say, smiling through my lie.

***

More wine. I had to have more wine. It was after two in the morning. I would be exhausted and perhaps a little hung over when the children got up tomorrow. But I had to keep reading. Julia was obviously more dangerous than I had known.

It happened. I am moving in. Anna and Matt are carrying my bags of clothing and mementos into their smallest guest room, the space that will someday be the nursery. And the best part? I didn't even have to ask.

One day after the usual entertainments, I used their spare bedroom to do some yoga. I needed to become my body, live in my bones and muscles instead of my brain. While I unfurled myself into a high flying crow, Anna and Matt crept in, watching me with interest and even a little envy. I carefully unwound the pose and pretended I wasn't annoyed at the interruption.

"How are you?"

"Excellent," said Matt, grinning. "Do you like this room?"

It was an odd question. Anna was staring at the floor looking as glum as Matt was elated. I had no idea what was going on, so I merely answered his question. "Sure," I said. "The high ceiling is great. It's got good light."

"Then how would you like to live in it? You spend so much time here, it doesn't make sense for you to stay in hotels and Airbnbs. The room is empty. We all have fun together. Why not stay?"

Why not, indeed. And now the spare-room-slash-nursery is furnished with a rustic, pinewood bed, a woven hemp floor rug, and a crazy Tiffany lamp. I have found my perch. A place where I can just be. A place that's safe from my past and my grief.

I spend all afternoon glorying in my new space. As the sun goes down, Anna and Matt knock on my door. They have another surprise for me. "We made you a special dinner and a cake," says Anna, her voice loud and brittle. "We're so glad you're here."

During dinner, Matt leaves to fight another work emergency. Anna grows pale and wan. She moves her food around her plate in a counterclockwise direction.

"Is everything OK?" I ask.

"Migraine," she mumbles. "I'm out of ibuprofen."

"I have some," I reply, being an accommodating housemate. "It's in the medicine cabinet. In my bathroom."

Anna thanks me and scurries off to the tiny bathroom they assigned to me. It's the one with the broken fan and moldy tiles.

While she's gone, I help myself to a sliver of cake. When she returns, she's wearing an odd, questioning frown. At first, I attribute it to simple pain. But it starts to feel like something more.

"Anna, what's wrong?"

"I looked in your medicine cabinet. You're not on birth control, are you?"

***

We are sitting in the middle of the living room. It is a relationship meeting. An inquisition. Anna has called it. And it is a Big Fucking Deal. I sit on a low ottoman. Anna and Matt recline on the couch. It is a perfect tableau of couple privilege.

Anna coughs and twirls her hair. Matt rubs her back, suddenly the supportive partner. No longer the bored, unsatisfied husband who began sleeping with me alone.

"I called this meeting because Julia lied to us about her birth control situation. She said she was on the pill. But now she says she is not."

Matt's hawkish face turns grave. He turns to me with hooded eyes. "Is that true?" he asks in a low, gravelly voice.

"Yes."

Anna shakes her head, as if she expected me to deny it. Her mouth opens and closes in an unflattering way, the opposite of an orgasm. "But why would you do such a thing? Why would you lie to us?"

I smile brightly. Calmly. "I don't know why my birth control choices matter so much to you. It's not like you're on birth control, Anna."

She sputters and clutches at Matt's hand as if it's a talisman. "But that's different. Matt."

Matt nods, moving closer to his wife. Erasing the distance between them. "Yes, Anna's right. We want a baby together. We invited you here for fun, to spice up our relationship. You had no right to lie to us."

I roll my eyes until they almost get stuck in my skull. "Did you tell Anna that you've been sleeping with me practically every time she goes out?"

Anna gasps, alternately blanching and flushing with shock. Her eyes well with hypocritical tears. "Matt, is that true?"

Matt sighs and rubs his temples with his hands. "I was going to tell you, I swear. And it's not like you said I couldn't be alone with her. Let's focus on Julia, OK? We can talk about us later."

Anna glares at me. "Yes, let's talk about Julia. Why were you trying to have a baby with Matt? Why? Tell me why?"

I glare back and pull out my trump card, my bloody, tragic trump card. I let my eyes fill with tears I have held back since I met them. "I had twins once. Beautiful girls. They died along with my husband in a car accident. Two years ago. I guess I wanted to care for a child again." And I wanted someone to care for me, too.

Matt and Anna stare at me with glassy eyes. Like most people in their late twenties, they are terrified of grief. They stiffen and chew on their tongues. Their pupils leak into wide inky pools. Their brains are frozen.

Matt, wearing his shock on his sleeve, murmurs, "Sorry. I'm so sorry. That's...unthinkable."

Anna shakes her head. "Yes, that's terrible. Terrible." She pauses. Regroups. "But that doesn't give you the right to deceive us. We don't want a child with you. We hardly know you!"

Matt gives me a sad, meaningful look. It could easily mean, I'll make it up to you later. But I won't let him. I'm done with his cowardice. Done with his half measures. Done with his possessive, privileged, barren wife.

"That's right," I say. "You don't know me very well. Certainly not well enough to live with. I'll find someplace else. I'll get a hotel room right now."

Anna's forehead creases with guilt. "No, you can stay. For a few days, anyway. Until you find someplace else."

***

I am in an Uber Pool on my way to another poly party. This time the hosts are Jessie and Micah Tunewell—rich, older business people from Silicon Valley looking for pretty young things, sexual conquests to show how edgy they are.

I sigh. I had hope for Matt and Anna. I was ready to feast on their relationship, to nourish myself on its soft, creamy center, to nudge Anna aside to make space for me, my future child, and my ghostly children.

I shouldn't have gotten complacent. I should have said I was using some form of birth control that couldn't be seen or felt. Like Depo. Or an IUD. It just might have worked. Or maybe it wouldn't have. Maybe Matt was just too soft and spineless, too much under Anna's thrall.

I look out the window and watch the world fly by. The sun is setting. Everything, even the trees, is tinged pink like watered blood. Micah told me Mann Gottlieb might show tonight. He is a billionaire investor with steady eyes and a square, heavy jaw.

The idea of this man—this Mann—is intoxicating. I am tired of trying to survive through my grief. All that money would make a soft place to fall.

16 WE SHOULD TALK

It was four in the morning. My mouth was sour. My head ached. The computer screen rippled and warped before my tired eyes, as if it were underwater. And yet I read on:

I thank the Uber driver and step across an immaculate green lawn, flush with chlorophyll. The party is at yet another large, unassuming house that is probably worth at least five or six million.

Jessie, my blond, bony emissary, greets me at the door. Her deeply grooved smile is sharp and contemptuous. Ostensibly poly or not, she is a wife. And I am a party favor.

"It's so nice you could come. Julie is it?"

"Julia," I say, taking in the crepey neck beneath her long, greyhound face. She must be well over forty, a fate that I, at twenty-four, cannot imagine. But she's also rich. My old Stanford friends are still unpaid interns or living at home while working for silly startups.

"Well, Julia, let me give you the tour."

I follow her like a puppy, moving from room to room. She shows me the buffet, the wine bar, and the bathrooms. And she points out a man with dark hair and an unyielding jawline, the man I thought was a rumor. He is taller than a geek should be, rangy yet strong. I stare perhaps a moment too long.

Jessie wags her finger, her lips tightening into a grimace. "That's Mann Gottlieb. He's a well-known investor. Try not to bother him. He has a lot of groupies."

Perhaps I don't look sufficiently convinced, because she points out a woman at the other end of the room. "See that woman over there?" I follow her bony finger to a short, plump woman with messy blond hair. She is holding a tumbler of wine. Her face is puffy, lost, and vaguely familiar.

"That's his wife, Helen" says Jessie, her voice full of gloating, as if she had just foiled me.

Instead of pouting, I shrug and smile. "She looks nice," I say.

Jessie rolls her eyes, as if to suggest Helen is no such thing. "Have a lovely time," she says, fluttering towards the buffet.

I follow an invisible line straight to Helen. I will use her to get to Mann.

***

Helen is obviously unhappy. Her mouth and eyes are droopy. She holds her wine like a shield, not drinking it. Her posture is defeated. I also realize why she seems familiar. She looks a bit like me, if I were much older and overfed.

In fact, she looks enough like me to be my sister. My sister who doesn't really exist. Ooooh, I am inspired. I have an idea that will create an instant bond between us. But for this to work, I must look distraught. I think of my girls and how I'll never see them again. Tears stream down my face.

I walk quickly and clumsily, aiming myself at Helen. We collide. She spills her wine.

"Oh my God, you look just like my sister."

Her face is wary but intrigued. "Oh, um, thank you. Older or younger?"

"Older," I say, holding back a sob. "I miss her so much. She died in a car accident five years ago. It was a drunk driver." I think of my girls again, and the dam breaks. I lose myself in my tears and my perfectly preserved grief. I allow Helen to herd me to a quiet couch.

I sink in next to her with a soft, sniffling sigh.

"What's your name?" she asks, both concerned and interested. Inside, I feel twin jaws snapping shut. I've got her.

"Julia," I say with a grateful simper. "And I'm sorry I broke down like that. It's been a tough year. A tough life, really."

"I'm Helen," she says, straightening her shoulders and smoothing her face. There's something slightly superior about her expression. She likes that I'm a mess. "Is there anything you'd like to talk about?"

I bite my lip and furrow my brow, pouring on the pathos. "Oh, if I talk about it, I'll just cry some more." Then I turn the conversation back to her. "So who do you know at this party?"

She looks like she doesn't belong here. And perhaps she really doesn't. Her older, tired-mom vibe probably doesn't mesh well with the poly scene. But she smiles stiffly and answers gamely.

"My husband knows the hosts, Micah and Jessie. I suppose I know them a little bit, but they're really his friends."

I see an opportunity to gain sympathy, to make myself seem harmless. "Matt and Anna, the couple I'm living with, know Jessie. I was sort of invited by osmosis."

"Are you dating Matt and Anna?" She seems surprised I'm dating, or was dating, a couple. She must be very new to poly. I bet it's her husband's idea.

"We're going through some issues. I don't really want to talk about it." She hasn't earned my story, not yet. Silence descends like a weary bird.

Helen looks into the distance. She wants to keep talking, but she's too dull and socially awkward to successfully change the subject. I allow my eyes to follow hers. They lead me exactly where I want to go. Mann, Helen's husband and my target, is watching us with a warm, speculative light in his eyes.

He approaches, and I feel a pleasant rush of attraction. He is everything Malcom, my poor, striving husband, had always wanted to be, but couldn't. He could give me a new life.

"I see you've made a new friend," he says, drinking me in. "Helen, can you introduce me to this lovely young lady?"

***

I can't believe Helen left me alone with her husband. She has obviously decided I'm too damaged to be a threat. So here I am, sitting next to Mann, who is visibly excited. I let myself casually brush against him. Oh, but he is strong. He could be my wall between me and the world.

He seeks out my eyes, smiling. "So how did you get into poly?"

His question is bold, even blunt, but his voice is gentle.

I relax into a shrug. I am so glad the true answer is, for my goals, also the right one. "My children died two years ago," I confess. "Twins. Lily and Serena. They were young, almost two themselves. They were my angels. Since then, I haven't had the energy for monogamy. Poly lets me give what I can, and take what I can accept."

I watch for signs of cowardice, of turning away. Instead, I see an empathy as strong and steady as sunlight. His eyes water. He takes my hand and squeezes it. I squeeze back.

"That's the worst thing I could imagine. My wife and I have two girls, twins. It's unthinkable."

Something inside me loosens. My grief feels lighter, as if I have found someone to share it with. We sit silently for a few moments, then our conversation grows like a tender, fragile plant. He tells me about his girls, I tell him about mine.

By the time Helen returns, I am floating in happy memories of my children, and learning about hers. She is a dark, pudgy cloud, holding a tray of food she doesn't need. She is my sad reflection and my instant nemesis.

In fact, I might just hate her. Her children are happy and alive. She has a kind, magnificent husband. And I can tell she isn't grateful at all.

***

Helen leaves me and Mann outside; she's going to pick up her twins from the babysitter's house. Since Mann invited me to stay over, Helen has been cooler to me. Studiously neutral. She drives away with a sour expression on her face, her hand folding into a halfhearted wave.

If I were going to pick up my children now, I would be ecstatic. Helen doesn't appreciate what she has. I think of my girls, and my eyes water for perhaps the thousandth time.

Mann notices. He takes my hand and leads me inside. And it feels like a miracle. His house is a cathedral built for some pale, secular god. The high ceilings and stark white open spaces are striking and otherworldly. I follow him quietly, my tears forgotten.

We climb a hardwood staircase to the second floor, which looks a bit more like a human home. We enter a minimally luxurious master bedroom with majestic windows. A bottle of pink nail polish sits on one of the bed stands. This must be where Helen sleeps.

"You can borrow some pajamas from Helen," he says, showing me a monstrously large walk in closet. Meticulously organized shelves and bins line the walls. Tasteful, professional outfits and simple dresses hang from an endless, titanium rod. I am intimidated by the sheer volume of this woman's possessions, like an immigrant at Target for the first time.

"Are you sure?" I ask, voice trembling.

Mann smiles and extracts a silky pajama set from one of the many bins. "Try this. It should be comfortable, and my wife doesn't wear it anymore."

"Thank you. I am so grateful. Your wife is an enormously lucky woman."

***

I feel glamorous in Helen's black, silky pajamas. They fit me perfectly. She must have been a lot thinner once, a lot more like me. Mann watches me cross the room. His eyes are intense. Knowing. I sit next to him on a white, microfiber couch, luxuriating in his presence.

"How are you feeling?" he asks, full of what I hope is genuine concern.

"Better, thank you. It's nice to get away from my problems for a night."

Mann frowns. A small crescent appears between his dark brows. "You'll probably see our girls in the morning. Will that bring back...memories?"

My tears well again. I don't try to stop them. "Good memories," I say with a brave smile.

Mann encircles me in his arm and pulls me in for a long hug. I feel sheltered. Protected. Valuable. Something I never felt with Malcom, who wanted to be strong, but was ultimately a weak, brittle reed.

"Can I ask you a question?"

"Sure," he murmurs.

"Are you and Helen poly? I mean, I met you at Jessie's party, but I don't want to make any assumptions."

His sigh is like a fresh breeze through a young forest. "We have an open marriage, but we're still working out the details. We're looking for a partner who will be patient with us both."

I smile. I can be patient. In fact, I'm excellent at it. "You don't have to answer this, but why did you open your marriage?"

His next sigh is longer and deeper. "Since we had kids, Helen hasn't been interested in sex. She just doesn't care about it anymore. I still do. Deeply."

Even better, I think, even better.

***

Anger cut through my wine-and-Xanax haze. I muttered a few curses, hurling them into the universe and sending them towards Mann and Julia. I couldn't believe Mann told Julia that I wasn't interested in sex anymore, as if

141

my physical pain were somehow a choice, as if he didn't stubbornly insist upon a single, prosaic act.

And why do women always have to be so fucking grateful? Shouldn't Mann have been grateful that I stayed with him? Of course, I already knew the answer. Women, as they age, are depreciating assets, while men add value with every year.

My eyes drifted towards the clock. Five a.m. The girls would be up soon. But I couldn't tear myself away. I had to read more, to drink all the poison left in the glass:

I am in one of the downstairs guest rooms, lying on a bed like a raft, when I hear Helen arrive with her children. Their soft girlish voices break my heart. Helen is brusque with her twins, herding them upstairs like cattle. I hate her just a little bit more.

I wonder if she's one of those women who never wanted children, who had them because she's supposed to, or because her husband wanted them.

She doesn't deserve them. Not at all.

***

I am floating close to the surface of sleep, dreaming of my Lily and Serena, when a light streams into my room. I am immediately awake. Since the fire and the nightmares that followed, I have been a light sleeper.

I shift myself into a sitting position. My door is ajar. Mann is watching me, his expression a mixture of soft and hard. We remain suspended in silence, our quiet eyes saying nothing and everything. He breaks first.

"I was just checking on you. Is the bed comfortable? Do you have everything you need?"

I glance at the sleek clock on the bed stand. It is four in the morning, the gray hour that is neither night nor day. "No," I say. "I don't think so."

I don't expect him to enter the room, but he does. He walks to me with a stride that's smooth and confident. He sits on the bed and takes my hand, running his fingers along the palm. "What else do you need?"

I look at him, and he knows. His lips brush mine. I let myself collapse. As we fall onto the silky sheets, he whispers, "STDs? Birth control?"

"No, none. And, yes, I've got it covered," I whisper back. Oh, he will be a wonderful father to my next child.

***

I knew it! She was trying to get pregnant. She was lying about the IUD. I started a pot of coffee. The girls were stirring, but I had a few more precious minutes to read:

One hour later, Mann is lying next to me, gazing at the skylight in the ceiling. The sky is shifting from gray to bluish pink. A new day is dawning. Maybe a new life. Mann cannot get comfortable. He is strangely agitated.

"The girls will be getting up soon. Probably Helen, too. I want to surprise them with breakfast."

"Really?" I pout slightly. Why does he want to surprise his selfish, ungrateful wife who has let herself go, who won't even have sex with him?

"Opening our marriage is hard for Helen. I'm not sure if she's going to be comfortable with…what happened tonight. Besides, I've barely seen the girls all week. You're welcome to sleep in."

I shake my head. "No, I'll get up with you. I'd love to have breakfast with you…and Helen and the girls. Besides. I'm a wonderful cook. I'll make something delicious while you play with your kids."

His face shifts from dull to light. His brown eyes glow with warm hope. "Are you sure?"

"Absolutely."

And the file ended. There was no more.

I dumped the dregs of my wine in the sink and poured myself a cup of coffee. Despite a night with not enough sleep and too much wine, I was painfully awake. My daughters were jumping in their cribs.

It was time to start the day. And decide what in the seven hells I was going to do.

***

While the girls played with their iPads, I wrote text after text. I wondered how I would convince Mann that Julia, his beloved third, was using him for his money, that she wanted to trick him into having another child.

She is lying about birth control.

She wants to break up our family.

She only wants you for your money.

We need to talk about Julia.
Julia has a dark side.
I have proof.
I have proof.
I have proof.

Everything I wrote read like the ramblings of a slightly unhinged, jealous wife who had been drinking too much. In other words, I sounded just like myself. The girls were beginning to exhibit signs of boredom. Rose was pounding on her iPad, and Briar was whimpering. I had to think of something fast.

I did the simplest, easiest possible thing. I uploaded Julia's poisonous memoir to the cloud and sent it to Mann with a short note.

We should talk.

17 CONFESSIONS AND DREAMS

The kids were napping, and I was trying to fall asleep. My hungover head was full and achy. My mouth was dry and stale. I had made a bold, irrevocable move by sending Julia's memoir to Mann. When I hit send, I practically heard a thousand alternate futures die.

Now Mann knew I had broken into her computer. I was certain—mostly certain—I had violated her privacy for a higher cause, not just my own jealousy. But I had doubts, cruel, useless doubts that prodded my motives and questioned my sanity.

I pushed them into a deep well and looked away. I was tired and muzzy from my sleepless night. It was time to rest.

Except I couldn't fall asleep. When I closed my eyes, I would see Mann's face, angry and disappointed, glowering at me. Or Julia's expression of shock and horror laid over a sly, triumphant smile. A little voice kept whispering, *You are wrong, always wrong.*

I tried to focus on the positive. I told myself the story I wanted to be true. Mann was a good, reasonable man. He loved our children. He loved me in his own way. Any sane parent or spouse would be disturbed by what Julia had written. And that same, good sane person wouldn't want Julia living with us for even one more day.

I drifted off imagining the hours after our inevitable confrontation. I held Mann's hand as he confessed his heartbreak. He desperately wished Julia had loved him, not just his money. He reluctantly concluded we had to let her go. For the children's sake and our own. I quietly agreed.

As Mann spoke in tense, sober tones about our new, post-Julia life, I smiled. The years I had spent at a job I hated had been worth it. They had proved beyond a doubt that I wanted Mann for himself.

I don't remember the rest of that dream, only that I felt relieved. And begrudgingly but truly loved.

***

"Wake up! Wake up!"

Rough hands pulled at the covers, exposing me to the light. Instinctively, I curled into a ball. I wasn't ready to leave my sleepy cocoon. I was still metamorphosing.

"What's wrong with you? The girls got out of their beds and they're destroying their room. They pulled every single book off the shelves."

My husband's voice was loud and sharp, not the loving murmur from my fantasy. His face was hard and angry. A deeply carved v shape formed between his eyes. "What?" I asked, confused. "I thought the girls were sleeping."

"You were sleeping. Or should I say unconscious? I can't believe you didn't hear them on the monitor. They could have gotten seriously hurt, and you wouldn't have noticed."

I pushed myself into a sitting position as a wave of shame crashed over me. I couldn't believe I had put my girls in danger. I guessed it was a combination of exhaustion and the residual effects of the Xanax. "Is Julia with them?"

"Yes, she is."

I moved to rise and join them. I had to go to my girls. I couldn't leave them alone with that horror. But Mann stopped me, placing his hands on my shoulders. "Stay in bed. Take a nap. You obviously need to rest."

I shook my head. Adrenaline jump-started my heart. I couldn't sink back into torpor, not now. "Did you get my email? We need to talk about Julia."

He sighed. "I don't want to do this now. I have an investors' meeting this afternoon. Can we talk later?"

I should have recognized the weary timbre of his voice and let him go. But my glimpse inside of Julia's soul had been jarring. Enlisting Mann, securing his agreement, felt desperately urgent. "What's more important? Your investors' meeting or your children's lives?"

He looked at me with a mixture of amazement and contempt. "What happened to the woman I married? The one who was so sensible? You need to get a hold of yourself. You're sounding like a nutcase."

I gasped. I wanted to shout, *How dare you?* Instead, I said, "You think *I'm* crazy? I simply read a document Julia wrote that suggests she's crazy. And dishonest. And manipulative. I do not want her around our children for even one more day."

Mann's hands on my shoulders squeezed tighter, an ominous pressure. Then, catching himself, he released me, balling his hands into fists.

"Damn it, Helen. The document you found was fiction. Julia is writing a novel. Her process is to start with real life and then completely distort it. I'm sorry your feelings got hurt, but that's what happens when you invade someone's privacy. You see things without context. It can make you, well, crazy."

I shook my head. Fiction? Really? But why use real names and places? Why make the plot something indistinguishable from real life? And what about all the other things I found using her real name on Google?

"Mann, it's not just the file. I also found her real name.

"You said you checked her out, but she's been lying to us. Her family didn't die in a car accident, she lit her goddamned house on fire. She was stalked by some violent internet trolls, the Angels of Vengeance, who could possibly still be stalking her now.

"And her sister who supposedly died? Doesn't exist."

I tried to catch my breath as Mann brought his hands together. The muscles in his jaw tensed. His cheeks flushed. "Helen, she told me about the fire and the Angels two days after we met. I also had an investigator check her out. I am confident she isn't a threat to you or the children. I didn't tell you because it is her story to tell. Hers, not yours.

"Maybe she didn't want to tell you because you're so jealous and judgmental. You obviously don't accept her. Why should she confide in you?"

I was suddenly dizzy and taking small, careful sips of air. I thought I had an ironclad case against Julia, a solid stool to sit upon. But Mann had knocked it over with a few words. I clung to her dishonesty, to the way she lied to me moments after we met.

"But she lied about having a dead, older sister…"

Mann interrupted, shaking his head. "She lied about having a sister *in her novel*. She wasn't talking about real life."

"She lied in her novel *and* in real life. Her so-called fiction is practically a transcript of our conversation," I snapped.

Mann stood and looked at me, the contempt in his eyes melting into pity. "Maybe you're not remembering accurately. We've all been through a lot since then."

I thought about all the wine I'd been drinking and the Xanax I'd been taking. Could my memory be blurring around the edges? "No, she lied to me about her sister. I'm sure."

Mann sighed and planted a kiss in the middle of my forehead. "You're exhausted and upset. We'll talk again when you've gotten some sleep."

***

I wandered downstairs just in time for dinner. The girls gave me quick hugs, then went back to pestering Julia, who was making a stir fry. Mann stood by the window, talking into his headset. My thoughts fizzed and sparked in a dizzying swirl of accusations and self-loathing.

I paced the room. I wanted to talk to Mann and Julia. But I dreaded it. My hands shook. My heart pounded. I had forgotten to take my blood pressure pills again. Instead of running upstairs for my pillbox, I popped into our wine cave and grabbed a bottle.

Julia watched me pour myself a drink through narrow eyes. She was sipping some kind of herbal tea. I took a large, burning swallow and watched Julia cover the dining table with fragrant, steaming bowls. I made plates for the girls. Mann collected the children with a tight smile.

As dinner unfolded, we adults spoke only to the children, commenting on their silly faces and big appetites. The tension between Julia, Mann and me was so brittle the smallest word could shatter it into a million bits of shrapnel. Better and safer to focus on the children.

Eventually, drunk on concentrated attention, the girls began misbehaving. They climbed onto the table. They spilled a bowl of rice. They even, somehow, broke a plastic plate. Mann declared bedtime. Without a shared word between us, Julia and I washed the girls, read stories, and tucked them in.

We silently padded downstairs, where I poured myself another glass of wine. I began searching my phone for a suitable book when Julia cleared her throat. It was an oddly meaningful sound.

"Helen," she said solemnly. "I'd like you to join Mann and me in the movie room. There's something I'd like to say."

***

Mann and Julia reclined on the couch while I sat on a straight-backed chair. They were the prosecution. I was the accused. Julia, holding a brown bag in her lap, made their case.

"Mann told me that you looked at my computer. I'm disappointed, and I feel exposed. But I can sort of understand. I would have done anything to keep my girls safe. I'm hoping that's where you were coming from when you invaded my privacy.

"Now, since you went through my life, you must know that my parents were drug addicts. They overdosed just a couple of weeks after I was born. I know addiction is a disease, and I'm always checking myself for signs.

"I ask myself questions all the time. Am I starting to use coffee as a crutch? Am I drinking too much? Am I using substances to stop an unpleasant feeling?

"I guess that's why I'm so sensitive to the signs of addiction in others. The early stages are so subtle that you can be sick without even knowing it. And that's why I have to speak up. I care about you and your precious children. I can't let you go down a dark path without handing you a light."

She paused and took a sip of tea. My fingers twitched. She sounded so sincere, like she really cared about me. I questioned the panic I'd felt earlier. Had I really overreacted? I replayed her memoir—or was it a novel?—in my head over and over again, remembering its arch, cruel voice. Was it really fiction like Mann said?

And what about her sister? Why would she lie about having a dead sister? And say that she looked just like me?

I was about to ask, when Julia spoke again. "I see you drinking too much, without even realizing. You sip wine while you're working, while you're relaxing, while you're playing with the children. You're going through about a bottle a night. I take out the trash. I know these things."

Mann frowned. "Julia, I'm supposed to take out the trash," he murmured. They exchanged sharp whispers while I tried to remember how much I had been drinking. I had finished a bottle last night while I pored through Julia's computer, but was I really drinking that much? I wasn't sure. I had never really thought about it.

"Yes," I said, "I have wine with dinner. But I don't think I'm drinking as much as you say."

Julia shook her head sadly. "There's more." She opened the paper bag on her lap and pulled out three orange prescription bottles. "I found these in your medicine cabinet. I know I shouldn't have looked, but you shouldn't have looked in my computer. And I guess we're family now."

She grimaced and continued, "That's a lot of Xanax. It's incredibly addictive. And it's dangerous when mixed with alcohol."

Before I could think, I snapped, "Give me those. That's prescription medication. I don't take it all the time. Only when I need it."

I expected her to make a big show of pouring the pills down the toilet. But she didn't. She handed the bottles to me, her face softly grave. "I was just trying to make a point," she said. "I think you should be more mindful of your consumption. And be open to the possibility that you could possibly have a problem."

Mann nodded his head and put his hand on Julia's back. "I know this isn't something you wanted to hear. But you should think about what she's saying. She cares about you. And the girls."

I nodded, still confused, clutching my Xanax like pearls. Did Julia really care about me? Was she genuinely concerned? And had I repaid her concern with suspicion? My thoughts were muddled and circular. I felt like I owed Julia for doubting her, for ripping the protective covering from her life.

I remembered the nanny cams that monitored the main living area, and allowed me to watch Julia and the girls during the day. And then I thought of my parents: my father's iron control and my mother's shrinking passivity. I had never wanted to be my mother, never wanted to be weak. But had I, without even realizing, become my *father*?

Something fluttered in my stomach. Perhaps Julia really was the innocent, honest victim, and I was the ogre, twisted by jealousy and fear. An overwhelming urge to confess surged through me.

I didn't think, I just opened my mouth. "Thank you for thinking of me and the girls. I'm grateful I really am. Now there's something you need to know."

***

I lay in bed, staring at the ceiling. Mann and Julia were downstairs talking and processing. I had taken down the nanny cams and plucked the GPS from Julia's car while they looked on, apparently shocked and numb. They thanked me for my honesty and suggested I go to bed.

"We have a lot to think about," Mann said.

I willed my breathing to slow, my pulse to steady. I couldn't bear to examine my own thoughts or motives. Desperate for peace, I tried to pour my thoughts from my brain. I focused on the hum of the water heater, the gentle whoosh of the night wind sliding over the house.

I imagined a stream burbling over a bed of pebbles. I carefully stepped into it. The cold water on my feet began as a shock and melted into a shiver. I felt the smooth shapes under my toes. For a moment, I was really there, listening to the water and the trees.

And then I was me again, heart thumping, awash in fear and doubt. I wasn't very good at visualization. I learned it from the therapist I saw during my maternity leave. Dr. Lorena Teague, an icily lovely women and an expert in cognitive behavioral therapy.

I closed my eyes and recalled her pale, cream-on-white office, her eggshell-colored couch I sat on while trying not to spill my coffee. She preferred to sit on a bone-white, high-backed rocking chair, an austere throne for a cool queen.

She always struck me as essentially *other*, an otherworldly creature peering out from a human skin. There was something glossy and seamless about her, as if every day pains slid right off her. It was a quality I coveted.

In our last session, the twins slept in their carriers while I quietly sobbed. Mann was traveling for business. He had left me barely enough money to cover groceries, certainly not enough for a babysitter. I was alone with the babies and afraid something would happen. A fall. An accident. A sudden sickness. And I was sure I would fail them when it did.

Like so many older parents, we could not rely on help from grandparents. My parents and Mann's father were dead. And Mann's mother had already begun her slide into dementia. All that stood between my children and some unspeakable fate was me. I was suffocating under the weight of obligation. For most of the appointment, I raged at Mann for leaving me alone, for turning me into a bulwark of last and only resort.

I raged and sobbed. The girls slept. And Dr. Teague watched. Eventually, when I ran out of epithets, she spoke. "You can't control your husband. The only thing you control is how you react to whatever is happening. The best thing you can do for yourself and your babies is to examine your feelings and choose to react in a healthy way."

Then she smiled wryly. Her face was no longer seamless. Lines streaked across her forehead and bracketed her eyes. "And ask your primary care doctor for some Xanax."

The memories crowded in my mind. I saw my mother and father arguing and getting drunk, Karl breaking a wine glass, a nurse changing my empty IV bag of liquid fire. I twisted and rolled in the sheets. I considered climbing out of bed and popping a Xanax, but I didn't. I smashed my eyes together and tried to will myself to sleep.

***

I was driving to Poppy's. The sun was achingly bright. I was fleeing the office, speeding towards my girls. I knew I had to pick them up. We had someplace important to go, but I couldn't quite grasp where.

I parked in front of Poppy's bungalow. Its pink exterior was strangely vibrant. It shimmered and shifted in the glare. When I knocked on the door, Poppy appeared. Or, I think it was Poppy. Her hair was blond, and she wore an apron. She looked at me with a quizzical expression and didn't invite me in.

"Um, who are you?" she asked.

I frowned. Was she stoned? Or worse? "I'm here to pick up Briar and Rose. The Gottlieb girls."

She shook her head. "No, I'm sorry. You're not Mrs. Gottlieb."

And then I smelled smoke, as if something inside the house were burning. "What's going on in there? It smells like something's on fire."

Poppy's hands were suddenly covered by oven mitts. "Excuse me, the cookies are burning," she said.

"But wait!" I called, my mouth filling with smoke.

Gradually, the dream faded away, but the smoky smell didn't. It got harsher, thicker. Was something burning in the house? I checked the monitor. The girls were sleeping. I checked the time. Three a.m. With a strange sense of déjà vu, I climbed out of bed and hurried downstairs.

18 AN IMAGINARY EVEREST

The kitchen was foggy with gray smoke. I gasped and coughed. The stove was on fire. Flames licked up and around the back burner. Julia's red tea kettle, rapidly blackening, sat at the center of the blaze. I watched the fire for a moment, hypnotized. Then something deep inside my lizard brain awakened with a snort and a shriek. *Put out the fire*, it hissed.

I obeyed, filling a large mixing bowl with water and dousing the flames. I did it again and again, until the floor was drenched. Once the fire was out, my hand began shaking. Wasn't this how Julia's children really died? I was sure I didn't have tea tonight. Almost positive, anyway. Did Julia?

I was chasing a smoky wisp of a thought when the ceiling lights flashed on. I turned around. Mann and Julia stood behind me, their faces slack with unreality. We watched each other for a long while. Mann finally broke the silence.

"What in the world just happened here? Why wasn't the smoke alarm on?" He directed the full force of his ire towards me. After all, I was the wife and responsible for all things homely. I tried to think. And then, to my horror, I remembered. It was the night I agreed to open our marriage. I had burned my first attempt at fajitas and switched off the smoke alarms.

"I don't know," I said, refusing to admit any more guilt. After all, I didn't leave the kettle on. That wasn't all my fault. I was sure.

Julia's face was distraught. I wasn't surprised. After all, this was how her children and husband had died. A cup of tea planned and then forgotten.

Mann was still fuming. "Helen, you must have left that kettle on. I didn't do it, and I'm dead certain that Jules didn't."

Mann was alluding to Julia's history. She was always tremendously careful of her tea kettle, keeping it in the cupboard instead of letting it sit on the stove. I didn't think Julia would do something like this, either. Except I knew I didn't do it. And Mann didn't drink tea, ever.

I recalled Julia's memoir, the dark, directed voice. Did Julia do this to blame it on me? Or to make Mann think I was setting her up? I took a deep breath and tried to ignore my racing heart. I shook my head slowly. "No, I didn't do this. It wasn't me."

Mann bit his lip. His left eyebrow twitched. "Given how much you drink and how much Xanax you're taking, how can you be sure of anything?"

I was trying to think of what to say when Julia, her face twisted with righteous rage, stepped towards me. "You put your children in danger! You got lucky! They could have...they could have..." She shattered into rough, barking sobs. Mann held her and rocked her.

I stared, mouth gaping. What could I say? What would they believe? I hadn't taken any Xanax. And I hadn't had wine since dinner. It must have been Julia. Or Mann.

"Go to bed," muttered Mann. We'll talk in the morning.

***

I was walking through a cloud of smoke, calling my daughters' names. "Briar! Rose!" I could barely see a foot in front of me, and yet I could breathe. My heart thrummed in my chest. I knew something was terribly wrong. I tried running through the fog when I tripped. I fell over a ledge and landed on the ground with an ear-splitting thud. I tasted something awful.

I awakened on the floor of my bedroom—was it still Mann's at all?— with carpet fuzz in my mouth. I leaped to my feet and checked the monitor.

It was Monday. I had overslept. Julia had already spirited the twins from their beds.

I showered quickly, dreading the work day and finding Julia and Mann, waiting for me downstairs. My face in the steamy mirror was bony and haggard. Black circles lined my eyes. Flesh hung from my cheekbones and puddled into incipient jowls. I looked thinner than I remembered. And haunted.

I scraped my hair into a damp, lumpy bun and threw on my usual work uniform. It had been getting steadily looser for the past couple of months. Today was some kind of tipping point. I needed a belt to keep my pants in place.

I should have been elated—I was finally closing in on my pre-pregnancy weight—but I wasn't. I was as anxious and as buzzy as a hive of angry bees. Last night felt wrong. I was sure I didn't make that tea. But Julia had seemed so certain and so impassioned. I doubted my own mind. My thoughts were somehow both hazy and cracked.

I took a deep breath and padded down the stairs. My worst fears peered out from the kitchen table. Mann and Julia were looking at me as if I were some kind of criminal. For the first time in months, the girls were confined to their playpen. Briar happily flipped through a book, but Rose looked forlorn.

Mann and Julia cleared their throats. The girls cried out for "Mommy."

"We need to talk," Mann said, taking the lead. His voice was harsh, revealing his parents' German roots.

I blew the girls kisses. "Mommy is busy right now." They whimpered and cooed.

I retreated deeper into the kitchen and poured myself a large cup of coffee, even as my heart danced in my chest, thumping out my doom. I sat across from Mann. Julia, tears tracing damp lines between her eyes and the corners of her mouth, looked away.

Mann sighed, his face softening. "Julia, why don't you take the girls outside?"

Silently, she rose and took my children. I watched her gather them one at a time and bring them into the back yard. Then I turned back to Mann. He was hard again, unyielding. I wasn't a wife anymore, I was problem to solve. A risk to mitigate.

He inhaled slowly and said, "Julia says she didn't leave the burner on under that kettle. I believe her."

I opened my mouth to say something, I didn't know what, but Mann stopped me. "Helen, for fuck's sake, let me finish."

I flinched. Mann rarely swore, and never around women. He continued, "I know opening our relationship has been stressful for you. I've been trying to be sensitive to that, even if it means walking on eggshells. But you need to find some way of coping that doesn't involve drink and drugs. You need to get help. ASAP.

"Jack Tremblay, my general counsel, said I could get a restraining order to keep you away from the kids."

I inhaled sharply. *Tremblay.* That was the last name of the divorce lawyer I had visited, the self-righteous woman who wouldn't take my case. The room shifted on its axis. I felt light and otherworldly, as if I were in a dream. I shook my head and murmured, "No, no, no."

Mann's lips curled with contempt. His eyes became brown, unflinching agates. He was the epitome of the stern CEO staring down a feckless employee. "I don't want it to come to that. The girls love you. But I will protect them from you. Understand?"

I nodded numbly. If Mann wanted to take the girls, I would have no defense. I may have been their mother, but he was a billionaire, the angel investor known for his good looks, obsession with ROI, and unassuming demeanor. He could hire the best lawyers, find the most sympathetic judges. He knew everybody who mattered. I didn't have access to much cash. How would I even begin to fight him?

"Now, I want you to go upstairs and bring me your bottles of Xanax. *All of them.*"

***

I opened the medicine cabinet where I kept my pills. I returned the bottles last night, after Julia's attempted intervention. They sat beside each other in a neat row.

I inspected them carefully and noticed something strange. Unsettling, even. One was a prescription from my OB-GYN, who functioned as my *de facto* primary care physician. She wrote me scripts for blood pressure medication and Xanax, even as she harried me to see a cardiologist, a psychiatrist and various other -ists.

But the other two were prescribed by a Dr. Alan Chesterson. Who the hell was he?

I took out my phone and snapped pictures of the bottles. An idea was forming in my mind, one that could prove my sanity and potentially reveal Julia. I pulled in a long, deep breath and released it in stages. I felt calmer and more centered than I had in days.

I would get to the bottom of this. I would fix my life, protect my children, and untangle—unwind—my marriage.

***

Mann took my arm, the first physical contact we'd had in weeks, and brought me to the smaller downstairs guest bathroom. His touch was firm and impersonal. It was hard to remember he had ever regarded me with sustained affection, that we had ever produced children.

"Dump them," he commanded.

I unscrewed each bottle and watched the pills hit the water. As I poured them out, my heart accelerated in small, panicked bursts. I didn't think I was a true addict who would commit an atrocity for another fix. But I could not deny that I would miss the Xanax and its cool, reliable comfort.

Now I would have to face the world as it was: hard and full of sharp edges. I could no longer drift. I would have to march uphill, alone. Mann had Julia. I had no one but my girls. And I would have to fight to keep them.

I held in my tears until I reached my car, waving a solemn goodbye to Julia and my dark-and-light twins.

***

At work, Brittany shadowed me like a blond wraith. Every now and then, she would materialize and ask innocuously barbed questions. Her lips curled into a rubbery smile.

"Do you need a new keyboard? Good ergonomics can help you type faster." *You are too old and slow.*

"Do you have reliable childcare? There's a mom in the engineering department who uses the center next door. It's super close and convenient." *You are coming in late and making me look bad.*

"Do you want to be considered for our departmental exchange program? Field sales support has an opening." *I want you off my team. Better you spend your time at luncheons in the Midwest.*

I waved off her fake concern. I understood her motivation, even vaguely sympathized with it. I was making quota, but just barely. The fiscal quarter would close in two days. I was almost certainly destroying her metrics. Perhaps she would have to make two different charts for her bosses: content production for the whole department and for everyone but Mann Gottlieb's wife.

Once again, I wondered what I would have to do to get fired. I cut-and-pasted in a fog, thinking about Julia. She had taken my insurance card at one point. Maybe she saw Alan Chesterson and pretended to be me. My fingers flew as I convinced myself this was what she had done.

When my break notification flashed onscreen, I got myself a huge cup of coffee—hammering heart be damned—and Googled Dr. Alan Chesterson. His Silicon Valley clinic roosted at the top of the page. I clicked through. His pale, square jawed face smirked at me from his web page. His features were heavy and vegetal. He looked like a sentient, carnivorous plant.

Caffeine coursing through my veins, I scanned his site. He had degrees from Stanford and Berkeley. He specialized in bipolar and borderline personality disorder. He had a long list of scholarly articles to his name. I Googled *borderline personality.*

I thought of Julia again, of her trauma and her drama and her tears. Was she legitimately mentally ill? Did she get much needed treatment under my name? Or was she simply creating a paper trail? I reflexively went to look at my nanny cam and sighed. I remembered I had taken it down in a futile gesture of goodwill.

I had felt tremendously guilty about spying on Julia. But maybe I shouldn't have. My head was starting to ache. I rubbed my temples. The timer on my screen counted down the remaining two minutes of break.

I sent a copy of Dr. Chesterson's page to my phone. I was going to make an appointment.

***

By lunchtime, I was practically vibrating from too much caffeine. My heart quivered. I could barely speak without gasping. I was breathless and restless, full of jagged-edged energy. I didn't trust myself to call Dr. Chesterson's office, not yet. I was afraid I would break down the moment I heard the receptionist's voice and tell her all about Julia and my most frightening fears. I would, in short, sound crazy.

Instead, I decided, I would work off my hysteria. I took the elevator to the company gym. It was there to keep us healthy—and onsite. Its shiny chrome surfaces and boldly colored motivational posters felt vaguely Orwellian. When I worked out, I was a corporate hamster running in a totalitarian wheel. At least it was free and convenient.

On the way to the locker room, I passed the blood pressure machine. A large, cheerful sign that said "Know your numbers" sat above it. I kept moving forward despite a twinge of guilt. I did not feel like worrying about my health. I had enough to worry about.

Hands shaking, I changed into my workout clothes: a navy blue T-shirt and black sweatpants. Like everything else I owned, they were loose. Out of curiosity, I found the scale in the back of the room. It was an old, doctor's office model with sliding weights. I stepped on, holding my breath. I placed the bigger weight and started moving the little one.

I couldn't believe it. A lone tear slid down my cheek. I weighed less than before I got pregnant with Briar and Rose. I was officially thin. Or, you know, thin for me. I should have been twirling and singing inside, dancing on a floor made of rose petals. But I wasn't. I was numb.

My shrinking body hadn't reignited Mann's love or made me more confident. I wasn't even more attractive. My face was haggard, my eyes somehow both tired and antic. My smile was bracketed by deep grooves. I turned away.

I located an elliptical machine and hopped on like a good little hamster. A soft techno beat played in the background. Closed-captioned news flashed on plasma screens. Celebrity deaths, natural disasters, cute pet stories zoomed by. I imagined making the appointment with Dr. Chesterson. I invented my lines and whispered them, climbing an imaginary Everest.

After half an hour or so, I was sweaty and slightly calmer. I took a shower, rinsing my oddly slender body, and wondered idly if I was thin enough to borrow Julia's clothes. As a mom, I had always gravitated towards self-effacing neutrals. The only statement they made was, "Don't look at me."

Maybe I would sneak into Julia's room sometime and have a clandestine fashion show. Maybe I would...*no*. I pinched my wrist until the blood welled just beneath the surface. Julia was not my friend or my roommate.

She was my enemy. Or my test.

***

Dressed again in my black-and-beige camouflage, I sat on a small bench beside the main parking lot. I looked around to make sure no one was near me. I didn't need anyone hearing that I was calling a psychiatrist.

I took a deep breath and dialed.

"Dr. Chesterson's office."

"Hi, this is Helen Gottlieb. I'd like to make an appointment. I should be in your system."

"Just a moment."

During a long interval of clicking and typing, I wondered if I had been somehow wrong. Maybe I had read the wrong name on the prescription bottle. Maybe I had the wrong Dr. Chesterson. Maybe I was somehow deluding myself, ginning up conspiracies where there was nothing but my own weakness and fallibility.

The receptionist's voice was filled with smiles. "Sorry for the delay. You missed your last two appointments, but the doctor would be glad to see you. When would you like to come in?"

19 IDENTITY

After making the appointment with Dr. Chesterson, I was anxious and drained. My fingers flew over my keyboard but accomplished little. Red notices dotted my screen. I minimized them and pecked away.

Soon enough, a shadow obscured half my desk. I turned around. Brittany was staring at me, her mouth carved into an unbending smile. Crimson lipstick stained one of her top teeth. Her hands rested firmly on her hips. She was not happy.

"Helen, are you *OK?*" The last two syllables were an insectoid whine.

"Yes," I said breathlessly, making a sudden show of rapid work.

She exhaled sharply, like a punctured tire. "You're falling behind again. Is there anything I can do to help you be more productive?" She threw the ostensibly helpful words like daggers.

I peered at her pretending to care. "No, I don't think so."

"Perhaps you could stay late and catch up?" It was an order in the form of a question. Normally, I would have said yes. Years of pleasant mediocrity, of being the good, obedient wife and the good, obedient patient, all told me to comply.

But then I remembered: I wasn't always this way. Before Mann and the kids, I was someone else, someone with a motorcycle, a love of stupid risks, and a surly attitude. Before I could think about it too much, I let her speak. "No way, I can't stay late tonight. Do you want me to work from home?"

"No, just get some rest. And think about what you need to be more productive." Her lips tensed and then loosened, as if she was going to say something but thought better of it.

As she walked away, my heart quivered and quailed. I said no. Firmly. And, miracle of miracles, Brittany backed off. I should have felt good and more in control. Instead, I was uneasy. My world was changing into something rougher and tougher, and so was I. I looked at the clock. Two more hours to endure.

I remembered how Xanax smudged my emotions, bringing them into soft focus. It smoothed my anxiety and slowed my heartbeat. I wanted just one pill, just for today. I opened my desk drawer and pulled out the bottle that had waited there for weeks.

I wondered if Brittany was still watching. Since Julia's intervention, I couldn't shake the feeling that my use of Xanax was somehow wrong. Suspect.

Before I could talk myself out of it, I dry swallowed a pill. It made a bitter trail down my throat. Bitter but somehow soothing. As it entered my bloodstream, I had the counterfeit feeling that everything, somehow, would be OK.

***

When I arrived home, no one came to greet me. I frowned. Usually, Briar and Rose would propel themselves into my arms. But not today. The house was silent except for the low murmur of distant conversation. I made my way to the dining table, uncomfortably aware of the white, sterile surroundings. Was this cool, barren space really where I lived?

Julia and Mann sat at one end of the table. They each sipped from a goblet filled with red wine. Probably a merlot based on its dark, purplish cast. The girls were strapped into their highchairs instead of perched on pillows. They strained their bonds when they saw me.

"Mommy!" howled Rose.

Briar merely smiled and gurgled. I kissed both of their foreheads and encouraged them to eat their quinoa and kale. The girls pacified, I sloughed off my jacket and draped it on a chair. Mann and Julia ate silently. The kitchen was blackened and slightly melted, but still basically functional. I helped myself to Julia's healthy cooking. I also poured myself a large glass from the open bottle of wine, a rebellion of sorts.

Mann and Julia beamed disapproval while I sipped and ate. I chattered with the girls while the grownups remained silent. The happy padding from my last Xanax was wearing off. Everything seemed brighter, louder, and harder.

When dinner was over, Julia and I bathed the girls. She was sweet to the children, but her posture was tense. There was something glittery and elusive about her eyes. I told myself to breathe. I would learn the truth soon enough when I visited Dr. Chesterson.

In the full-length bathroom mirror, I caught a glimpse of Julia and me together. She was younger and smoother and vastly prettier. She was mother and I was the crone. Her cheeks were pink and plump. Mine were pale and hollow. Nothing had changed.

After we put the children to bed, Julia followed me downstairs, where Mann was waiting. "Do you really think you should be drinking wine? After what happened?" she asked.

Mann nodded, frowning. "I think you should give it up."

I shrugged. "I'm not an alcoholic. I didn't set the kitchen on fire. I think you both are overreacting."

Mann scowled. His eyes hardened. "You're acting like a defiant teenager. Your drinking could be putting our children at risk."

Now Julia was nodding, her impossibly shiny hair bouncing along. "You know what happened to me and my children. How can you not take this seriously?"

"I am taking this seriously. But you're not taking me seriously. How many times do I have to say that I didn't leave Julia's fucking kettle on?" My hand flew to my mouth. I hadn't meant to speak so loudly, or so coarsely.

I opened my mouth to apologize, but it was too late. Julia was crying. She ran away, leaving me with Mann's rage.

"I didn't leave that kettle on, and neither did Julia. You, on the other hand, have a credibility problem. You're acting like an addict."

"I'm not an addict!" I yelled. "And you always take her word over mine. Always!"

Mann's biscotti-colored face darkened to a blotchy rose. "I'm done with this. Let me make it simple for you. You will stop drinking and taking all drugs. Or I will get a restraining order, and I will take the children. Period."

***

I climbed the stairs slowly, leaving Mann alone. It was happening. My worst fears about our open relationship were coming true. Mann had found a replacement for me. An upgrade. A better version. I don't know why I was so surprised. Mann's signal talent was finding the next best thing.

I entered the bathroom and closed the door. Then quietly, with all the shame of a secret not-exactly-an-addict, I took ten Xanax from my pocket. I had brought them from work. They would be my emergency stash.

But where could I put them? Was there anywhere Mann and Julia, now convinced I was a hard-core druggie, wouldn't look? I scanned the medicine cabinet, and the answer was obvious. My bottle of blood pressure pills.

I dropped nine pills into the bottle and one pill into my mouth. I would be seeing Dr. Chesterson tomorrow. I would need to be alert and ready for anything. I couldn't afford to thrash in bed all night, sick with worry.

I climbed under the covers and listened to the house. Raindrops plinked against the roof. I focused on them and not the shambling wreckage of my life. I slipped below the surface, diving into a place that was warm and dark and soothing. An underwater womb.

But when I changed position, I was sitting on a hard bench. A thin, pale-haired woman was looking down at me from behind a large desk on a dais. She was wearing a silky judge's robe, and her eyes crackled with malicious energy.

It was Jessie, Micah's wife and hostess of the poly party where Mann and I met Julia. I gasped, and her face split into a saw-toothed grin. "I told you to watch out for her," she said, cackling.

"Yes, you did," I mumbled.

"I can't believe you didn't even ask me what her big, bad drama was. Rule number one of poly is, 'Always ask questions.'"

I stared, uncertain what to say. Jessie pulled a gavel from her robe and slammed it down on the desk. I jumped and cringed.

"You didn't ask questions because you're an unfit mother!" she shouted, as her face twisted and stretched to resemble Agnes, the divorce lawyer. "I am awarding custody of your children to Julia Weatherstone!"

I opened my mouth to scream, 'Nooooo' when I started coughing. My mouth was dry, my eyes were sticky. I was awake at three a.m. And that is how I stayed for far too long.

***

Of course, I overslept. Rushed and groggy, I hurried downstairs and found Julia eating breakfast with the girls. I kissed Briar and Rose.

"Oh, Helen! I have something for you," she said, holding up a tall, cold glass. "It's a banana-chia smoothie. It's great for stress."

I took the glass. The liquid inside was buff-colored and viscous. It had a neutral, empty smell. I brought it to my mouth and then froze. I was virtually certain Julia had been using my name to get multiple prescriptions for Xanax. And she had already convinced Mann I was an addict.

What if there were more pills? Or different pills? What if Julia was trying to get rid of me? The smoothie would be a perfect vehicle for an overdose. And she and Mann could very credibly say I had done it myself. I could feel my face burning with dread. I took air in small, frightened sips.

Julia looked at me with wide eyes. "Are you OK?"

I nodded, still clutching the smoothie. "Big day at work," I squeaked.

"You should drink up. I know the past couple of days have been hard. I'm sorry for my part in it. That's why I made you this shake."

"Can I take it to go?" I asked, trembling.

"Sure. Thank you." She brought me a lid for my cup of death. I carried it like unexploded ordnance, calling goodbye to the girls. I drove until I lost sight of the house and then emptied the drink into the closest sewer drain.

I decided I would leave the cup in the car. Perhaps the residue was evidence. Something I could test. Something I could use.

***

Dr. Chesterson's waiting room was a study in pale blues. I guess they were supposed to be calming. Several other patients perched nervously on chairs, gazing into their phones. They were all attractive women in their twenties or early thirties, all wearing edgy, fashionable clothes. I was by far the oldest and frumpiest one in the room.

I picked up a magazine from an end table and flipped through it. It had a quaint, older feel. I checked the date on the cover. It was five years old. I supposed doctors' offices didn't need to provide magazines anymore, now that everyone had smartphones.

I tried to read the *New York Times,* to lose myself in the horrors of the day. But I kept reading the same passage over and over again. My own life was horrifying enough. I could easily imagine the stern-but-handsome doctor from the website greeting me with a sort of puzzled alarm.

"You're not Helen Gottlieb," he'd say, reaching his hand under his desk for the panic button.

"No, wait!" I'd reply, launching into a story of identity theft that was both pointless and incredible. Julia had Mann, who had enough money to do anything he wanted. Why would she need to drug my smoothie?

Yes, here in this office amidst so many neatly put together patients, I was feeling paranoid and unmoored. Perhaps I should have been going to therapy all along. Perhaps I should have worked on myself instead of obsessing over my marriage. Perhaps I should have…

"Helen Gottlieb?"

I gasped. A dark-haired nurse with hair bound into an intricate bun, motioned to me. She wore a gold bangle around her wrist in the shape of a snake. I followed her down a dull hallway lined with more sickly, pastel blues.

"It's nice to see you again, Helen," she said, glancing at her chart.

"Um, sure." I smiled weakly. I wasn't going to burden her with my strange tale.

She bade me sit at a small triage station, where she took my vitals and wrapped a blood pressure cuff around my arm. Fear poured through me as the cuff constricted. I was transported back to my prenatal appointments, where my safe, seamless world had begun to crack.

"Oh my," tutted the nurse, whose name tag read Cassie, "that's a little high. Especially for you."

I shrugged. She was comparing my blood pressure to Julia's. The woman probably had the cool, slow-moving blood of a basilisk.

I followed Cassie while she dutifully recited the dangers of high blood pressure, the importance of a healthy diet, and how I should follow up with my family physician. She opened the door to the doctor's den, and I gratefully entered.

Unlike the waiting room and the nurse's station, which were entirely bland, this space had a decidedly masculine point of view. Dark-paneled walls offset a bright picture window. Leather-bound books lined floor-to-ceiling bookshelves.

"Thank you," I said, dismissing Cassie and sliding onto a buttery couch. I felt strangely calm, as if all my planning and plotting was finally over. It was time to wait.

***

The couch was soft and inviting; I leaned into the armrest like a lover. My eyes fluttered and closed. My thoughts were drifting into a jumbled dreamscape when I heard a rough coughing bark.

I awakened to a surge of adrenaline. The man staring down at me was older than the picture on the website, his features heavier. In his suit jacket and button-down shirt, he looked like a disappointed professor.

"I'm sorry," I muttered to head off a scolding. "Your couch is so comfortable."

He coughed again and sat down at his desk, paging through what must be my file. Finally, his eyes found me and squinted. "Helen, you look unusually tired. Is there something going on?"

I blinked. I had never met this man before. And yet, here he was, telling me I looked tired. Yes, as my body shrunk, I was becoming a bad copy of Julia. But we're not identical, not even close. Or were we?

"Yes," I said, my voice round with shock. "There is something going on. You see, I've never met you before. My husband's girlfriend has been using my insurance data to visit doctors. I think she's getting prescriptions in my name."

Dr. Chesterson's face shook. His small jaws swayed. His expression darkened and creased. "That was not what I was expecting. But your assertion is not correct. We have met before. I have records in this chart."

"But it wasn't me…"

"Aren't the last four digits of your social security number 6273?"

"Yes, but…"

"And don't you live on 627 Briarcliff Lane?"

"Yes, but…"

"And aren't you five-foot-three? And one hundred twenty-five pounds? With blond hair and green eyes? And allergic to Narcan?"

"She looks a lot like me. That's why she thought impersonating me was a good idea. She's getting prescriptions to make it look like I'm a drug addict. By the way, what's Narcan?"

Dr. Chesterson sighed. It was the sound of a man who had heard too much bullshit from too many people, the sound of a thick, deaf wall.

"I've heard enough, Helen. I am not going to enable this fantasy. When you are ready to work on your issues, make another appointment. I will be happy to see you."

"But…"

He left me as brusquely as he came. I sat paralyzed, shocked at how impossible it was to prove that I was, in fact, me. Then, still sitting on the doctor's couch, I Googled Narcan.

20 A DESPERATE CRY FOR HELP

Narcan. Trade name for naxolone. A medication used to block the effects of opioids, especially in overdose.

As I wove through traffic, the toxic knowledge wove through my brain. Julia had told Dr. Chesterson that I was allergic to Narcan. She had obtained God-knows-how-many prescriptions for Xanax. And yet she still prepared my food, my children's food, my husband's food. It was ominous.

But Narcan wasn't an antidote for Xanax. Why would Julia tell the doctor I was allergic to it if she wanted me to OD on Xanax? Was I missing a piece of the puzzle? Was she seeing other doctors, getting 'scripts for Oxycodone or something similar in my name?

I drove faster and faster as my brain twitched and spun. The sun was too bright, the world around me was too sharply resolved. It had the brittle quality of frosted glass. I was sure it would shatter at any moment. I took a deep breath, ignoring the flutter in my chest.

I'm not sure what I was expecting when I poured my secrets all over the doctor. That he would help me? Save me? Protect me from Julia? I should have known better. Julia is twenty-four years old and beautiful. Men are programmed to help women like her, not women like me.

Four miles until my exit. If I didn't have children, I would have kept driving. I had given up on Mann. He was no longer mine, if he ever was. He was happily lying in Julia's sticky web. And Julia herself sat in my home like a sleek spider, hoping to turn my husband into a widower.

After my visit to Dr. Chesterson's, I could no longer deceive myself. I wasn't just a jealous, paranoid wife and a failure at open marriage. No, I was Julia's prey. And so were my children. I had to go home, watch over them as long as I could, and figure out some kind of plan.

If no one was going to rescue me and my girls, if I was too old and unattractive to be seen and heard, I would have to do it myself.

I remembered the smoothie cup in the glove box. Maybe I already had what I needed.

***

My girls greeted me with coos and smiles. Their unbridled joy tore at my heart. They were the only people alive who truly loved me. I followed them into the back yard while Julia remained in the kitchen, cooking.

Briar shyly showed me a slug, while Rose tried to squish it. They squabbled, I gently held them apart until a passing butterfly broke the angry spell. Inside, Julia brought steaming plates to the table, bursting with nourishment and, just maybe, death.

I told myself that Julia loved the girls. They were so much like her own. Perhaps she could even look at them and see her memories alive and smiling. As much as she wanted to be rid of me, she wouldn't, couldn't, hurt them. Would she?

A soft hiss cut through the quiet. Mann's Tesla pulled into the driveway. He slipped out of the car and into the house. Through the patio doors, I watched him pull Julia into his arms. She melted against him, pliant and poisonous.

Rose kissed my cheek. "Daddy home. See Daddy."

I sighed and brought the girls inside, where they greeted their father with a fresh burst of enthusiasm. I felt a twinge of shame. He was a good father. He loved them. I couldn't just take them and run. I would have to, somehow, stay alive, discredit Julia, and get her out of my house.

The enormity of the task made my stomach lurch. Mann must have noticed the greenish look on my face. "Are you OK?" he asked, his voice laced with annoyance, as if I were a poorly performing app.

"Yes, I'm fine."

He came closer and whispered in my ear. "Are you in withdrawal?"

"Jesus, no. I'm not an addict."

Mann stepped backwards, stung. Julia beckoned us to the table. We helped the girls into their booster seats. I watched Julia fill her plate, carefully noting which dishes she chose. I made up plates for Briar and Rose that mimicked Julia's. I even made a small plate for myself.

Mann focused intently on his food, occasionally glancing up to engage the girls. But Julia must have noticed my caution. "Aren't you hungry?" she asked.

I shrugged. "Not really, I had a big lunch."

Her eyes glowed with fraudulent concern. "You need to keep your strength up. Change is exhausting. That's why I made you these creamed turnips. I know how much you like them."

Mann looked up, pinning me with his gaze. I ignored him, finding the turnips with my eyes. They were a creamy butter yellow and smelled vaguely of cilantro. Of course, I liked them. They were delicious. But today they made my stomach do a slow roll. Were they really turnips, or something else?

I shook my head. "They look wonderful, but I'm just not hungry. I'll have some later."

Julia frowned. "You're looking thin, Helen. You've got to start taking care of yourself," she said, sliding her eyes towards the girls.

"Thank you for your concern. But I'm just not hungry."

As silence descended, I helped the girls eat a few more mouthfuls and freed them from their chairs. I led them to their bath and Julia, presumably to protect them from their drug-addled mother, followed closely.

Watching Julia's supple form, it was hard to believe she had managed to impersonate a thirty-nine year old woman like me. Her charts at Dr. Chesterson's office were flawless: low weights, measured pulse rates, stellar blood pressures.

I smiled. Her perfect health had betrayed her. Even if there was no suspicious residue in the smoothie cup, I had her data. And I was legally entitled to it.

***

Mann sat at the table, sipping Cabernet and pecking at his phone, while Julia and I cleaned up. Despite the palpable tension between us, we worked like a seamless machine. I loaded the dishwasher while she cleaned the plates by hand.

When we were done, Mann poured Julia a glass of wine. She took a large, eager sip. I imagined her drinking my blood. I turned away and gathered up the laptop and gym bag I'd brought home from work. I was better off hiding upstairs, where I could be close to the girls and learn how to obtain my medical records.

I mumbled a quick goodnight and almost got away. Almost.

"Helen? We need to talk."

Mann was once again staring at me like I was an under-performing employee. I sighed and returned to the dining room table. He and Julia were sitting comfortably, sipping wine. I stood at attention. Waiting for my orders.

I watched them mutely. Mann coughed and Julia stroked her wineglass. Finally, he spoke. "We need to know you are going to get help for your, um, issues. You need to tell us the therapist or program you choose, and give us regular progress reports."

Julia blinked and added, "Accountability is important." Her tone is soft, sweet, and utterly false.

Anger crackled through me, short-circuiting my sensible fear. I knew I should say something noncommittal and scurry off to bed. But the idea of being accountable to Julia made me want to shriek.

I glared at Mann. "If we're all going to be accountable, how about holding Julia accountable for fraud?"

His eyebrows flew together like angry hawks. "Yes, we all know Julia borrowed your insurance card. She said she is sorry I don't know how many times. It is a dead issue. You should…"

"She has been seeing a psychiatrist and pretending to be me. She's been getting prescriptions for Xanax and God-knows-what-else in my name."

Julia flushed and sorted. "That's ridiculous."

"No it's not. And I have the medical records to prove it. She is disgustingly healthy. I, as you know, am not," I breathed through the lie. I would have the records soon. I was sure.

Mann frowned and turned to Julia. He no longer respected me, but he still respected data. "Jules? Do you have any idea what she's talking about?"

Julia shrugged. "Addicts tell stories. They're not lies, really. Just wishes. Helen's just saying what she wants to be true."

Mann's eyes flickered back to me. "Can you show me the records?"

I took another deep breath. Perhaps I could actually sway Mann. Perhaps his rational side, and not his love for me, would be my salvation. Hope, lighter and more fragile than fear, beat in my chest.

"I'll send them to you tomorrow. Even better, I'll have the doctor's office send them. You'll see."

**

Hope would not let me sleep. It forced me to listen for signs of an argument between Mann and Julia. It whispered how I would go back to Dr. Chesterson's office and demand my records and repeated the sequence over and over again. It made my whole body shake.

I crept out of bed and padded to the bathroom. I opened the special bottle of blood pressure medication, the one that contained the Xanax. I knew I wouldn't be able to sleep without it. Julia was wrong. I wasn't an addict. I just needed to take the edge off, to turn my spiky fears into fuzzy little worries.

And yet I still couldn't rest. I watched the girls sleeping on the monitor and imagined what Mann would say when he saw the medical records. I'd had a checkup a few weeks before we met Julia, where I had weighed in at one-hundred sixty pounds. The date on the first prescription from Dr. Chesterson was just one month later. Even Mann would recognize that I didn't lose more than forty pounds in a single stinking month.

I was so consumed by hope that I didn't notice the footsteps. Julia opened my door. Her face was pale and streaked with tears. The moonlight streaming through my window made her shine like a goddess.

She walked towards me, a hungry angel, and sat down on the edge of my bed. I instinctively shrunk back. What did she want?

"Don't be afraid," she said, reaching for my hand. "I know what you're going through."

When I didn't answer, she continued, "Deep down, you're afraid you're going to hurt your children. You're afraid you're going to cause a terrible accident like I did."

I shook my head. "No, that's not what I'm…"

She squeezed my hand tighter, interrupting. "I'm not going to let you do it. You are addicted to Xanax and opioids. You've been getting drugs from multiple doctors. You need help."

I gasped and squeezed back. Hard. "But that's not true. You're the one who…"

"You need to check into rehab tomorrow or I'm going to call Child Protective Services. I'll show them all your prescriptions. Then they'll make you leave."

Now my eyes were damp. How could I convince Child Protective Services that Julia was trying to erase me if I couldn't even convince my husband? What if they drug tested me? I had no idea how long the Xanax would stay in my bloodstream.

I watched her, as my heart trembled. Her fingernails dug into my palm. Her eyes glittered and bulged. "Thank you for caring so much," I said.

And she smiled.

***

It killed me to leave the children in the morning. I thought about running, but I had nowhere to go. I was the only child of deceased parents. I had no friends who would reliably do more than like and share.

No, I had to stop Julia and turn Mann against her. And that meant pretending everything was OK. Mann and Julia were eating breakfast while I kissed Briar and Rose goodbye. I wiped a tear from my eye. And then another.

"Are you going to get help today?" asked Julia wearing an expression of ersatz concern. Mann looked down at his phone.

"Yes, I'm going to get help. A lot of it."

I hurried to the car, my heart echoing in my ears. But I didn't drive to work. I had to get my medical records—really, Julia's records—from Dr. Chesterson's office. They were my armor, my proof that Julia was the dangerous liar, not me. I would send a copy to Mann and keep a copy for myself.

I drove straight to the medical center. The weary-looking receptionist eyed me with suspicion. "Do you have an appointment?" she asked.

I shook my head. "I'm here to get a copy of my medical records."

"Uh huh," she said, reaching under her desk for a clipboard. "Fill out these forms."

I scribbled my information as fast as I could. My heart flipped and fluttered. I was manically hopeful. Something would finally go right. I would have tangible proof that Julia was doing something irrefutably wrong. My husband might even protect me and our children.

I returned the clipboard to the receptionist. My fingers were slightly moist. The receptionist clicked her tongue and flipped through the pages. Her watery blue eyes blinked. I shivered. Was something wrong?

"Is everything alright?" I asked.

She looked at me, her face a portrait of distraction. "Um, yes, ma'am. We'll text you when your records will be ready."

"And when will that be?" I held my breath. I was hoping I could get them this morning, so I could talk to Mann before we saw Julia at home.

"In about thirty days, give or take."

My heart stopped and started, stopped and started. I didn't have a month to get Mann on my side and keep Julia from destroying my life or worse. I barely had a day.

***

I had never been to a police station before. It was a busy, dirty hive taut with potential violence. Loud, uniformed men shouldered their way in and out of hallways. The ceilings were low and lined with greenish fluorescent lights.

Clutching the cup that had once contained the possibly drug-laden smoothie, I waited in line to speak with a square-jawed woman working behind a thick wall of bullet proof glass. Her large, brown eyes were both warm and skeptical. Her lips wore a wry, seen-everything smile.

"How can I help you?" she asked, her voice scratchy and jocular.

"Um, I think, uh, my husband's girlfriend is trying to drug me. My name is, um, Helen Gottlieb."

Her eyes widened, and her sculpted eyebrows rose ever so slightly. "Go wait in the lobby to your left. I'll be with you shortly."

I sat in a hard, metallic chair alongside men and women who looked just as desperate as me. As a group, they were harder and more easily startled than the people I usually saw around town. Their movements were quick, their expressions hunted.

The air had a close, acrid smell, a mixture of stale coffee and dread. I rubbed my nose and nervously scanned the room, much as everyone else did. I flinched at every sound. Was I really doing this? Was I going to accuse Julia of maybe committing a crime?

"Helen Gottlieb?"

I followed the sound of my name. It was the woman from the window. She wore a black suit, a pink blouse, and a name tag that read Janet Rosso. She was shorter and rounder than I had expected.

"Yes," I said. "That's me."

I followed her down a gray hallway to a small windowless room. I sat down at a dull steel table and took a deep breath. My heart was stuttering, and my head felt as light as a balloon. The walls seemed to be closing in. If I were a suspect, if this were a real interrogation, I would have cracked.

"Can I get you something? Coffee or water?"

"No thank you." I didn't want her to leave. I didn't want to be alone in the tiny room.

She took out a pad of paper and opened an app on her phone. "Hi Helen. I'm Assistant Investigator Janet Grosso. Let's talk about what brings you here today. Do you mind if I record our conversation? And if I take notes?"

"Um, that's fine. I expect you to."

Up close, Janet's face was smooth under a thick layer of makeup. She was ageless, anywhere between twenty-five and fifty. She led me through a series of questions, starting with my name and Julia's name, and touching upon all the major milestones on the path that had brought me here.

She nodded sympathetically in all the right places. I talked volubly, like a woman without a friend in the world. I let the story pour out of me while she wrote on her yellow pad. When I was finished, I felt drained. Empty.

"You certainly have a complicated situation. It can't be easy." Her voice was buttery and even. It didn't give anything away.

I nodded, tracking her eyes. Would this woman be my savior? Would she be the one to set me free?

"Have you and your husband tried couples therapy?"

I blinked. "What?"

She regarded me with a calm, purposeful stare, as if she were a zookeeper and I a raging chimp. "You're clearly very emotional, which is understandable in your situation. But everything you're telling me is pure speculation. It's your word against Julia's and perhaps your husband's."

I took a breath, but she cut me off. "You have a lot of resources that most people don't. You could hire a family therapist or a divorce lawyer or even a private investigator. You have a lot of options for working something out with your husband, something better than what's happening now."

"But she committed fraud! And the smoothie cup..."

"Ma'am, I'm going to be honest with you. Your story is awfully convoluted. I'm sorry you're going through a rough patch right now. But dysfunctional relationships—no matter how awful they are—are not a priority for this department. We have a lot of serious, violent crime in this area. More than someone like you would suspect."

Someone like me. I wanted to scream, but I knew better. Mann's name was known even inside the police station. Because I was Mann's wife, I was assumed to be rich and powerful, the kind of person who could pay a lawyer or a fancy therapist without maxing out her credit cards. If only she knew, or believed.

"Thank you for your time," I said, standing slowly. But inside I was shaking. I didn't know what I was going to do.

21 THE OTHER ONE

Like a cow moving through the slaughter chute, I drove to work. I had no proof. And I wouldn't have it for thirty days. I was stuck. I had no plan, no idea what to do next. So I followed my routine like a zombie.

I pulled into the WorldFeed lot an hour late and walked slowly towards the giant double doors. The slogan "Productivity and personal growth" flashed above them. My legs felt strangely light and wobbly. I considered sinking onto one of the many benches surrounding the main building, but force of habit carried me onward.

At last, I passed out of the warm sun and into the air conditioned womb. I shivered slightly and hitched up my pants, which were sliding down my hips. My weight loss had done me no good whatsoever. Thinness was no substitute for youth or good judgment.

As I wandered through the beige-walled labyrinth to my desk, I thought I heard whispers. They trailed me like rustling leaves. At first, I thought I was being paranoid. My interactions with Mann and Julia had put me on high alert. My heart boomed in my chest. I was a bomb that even a soft breath could set off.

But the whispers didn't fade, even when I told myself to ignore them. They grew louder and picked up a low-pitched murmur. It was as if people were talking about me. I craved a Xanax more than anything.

I still had a bottle left in my desk drawer, my emergency stash. And today felt like an emergency. I picked up my pace. If I could only get to my desk, I could stop the panic building in my throat.

But my desk was not an oasis, after all. Two women wearing skirt suits were standing in my work space. They had the formal, vaguely anachronistic look of HR. The taller woman, who had the stern visage and broad shoulders of a prison matron, was clutching my Xanax and peering at me from acidulous eyes.

***

Brittany smiled at me with the glee of a cat toying with a mouse. The larger, gray-haired human resources rep named Nancy leaned against the door, presumably so I couldn't escape. Ashley, a short, very young-looking blonde, perched in the corner and took notes.

I sat across from my boss, sweating silently. I had no idea what was happening. The Xanax was a legitimate prescription, at least as far as they knew. I wondered if Mann or Julia had called HR and told them I was an addict. Why else would they have searched my drawers?

"Do you remember your employment contract?" asked Brittany in a crisp, chipper voice.

I nodded. "Vaguely. It's been a few years."

"Six to be exact."

I groaned inside. I could not believe I had spent six years of my life in this stale, gray box. And then a small flame flickered to life, and I watched it dance. Despite the nightmare my life had become, the idea of possibly being forced to leave this job made me happy.

Brittany's eyes widened, and her forehead creased. She was bursting to speak, waiting for acknowledgement. I nodded.

"Helen, the employment contract you signed specifies WorldFeed as a drug free workplace. We prohibit all illegal drugs as well as pharmaceutical drugs that could have a damaging effect on judgment or productivity."

I frowned. "I have a valid doctor's prescription for Xanax. What's the problem?"

Brittany coughed. Or maybe she snorted. "Xanax is one of the drugs on our prohibited list, prescription or no. Employees may not take benzodiazepines, opioids, or certain stimulants on site. It's a safety issue."

I shook my head. Although I didn't care about the job, I was angry. "But what gives you the right to search my desk? Did someone tip you off?"

Brittany regarded me as if I were a slow child. There was even a touch of pity in her gaze. "Your desk, your workstation, everything here is company property. You have no right to privacy. Not here."

I sighed. Ownership was the ultimate trump card. As Mann's wife, I should have known that. "So what happens next?" I asked.

Brittany's mouth curled into something that could have been a frown or a smirk. "I've been concerned about your performance for a long time. You're a talented writer, but I don't think you're a good fit. When I consider this additional issue, well…I think it's time for us to part ways. Nancy and Ashley will show you out, and make sure you get all your insurance forms."

My eyes darted between Nancy, Ashley, and Brittany. My heart raced. I couldn't tell if I was terrified or excited. My heart skipped and jumped. I took a deep, shuddering breath. I felt too speedy, like I was about to fly off the surface of the planet. Everything was moving too fast. Everything was too hard.

"Nancy," I said, my voice surprisingly steady. "Give me back my Xanax."

***

Newly unemployed, I took the long way home. The rhythm of driving, of starting and coasting and stopping, was oddly soothing. I felt calmer than I had any right to be. I had taken one Xanax, but it was no worse than driving after having one glass of wine. Or so I told myself.

I found myself driving in circuitous circles through suburban warrens. I passed by small bungalows worth millions, digital playgrounds, and palm trees. I couldn't go home, even if Julia did have my girls. If I went home, she would know I had been fired. It might prompt her to call Child Protective Services. And I was pretty sure Mann would back her up. After all, I didn't have any proof, and I wouldn't for a month.

I wondered if I should sign up for rehab, even though I wasn't the hard core addict Julia and Mann thought I was. After all, I wasn't a model of flawless self-control. I was routinely taking one or two Xanax each day, along with a glass or two of wine. Perhaps I could benefit from a few weeks in rehab, if I knew I wouldn't lose my girls.

No, I thought, rounding a corner slightly too fast, that wouldn't work. Going to rehab would simply label me as an addict. It would be easy enough for Julia to engineer a "relapse" by slipping something into my food or getting more prescriptions.

I turned on the radio, grateful for my Xanax buffer. My life was like a shattered windshield. I couldn't see through it or even around it. As I passed another row of bungalows, I felt a vague déjà vu. I had been here before. I trawled my mind for answers.

And then I found one. Matt and Anna, Julia's exes, lived in this neighborhood. I had taken Julia here to pick up her things. I had felt like a getaway driver at the scene of a sordid crime. And perhaps I had been. After reading her account of nearly tricking Matt and Anna into having a child, I had no idea what was really true.

I slowed to a crawl and scrutinized the houses. They all looked so similar in their suburban, Northern Californian way. There was no way I would guess correctly. And I dreaded knocking on the door of the wrong house, intruding into someone's quiet day.

Was it time to give up and book time in rehab? Or head home to whatever Julia might have in store? Or even call Mann? Tell him my medical records wouldn't be ready for an unbelievable thirty days?

No, I couldn't. All of those choices felt futile and dangerous. They were paths away from my girls and towards a lonely life in a studio apartment by a hotel overpass, or a quiet, solitary death. I was about to start sobbing along with the radio when I had an idea.

I pulled over and looked through my phone. I had mapped the location when I drove there with Julia. Maybe I had saved it. I opened the app and scrolled through recent locations.

And there it was. The address, labeled *Julia's crazy exes*. I exhaled slowly and gratefully. And then I drove.

***

Matt and Anna's house had changed. The grass was uneven and unkempt, patches of overgrown green mixed with dry, yellowing weeds. The trashcans out front were full. The windows were dark, hooded eyes. Bicycles lay in the driveway like orphans.

My heart revved, and I shivered as if I had a fever. How could I survive so much fear? I took a deep breath, counting down my inhales and exhales. I wouldn't give up now. I would force myself to try. And Matt and Anna were probably at work. They were probably crazy-busy and had fallen behind on the yard work. Chances were I wouldn't see them at all.

I stepped out of my van and walked slowly to the front door. I kept telling myself that no one was home, that I was checking a box. If she wasn't home, I would find Anna's email address somehow. I would write her, not Matt. I would divulge just enough for her to find me.

It was go time. I was standing on the front step. A dog yapped in the distance. I tapped the doorbell. It echoed and chimed. Mentally, I prepared to run. I shifted my weight to my right foot and was about to turn around when the door opened.

The woman standing before me was a caricature of the Anna I had met a few months before. Her hair was frizzled where it had been sleek. Her face was gaunt where it had been lean. Cheekbones protruded like fists. Her sporty clothes hung from a sickly frame that had once been taut and athletic.

"Oh," she said in a dry, reedy voice. "Do I know you?"

"Um, I'm sorry to bother you," I stammered. "I helped, er, Julia move some things out of your house. She's living with us—me and my husband—now. Can I ask you some questions about her? I promise it, um, won't take long."

She watched me through red, swollen eyes. I shuffled my feet. Would she let me in? I looked down and then away. She seemed as fragile as a deer. I didn't want to spook her.

"Sure," she said softly. "Come in."

***

The inside of Anna's house was even grimmer than the outside. The overhead light was dim, as if several bulbs were burnt out and hadn't been changed. The air was stuffy and smelled like coffee and stale sweat. The end tables covered with paper coffee cups. Weights, resistance bands, and other exercise equipment were scattered on the floor.

"Sorry for the mess. Can I get you some coffee?"

"Um, sure, that would be great," I said, hoping the kitchen would be less depressing. As I followed her across the threshold, a tiny ball of fur growled and nipped at my feet. It looked like a Chihuahua, but with long fur.

I froze and extended my hand so the dog could sniff it and, hopefully, find me acceptable. The bit of fluff snarled and bared her teeth. I pulled my hand away just as Anna snatched up her dog.

"Sorry about that. Masha is a rescue. I just got her."

Anna whisked the dog into a small crate, and I sat down at a flimsy card table. As Anna made coffee in a small, white pot and Masha whined, I looked around. The kitchen was strangely barren. There were no knick-knacks or wooden shakers. The sink and the dish rack were empty.

As she worked, I tried to think of something to say, but my casual social skills were out of practice. The silence grew hard and oppressive. I was about to ask her about Matt when she set out two steaming mugs along with a carton of milk and a bowl of sugar.

I fixed my coffee and went to take a sip. I noticed the edge of the cup was chipped. I was turning it around to find an intact rim when Anna sniffled. "Sorry about that. Matt moved out last week. He took all the kitchen stuff."

She collapsed into rough, barking sobs that set off her dog. As they howled together, I did what I could, patting Anna gingerly on her narrow, bony back. I wondered if I was seeing my future.

***

"Tell me about Julia," I asked as gently as I could.

Anna sniffled and wiped her nose. Her cheeks were blotchy. Her eyes were red and swollen. "Matt and I really wanted to try non-monogamy. It sounded so reasonable and yet so adventurous. We talked about it all the time. It made us feel freer. More open. Better."

She smiled wryly. "We knew some people who were into poly. We went to their party, and met Julia. She was a fantasy. A unicorn. She seemed like she was interested in me and Matt equally. And Matt was wild about her.

"We talked and drank and danced for hours. The three of us together felt so perfect. Like fate or something. It probably was crazy—no, it definitely was crazy—we brought her home that night. Matt and I had our first threesome. We had fun. Matt was delighted. And I got through it somehow. I felt strong, as if I had stretched my boundaries and grown as a person."

She laughed bitterly. "After that, Julia just fell into our lives, like the missing piece of a jigsaw puzzle. I enjoyed her company. Matt enjoyed her company and the sex. And I enjoyed that Matt was enjoying himself. Or, you know, that's what I thought."

"Everything seemed to be going well until Matt and I decided to get pregnant. Once we told her, it was like a switch had flipped. Julia started pushing me to drink, and smoke weed, and take ecstasy. I wasn't interested—nobody does that when they're planning a baby—but she kept pushing.

"She also laughed at my fertility charts. Said it was a waste of time, that I would get pregnant naturally. She took Matt out on dates whenever I was ovulating. She made me delicious, gorgeous-looking meals that made me feel loopy and out of it. One time I fell asleep for eighteen hours. I wondered if she was drugging me.

"I even said something to Matt, but he said I was just being jealous. I even sort of agreed. I didn't like Julia nearly as much as he did. I tried to do better, to be less suspicious, and give her the benefit of the doubt. And then one day I got a terrible migraine.

"Did you know that you aren't supposed to take ibuprofen if you're trying to get pregnant? Well, I was out of acetaminophen when my headache hit, so I checked Julia's medicine cabinet. I did find some acetaminophen. And some prenatal vitamins. But I didn't see any birth control pills.

"This time, I didn't say anything to Matt. I just spent time with Julia and waited for an opening. I found my moment when we were eating the dinner I had insisted on cooking despite my head. Out of the blue, without a breath of warning, I asked Julia how she liked her birth control pills. Without thinking twice, she said she didn't take birth control pills.

"The look on her face said it all. She had slipped and slipped hard.

"And then it was all over. We had a meeting with Matt. She confessed quickly, which shocked me. I thought she would have just said I was lying. But no, she cracked open her soul. She told us about her two children who died in a drunk driving accident. She was so sad. I wanted to be angry at her, but I just couldn't. Matt couldn't, either. We said she could stay with us, for a while."

"Did she say anything about a sister?" I asked.

Anna shook her head. "She left about a week later. To live with you. At the time, I was relieved. But Matt was confused. He'd had feelings for her. He missed her. He was so distraught, he couldn't…Well, we decided to put our pregnancy on hold. And then he said he needed some time and space to think.

"We agreed it would be a trial separation, but he took everything he owned. Everything. I'm still getting used to it. I'll be seeing a therapist tomorrow. I hope she can help."

Anna dissolved into tears again, gulping and gasping. This time I hugged her. I didn't think I could help her. But maybe, just maybe, she could help me.

22 SLOW MOTION DISASTER

I sat in my car outside Anna's house, hopeful and afraid. Anna was still inside, jogging on a treadmill, trying to outrun her sadness. She was another flavor of me, a woman who had failed to please her husband. A woman who had lost to Julia.

She said she'd talk to Mann if I wanted, explain what Julia did to her and Matt. I was grateful. It changed things a little. I didn't have data, but I did have a witness. Maybe I could still persuade Mann that Julia was deliberately trying to take my place, to make me go away.

My heart pounded insistently, as if it was trying to tell me something. I took slow, deep breaths and ignored it. Then I pulled my phone from my bag. I was going to text Mann. I was going to tell him what I'd learned.

I told myself I had married him for a reason. He was good, reasonable, and caring. He loved our children and cared about them. He was smart. He would understand.

Hi Mann, are you busy?
Sort of. What's going on?
I talked to Anna.

Who?

Julia's ex. The one who supposedly mistreated her.

OK

Julia might have drugged her. And she was trying to get pregnant.

Maybe her ex has an agenda. We don't know her.

Do we really know Julia? Are we sure?

Did you get the medical records?

I filled out the forms. Won't have them for 30 days.

Huh.

Listen, Julia threatened to call CPS on me.

She's just being overprotective. Meeting now. Talk later.

I stared at my screen, tears in my eyes. He didn't say that he loved me. And his responses were so ambiguous, I didn't know what to make of them. Did he provisionally support me but wanted to make sure he had all the facts? Or was he trying to keep me calm, to stop me from causing trouble?

I started my car. I couldn't sit here in front of Anna's house forever, she might think something was wrong. And she would have been right. As the van rumbled to life, I realized there was only one place I could go. One place where I had to go.

Home. I wasn't ready to call rehab, not yet. I needed time. Just a little more time.

***

My house loomed in the distance. A cool white castle on a bright green mat. I realized that I didn't really consider it home, that I never had.

It had always been Mann's house or, when I was feeling especially impoverished, Mann's mansion. When we first moved in, he had wanted to split the utility payments with me. Only when I showed him my pay stub did he finally back off.

Counting slowly backwards from ten, I slowly pulled into our driveway. I got out of the van. But instead of rushing inside like I usually did, I stood on the lawn, inspecting the house and the yard, like I was saying goodbye. The grass was a vividly healthy green, made all the more vibrant by the cloudy sky. The house was all hard angles and stark planes.

In the second story window, the one that looked out from the girls' room, I saw a dim, familiar shape. It had the hazy, barely-there presence of a ghost. It had to be Julia. Fear flowed through me. My heart shuddered and my hands shook. Yes, despite everything, my body had an apparently unlimited supply of liquid fear.

My children were with Julia. I had no more time to waste. I walked quickly into the house. The downstairs was dark, except for the anemic, cloud-filtered light. I hung my bag on a sturdy, white-painted rack. I fast-walked to the staircase. As I climbed, I heard muffled sounds. A female voice was speaking urgently. Intensely. As if there was an emergency.

I ran towards the girls' room. The door was slightly ajar. Julia was speaking into her phone, her voice jagged with distress. I paused, listening quietly. Holding my breath.

"I was watching the kids for my...friend. They're both two. Twins.

"They were playing in their room.

"I went down the hallway to get diapers.

"When I came back, I found them playing with open pill bottles.

"They had opened them, somehow.

"Vicodin and Xanax. My friend has a drug problem. But she said she was getting help.

"They're going through a phase. They put everything in their mouths. Everything.

"I don't know if they swallowed the pills.

"I have no idea how many pills were in the bottles.

"They're playing. They seem normal but sleepy. It's almost nap time.

"OK, thank you. I'll look out for the ambulance."

Julia ended the call. My head was buzzing with fear. How was this possible? Except for the pills hidden with my blood pressure meds, I didn't have any Xanax at the house. Certainly no bottles. And I'd never taken Vicodin ever.

What was Julia playing at? Had Briar and Rose actually been poisoned? I burst into the room, wired and breathless.

"Julia, what the fuck is going on?"

***

Julia slid her phone into her sweater pocket. She squinted, as if she struggled to see me.

"You're home early."

I shook my head. She was way too calm and still for what I had just heard. Briar and Rose leaped up from their toys and hugged my legs. My heart cracked open. I wanted to pick them up, to tell them everything was going to be alright.

But I couldn't. I had to know what had happened. I led the girls back to their toys. I encouraged Rose to push her truck, and Briar to strip her Barbie doll.

"Julia, did you see Briar or Rose ingest pills? And how did they get into pills in the first place? You know there are no bottles of Xanax in this house. And I don't take fucking Vicodin. I've never taken it. Do you?"

Julia smiled grimly, baring her teeth. She slowly reached into her pocket and pulled out two bottles of pills. "Your name is on these prescription bottles," she said. "And the girls *could* have gotten into them. And isn't that the real point?

"You're an addict. Addicts are careless. And selfish. I could see you leaving your pills on top of the diapers, or next to the girls' toys. Maybe you were high. Or maybe you just weren't thinking about anyone but yourself."

I shuddered. She still hadn't answered my question, the only important question. "Julia, did the girls take any of those pills."

She shrugged. "Of course not. But like I told you, that's not what matters here. You're an ungrateful woman who needs to get off drugs. For your children's sake. And I'm going to help you. Your husband is going to help you."

I heard sirens in the distance. I saw the red lights through the window. And I knew her help was going to hurt. A lot.

***

Julia and I rode together in the ambulance. She had handed the pill bottles to the paramedics, who were rightfully too busy to hear my explanations. Nevertheless, I felt like a suspect, perhaps on my way to the police station instead of a hospital.

As the ambulance bounced along, I held Briar, who buried her head in my chest. Julia bounced Rose, who found the clatter and chaos exhilarating. The paramedics took their vitals and talked with someone at Saint Mary's Hospital.

"Julia, this is insane. Why won't you just tell the truth? The girls didn't take any pills." I whispered.

"They could have. You need to admit you have a problem and get into a program."

I had no idea what kind of procedures the doctors would do to the girls at the hospital. Would they pump their stomachs to expel poison that wasn't there? Give them an antidote? Perhaps if I admitted I was an addict, if I took the blame, Julia would tell the truth and my children could go home.

But then, as an admitted addict, I would have to seek "treatment." I would be locked in a treatment center while Julia had my girls. I couldn't risk it, could I?

Meanwhile, Rose played with a stethoscope and Briar started to cry. I rubbed her back and listened to the sirens blare. As we weaved through early rush hour traffic, my phone chirped and chirped again.

I had texts. From Mann.

What just happened?

Why was there an ambulance at our house?

What have you done?

***

Dr. Lena Swenson, a hearty blond woman who stood over six feet tall, examined the girls who were more than a little cranky.

"It's past their nap time," I explained. "They're tired."

The doctor said nothing and checked the girls' heart rate and blood pressure. She looked in their eyes and down their throats. Julia and I held them down while a nurse collected their blood. The examination seemed to take forever. Rose pulled at the stethoscope and grabbed the doctor's glasses. Briar cried and squirmed at the slightest touch.

Julia remained silent. Her face was calm. She looked peacefully certain, as if she would get away with all her lies. I would have to talk to Mann. If he could talk to Anna, maybe he would understand just how noxious Julia was, how dangerous.

Even if she did have a tragic past, that didn't give her the right to destroy my present. It didn't give her the right to tell aggressive, malicious lies. And it didn't give her the right to judge me as "ungrateful."

Grateful. How I hated that word. I heard it often during my recovery from preeclampsia. Friends were always telling me to be grateful for my healthy children and supportive husband. I had no right to complain about my ruined health, about the pain that was driving my husband away.

Finally, the exam was done. Rose bounded into my arms. Briar hugged my legs. Julia's calm expression crumbled into a scowl. I supposed she was irritated that the girls, despite everything, seemed to prefer me. My eyes stung with tears.

"Mrs. Gottlieb?" asked the doctor.

"That's me," I said. Julia's scowl deepened, as if she had been slighted.

"Your girls seem to be fine. I don't see any evidence they ingested pills. But I would like to observe them while we wait for the results of the drug screen. Just in case. Go to the nurse's station down the hall. They'll get them checked in."

"Thank you," I said. "Thank you."

I exhaled. Relief flooded through me. I had professional validation the girls were fine. Almost certainly fine, anyway. And they would be carefully monitored overnight. I would sleep in a chair beside their beds. I wouldn't ever want anything besides their well being ever again. I would, at last, be grateful.

"But what about the pill bottles?" asked Julia in a loud, shiny voice. "How can we be sure Helen—Mrs. Gottlieb—doesn't leave her medications lying around? How can we be sure she gets treatment for her addiction?"

The doctor's pale face froze. Her white-blond eyebrows crept upwards. She was obviously uncomfortable. "We report to Child Protective Services according to strict legal guidelines," she explained. I was cheered she didn't answer Julia's question.

The doctor, no doubt eager to get away from potential crazies, said brisk, hurried goodbyes, and pointed us towards the nurse's station. As she swept out of the room, I gathered up Briar and took Rose's hand. I looked at Julia through cool, narrowed eyes.

"You can go home if you want," I said, futilely hoping she might leave.

Instead she shook her head. "I'm going to stay right here. Someone needs to protect those girls."

I was about to reply when Mann appeared in the doorway, his expression bleak, as if he was expecting something terrible. The girls, who had begun to wilt, immediately perked up.

"Daddy!" squealed Briar, reaching with her soft, pale little arms.

"Pick me up!" whined Rose as Mann managed to collect both girls in his arms, smiling weakly. He looked at me and then at Julia.

"What happened?" he asked.

Julia explained that I had left improperly closed bottles of Vicodin and Xanax where the girls could find them, open them, and even consume them.

I snapped that Julia was lying. "That is bullshit. The pills belong to Julia. She got them from doctors I've never seen by pretending to be me. Once you see the medical records, you'll know.

"She called 911 to frame me. To make you think I'd put the girls in danger. But the real danger is her. All I can guess is that she's so traumatized by her loss she isn't thinking straight.

"Oh, and she told me the girls didn't eat any pills. *She told me.*"

Mann rubbed his bare chin. When he had a goatee, he used to play with it when he was nervous or had a difficult decision to make. He regarded me with soft, uncertain eyes. "Let's get the girls settled. The doctor wants to observe them overnight. It can't hurt to be safe."

After completing an endless series of forms, we tucked the girls into their cribs on the children's floor. Of course, they began immediately demanding snacks. The nurses told us how cute they were. My heart began to unclench. Maybe, somehow, everything would be OK.

"Mann, do you want to stay with the kids, or should I?"

He looked at his shoes, at the girls, at Julia. Everywhere but at me. He opened his computer bag and pulled out a sheaf of papers. They were notarized and covered in small, dark print.

"I'm sorry, Helen," he said. "This is a temporary restraining order. You have to stay at least one hundred yards away from me, Julia, and the girls."

I stared at him, clutching the papers. I couldn't breathe. My worst fears had come true. The world had cleaved, opening an abyss at my feet. I wanted to fall in. Instead I asked, "Why?"

Mann shuffled his feet. "It's only temporary. Until we can get things figured out. Get you some help. We'll talk later, on the phone, when the girls are home. You should go now. Go to the house and get your things."

***

I gathered my things in a fugue, packing bags for what could be a long, dark trip. I took my pills, some clothes, my devices, an external drive with pictures of Briar and Rose. When I was done, I went into the girls' room and cried until the sky turned pink.

As I made my way down the hallway, I paused outside Mann's home office. The door was ajar. His desk was the focal point of an open, airy space. It reminded me of him: expansive, open-minded, and focused like a laser. I realized I hadn't stepped into it since the day we met Emma.

I looked at the safe against the wall. It contained Mann's end of the world stash, what he called his *Walking Dead* fund: fifty thousand dollars and a handgun. Today seemed like the end of my world. *Perhaps I should take them.*

I stood there, silently deliberating, for more than twenty minutes. But, in the end, I couldn't do it. Neither the money nor the gun would help my girls, or help me get them back.

***

I checked into a small, dingy motel in Mountain View that was still exorbitantly expensive. My room smelled like smoke. The walls were beige dapple with brown water stains. The bedspread was dappled with flowers the orangey-yellow of fresh vomit.

Mechanically, I put my things into the rickety dresser, taking in the wreckage of my life. No job. No family, except for distant, barely thought-of cousins. No friends. No children. I now had the life Julia had before she met me and Mann. And Julia had mine.

My heart fluttered as I thought of Julia and what she had done to me. What I had let her do to me. My face flushed. My hands clenched into fists. I tried breathing slowly. Long inhales and longer exhales. Visualizations. Affirmations.

But nothing could exorcise my burning rage. Nothing except for one or two things. I used my phone to order dinner and a bottle of wine. And then I took the bottle of Xanax from my purse. I swallowed one pill. Then two.

As the ersatz calm flowed through my veins, I positioned myself by the window and watched the parking lot, waiting for my delivery. I could practically taste the first bite of the wine on my tongue and the smooth sweetness that came later.

My life was a slow-moving disaster, a still life of regret. I had nothing but my pills and my wine. If I was going to be punished as an addict, I would be one.

23 RELUCTANT HOPE

My dreams were turgid sludge. A dark, turbulent sea of monstrous silhouettes. A sweaty, panicked run through a narrow hall. I woke up with a pounding pulse, dry mouth, and aching head. My legs were tangled in damp, twisted sheets.

It was two in the morning, and I was already regretting the Xanax and the wine. *Regret. Isn't that what addicts do?* whispered a snide little voice that sounded like Julia. I unwrapped myself from the sheets and stepped out of bed. Woozily, I made my way to the bathroom and poured myself a glass of water.

I sipped the cool liquid and stared at my exhausted face. Lank hair. Furrowed forehead. Bloodshot eyes framed by puffy lids. I looked old and defeated. I was thirty-nine, but I might have been fifty-nine. I had no idea how I was going to survive the coming days or weeks. I was overwhelmed. Drowning.

I eyed my bottles of Xanax. Xanax is from the benzodiazepine family. It was designed to have a high overdose threshold, to be safer than barbituates. But what if I took them—a lot of them—with wine?

I shook my head as if to shake away the dark thoughts. No, I couldn't do that to my girls. I wouldn't. I would find some way forward, some way to sanity. Some path to a normal, post-divorce life. Yes, after everything, I was ready to divorce Mann. I couldn't stay with him, not after the restraining order. Not after he believed Julia over me.

I turned on the shower and stepped in, washing away bad dreams. I allowed my muscles to relax, my thoughts to bend and melt. By the time my skin was red and wrinkly, I was ready for bed again. I dried myself with a tiny towel and slipped on a fresh T-shirt and sweats.

I was almost in bed when I heard the knock at my door. Three loud booms, one after the other. And there was nothing tentative about them. Whoever it was was not concerned about disturbing my sleep. I froze and waited, hoping he—it had to be a 'he,' right?—would go away.

Then it happened again. Three knocks, even louder this time. Was it the police? Had Julia contrived some way to have me arrested? I listened carefully. No one was yelling for me to come out.

I waited some more, suspended in silence. I heard no more knocks, just the low hum of the air conditioner, and the drip of water in the sink. Was the intruder gone? I gathered up the threads of my courage and padded to the door. My heart shuddered as I peered through the peephole.

A man in a long-sleeved black shirt, black jeans, and a lizard mask was standing before my door, arms crossed in front of his chest. He was tall and muscular, casting a long shadow under the thin, outdoor lights.

Startled, I stepped backwards and fell, twisting my ankle. I hobbled to the bed stand and picked up my phone. I thought about calling the police. My finger hovered over the keypad. But I stopped.

What if the man was gone by the time the police arrived? Would they believe me? Or would they snicker at the empty wine bottle in the trash, the Xanax on the sink. If I was going to divorce Mann, I didn't need a police report on file showing I was a crazy lady who drank too much and imagined things.

I sat on my bed, holding my phone. I would wait. If I heard the man try to break in, I would call 911. If he just stood there, I would do nothing. Surely, he would get bored and go away.

For what seemed like hours, I existed in a tense sort of limbo, both exhausted and wired. Every ten minutes or so, I would stand up and look out the peephole. He was always there. Eventually, my terror blurred into tedium.

I rubbed at my eyes and yawned as sunlight peeked through the curtains. I told myself I could wait.

Wait, wait, wait.

***

I awakened with my cheek pressed into my phone. The room was light and hot. My head throbbed gently with an echo of a hangover.

I scraped myself out of bed and dragged myself to the door and looked out the peephole. The masked man was gone. The parking lot was exactly as it had been, filled with small, energy efficient hybrids and rental cars. My big white van was the lone, out-sized outlier.

I exhaled with relief. The man had been oddly familiar in some way just out of my grasp. But I didn't want to think about it. I told myself he was some random lunatic who had seen too many superhero movies, or something. Or maybe he was a genuine stalker who simply had the wrong room. Either way, the crisis was over.

As my relief faded away, I thought of my girls—and the fact that I couldn't even call them—and started to cry. I sobbed for about twenty minutes, taking long, gasping breaths. My heart fluttered and skipped, but I no longer cared.

Finally, my body collapsed. My eyes ran out of tears. Limp and exhausted, I considered falling onto the bed and into the mute darkness of sleep. Instead, I hauled myself to the bathroom, an incremental victory.

My face was pink and puffy. My cheek was deeply creased from sleeping on my phone. My tongue was still dry from last night's excesses, and an invisible band tightened around my head, encircling it in pain.

I took another shower and put myself together one piece at a time. I dried and ironed my hair. I covered my face in base. I drew on eyes and lips until I looked like a better version of myself. I even pulled on work clothes—they hung on me, I had lost even more weight—for some future job I couldn't even imagine.

Inspired by my outfit, I set up my computer and turned on the wifi. Still without a plan, still paralyzed by my losses, I stared at the screen. Mindlessly, I opened my browser. Facebook appeared, along with numerous status updates from Mann and Julia.

I devoured every one, watching my children from afar. I clicked between pictures and videos and paged through Julia's entire timeline. My eyes swelled again. An ocean of tears ruined my makeup and my resolve.

***

I walked on the shitty hotel treadmill, climbing a steep, imaginary hill. I had chosen the dingy hotel gym—home to a single treadmill and a small collection of free weights—over more Xanax and wine. It was a good choice. One that boded well for the future.

As sweat soaked through my bulky white T-shirt, I tried to think of a plan. Clearly, I could expect no help from Mann, financially or otherwise. I had very little money, no permanent residence, and no job. Even worse was the temporary restraining order I had no idea how to undo.

Something, somehow, would have to change.

I desperately needed a lawyer. But how would I pay for one?

Money. I needed money. I supposed I could apply for unemployment insurance. It wasn't much, but it was something. And I owned the van outright. The title, sitting in the glove compartment, was in my name. It was something I could sell.

And then, as I walked, I remembered something I had seen on a poster during the latest WorldCom charity drive. Something slid into place. I had an idea.

***

Sitting in the Legal Aid office, I felt like a fraud. My husband was Mann Gottlieb, one of the richest men in the Valley. And I was his wife. What right did I have to be here, among the real poor? The deserving poor?

But I was unemployed. And my bank balance didn't lie. While I theoretically had access to Mann's millions, we had no joint accounts or credit cards. I had no idea what he did with his money. We existed in separate classes, different spheres.

I looked around the waiting room. It was crowded. People of all shapes and sizes perched on mustard yellow chairs probably scavenged from some failed corporate giant. They tapped aggressively at their phones or tapped their feet or rubbed at their hands. Together, they smelled like anxiety.

Were they all like me, I wondered, caught up in a complicated, multi-threaded nightmare they couldn't imagine ever untangling? I forced myself to look down at my phone, to stop staring at my fellow desperadoes.

I looked down at my phone, playing multiple rounds of Sudoku. Time slipped by in small, unpredictable dollops. I reconciled myself to a long wait. I felt the weight of the restraining order in my computer bag. I needed someone to help me. To save me.

Without really meaning to, I imagined a man. Someone like Mann, but older and wearier. Warier, too, with a wry, wrinkled grin and a dimple in his chin. He would be experienced but only moderately jaded. Rumpled, but, except for a small paunch, fit.

Needless to say, my heart sank when a fresh-faced girl in a short, lime green skirt and ponytails called my name.

***

The baby lawyer's office was tiny, but surprisingly and solidly real. Whiteboards and cork boards lined her walls. Boxes of files covered every available surface area except for her chair and mine.

"Hi, I'm Beatrice Garcia, and I'll be your lawyer today. Let me take a moment to go over your paperwork." Her voice was not as high as I had expected. It was actually somewhat pleasant.

I nodded and handed her my clipboard of hand-completed forms. She put on a pair of tortoiseshell reading glasses that made her look like a little girl playing dress up. She paged through the forms, her tongue poking out of her mouth.

I wondered what she was thinking as she read my story. Perhaps she would be like Agnes, the divorce lawyer who had called me a terrible mother. Those words had carried a dreadful authority coming from fifty-something Agnes. Would they sting as much coming from this little sprite of a girl?

She read slowly, taking copious notes like a student, dutifully completing an assignment. Perhaps Briar and Rose would look something like this someday: studious, earnest, and completely untested.

The silence lengthened and grew. I assumed she was about to tell me how sorry she was, how she couldn't take my case. After all, what young lawyer in her right mind would willingly take on Mann and risk her future career? I wouldn't blame her, really. Self-preservation is a very reasonable stance.

I glanced down at my phone and started paging through job boards. I had to get a job, I needed the money. But all the listings were startups looking for interns and other youngsters who could dedicate their entire waking lives to enterprise infrastructure.

I was scrolling past an ad for a hard-charging self-starter who was not afraid of late nights and multidimensional collaboration when my lawyer spoke, her eyes white and wide.

"Oh my God, you're actually married to Mann Gottlieb? This isn't a hoax?"

I sighed. "I'm Helen Gottlieb. Mann's wife. For now."

"Is everything you wrote here, um, true?"

I nodded. "Yes. And I know it seems absurd that I came here. But Mann and I keep our finances strictly separate. I just lost my job and…well, I'm broke. I didn't have any place else to go."

"Wow. This looks like a tough situation. Let's see if we can break it down."

My eyes widened. She sounded competent and practical with no inclination to judge. "Um, OK," I replied, still skeptical.

"Let's start with the restraining order. That sucks, but we can deal with it. I should be able to schedule a hearing within ten days or less. Oh, and I'll need to subpoena your medical records to verify your story.

"You'll have to fill out some more forms. Sorry about that."

I shook my head slowly, amazed and grateful someone was finally taking charge of my intractable mess. "No, don't apologize. Forms are OK. I love forms."

"Also, I'll take a closer look at Julia. I know an investigator who owes me a few favors.

"And we'll need to prepare your divorce filing. I'll need bank statements, DOBs and social security numbers for your children, the usual. More forms."

"Great!" I practically chirped. I had misjudged the young woman, her bright, too-small clothes, and messy desk.

It was fitting that she would be the one to help me get my daughters back. My children could do worse than turning out like her.

***

I returned to the motel filled with reluctant hope. I stood straight and tall as I walked through the parking lot. There was a route back to my girls and some semblance of sane, normal life. I just had to follow it.

As I climbed the stairs to the second floor, my legs felt fresh and springy. Even my heart obeyed, beating normally. I was filled with more energy than I'd had for months or even years. I didn't trust it.

I decided I would go to the gym and work it off. I wanted to fall into bed exhausted, too spent to worry about the coming legal wrangle, my diminishing bank account, or the strange, masked man.

I pulled my passkey from my wallet and…something was wrong. A yellow Post-It note sat right above the lock, filled with scrawl. I plucked it from the door.

Julia Logan. We found you.

***

I turned my room into a fortress. I locked the windows, closed the curtains, and pushed the dresser against the door. I put the Post-It note in a plastic bag. I also left a lengthy voicemail for Beatrice the baby lawyer, the one person who might believe me.

Julia Logan had become Julia Weatherstone to escape the Angels of Vengeance, Internet vigilantes who wanted to punish her for what had happened to her twins. Now, they thought I was Julia. And they were after me.

I turned on my laptop and devoured every piece of information on them I could find. Each article was more frightening than the last. They were strict Old Testament Christians. In fact, they were an official church, a 501c3 organization with a pack of snarling lawyers and a donation button on their website.

They believed they were God's vengeance on Earth, and they judged without mercy. They were allegedly responsible for all kinds of Internet

205

nastiness—doxing and swatting and malicious calls to Child Protective Services. Even worse, they were associated with a handful of suspicious deaths.

I peeked out my window. Even in the daylight, the parking lot was filled with shadows. It was going to be another long, sleepless night.

24 A TERRIBLE IDEA

Over the hours, my obsession became a routine. I looked out the window. I scanned the parking lot. I sat at the computer, reading more terrifying articles about the Angels of Vengeance. They were so frightening, I began to have some empathy for Julia, who had once fled a masked man of her own. Not too much empathy, though. I peered out the peephole. I rested on my bed, counting breaths and telling myself to be calm.

I repeated the sequence, again and again. Eventually, I grew hungry. But I was afraid to order anything. What if the masked man was watching? Would he follow the delivery person to my room? Would he skip the ridiculous lizard mask and just pretend to be ferrying food?

Stomach whining, I caved and ordered sushi, an indulgence I probably couldn't afford. I waited anxiously, oscillating between the window and the door. When a young man in a red cap finally appeared outside my door, I chained the door and opened it just a crack. I signed the bill. He left the food on the welcome mat, his face a jaded void.

I pulled the food inside my room-cave and devoured it, lips smacking. I hadn't eaten since this morning. I forgot about the masked man and the

Angels of Vengeance as long as the fish and rice lasted. I ate, chewed, and swallowed, losing myself in consumption.

Afterward, my belly full, I lay on the bed. I explored Facebook on my phone. Everyone was #Grateful. My thoughts turned bitter. I had nothing to be #Grateful for. And then I gasped. Actually, I did. As long as the Angels of Vengeance were stalking me, assuming I was Julia, they wouldn't be anywhere near my girls.

I held onto that thought as I slipped back into my routine. Window. Desk. Door. Bed. I yawned as I cycled through my stations. As I lay on the bed for the last time, I thought of my children. And I fell asleep.

***

I was in a huge department store, walking unsteadily between brightly colored displays. I pulled a filmy Creamsicle-colored shirt from an overstuffed rack. Anxiety had honed my body into a blade. I needed a smaller sheath.

I wandered from rack to rack, dizzily grabbing garments. Dresses. Shirts. Jeans. Pants. I gathered them all in every combination. When my arms were full, a dark-haired woman who reminded me of Poppy led me to a beige changing area.

I pulled outfits on and off, spinning and twirling. I felt hard and light. Fresh and new. Like a butterfly that had just chewed its way out of a chrysalis, I was testing my wings. I gave them a small flap, and then another. I was almost ready to fly.

I finally decided on an indigo blue dress. It was like the dress I had bought with Julia, except now I was wearing the impossibly small size. I smiled at the new me in the mirror. My face blurred and sifted. I looked younger, softer. Almost like Julia, but still recognizably me. I was happy. Almost rapturous. Renewed.

Heavenly music swelled in my ears as I carried my purchases to the register, still wearing my miraculous blue dress. The cashier was familiar, an older woman who reminded me of Agnes, the judgmental lawyer. And yet I was still happy. I handed her a golden card. She smiled for a moment. Just a moment.

Then her face closed in on itself. Her smile wilted into a frown.

"What is your name?" she asked in a dark, cool tone.

"Helen Gottlieb," I replied, trying to hold onto my joy.

"No," she said, shaking her head. "You are lying. Helen is older than you. Fatter. Sadder. And she is a mother. You are not Helen Gottlieb at all. You are Julia Weatherstone."

"You're mistaken," I cried. "I am Helen. I am!"

The Agnes cashier shook her head and waved at something behind me. I turned, following her eyes. Two policemen, each holding a snarling dog on a leash. They were tall men with closely cropped hair, thick jaws, and narrow eyes.

I ran. And I ran.

***

Dogs barked and snarled behind me as I ran through the store. I could see a door in the distance, alight with hope. I toppled Mann-shaped mannequins and barreled through displays. I dropped my purchases. My legs pumped. My heart pounded.

As I got closer to the door, I nearly choked with hope. I was going to make it. I was going to escape. But then I heard something loud and explosive. A car backfiring? A gunshot? I stopped and looked behind me. The police had raised their guns.

I dove into a bin of silky bras and…I awakened. On the bed. In a pool of sweat. The room was dim but not dark. It was morning, but extremely early. I took my phone from the bed stand and saw that it was five a.m. before the red battery sign flashed, and it flickered off.

I rubbed and blinked my sticky eyes, slowly coming alive. My heart was slowing, ever-so-slightly. Until I heard the loud, echoing thud of someone banging on my door. I immediately thought of the masked man. The Angel of Vengeance. I was sure he had finally arrived.

I peeled the sodden sheets off me and threw on a clean sweatshirt and yoga pants, my only armor. Then I took a deep, unsteady breath and went to the door. I approached the peephole and brought my eye to it.

My heart nearly exploded. It wasn't the masked man at all. It was something else entirely.

It was Julia.

***

Seeing Julia inside my tiny, cluttered hotel room was surreal. She looked smooth and gilded, as if she had recently been to a spa. Her hair was done up in a complicated braid. Her clothes were perfectly tailored and utterly forgettable. She was a slender, supple echo of Mann.

Compared to Julia, I no longer looked fat and frumpy, everybody's overworked and overlooked mom. Now I was her sick, haggard reflection, the crone to her maid. I ached imagining how much the girls loved her beauty. Of course, they wanted their Julia Mommy. Of course.

She sniffed the air and wrinkled her nose. My night sweat must have poisoned the air. Without saying a word, I opened the window. Julia followed me. She sat down at the tiny table that doubled as a desk. I perched on the bed.

"How did you find me?" I asked, dispensing with the small talk.

She shrugged, smiling like the victor she was. "Mann is the guarantor on all your accounts. He gets your statements. I have his passwords. He likes to share."

I groaned inside. When I married Mann, my credit was bad. Too many student loans, a studio apartment blessedly free of roommates, a motorcycle I couldn't really afford. It was shocking how those quick decisions, those scrawled signatures, had haunted me for the rest of my life.

"Wonderful," I said. "You found me. What do you want?"

Julia smiled. Her teeth looked whiter than I remembered. Shinier. Had she gotten work done? Veneers? "I know you're going through a tough time. Mann said you lost your job. That must be a terrible blow."

Her voice was emollient with fake sympathy. I nodded, not trusting myself to speak.

"I know you need money," she continued. "I've been there. I've been broke. I'd probably still be there if it wasn't for Mann's generosity."

I shook my head, anger shooting through me like lightning. "Mann's generosity? What about mine? I let you into our lives. I shared my husband."

Julia sniffed. "You accepted me begrudgingly. Because you had to. You did it to keep Mann and your house and your boring, rich suburban life that you weren't even grateful for."

I sighed and seethed. There were so many important things to say and to ask, but I couldn't suppress my annoyance. "So now you've stolen my boring life? And it's OK because you are fucking grateful?"

Julia smiled, her face an infuriating mask of calm. "Mann and I won't be boring together. We'll be stellar. We'll start a charitable foundation named after my dead daughters and your live ones. We'll travel all over the world, spending his money on worthy causes. It will be exciting and educational. And good for your girls, too."

When she mentioned the girls, I snapped out of my rage. What was I thinking? I had to handle Julia carefully. Gingerly even. She was with my children. She could hurt them. "Julia, why did you come here?" I asked as calmly as I could.

Julia opened her bag and took out her checkbook. "Mann doesn't want you to suffer.

"He would like to offer you some money to get back on your feet again, and get some help for your drug and alcohol problems. I can write you a check for two hundred thousand dollars right now. In return, all you have to do is sign a few papers, just a basic post-nuptial agreement and a promise to get treatment."

I stared at her. The money was shockingly tempting. I would no longer be 'this close' to being homeless. I could take my time finding a job. I could put a down payment on a one-bedroom condo where the girls could visit semi-comfortably.

But I knew two hundred thousand dollars was loose change to Mann, who had billions. And the woman before me was Julia, a nightmare of deception. As far as I knew, she and Mann were the only people who knew where I was. I wondered if she had somehow sicced the Angels of Vengeance on me with a gently misdirecting email or tweet. And I did have a lawyer who seemed competent, and who might even believe in me.

No, I couldn't give my twins to Mann and Julia without a fight, even if it would be bloody. I had given up too much already. "No thank you, Julia," I said calmly. "I have other plans."

Julia blinked and stared. Her mouth drooped into a small, vacant 'o.' Clearly, she hadn't expected my response. Emboldened by her confusion, I attacked. "Julia, why did you send the Angels of Vengeance here?"

She blinked again. "What are you talking about? I haven't heard from those psychos since I stayed in Chico."

Her face was still a cipher, a complete blank slate. Of course, she wouldn't give anything away. She hid her emotions better than I did. She had the power of persuasion and finely chiseled goals.

I shook my head. I knew I wouldn't learn anything from talking to her. Higher blood pressure or a quivering, anxious heart would be all I'd get for my trouble. And I had to stay healthy for my girls.

I took one last look at my lovely nemesis. Was I ever this young and pretty and hard and focused? I didn't think so. My entire life had been stumbling from one good enough situation to the next.

She was more than a match for me. She was my superior. And I never wanted to see her again without impartial witnesses.

"Goodbye, Julia," I said. "Tell Mann I said no. Tell him I said hell no."

***

I walked on the motel's lone treadmill, forcing myself to think. Julia's visit had left me shaky and breathless with a fluttering heart. Its pounding beat echoed in my ears, a scattershot metronome for my thoughts.

I was fully exposed, a red dot on a white map. Julia and Mann knew where I was staying. So did the Angels of Vengeance. Therefore, logically, I should go someplace else. Honestly, I should have packed up and left as soon as the masked man had departed.

But desperation held me fast, like a butterfly pinned to a mounting board.

Mann got all my credit card and bank account statements. And Julia could access them, and tell the Angels where to find me, perhaps even posing as Helen Gottlieb, the disgruntled wife. I needed the anonymity and security of physical cash.

I supposed I would have to sell my van. I would be sad to part with it. Its uninspired, boxy frame had been a daily part of my daughters' newborn lives. I used it to take them to pediatrician appointments and to the park. To Poppy's house and then to work.

With cash I could find someplace off the digital-financial grid, someplace I would not be found. I could plan my next moves unobserved. I knew there were buses and plain old metered taxis. It would be like hiding in the past.

I would look for work and try to survive until the hearing on my restraining order and the looming epic of my divorce. I would see my girls — legally — and start searching for a living arrangement that would allow me to have them for days or weeks at a time.

It was a good plan. A sensible plan. I told myself I should feel calmer. But I didn't. My hands shook. My lungs tightened. My heart flailed. I increased the incline on the treadmill, hoping to beat the fear out of my body. My throat tightened. My chest ached.

And then, as my vision blackened around the edges, I thought of something else. A terrible idea that was, just maybe, a little brilliant, too.

***

The day passed in a pall of waiting. The sky darkened from a faded pink to a bruised purple. I looked out the window of my room. My van remained in the parking lot. I ate from a Styrofoam container of dehydrated noodles I had picked up from the gas station across the street.

My mind was achingly sharp, unbuffered by Xanax or alcohol. I needed to be alert. And I was dressed in my best, most authoritative clothes. I had to sound sane and look sane. As the purplish light shaded into gray and then black, I watched for cars.

Several tiny, electric cars left the lot. Another entered. Its occupants, a mother and child lugging oversized bags, were not who I was looking for. I blinked my eyes, focusing on the lights streaming down the road.

I didn't think it would ever come. But it did.

An American-made car, the big, gas guzzling kind that still prowls the Midwest, pulled into the lot. It parked in the back, far from the lights. A shadowy figured emerged, tall and likely male. He carried a briefcase. I crossed my fingers. Not too much longer now.

When the knock came, I almost jumped. Bang, bang, bang. Just like two nights before. The sound paused. I waited. Bang, bang, bang. There is was again. I inhaled deeply and walked unsteadily to the door.

I looked through the peephole. The masked man was back.

I took another deep breath. And another. And then I opened the door.

25 JULIA REDUX

If I squint, I can see my children running along a carpet of parched grass. Light and dark. Sunny and brooding. Lily and Selene.

But they're not my children at all, are they? They're not Lily and Selene. They're Briar and Rose. And they belong to Helen, that horrible, ungrateful cow. It is hard to express just how much I dislike Helen. She is middle-aged, entitled, and oh-so-smug. And she has no idea how lucky she is.

I watch Helen's children play on the patchy lawn with Poppy, the glorified babysitter. Poppy used to run a daycare, and then she shut it down when Mann funded her startup. But she'll still watch Briar and Rose.

Honestly, I don't like leaving the children with Poppy, who is fake and over-familiar. She's always calling Mann, supposedly asking about startup business. And she's aggressively poly, always hinting that she might want to date me, or Mann, or preferably both.

But this morning, I had no choice. I couldn't have brought the kids to Helen's grimy little room, after all. So now I'm here. And Poppy has just spotted my car. It's a Tesla X-class, so quiet that sometimes people don't hear it pull up. I paste on a smile to equal Poppy's and open the door.

"Julia!" she cries. "It's so good to see you!"

"Poppy! Great to see you, too!"

She gives me an airy hug and kiss that I do my best not to cringe from.

"So how's Helen? Is she finally adjusting to the whole poly thing? I know it's been a tough transition."

I smile like a Sphinx. I want to preen for just a moment, to bask in my success. I want to shout that Helen and Mann are on the brink of divorce. But I know I have to be discreet. "I don't know," I say. "I hope so. I'm just grateful for what I have."

Poppy nods, her shiny black hair glistening in the sun. "It's tough being the third. I'm still with Stephen and Laura. They can get so wrapped up in each other sometimes that they forget I have needs completely separate from their identity as a couple."

"Uh huh," I say noncommittally. Poppy for all her talk of transgressing norms is a conservative soul. She tiptoes around Stephen and Laura's marital bond. She treats herself like the other, like a citizen of a lesser land.

Poppy looks lost for a moment. I glance at the girls. They are still picking dandelions. They have not bothered to greet me. I even heard Rose murmur, "Where's Mommy?" Oh well, they'll get over it. I'm doing them a favor. Helen is an awful mother. Her children don't deserve that. No children do.

"Um Julia? Did you have a chance to look at my new learning portal? The one for teaching two-year-olds to read? I tried some of the apps on Briar and Rose, and they love them. Mann said you'd check them out."

I don't like the way Mann's name sounds in her mouth. She's flaunting it, as if her relationship with him is on the same level as mine. "I'll try to get to it," I say, faking another smile. "Things are crazy busy."

Poppy nods, understanding her dismissal, and helps me round up the children. When they are safely in the car seats, she regards me with an aggressive, appraising grin. As I open the driver's side door, she says, "I really hope you love the apps. And tell Helen I said Hi!"

As I drive away, I decide Poppy will be a new character in my fictional memoir. It's part novel, part memoir, and all me. I can already see the scene. She is on her knees, sobbing and humiliated. Rejected. Mann stares down at her, his face soft with pity.

I smile. And, for the first time today, it feels good.

***

When the children and I arrive home, Mann is waiting for us. He loves us. All of us. And that includes me. Knowing that he never came home at lunchtime for Helen makes my insides all warm and fuzzy. She never got him, never pleased him, like I do.

He is such a wonderful father. I watch him scoop up his children and nuzzle their hair. His affection is fluid and natural, utterly unlike Malcom's clumsy interactions with Lily and Selene.

Mann is the real, genuine thing. And Briar and Rose know it. They stroke his ever-so-slightly graying hair with their childish hands and plant wet kisses on his rough cheeks. They remind me so much of Lily and Selene that it seems like my heart is going to burst.

I remind myself that it has been two years since my twins were this age. If they had lived, they would be four going on five, chatty little pre-K girls trying on different attitudes. My eyes well with tears. I blink them away, along with my old family, until all I see is the new in painfully crisp relief.

After the children scurry off to play, Mann sidles up to me and takes my hand. His grip is firm and assured. It makes me feel safe and cared for. I squeeze him back and sigh. His lips brush my ear. His breath is warm and inviting.

"Did Helen take the money?" he asks.

I pull away. I don't want to talk about Helen. Not yet. He takes my hand again. Harder this time. "Tell me," he insists.

"No, she didn't. She has a lawyer. She wants more. She's a gold-digging whore, just like we thought."

He strikes faster than a cobra. His hand slaps my face. Hard enough to sting, but not hard enough to leave a mark. I gasp. My face becomes a question.

"Jules," he says softly, "she's the mother of my children. Don't talk about her like that."

I am incredulous. This is the man who asked me to impersonate his wife. Who told me he loved me and not her. Who said I was a better influence on his daughters. Who demanded I practically burn the house down and pretend that Helen did it.

I swallow my anger and reach for the hand that slapped me. I give it a gentle little squeeze. It is the hand that feeds me, after all. The red mark on my cheek will fade; I will remain.

Mann and I shift our attention to the children. He plays with them, pulling squeals even from shy little Briar, while I make their lunch: organic peanut butter and locally produced jam on Ezekiel bread with sliced grapes and celery sticks. I pour distilled water into BPA-free sippy cups.

At lunchtime, Mann is as laser-focused on his children as he is on his many companies. He asks them to name objects and tosses celery sticks in the air. The action takes on the quality of a movie. He is our director. The girls are the stars. And I am the producer, making sure all the props are in good working order.

When all that's left of lunch are crumbs, we herd the children into the bathroom to brush their teeth and then chase them up the stairs. They are full of food and giggles. They listen to their stories and nestle into their blankets. As their eyes close, mine begin to sting. With their features slack and unformed, they could be my angel babies. They could be mine.

I must be staring too long or too intently. Mann takes my hand and leads me out of the room. At the foot of the staircase, he kisses my bruised cheek. I follow him into the kitchen, where he retrieves his computer bag from the table.

"Don't you want to have grown up lunch with me?" I ask, hating myself for the slight whine in my voice.

"Sorry, Jules. I have a big meeting."

He brushes by me, so close we almost touch. I can smell his musky, coniferous scent. Like smoke and pine. "When will you be back?" I ask breathlessly.

He shrugs. "I don't know. Hug the girls for me." Then he blows me a kiss.

***

While the children sleep, I run through a tough yoga routine. I fly like an angry crow. I balance on my hands like a willow unbent by the wind. When I am done, I check the monitor. Lily and Selene…no, Briar and Rose, always Briar and Rose…are still sleeping.

I bring the monitor downstairs. The house is big and lonely: a beautiful prison. For a wild moment, I want to leave. I want to drive into town and wander around, gaze at the sky, be the young, twenty-four-year-old woman I physically am.

I want to drift into bars and flirt with college guys.

I want to drink, just enough.

I want to take pictures of my lean, yoga-hardened body and share them on social media. Look at me, they would say. Look at me.

But I can't. I can't ever be myself on social media again. Even if I did it as Julia Weatherstone, I know they would scent me. The Angels of Vengeance are Internet trolls who believe they have a mission from God. They are young, pale men with gangly limbs and soft, swollen bellies who judge women like me.

I imagine them in front of their computer screens, their mouths filled with the sweetly metallic taste of self-loathing. They type furiously, punishing their keyboards. They float through digital currents like so much unwanted trash.

First they find my picture: blonde, smiling, too pretty for them. They assume I am the kind of woman who would reject them, and they hate me for it. I am like an ex-girlfriend, only worse, because I never put out.

And then they find my tragedy. That something terrible happened to me vindicates their worst suspicions about me. Not only am I the sort of woman who would reject them, I am also the sort of woman who would watch her family burn.

They don't care that I was asleep when the flames from my melted tea kettle caught the drapes. That I inhaled almost enough smoke to die. That my lungs blistered and boiled. That I still grieve every day.

No, all they care about is their judgment. About being heroes. About taking me, someone who certainly would have rejected them, down. They are gleeful and merciless and unrelenting. And now they are after Helen, the older sister I never had. I don't know why I told that lie. I'm not a liar. But it was inspired, perhaps even prescient.

I got the idea of pointing the Angels in her direction after she lost weight. Without the extra fluff, she is almost exactly my size. She really does look like my much older sister. Her face is the ghost of my worst possible future. A warning.

I took a few iPhone pictures, created a new online presence. Posted a comment or two. Ultimately, it was easy. A few cryptic comments on the right message boards was all it took to tip the scales.

And Mann didn't ask me to do it, either. It was all my idea, something that could help our fragile little family. I wonder if Helen believed me when she asked about the Angels and I made my face go blank. It doesn't matter either way, though. The Angels are convinced. They are hers now, just like her husband and children are becoming mine.

Eventually, they will scare Helen so badly that she runs away from me, Mann, and her children. They love to frighten people, after all. It makes them feel powerful. Or maybe something unexpected will happen. Something irrevocable. An ending, hard and clean.

Then perhaps the Angels will go away. I will get to be me again, and also Helen. I will occupy Helen's space in the world, but differently. The children, her children, will be happier. Mann will be happier. Together, we will be free. We will travel the world and dance on mountaintops and give money to worthy causes. We will create. And it will be good.

My grief will fade. I will no longer feel lonely, like I am missing something. And, most of all, I will be grateful.

***

I am restless, ever restless. Briar and Rose are still sleeping. Without their constant din, I slip back into grief. I need a distraction. Something to occupy my mind. To give me the illusion of control. I drift down to my downstairs room, which I am coming to resent. Helen is gone, and Mann still hasn't invited me to share the master bedroom upstairs.

For a brief moment, I can see how gratitude can slip away. I tell myself it's like a habit or a muscle. It must be continually maintained. I pause and make a list of everything I'm grateful for.

This beautiful room with a garden view and my very own bathroom.
Briar and Rose, the children who are almost my children.
Mann, the man who is almost my husband.
This big, airy cathedral of a house.
The allowance that Mann lets me use for homey little purchases.
And my joyful little secret, the one I can't yet, don't yet, believe.

Feeling calmer and more in control, I enter my room and sit down at my small, hardwood desk. My Mac Book chirps a happy hello. It is time for me to Write. Until recently, it has been a way to reinvent my past, to shape the story of my life into a new and better form. In it, I am stronger, harder, and less introspective.

But today I don't want to change my past, or even think about it. I want to change my future. I click open the file called The Story of My Life and start a new section, dated one month from today.

I just got the most wonderful news. Helen has left us. She met a biker and—can you believe it?—fell in love. She sent a text to me and Mann. She says she's given all she can to us and the children. She wants me and Mann to take care of Briar and Rose while she travels. And she doesn't even want any money.

Mann is so relieved. He was terrified of an endless court battle. I think he wishes Helen would have wanted to see the girls. But I'm here for him. I'll be the mother those girls deserve, the mother I couldn't be to my own twins. Without the shadow of Helen looming over me, I will be able to truly love them. It will be almost like having Lily and Selene back.

Mann wants to take some time off to travel with me and the children. He got into the habit of working long hours so he could avoid Helen. But now that Helen's out of the picture, he wants to stop making money and start his own charity. We will visit underprivileged places all over the world and decide which ones inspire us the most.

Of course, we won't do all this immediately. I have some news for Mann. Very special news. I will have to stay close to medical care of some kind for the next seven or eight months...

I stop typing and listen to my body. I am more tired than usual. My breasts ache. I feel heavy and weighed down. I have tried not to think about the possibility that I may be pregnant. But the idea is deafening in my brain, silencing all other thoughts.

My doubtful secret could be real. My happy future could be happening right now.

I rush to the bathroom and pee on a stick. I wait, on the cusp of so many tomorrows.

I drop the stick in the trash, defeated. It is not my time yet. Almost but not quite. I return to my Writing.

Mann wants to name his new foundation after Lily and Selene. I don't know how I feel about that, but I'm so grateful he is always thinking of me.

***

Briar, Rose, and I are eating dinner. I made a free-range chicken parmigiana with an arugula-feta salad. The sauce is homemade from tender heirloom tomatoes I got at the Farmer's Market. The little ones are quiet, inhaling their food. They have marvelously broad palates for two-year-olds.

I am hungry, sipping hot tea to trick my stomach into thinking it's full. My plate and Mann's sit in the oven, untouched. I can't eat, won't eat until Mann comes home. But he is late. He texted a few hours ago. It was a vague and unsatisfying message.

Unexpected meetings. Probably late. Feed the girls. Love you.

Stomach growling, I put Briar and Rose into the bathtub and then into bed. They are more subdued than usual, asking for their mommy. I can't understand why they miss Helen. When she was here, the children overwhelmingly preferred me. Helen was a whiny, pudgy lump until she became a nervous drunk.

Oh well, I tell myself, they'll get over it. The house is quiet again, and I feel twinges of restlessness. I want to text Mann and demand when he will be home. But I can't do that. It's the kind of thing Helen would do. And I am not like Helen. I am reasonable. Grateful. Patient. Not even remotely entitled.

I go to the yoga room and stand on my head. The blood rushes to my brain. My head pounds slightly and my arms quiver. I focus on keeping my balance. Then I run through my favorite Ashtanga series until my breath comes in hot gasps. I collapse on my organic hemp mat and listen to the blood whir in my ears.

I listen to the thick silence of the house. I strain my ears for the quiet, barely audible approach of Mann's Tesla. I jump up when I hear a low hum that could be the garage. I look out the window, searching for lights and...nothing. Cool air is rushing through the vent on the floor. The noise was the air conditioner, nothing more.

Cool and slick with sweat, I pad downstairs and take a shower. I put on my new blue kettle—no more red ones for me, I refuse to keep thinking about the fire—and make some tea. I sip and sip as time slows to a limp. Minutes are elastic. Maddening.

I finally break down and text Mann.

How's your nite?

I hate that I am so needy. I put my phone into airplane mode and turn on the oven light. I look longingly at my food. My stomach whines and howls. I tell myself I can look as soon as I have finished washing the dishes. Unlike Helen, I give every plate and cup my undivided attention. I am mindful of the soapy water on my hands, of the smooth ceramic against my skin.

When the rack is full of hygienically clean dishes, I quiver with excitement. Will there be a text from Mann waiting for me? I bring my phone back to life, and I hear the chime that is the music of my life.

Late meeting with Poppy & the edu startup. U should rest. xxx

I remember Poppy's glossy, blue-back hair. Her pale skin. Her cherry, gloating smile. Something like jealousy, hot and unworthy, pours through me as I devour my dinner and Mann's, stabbing every morsel as if it were my last.

***

My belly is taut and distended. My breath is short and quick. My heart rate is oddly fast. This overstuffed, overheated feeling is distantly familiar. It has been forever since I binged on food. I want to go to bed, but I know I will have nightmares.

Instead, I watch the weather station. A storm front is moving through. Clouds will roil and flashes of lightning will streak the sky. As the blandly blond weatherman points at the map, I hear the low rumble of thunder and the thrum of raindrops on the roof. I am momentarily cheered. The gloomy weather suits my mood.

It suits it so well that I poke around Helen's closet looking for a rain jacket and boots. She's just the type to have something for every contingency. I find a hideous pea-green poncho and some LL Bean duck boots. Oh well, I suppose borrowers can't be choosers. I pull them on and shove the monitor into the front inside pocket.

I leave the lights off and step onto the deck. Raindrops pour off the awning and explode onto the treated wood. The world around me is layers of charcoal and black. The moon has been blotted out. The air is fresh and moist. I drink it in.

The thunder is louder now, a rare treat in this arid place. Then a flash of lightning illuminates the yard and...what? A man in a green lizard mask is standing beside the pool. The Angels have found me. Adrenaline seizes control of my body, and I leap back into the house, locking the door behind me.

I tell myself it will be different this time. Mann will protect me. He has the resources for lawyers and security guards and alarm systems. I grab my phone and send him a quick text.

They found me. I'm scared. Please call.

A second goes by, then ten seconds, then a full minute. And then five. Mann does not call or even text back. But now someone is pounding on the sliding door leading to the deck. It is him. The door is sturdy, it must be sturdy, but it shakes ominously in its frame.

I am not an idiot. I give up on Mann, for now anyway, and call the police.

26 JULIA ROARING

The police, a short, brown-skinned woman and a tall, Asian man, treat me like a suspect. They keep asking me how I know Mann and if I have permission to be in his house. After all, I am not—not yet—the legal wife.

My answers are off-balance and awkward. "I'm his friend, um, his girlfriend. Sort of second wife," I sputter.

The female officer, whose last name is Bedi, frowns and sniffs. "I thought Mann Gottlieb only had one wife. An older lady. Nothing like you."

I shake my head. "Please call Mann and ask him. He and his wife are having problems. I live here now."

Officer Bedi looks sideways at her partner, Officer Lee. They are both soaked. Rainwater is still dripping off their dark blue slickers onto the pale bamboo floor. "We thoroughly searched your back yard," says Lee, mouth pursed. "We found no evidence of an intruder."

Bedi nods, finishing his sentence, "And no evidence that anyone broke in."

My hands begin to turn numb. Against my will, I remember the aftermath of the fire. Two detectives questioned me for hours, trying to find some evidence that I was to blame. When I started crying and clawing at my eyes, they finally believed me. And packed me off to the psych ward.

My eyes slide between Bedi and Lee. I want to tell them about the Angels of Vengeance, how they are after me, how they send masked men. But I can't imagine their stolid, skeptical faces looking anything but incredulous. Best case, they will "write a report" and "add it to the database."

I sigh softly. I wonder if Helen convinced the Angels she really was herself and pointed them back at me and her vulnerable children. A terrible thing, but not entirely out of character. She is a monster of selfishness.

My blood is fizzy with fear as I thank the officers for their time and walk them to the door.

"Are you sure you're alright?" asks Bedi, her eyes and voice uncomfortably sharp.

"Yes," I murmur. "I am."

***

Mann has not returned my text. I even broke down and called him, leaving a voice mail message. Still nothing. I imagine him sharing chai lattes and vegan cookies with Poppy, talking about investment tiers and revenue growth, their dark heads coming together like magnets.

No, I tell myself, this is unacceptable. I pinch the underside of my wrist. I will not be a jealous wreck like Helen. I will be secure in my own worth. Mann is a very busy man. Maybe he turned his phone off so he could concentrate on a meeting. Maybe his battery ran down. Maybe he's taking a lengthy, voluminous shit.

I walk upstairs and visit Briar and Rose. They are suspended in that kind of deep, motionless sleep that only children can obtain. For a moment, I envy their oblivion. As always, I let my eyes go out of focus, so I can finally see Lily and Selene.

Of course, I surrender to tears. As sweet as Briar and Rose are, they aren't really mine. They will always belong to Helen and Mann. They will never love me the way my children did. I wipe my eyes and close their door, clutching the baby monitor like a security blanket.

I find myself drawn to Mann's office, missing him and my usual confidence in him. I need to reconnect with my feelings, to be in a space that belongs to him. To touch his things. To breathe him in. As I move down the hallway, I notice his door is slightly ajar.

I pause, my thoughts flickering back to the man on the patio and the police. Did I leave the door open? Or did the officers when they did the cursory check of the house? I step towards the open door, and my skin prickles with fear.

No, I remind myself, there's no one here. The man is gone. He must have climbed over the fence. Or something. Or maybe he wasn't even here. Maybe my mind made up a story—a very visual, powerful story—to distract itself from obsessing over Mann.

I remember how Helen was afraid of everything. She was constantly worried that Something Bad would happen to her or her children. She was terrified that Mann would leave her, that I would usurp her place. I giggle out loud. Yes, I suppose she was right to be scared. She was the prey, and I am the predator.

"I am the predator," I whisper as I push my way into Mann's office. "Low lights," I say to the empty darkness. The recessed ceiling lights produce a soft, warm glow. I can see his floor-to-ceiling bookshelf and the enormous drafting desk supporting three wafer-thin monitors.

Everything is buff or white, a pale-on-pale elegance that is the essence of Mann, a perfect, unsparing minimalism. The only discordant note is the squat, gray floor safe, an orc among decorative wood elves. Like the door, its slightly ajar. And, I think, it is empty.

My fear trickles back, even as I step closer to the safe. I don't know what Mann kept in it, but it must be—must have been—valuable. I need to make sure it is really empty, that my mind isn't toying with me again.

I take one step and then another. But before I can look inside, something cold presses into the back of my neck. And a deep, mechanical voice says, "Get down. Now!"

I drop the monitor onto the floor and sink slowly to my knees.

***

I am stuffed with fear and rage. I was certain I was the predator, but now I am the prey. The cool object digs into my neck. The pressure is almost painful for a moment. And then it's gone.

The shadowy man moves around the room until I can see him from the corner of my eye. He is wearing a lizard mask, a black shirt, and black pants. He is short, not much taller than me. His movements are agitated and spastic, like an exposed nerve. And, in his right hand, there is a blunt-nosed charcoal-colored gun.

I am sure this is the man I saw, the Angel of Vengeance. My heart revs and sputters as my mind gropes for a plan. I decide my best chance is to convince him I am Helen, to sow doubt and uncertainty.

Who else would be here in Helen's house, caring for Helen's children, but Helen? I don't have her driver's license, but I know where she keeps her birth certificate and her other, special documents. I know how she talks, how she moves, how she depends on Mann.

I let my voice go dry with fear. "What are you doing here?"

"What are *you* doing here?" asks the man, his voice booming through a curtain of static.

"Waiting for my husband to come home. I'm Helen Gottlieb. Who are you?"

The man laughs. The sound is both tinny and dismissive. "Helen Gottlieb. Uh huh. Yeah. Sure you are."

Despite the danger, I am wildly offended. My cheeks flush, and I snap as if I were talking to a misbehaving boyfriend. "This is my house," I snarl. "I am here with my children. You are the intruder in this interaction, not me."

The masked man abruptly stops moving. I can't see his expression, but his stillness suggests he is examining me. Assessing me. Dissecting me. "You are a good actress," he says. "Totally committed to your role."

I let my outrage carry me along and serve my goals. "There's no part to commit to. I am Helen Gottlieb." I pause and then allow my voice to soften, just a little. "Why don't you tell me what you want? Maybe my husband and I can help."

The man shakes his head. "I don't think so."

He raises the gun slowly, so its barrel is pointing at my forehead. I stare into it, hypnotized as if by a poisonous snake. I picture myself dissolving and floating through the dark tunnel, disappearing into the metal tube. I wonder if there is a bright, white light at the end of it, and then I laugh.

Really, what should death matter to me? My two daughters went through it. I realize I can, too. I giggle and snort. Tears stream down my cheeks.

"What is so fucking funny?" asks the man, his arm starting to shake.

I laugh and smile and practically sing. "There's nothing you can do to hurt me. Nothing!"

The man shakes his head. "Well, you hurt me plenty."

I am trying to decipher exactly what he meant by that when he pulls off his mask. Under an oily snarl of blond hair, I see that he isn't a he at all. He was just talking through a mic and a cheap voice synthesizer, the kind kids get for Halloween. And I laugh even harder.

"Hello, Helen. I guess you're just ignoring the restraining order?"

"Fuck the restraining order. We have to talk."

***

Helen glares at me, and I glare at her. She is gaunt and wild-eyed. Her chest is rising and falling with quick, shallow breaths. I never really believed she was a hard-core, child-endangering addict; it was just a story.

But now I wonder if my story was, in some essential way, true. She looks like she's on something hard and fast, like coke or meth. And the fact that she is here, waving a gun at me held in one dainty, gloved hand is making me question a lot of assumptions.

"I have a lawyer, you know," says Helen almost smugly. "She's going to get proof that you committed fraud to destroy my marriage and my life. And then she's going to talk to her friend, the assistant district attorney."

I am incredulous. "If that's true, then why are you here? Dressed like that and holding a gun?"

"Because I'd rather you just do what I want."

I have no idea what she wants, but her eyes are wide and glittery. A deep, mossy green. Just like mine. If I let my eyes go out of focus, she really could be my sister. Or me, fifteen or twenty years from now. It's what inspired the first lie I told her, the tragically deceased older sibling I made up when we met.

I shake my head, confused. "What are you talking about?"

She blinks, lips curling into an unattractive snarl. "I talked to the Angel of Vengeance you sent to my hotel. You told them I was you."

"I didn't send anyone to your hotel," I lie. Despite the danger I am in, I cannot resist needling her. "Look, Helen, I care about you. All I want is for you to deal with your addiction and get the help you need."

"I am not a fucking addict!" howls Helen. Really, she protests too much. If she wasn't almost an addict, teetering on the edge of the abyss, it wouldn't have been so easy to frame her.

I shrug my shoulders. "That's what addicts always say," I reply, watching her face twist with fury.

As her chest heaves with broken breaths, I seriously consider grabbing for the gun. She won't shoot me. She's too weak and uncertain. But the moment passes. She calms quickly and tosses a black leather bag in my direction.

"You want to know what I want? Look in the bag."

The bag is simply designed and made of buttery leather. It obviously belongs to Mann. I unzip it, exposing crisp bricks of cash. "What's this?" I ask.

Helen flashes a bitter smile. "Mann likes to keep cash around in case of a zombie apocalypse. He kept it in that safe over there." She points at the safe and rolls her eyes. "I always thought of it as his money. But it's my money, too. At least for now, while I'm still his wife.

Helen watches me, shaking her head. "I'm sorry about what happened to your children," she says in a low, quavering voice. "I can only imagine what that would feel like. And then being stalked by the Angels? You can't possibly be in your right mind."

I stifle the urge to contradict her facile psychoanalysis and nod. She continues: "I want you to take the money and leave. If you go tonight, I won't press charges for fraud. You won't go to jail."

Of course, her offer is ridiculous. Why should I take a small bag of cash when I have Mann and his billions? He won't let me go to jail. I open my mouth to tell her exactly what I think of her sad little offer when she brings a finger to her lips.

"You know, the Angels want me to kill you."

I practically roll my eyes. Of course they do. They remind me of Malcolm. They think the world owes them wealth and attention. But they won't do the work. "Yes, that seems like their style. Get someone else, some credulous fool, to do their dirty work. Well, go ahead, Helen. I'm ready."

"Dammit, Julia, I don't want to kill you. If you take the money and go, I won't tell the Angels you are still alive. They'll think you're dead, at least for a while. All you have to do is leave this house and my children. For good."

I shake my head slowly. Helen is so deadly earnest, so ploddingly sincere and convinced of her own virtue, that I want to see her squirm.

"Are you sure you don't want to shoot me? I bet you'd find it very cathartic."

"I'm not going to shoot you," snaps Helen, her face exasperated. "At least, not while my children are asleep in the next room."

My strangled giggle surprises even me. "You'd wake them up for sure!" I gasp. "Unless, you know, you have a silencer or something."

Then Helen snorts, and we are both laughing like children. The hilarity builds until I realize the gun is not pointed at me. I leap to my feet. "Back on your knees!" shouts a suddenly humorless Helen.

We are silent for a long moment. The rain pummels the roof. Thunder rumbles like echoes from a terrible dream.

***

The power flickers off and on. Lightning flashes in the windows. Helen is still staring at me, like she doesn't know what to do. She obviously isn't very good at being in charge. After all, she has spent the past ten years or more barnacled to Mann.

Perhaps I can take control. Perhaps it will be easy.

"Helen, we both know you're not going to shoot me," I say, standing slowly.

Her hand starts shaking. The gun is an unsteady blur. "Don't be so sure!" she squeaks.

Emboldened, I take a step towards her. And then another. "Why don't you put down that gun? We both love Mann, right? Why don't we call him, ask him to come home and work things out."

Helen's face turns from pink to white. The muscles in her arm are twitching. Her will is collapsing. I am sure she is going to drop the gun and melt into my arms. I am, or was, her sister wife, after all, and the third and missing piece of her marriage.

The gun in Helen's hand explodes. Its roar blots out the sound of the rain, of the thunder, of everything. A bullet whizzes by my cheek and crashes into the wall. Helen looks as stunned as I feel. A high, sonic whine still echoes in my ears.

"What the fuck, Helen?" I yell to hear myself over the aural ringing. The world around me feels surreal. Bland, stolid Helen fired a gun in the house where her children are sleeping. Or were sleeping. I look down at the monitor I dropped on the floor. The children are rolling in their beds, whimpering, then crying.

Helen's cheeks are red again. She looks wild. Unhinged. "I don't want to hurt you, but I need you to stay put!"

The children's cries, louder now, are piercing and plaintive. They remind me of Lily and Selene. Helen can't possibly want them to keep screaming. No mother would.

"What about the children?" I ask. "They're awake and crying. Let me help them go back to sleep."

"No!" shrieks Helen, her finger on the trigger. "You've done enough! They'll get themselves back to sleep."

We wait in silence as the girls' cries fade to sniffles. The power flickers again, but this time it fades to black. A door slams. Helen screams. I lunge forward, blindly. I focus my entire being on taking that gun from Helen.

I fall into her, and we crash to the floor. I grab her wrist and she grabs mine. I can hear her breathing. It is loud and fast, as if she is hyperventilating. I try to pry her fingers from the handle of the gun, but she is surprisingly strong.

As her breath accelerates, I hang on. All I have to do is wear her down. I hear the creak of a door on its hinges and heavy footsteps. I try to hang onto Helen and look around the room at the same time. Someone's pulling me away, throwing me onto my back.

A gun explodes, but not the one in Helen's hand. I smell a bitter acrid smoke. My arms stop working, and suddenly I cannot breathe. Helen is lying on her back beside me, gasping for air. I touch my chest. Something is warm and wet and the consistency of hamburger. My vision is fading. A cool exhaustion is sliding over me. Where is the pain?

Where is the pain?

I try to stay awake as a tall, masculine figure kneels beside me. He is wearing a lizard mask like the one Helen wore. His voice is a staticky, synthetic blur.

"Poor little Jules. Poor, sweet, little Jules."

27 REVELATIONS, PART 1

I learned something about myself the night Julia died. I am apparently not a killer. When she lunged at me, I felt a terrible sadness and horror. I was frightened for myself and my children. But I could not pull the trigger. Not even to save my own life.

I struggled mightily, though, trying to keep the gun I had taken from Mann's safe away from Julia's cruel little hands. And I succeeded for a while. She wasn't as strong as I thought she would be. And yet she was strong enough. She would have defeated me eventually if the masked man had not appeared.

Even in the dim light of Mann's office, I could tell the stranger was wearing a lizard mask. The shiny green plastic of the snout reflected the lightning like algae on a pond. I wondered if he was the same Angel of Vengeance who had visited my hotel room. That man had been a zealot, but oddly calm and contained.

He asked me to kill Julia. Apparently, he didn't trust me to do the job. And he was right. The masked man, whoever he was, pulled Julia off me, threw her onto her back and shot her. He was stronger than someone who spent their life trolling broken women on social media ought to be.

The roar of the gunshot obliterated my hearing. A dull cacophony echoed through my ears. My head and face were spattered with something warm and wet: *Julia's blood.* I did not feel even a whisper of triumph that my adversary was likely gone forever. No, all I felt was sorrow and a deep, soul-clenching revulsion.

My chest tightened as the man kneeled beside Julia and pushed a strand of hair out of her eyes. His movements were surprisingly tender for one sworn to hold fallible humans to a more stringent moral accounting. I supposed he was religious like my mother. Perhaps this Angel believed that death had expiated Julia's sins, that she had returned to a pristine, innocent state.

Or maybe he was just a murderous sicko who thrilled to the power of his gun and the way it tore through lives like tissue paper. He put his masked head to hers and murmured something through his synthesizer. All I could make out was a static hiss. She emitted a soft, wet groan while he hovered over her.

I pulled myself into a sitting position. The simple motion sent my heart into overdrive and my breath into short, staccato gasps. The masked man lingered by Julia's side, squeezing her hand.

Julia, with her blank eyes and ruined chest, still eclipsed me. If it weren't for the children, I would have taken advantage of my invisibility and quietly backed out of the room. But I couldn't leave my girls alone in a house with a murderer. I had to watch this dangerous man until he left the house.

And if he wouldn't go, I would have to make him.

***

My body rebelled against my belated courage. My stomach twisted with the nausea that had been my constant companion during pregnancy. My pores opened and drenched me with slick sweat; the gun was slippery in my hands. If the lizard man had made a sudden movement, or even a sudden noise, I would have lost my grip.

But the man remained silent, a still life possessed by Julia's corpse. I felt sick and dizzy as I quickly wiped my hands and wrapped them back around the gun. I imagined the man shooting me, then taking my children. He had a good reason to judge me. He told me to kill and I agreed.

234

I gasped at a small explosion of thunder and lightning. The power flickered on and off. In the ghostly strobe, the man finally turned to me. I struggled to inhale enough air, to keep myself upright and conscious and away from the beckoning darkness. More static came from the mask, a strange wheezing sound I recognized as laughter.

"You disappointed me. I really thought you were going to kill her."

A flash of anger burned through my fear. I swallowed it down. He also had a gun and was prepared to use it. I couldn't afford to antagonize him. "I guess I'm not much of a killer," I said in a high, gently pleading voice.

He snorted. "When I came to see you, you told me all about Julia, how she was threatening your husband and your children. You sounded like a Fury, a woman possessed by revenge.

"Instead, you're just another weak woman. Just another helpless mom who won't do what it takes to protect her kids."

I opened my mouth to interrupt and then closed it again. Maybe he was right. Maybe I should have killed Julia and fulfilled my bargain. He took a step closer. I took a step back, conscious of the trigger under my finger pad. I still had time to redeem myself.

"I know something about you, Helen," he said in his strange, synthesized voice. "More than ten years ago, you went to the ER with your boyfriend, Karl Wilson. You had a broken cheekbone. A mild concussion. Then just two months later, Karl disappeared.

"You were living with Karl, but you never filed a missing person's report. Never made a peep. Instead, you just moved out and put his stuff into storage.

"When you were celebrating your engagement to Mann Gottlieb, Karl's mother was printing out flyers with tears in her eyes, mourning for her missing son.

"Helen, you say you're not a killer. Are you really sure about that?"

***

My heart fluttered, and I strained for air, trying to fill my lungs. I supposed the lizard man was trying to convince himself that I had killed Karl, so he would have an easy reason to kill me, too. As an Angel of Vengeance, it was his job to judge. To condemn.

I wondered if the lizard man had actually known Karl in some way. The Angels of Vengeance spewed just the kind of self-righteous, hyper-masculine bullshit he would have loved. The possibility of this gruesome coincidence struck me as wildly hilarious. I strangled my laughter, turning it into a strangled cough that made my chest tighten and ache.

Before I collapsed into a wheezing mound, I glanced at my sleeping girls on the monitor. I reminded myself that I had to survive.

"I don't know what you think you discovered online, but I didn't kill Karl," I said, trying to sound credible and confident.

The lizard man hissed. "Doing nothing can be just a deadly as taking action. You could have left Karl, but you didn't. Instead, you waited. You toyed with him.

"Something tells me that Karl would still be alive today if…" A series of digital tones cut him off. The phone in his back pocket was chirping, trying to tell him something. I willed him to look at it, to become distracted.

Perhaps I had just enough adrenaline in my veins to convince myself I could take his gun.

But he ignored his phone. "Silly Helen," he said. "We're holding guns on each other. You didn't expect me to lay down my weapon just to check my damn phone, did you?"

I shrugged. Honestly, I sort of did.

The lizard man raised his gun slightly, so the barrel was pointing towards my heart. It felt as if something gave my chest a hard squeeze. I gasped and tried to keep my sweaty face impassive.

"Are you expecting something important?" I asked, as coolly as if we were coworkers at the company coffee bar.

It was his turn to shrug. "I wish I could read that text. It's the love of my life. She is strong and independent. Nothing like you."

I ignored the barb and focused on my breathing. I had to make him see reason, give him a good reason to go. "You're right. I'm sure your girlfriend or wife is nothing at all like me. And now that Julia's dead, you should probably leave. Let me deal with the fallout."

And the fallout would be extreme. I was violating a restraining order. My hands were covered with gunshot residue. It would take time—perhaps a lot of time—for the police to realize that I didn't shoot Julia, that it wasn't my gun.

The lizard man cough-laughed through his synthesizer. "I might leave you here alive. But I need a better reason than that. Try harder."

***

I stifled a groan. This man was playing with me. I was certain this encounter was going to end in violence and, probably, my death. A cold resignation seeped through my body, weighing me down.

But I was going to play his game, anyway. What else could I do? I forced my brain into gear, tried to put myself into his shoes. What did the lizard man want? What did he need? I imagined him huddled in his parents' basement hunched over his computer, dreaming of a life he wasn't either skilled or hopeful enough to achieve.

My eyes slid around the room, searching for some kind of answer. And then, improbably, I had it. "See that black bag over there? The one on the floor?"

The lizard man grunted in the affirmative.

"There's fifty thousand dollars inside. You're right that I'm weak. I was going to give Julia that money so she would disappear, and I wouldn't have to kill her. But now she's dead. So the money's yours, if you leave now."

The lizard man laughed through his synthesizer, an oddly menacing sound. "Fifty thousand dollars? C'mon lady. You are the wife of Mann Gottlieb. If you're going to bribe me, you've got to do better than that."

I shook my head. "Sorry, the fifty thousand is all I have. My husband is kind of weird and paranoid about money. We have completely separate financial lives."

The lizard man laughed again. "No secret accounts? No expensive jewelry? No credit cards you can use for a quick retail boost? I don't believe you."

I huffed, anger overtaking fear. "Believe me. Mann hates to share. There's a dent in my van. It's been there for more than a year because I don't have the money to fix it."

The lizard man rolled his shoulders in a way that felt skeptical. "I'm sure he would have given you the money if you asked nicely."

"No!" I blurted. "I didn't want to ask my husband for money as if I were a child! I wanted us to be equal partners. I wanted us to share everything."

"You? You're a mid-level public relations hack and a mediocre mom. How could you be equal partners with Mann Gottlieb, the lion of Silicon

Valley, the man who single-handedly created a million jobs? I just don't see it."

While I struggled to come up with a rebuttal, something about how professional success is not the sum total of a person's worth, a cold wave of nausea cleaved through me. My heart made a tight fist in my chest, and a hard, unyielding pain battered its way down my neck and along my arm.

Oh God, I was having a heart attack.

28 REVELATIONS, PART 2

As always, my heart hammered in my chest. But this time the dull thud was accompanied by a pulsing agony, as if a giant were crushing my torso in his over-sized hand. The pain and pressure brought me to my knees. I gasped, clutching the gun in defiance of my aching arms.

The lizard man loomed over me then gently pushed my shoulder. I toppled backward like a broken doll, still clinging to the gun as if it could still save me. "Poor Helen," he muttered. "I always worried something like this would happen to you. You were always so bad about taking care of yourself."

He reached down and pushed a strand of hair out of my eyes as I struggled for air. There was something about the way he moved, about the strange mixture of rough and tender, that was deeply familiar. Then he pulled off his mask and vocal synthesizer.

Oh God, it was Mann.

Mann. Mann. Mann. Mann.

He loved Julia, but he killed Julia. He said he got a text from his true love, but wasn't that Julia? No, it couldn't be.

He killed Julia. He killed Julia. He killed Julia.

And he had tried to get me to kill Julia.

Despite the crushing pain in my chest, all I could think was *why, why, why, why?*

I glanced at the monitor. The girls, still thankfully in their beds, were stretching and babbling. Then I looked up at Mann, who was gazing down at me with a mildly contemptuous expression on his face.

I struggled to sit up, but the heaviness in my chest pinned me to the ground. Sweat beaded around my hairline. It hurt to breathe. "What the hell is going on?" I gasped. "What did you do? Why did you kill Julia?"

Mann shook his head. He pressed the center of my forehead with cool, dry lips. "I made a terrible mistake," he said, his voice a melancholy sigh. "I'm sorry, honey."

I reached my hand towards my chest. Even this slight movement was excruciating. I began to shiver; my teeth knocked together. Sweat, commingled with Julia's blood, trickled down my face. "I'm sick, Mann. I think it's my heart."

He stroked my hair. "Everything will be OK. We can still get back on track." He kissed my neck and my ear. The weight on my chest grew heavier. I wondered if this was how I was going to die: here, lying on the floor, with my prodigal husband finally returned.

I could hear Briar and Rose on the monitor, cooing in their sleep. I wanted to hold them one last time but doubted I could manage it. My arms were crushed by the same constricting force that bound my chest.

I sighed. I was sure I was experiencing my last memory, my last few moments on earth. I was wracked by pain but also strangely numb. Mann was many things, but he was a good father. He would care for my girls. And they would definitely not go to Julia. He killed her, after all. Did he do it to set me free, to set us free?

And who was the "true" love he talked about from under the lizard mask? Was it a memory of me, the old, tougher and more adventurous me?

I forced my mind to stop whirling. I had so little time left and so few options. The only choice before me was how I was going to die: screaming and railing or measured and deliberate. Despite everything, I decided to make a gracious exit. I would give Mann a deathbed story to tell the girls, a pocketful of heartfelt last words.

"I love you," I said, "for everything you've done for the children. I am grateful that you will be there for Briar and Rose. Tell them I love them. Tell them I will be with them always."

Mann nodded and gave my hand a quick squeeze. Through the pain, I detected something brusque about his touch. Something calculating. Something that reminded me he had been the lizard man. And I couldn't let it go.

Mann kissed me again with his cool, dry lips. "I told you everything is going to be fine. I'll call an ambulance, and they'll take you to Stanford. Now give me the gun."

I wanted to do it. I was sick and exhausted, my burden too great. I imagined myself passing the gun into my husband's capable hands, letting the heavy weight of responsibility pass to him. But one of those hands still held another gun, the one he used to kill Julia.

Was he really going to call an ambulance? Could I truly believe him?

"No!" I yelped clutching my weapon and inching away from my husband. I couldn't put myself at his mercy until I knew more.

"Helen," he said, frowning. "Don't be absurd. I'm not going to hurt you. Give me the gun."

"Not until you tell me what's going on." My voice was a hoarse squeak, and my breath came in tiny sips. Pain thundered through my body, radiating from my chest to my back, arms, and hands. But I stood my ground, metaphorically speaking.

Mann muttered to himself, a harsh, guttural curse. He raised his gun and touched the end to the center of my forehead. "Oh Helen, my infinite disappointment of a wife. You ruin everything."

"What is that supposed to mean?" I asked in a breathy groan.

"It would have been so much better if you had just killed Julia like you were supposed to."

***

I moaned, the pain would not relent. My life was crashing down around me, breaking off into strange, molten chunks. I was going to die, or something worse. And what would happen to the girls?

"Why did you want me to kill Julia?"

Mann cut off my strangled questioning with a short laugh. "You destroyed her, you know. All Julia had wanted out of life was simply to be like you: a happy, ordinary mother with ordinary children.

She was gentle. She was creative. She would have been your friend if you hadn't twisted her with your obsessive jealousy.

"You infected her. You made her dark and selfish and grasping. Just like you. It's your fault she's dead. If you had just taken the money and disappeared, left the girls to me, she would still be alive right now. But you never make things easy, do you?"

The pain was overwhelming, but my anger punched through it. "I didn't force you to shoot Julia. And if I was all that bad, you could have grown some balls and left me. Maybe it would have been for the best."

Yes, Mann's deciding to leave me had been my worst nightmare. But now, lying on the floor of Mann's office, holding one gun in my shaky, aching hand and staring into the barrel of another, I realized I believed what I'd said. It would have been better had we separated. Infinitely better.

Mann snorted softly. "How could I have possibly left you? We never signed a prenup. And you don't deserve half of all the value I created over the past ten years. You were a parasite. Just barely competent enough to work a mediocre little job and take care of small children.

"I used to think you were a strong woman, someone who wanted me, not my balance sheet. But something happened when you got pregnant. You changed.

"I was hoping Julia's little deceptions would help you see the light. You should have signed the post-nuptial agreement, taken the money, and disappeared.

"Since you didn't, I made another plan. I kept track of what Julia was doing with the Angels of Vengeance. It was easy enough to step into the scene they'd prepared. If you killed Julia, I could have killed you defending Julia and our children. It would have been perfect."

The room spun. I felt distant and unreal. "But why did Julia have to die?"

Mann smiled ruefully. "She was passionate and desperate and exciting, sort of like you used to be. Once I disappointed her, she would have found a way to damage me or the girls. It was time for things to end."

A scream burned in my throat. "Mann, you didn't end things, you murdered her. You're a murderer!"

Mann shook his head. "You never really wonder what happened to Karl, do you?"

I struggled to breathe, then said, "He was bad for me. We had a bad relationship. I was glad he disappeared. Glad, OK! Why are you so obsessed with him now?"

Mann clicked his tongue, gently chiding me. "I got rid of Karl. I ended his toxic existence so you could be free. And you never even said thank you."

I took small sips of air, each one cutting like a ragged-edged knife. "You killed *Karl*?"

He smiled ruefully. "I knew he was hitting you. I knew he was a lowlife. And I was bored. I wanted to do something utterly disruptive. Something that would divide my life into before and after.

"It was surprisingly exciting. It put my whole life into perspective."

I opened and closed my mouth, trying to remember the last time I saw Karl, but I couldn't even remember his face. I just came home from work one day, and he was gone. A small part of me had missed our passive-aggressive cat-and-mouse games. But a bigger part of me was relieved it had to stop.

I swallowed a mouthful of warm saliva, and my chest clenched. "How did you kill him? How did you, um, get rid of his body?"

He smiled again. "He was a housepainter, don't you remember? I asked him to spread out a tarp and lie down on it. I couldn't believe he was so submissive; he just did what I said.

"Ironically, I used the gun you're holding now. One quick shot to the back of the head. It was neater than I expected.

"And who says I got rid of his body?"

I nearly choked. "What do you mean?"

"I brought him to my workshop, the barn behind the beach house in Capitola. I'd been reading up on the ancient Egyptians—fascinating culture, by the way—and I decided to do some experiments. I wanted to make a talisman, a memento of what I did. And I succeeded. I preserved him.

"Most of him, anyway. I fed some of the squishier bits to the neighborhood dogs.

"Now he's in our attic packed in the Yeti cooler. For the longest time, I wanted to show you, to reveal the part of me that was capable—is capable—of anything.

"First, I waited until we were married. Then I waited until you had the children. And then I waited for you to turn back into the woman I married, the passionate one who loved all of me no matter what and didn't give a damn about my money or the state of her van.

"I knew we were over when I realized you were too conventional, too small minded to appreciate what I'd done with Karl."

I tried to speak, but all that came out was a high whistle. Karl—what was left of him, anyway—was in our fucking attic, and he'd been here for years. I'd always known Mann was different from other people. Smarter. More successful. Utterly confident. But perhaps he was different in other ways, too. Monstrous ways.

"Mann, you're sick," I gasped. "You need help."

Mann shook his head, as if I were a slow student. "The latest research says personality is genetic. Your parents must have passed along their narrow, conventional mindset along with their predisposition for heart disease."

My chest clenched again, and my eyes filled with pointless tears. My parents had been simple, ordinary people, awful in simple, ordinary ways. I clutched at my gun with both hands, sending a cascade of pain down my arm. I was about to die a simple, ordinary death, and yet it felt deeply, achingly unfair.

Mann, keeping his gun trained on me, plucked the baby monitor from the floor. "You know, I shouldn't have reproduced with you. The girls seem fine now, but who knows what bad snippets of code you passed onto them. Only time will tell."

Adrenaline flooded through me. I was suddenly sure he was going to hurt the girls. He said he was capable of anything, and I believed him. For the first time, I knew I could put him down.

"What are you going to do with the girls?" I asked, conscious of the cool metal beneath my finger.

"Oh no, I won't hurt our children. I'll make sure they're taken care of. But they're not going to be my only legacy. You see, I found a woman who is truly worthy of my investment. She is beautiful, brilliant, and ambitious. And enthusiastically poly.

"She'll make a great stepmother for the girls. And I think even you'll approve. It's Poppy."

Poppy was his true love. Of course. *Of course.*

My mind flashed to her dark, glossy hair and knowing smile. She ran a daycare center and some kind of software startup all by herself. Children loved her. My children loved her. He was right. Poppy was an upgrade.

Mann must have seen something shift in my expression because he visibly relaxed. "Yes, I knew you'd approve. When you die, she'll keep your memory alive. Of course, you'll get the blame for shooting Julia. After all, you're a borderline personality with addiction issues.

"And you'll probably be blamed for killing Karl. You were the last person to see him alive."

He smiled at me. It was almost tender. "Helen dearest, I know you're not going to shoot me. You *hated* Julia, and you couldn't kill *her*. So let's make the most of the time we have left. I could put my arms around you while you take your last breaths. I could show you pictures of the girls when they were babies. I could even bring them in to see you for one last…"

My finger twitched. My shoulder screamed. The air around me roared and fell silent. It smelled like burnt crystals, harsh but pure. The red blossom in the center of Mann's forehead wilted and liquefied. Blood dripped into his eyes as he toppled backwards onto the floor.

The pain intensified, and my thoughts began winking out, one by one. I heard mournful howls just outside the house, and bright, colorful light pulsed through the window. The police had arrived. Someone in our quiet neighborhood must have heard the shots and made the call.

I closed my eyes and one, final thought flickered through my synapses. *What have I done? Who will take care of the girls?*

29 LIFE AND DEATH

I was supposed to be floating above my body, following a bright, beautiful light. I was going to follow it out of this life. It would lead me to my broken family, miraculously healed by the light. I expected to see my parents and grandparents waiting for me in a small, grassy clearing full of luminescent butterflies. Would my father still be yelling? Would my mother be drunk?

I wondered if I would see Julia, if she would be laughing with her children, reunited at last. I didn't like Julia alive. But dead? I sort of wanted to see her. I bet she would be a different person freed from her grief.

And I dreaded a post-mortem encounter with Mann. I could imagine him standing there, smirking. After all, our near instantaneous deaths were something of a cosmic joke. Perhaps he would laugh when he saw me. Or maybe he would sulk that I got him before he got me.

Or maybe he would be full of rage that our children were orphans.

Even in the twilight between life and death, I worried about Briar and Rose. I left them alone. Without a father. Oh, I didn't want them to be raised by a murderer who kept my ex-boyfriend's corpse in the attic. But, without me and Mann, where would they go? Mann and I were both from stunted families. No obvious relatives were waiting in the wings.

Mann had a much-younger brother in Hamburg, Germany I had met at our wedding. He was, as far as I could remember, a single man who enjoyed frequent travel to the South American rain forests. And my family tree was utterly barren. I was the only child of an only child.

And yet, while I feared for my children, I was grateful they were alive. The police would find them, and take them somewhere. They would be safe. They would inherit Mann's wealth.

But I didn't see any of that. The light that hung above me was an anemic little thing, a cool yellow blur. I didn't want to get near its chilly presence. I made myself small and quiet, hiding in the darkness until, slowly, it went away.

***

No, I didn't die after all. Someone must have plucked the blockage from my heart. I was groggy, swaddled in cool blankets. My chest ached as if I had been cut open and sewn back together. My throat was scraped raw. But the crushing weight was gone. And I could breathe. I would see my girls again.

My eyes were dry and crusty. I opened them and blinked into a dimly lit space. A hospital room. Machines beeped and purred. White curtains surrounded my bed like ghosts. A piece of dark furniture lurked like a sleeping panther. I blinked some more, but my vision was still hazy. I tried to rub my eyes, but my right hand wouldn't move.

I squeezed my eyes tightly together and allowed myself to think terrible thoughts that brought me to tears. My eyes finally cleared and my surroundings crystallized in sharp relief. I was indeed in a hospital room. And I was handcuffed to my bed.

Even more disturbing, there was a chair beside my bed. And it was occupied by an elegant woman in black. She wore a close-fitting shirt and short skirt with glossy patent boots. Her hair was as dark as a raven's wing and pulled into a tight bun. Her lips were arterial red. She was…Poppy.

"Poppy?" I asked in a dry rasp. "What are you doing here? Do you know where my girls are?"

She sniffed and a single tear trickled down her pale cheek without smudging her mascara. "You killed Mann. You ruined my future."

And then I remembered. Mann had been planning to marry Poppy— or, at least, reproduce with her. I sighed. "Mann wasn't exactly the ideal husband. Perhaps you dodged a bullet. But, seriously, do you know where Briar and Rose are?"

Poppy rolled her eyes, something I had never seen her do before. "Briar and Rose are *your* children, full of your genetic flaws. Don't ask me where they are."

My heart began to pound, my chest to ache. "I'm in a hospital room. I've just woken up from something. Please. Tell me what happened to my children."

Poppy shook her head. "I can't help you. But maybe she can."

A nurse pushed through the curtain around my bed. She moved with a supple confidence that made her loose scrubs look like high fashion. Her blond hair was neatly piled on her head and pinned away from her face. It was Julia.

"You're alive!" I gasped.

"Do you think a little gunshot wound could stop me?" she asked, smiling.

My panic intensified. "Julia, have you seen Briar and Rose?"

Julia's smile grew wider, more beatific. "They're just fine. Your children are just fine."

I felt like my heart was about to explode. "Yes, but where are they?"

Julia approached the bed and took my hand. "They're with Lily and Selene. And Karl, your old boyfriend."

Again, the giant hand wrapped around my torso and squeezed. Julia stroked my hair, and I tried to scream, but I couldn't breathe. Something was stuck in my throat.

***

A nurse who looked nothing like Julia pulled the ventilator tube from my throat. "Take a deep, slow breath," she said.

I did as she said, gasping and thrashing. My throat was raw, throbbing with every gurgling breath. The nurse, a young woman with smooth, beige skin, nodded encouragingly. I opened my mouth to speak, but all that came out was a phlegmy whistle.

"You've been through a lot," said the nurse. "Try to rest." But I didn't want to rest. I needed to wrap my hands around reality. I needed to know exactly how sick I was, where the girls were, if Mann or Julia was somehow still alive.

I opened and closed my mouth like a fish starved for oxygen. I mouthed, "Tell me what happened. Please." The nurse shook her head, smiling like a patient adult indulging a toddler. She adjusted one of the many devices now connected to my body, and a wave of sleepy euphoria passed through me.

But I didn't trust it! I tried to fight the dreamy lethargy. I kicked at the sheets and pinched my wrists. It wasn't enough. I slipped back under the surface into a warm, womb-like darkness. I dissolved into drugged exhaustion, falling and falling.

As I fell, my thoughts were weighted and slow. My dreams were all dark shapes and elusive fears. I tried to swim up and away from something I couldn't recognize or even understand. It didn't work. I kept drifting downwards. And yet I knew I had to keep trying and moving.

I rested fitfully for hours. Maybe even days. When I awakened again, groggy and dry-mouthed, the nurse was accompanied by a doctor, a thin man in rimless glasses, holding a clipboard. His skin was pallid and soft, as if he had spent his entire life indoors.

"Hello, Mrs. Gottlieb. I trust you're feeling better?"

I blinked my crusty eyes. I was forgetting something important, but my thoughts were a jumble of shadows, just out of reach. "Um, sure?"

He chuckled at my uncertainty. "You were seriously ill. We found two blood clots in your lungs and two in your heart. We have you on blood thinners. Do you have a family history of blood clotting disorders?"

My hand reached blindly for the stitches on my chest. "My father had a heart attack."

The doctor scribbled something on my chart. "We'll have to get you in for genetic testing. For now, I want to see you walking around. It's time to rebuild your strength, get your blood flowing."

Then something clicked. "What happened to my husband? Where are my children?" I blurted in a high, crackling howl.

The nurse frowned, and the doctor shook his head. I watched them exchange pointed looks as the machine tracking my heart rate began to beep faster and faster. The doctor cleared his throat. A decision had been made.

"Mrs. Gottlieb, your husband is dead. Your children are staying with your friend, Poppy Maxwell."

I wanted to scream that Poppy was not my friend, she was yet another polyamorous beauty who had wanted my wealthy, merciless husband. But I didn't. I swallowed my shock and let it burn down my throat.

All I had to do was get out of the hospital and take my girls back. And, remembering my final moments with Julia and Mann, stay out of jail.

***

After a quick exam, the nurse helped me out of bed and sent me, along with my rolling IV pole, for a walk through the hospital.

As I moved, as cautious and gingerly as the invalid I was, I thought about Briar and Rose. Perhaps Mann had been right. Perhaps I had passed along a genetic curse. Perhaps he could have had healthier, luckier children with Poppy or even Julia, our doomed third.

I told myself that the girls would be fine with Poppy. After all they used to spend every day with her. She loved children. Her relationship with Mann, whatever it was, wouldn't have changed that.

I was still amazed—and horrified—that Mann had fallen in love, or obsession, with Poppy during his infatuation with Julia. I supposed it was logical. After all, we were poly. He hadn't betrayed my trust by getting together with her. Not technically, anyway.

No, he had betrayed my trust by having an intense relationship with Julia and rubbing it in my face and encouraging her to steal my identity. She had tried to take my place. And, in a strange way, she succeeded. Mann came to have the same contempt for her that he'd had for me.

I recalled Julia's face and her sad, passionate eyes. She had envied me so much she became me. She really was my almost-twin. I pitied her now and hoped she was at peace. Perhaps she really was with her twins.

As I neared the end of the hallway, an alcove filled with vending machines, I wondered when the police would come for me. I had shot my husband after all, even if he had shot Julia. I hoped they knew I didn't shoot both of them. They must, or I wouldn't have been left alone.

I tried to remember if I'd said anything to the police that night. But my mind held only brief, jagged flashes. Loud, male voices screaming. Cops working alongside the paramedics. Ripping, tearing sounds. Someone rubbing my face and my hands with soft cloth.

I turned and walked back towards my room. Just thinking of that night was making me lightheaded. My arms shook, and my legs wobbled. I wanted nothing more than to get back into bed. I was listing badly to one side when the nurse intercepted me.

When we reached my door, she said, in a voice barely louder than a whisper, "The police are here to see you."

***

I sat in bed, attempting to look as dignified as one can look in a hospital gown. Detective Janet Grosso, apparently promoted from Assistant Investigator, sat in a metal chair beside my bed. She read me my rights so softly and gently that I didn't even think to call my young lawyer.

She looked both hard and kind. Her makeup was faded and cracked as if she'd slept in it. And she seemed older. I wondered if she remembered me and my panicked visit to the police station, clutching my dirty cup.

My mind buzzed and whirred as she ignored me. She stared down at an iPad, tapping and swiping. Perhaps this was an attempt to catch me off guard? To see what I would volunteer under the pressure of silence?

I waited for her to speak. One thing I had learned from Mann was never to make the first offer. I closed my eyes for a long time and opened them. When I did, the detective was staring back at me. "You know, you really look a lot like your husband's girlfriend."

"I would say she looks like me."

The detective's eyes widened and then narrowed. I had clearly deviated from her script. "Well, Officer Bedi thought so, too. She answered a call at your house and met, uh, Julia Logan, also known as Julia Weatherstone. The forensic evidence says your husband shot her. Is that true?"

I nodded. "Yes. Yes, it is."

The detective nodded, too. "Do you have any idea why your husband would want to shoot her?"

I gaped and almost unpacked the whole, twisted tale. Mann and I exploring polyamory. Mann and Julia falling in love. My endless, hopeless jealousy. Julia deciding to replace me and twisting herself in my image. Mann's deciding to get rid of us both. And Karl's desiccated corpse, shot by the same gun I used to kill Mann, moldering in the attic.

Instead, I shrugged. "I'm not sure. They had a very volatile relationship. Big highs and lows."

Detective Grosso's expression was as incredulous as her tone. "I know why *you* would want to shoot her. You said she had stolen your husband and might be trying to poison you."

I shrugged again. "Clearly, I didn't know my husband as well as I thought I did."

"Indeed." The detective went back to her iPad and swiped some more. Then she showed me a picture of a woman. Her hair was a glossy, raven's wing black, and her lips were a cherry red bow. It was Poppy. "Do you know who this is?"

A bolt of adrenaline crackled through me. "Yes. That's Poppy Ralston. She owns a daycare. She was our children's babysitter. I think she may also have been having an affair with Mann."

Detective Grosso watched my stricken face as if it was a weather vane. "Why did you shoot your husband?"

I stared at the detective who stared back at me, waiting for my reply like a spider waiting for a juicy fly. I blurted, "I saw him kill Julia! He was acting strangely. I was worried he would hurt me. I was worried he hurt the children. When he pointed his gun at me, and I…just…just reacted. I guess it was self-defense."

The detective's eyes sparkled like a hound scenting blood. "What were you doing in the house that night?"

"Breaking a restraining order," I said, feeling heavy with resignation. "I wanted to see my children."

"You were dressed like a ninja and wearing a mask. Your husband was dressed the same way. Why?"

I sighed, increasingly sure I was going to jail. "I didn't want Julia to recognize me if she caught sight of me. A group called the Angels of Vengeance had been stalking her. You know who they are? What they wear?"

The detective nodded. I continued, "I thought dressing like one of the Angels was a good disguise. Maybe Mann thought so, too."

The detective paused, her face thoughtful. I twisted the thin hospital blanket in my fingers. I felt guilty. Maybe if I had been a better wife, if I had snapped back from the birth of my twins, none of this would have happened. Mann and I could have continued our lives together. Perhaps he would have showed me Karl. I wondered if I would have stayed.

"Julia told Officer Bedi that she saw a man in a mask outside her, um, your house. The officer thought Julia looked so nervous that it stuck with her. Bothered her. She went back to your house for a second look. I guess she saved your life."

I nodded slowly, breathing in and out. But my heart, now clot free, took off like a shot. The soft background beeping of the machine that tracked my heart rate grew louder and faster. It was as if I was plugged into a lie detector, or a fear detector.

I asked the only question that seemed to matter. "Am I in trouble?"

Janet Grosso sighed, long and deep. "I guess we'll have to see."

***

Poppy finally came to visit, bringing my girls along. She was less glamorous in person than in my imagination. Her hair was messy, as if she'd slept on it, and her face was puffy. Her jeans were even slightly too tight.

I smiled at her awkwardly. Was she mourning Mann? Was she distraught that he was dead—that I killed him? Were they really blissful soulmates, or had they shared some form of dark, complicated love? I took a deep, shuddering breath and focused on the children. They smiled shyly. I hugged them tightly.

Briar patted my arm, and Rose giggled. They pulled at my IVs and snuggled into my adjustable bed, pushing all the buttons they could reach. I laughed. They laughed. Even Poppy laughed, her voice a low rasp.

When the girls had adjusted to the room, Poppy pulled toys out of her bottomless diaper bag to amuse the girls. "I guess we should talk she said," smiling ruefully.

"So the girls are staying with you?" I asked.

"Yeah, we've been having fun."

The conversation halted there. I cuddled the girls, allowing the pause to grow cavernous. Poppy squirmed slightly. A small, dark part of me enjoyed her discomfort as she bit her soft, pink lips, working up the courage to speak.

"Listen Helen," she finally said in a soft, confidential voice. "I know you probably don't care, but my startup is in trouble. Now that Mann is gone, his partners don't want to give me the next round of funding. I decided to sell my house to save the company. I listed it yesterday, and within four hours I got an offer. I have to move out this week.

"I'm sure you want to go home with your kids. But you're ill, and you need time to recover. I can't imagine what you've been through."

I nodded, unsure what my situation had to do with her ailing startup. In truth, I had very little sympathy for this young, healthy woman in front of me who could no longer extract money from my dead husband. A small, twisted part of me wanted her to fail, wanted to see her return to the world of the painfully employed.

Poppy sighed softly. "I know we weren't exactly friends. But I adore your children, and I have an idea that would be great for all of us. I was thinking I could stay with you and the kids for a few weeks, while I look for an apartment and a workspace. I'd help you with the girls while you recover. It's a win-win."

I sat silently, allowing this strange offer to sink into my mind. Poppy's eyes glimmered, and her mouth softened. I wondered if she was holding back tears, grieving for Mann and her startup and the glorious life they would have had. Rose tugged hard on my IV line, sending a hot, tearing pain along my arm.

"No, sweetie," I said, grasping her pudgy hand and kissing it. Something about the warm weight of the girls made me feel fractionally more alive, more hopeful. I did want to get out of this hospital, to be home with my children and begin reassembling my life from the charred bits and pieces.

Of course, the idea of sharing my home with Poppy made my stomach squirm. Had she known about Mann's decision to get rid of me and Julia? I didn't think so. But how could I be sure? My pulse sped up and Rose hummed in rhythm with the quickening beep-beep-beep of the heart monitor. The children were already staying with Poppy; they were happy and healthy. If I said no to Poppy's offer while I was mired in the hospital, where would they go?

Briar wrapped her arms around my neck. I tried to shift her weight, but I was too weak. The heart rate monitor shifted into an even faster staccato. Hungry for air, I gasped for breath. If I wanted to go home with the girls, I would need help.

Poppy was here. She was willing to help. And I wouldn't be sharing a husband with her, only some painful memories.

"OK Poppy," I said with exhausted resignation. "Let's give it a try."

30 THE BITTER END

I returned to my house—Mann's house—weak and haunted. I was a ghost of myself seeking phantoms of my husband and my old, illusory life.

Poppy drove the girls and me back from the hospital in her lemon yellow Tesla. After more than a week indoors, the bright sun was an assault. For the entire, traffic-clogged trip, I covered my eyes, wondering if the car had been a gift from Mann, a special perk for his special girl.

Of course, the girls were restless and out of sorts. Rose bawled and Briar drooled. They had become accustomed to Poppy's house, and they hated change. When we pulled into the driveway, I thought I saw motion and a flash of golden hair. For one horrifying moment, I wondered if Julia was home.

"Helen, are you OK?" asked Poppy, her face a convincing mask of concern.

I shook my head. I was returning to the scene of the crimes. The place where I watched Julia die, where I shot my husband, where Karl's remains might be waiting in the attic. My heart fluttered. I felt dizzy and unreal, not believing that my life had come to this.

Poppy blinked and shook her head. "Sorry, stupid question. Of course you're not OK."

Poppy wrangled my squirming children inside, while I walked slowly behind. I watched Poppy calm each girl and settle her with a favorite toy. My eyes stung and watered. If I squinted, Poppy looked like Julia. For a moment, I saw Julia as she was in Mann's office, eyes wide and questioning, face spattered with blood. My vision browned out around the edges, and I stumbled, reaching my hand towards the floor.

Poppy rushed towards me, propping me up. I shrunk from her cool hands, hands that had cared for my children, hands that had caressed Mann. I wondered what she would have thought about Karl's remains. Would she have recoiled in horror or simply shrugged, telling herself Mann was an extraordinary man with concomitant failings?

Poppy glanced at the girls, who were miraculously playing quietly together. "Briar and Rose! I'm going to help your mommy upstairs. I'll be back in a minute!"

I let Poppy support me as we climbed the stairs. The house felt too bright, too open. The stark, white walls and carpet a perfect contrast with blood. I closed my eyes and followed Poppy blindly to the master bedroom. The room was bigger than I remembered, and tidier. The bed was made. The air smelled like roses.

"Can you manage from here?" asked Poppy, her words a rushed apology. "I've got to check on the girls."

"Of course," I said, waving her away.

I wanted to take a shower and wash the last traces of the hospital from my skin. I wanted to go downstairs and play with my girls, show them I was still their mother. I wanted to ask Poppy if the girls knew what had happened to their father, if they knew that Julia was gone. I wanted to climb up to our attic and find the old Yeti cooler and see if it really did contain Karl.

But I did none of the things. I let myself fall onto the enormous bed and drift into a restless sleep.

***

Although they were dead, Mann and Julia were still with me. The warmth of Julia's bloody spatter on my neck. The gaping hole in Mann's forehead. The

258

dull blankness in Mann's eyes before he collapsed. The images were brighter and more vivid than my poor, muddled thoughts. They were sharper, too, and redolent of terror.

Like a Victorian invalid, I took to my bed. And, like modern homo sapiens, I took my drugs. Beta blockers. Percocet. Ativan instead of Xanax. They didn't erase my memories, but they pushed them into the fog.

Unfortunately, I was there with them. I could barely remain awake when Poppy brought the girls to my bedside for short, poignant visits. Rose would give me a quick kiss and bound away. Briar would hug me tightly and then ask Poppy to pick her up. Poppy would flash a tired smile. Sometimes, she would inquire after my health. I would smile and lie until she went away.

While I wandered the fog, Poppy carried our domestic load. She kept the girls fed and clean and alive. She forced me to see Beatrice, my lawyer, when she appeared on our doorstep. She even helped Micah and Jess plan Mann's funeral, playing the grief-stricken widow to perfection.

God help me, she reminded me of Julia. She was so ready and eager to take my place. Anyone who looked at us would assume she was Mann's true widow. And maybe, in a way, she was. According to Beatrice, Mann's lawyers were still searching their files for his will. Perhaps he left everything to his new love. Perhaps my house was really her house.

As the days wore on, my sense of time began to decay. I would sleep through the morning and afternoon and wake at dinnertime. One evening, feeling exceptionally brave and alert, I rose from my bed. My legs felt weak and my breath short, but I felt shockingly alive. I walked slowly to my closet and pulled on a robe. Then I began the long trek downstairs.

By the time I'd reached the landing, I could hear high, cheery laughter. Poppy and my girls were giggling. The sound pierced my heart. By coddling my fears, I had neglected my children. I was certain they were already forgetting me and attaching themselves to my latest replacement. My heart sped, and I considered going back upstairs. Clearly, the girls didn't need me. Nobody needed me.

I took a deep breath and pinched the inside of my wrist. I wasn't going to succumb to self-pity. I wasn't. I quietly made my way to the dining area where the girls were putting their fingers into a violently orange vegan mac 'n faux cheese and trying to smear it on Poppy. I stifled a laugh.

The girls looked genuinely happy, and I exhaled a breath I didn't even know I was holding. And Poppy looked shockingly exhausted. Her face was puffy, and the flesh under her eyes were the color of faded eggplant. Her Stanford T-shirt was too tight, clinging in awkward places.

I took a moment to savor Poppy's casual imperfection. It made it easier to believe that she was just a bright, decent young woman who fell in love with a powerful and deeply flawed man. Perhaps she really was just doing what she believed to be the right thing. Perhaps she wasn't looking to steal my daughters' birthright. Perhaps, now that Mann was gone, I had nothing to fear.

Smiling, I stepped around the corner and coughed loudly. The girls turned around and squealed, "Mommy! Mommy!" Poppy's eyes were wide and glassy, but her lips curled into a slow, lopsided smile. She had the somewhat dazed and hopeful expression of an adult marooned with children when another adult enters the room.

"Hello Helen," she said. "I'm glad to see you're feeling better. The girls really miss you!"

"Miss you, miss you!" the girls chorused.

I pulled up a chair and inspected the girls' dinner. Gluey, orange mac 'n cheese and limp, soggy kale. I stifled a giggle. No wonder Poppy was facing a rebellion.

"Who wants peanut butter and jelly sandwiches?" I asked, grinning.

"I do! I do!"

I took a deep, even breath and walked slowly yet purposefully to the kitchen. I spotted a bottle of red wine on the shelf and thought about opening it. "Poppy!" I called. "Do you want any wine?"

"Yes!" she called. "Um, I mean, no. No thank you," she said.

I imagined the soft, fruity tang of the wine, how it would go so well with the Ativan I was taking. And then I remembered my time with Julia, how the wine and Xanax made me vulnerable to her desperate plots. So I left the bottle where it stood and made my children's sandwiches with organic strawberry jelly, hand-ground peanut butter, and sprouted bread.

The girls dug into their sandwiches with hungry zeal, painting their mouths with crumbs. Poppy's eyes fluttered closed for a moment. She really did look terrible. She could have passed for thirty, my younger sister instead of my nearly-daughter. My daughters must have been draining her energy like sweet little, sticky-fingered vampires. In that moment, I felt for her, even as I had once felt for Julia.

I groped for small talk. What beyond Mann and the children did Poppy and I share? But all I could remember was her old Facebook profile and her unique relationship status. I shrugged. I was all the fodder I had.

"So Poppy," I said, waiting until she opened her eyes. "How are Stephen and Laura?" Sam and Laura were the married couple Poppy was, as far as I knew, still dating.

Poppy shrugged and, it seemed, her eyes grew vague and misty. "Oh, that's over now. I was spending so much time on my startup that I didn't have enough time for proper relationship maintenance. We're still good friends, though."

I nodded, my eyes narrowing. I wondered if Mann was the real reason she left Stephen and Laura. I pinched the inside of my wrist again. She was hurting and Mann was dead. I had no reason to be resentful.

I offered the only sure comfort I could. "Are you sure you don't want some wine?"

Poppy opened her mouth and then closed it, as if she had wanted to say something and then thought better of it. The flesh around her eyes crinkled with worry. Briar and Rose plucked cold food from Poppy's plate, which she obviously hadn't been eating.

How could she eat so little and still manage to look so puffy? And then I suddenly understood. The straining buttons. The overstretched jeans. The queasy expression on her face. Briar and Rose were going to have a sibling. Mann was going to have a posthumous child.

***

I took long, slow breaths as everything fell into place. No wonder Poppy was so solicitous. She wanted a place for her child beside Mann's children. She wanted to share my widowhood and Mann's money. Or maybe Mann's will, once found, would leave everything to Poppy and his genetically superior, golden child.

I was about to ask Poppy if my conjecture was true, if she really was pregnant, when wind chimes echoed through the house. My heart sped. The last time I had heard them was when Emma came to the house, showing off her strong shoulders in an ill-fitting sundress.

I leaped up to check the security camera, and my heart fell. Detective Janet Grosso and a tall, bulky man were at the front door. I wondered if they were here to arrest me, to out an ellipses at the end of my life. After all, Mann was a more credible source than I was, even from the grave.

I rose slowly from my seat and nodded at Poppy. "Get the girls ready for bed." I kissed Briar and then Rose, not knowing when I would get to again.

When I opened the door, Detective Grosso smiled as if she had a special secret. "Good evening, Helen. We've talked before. This is my partner Emmett Hale," she said, motioning to the large, balding man by her side. "Can we talk to you for a moment?"

I shrugged. Beatrice was finding me a criminal lawyer, just in case. And she told me firmly that I never had to talk to the police, that I'd be better off if I simply didn't. But the uncertainty of the investigation clouded my future. I craved closure, even if it was catastrophic. And I was also curious. I wanted to know what they knew.

"Come in," I said, leading them to a small sitting area that remained relatively free of toys. They struggled to settle themselves in the white, angular chairs that Mann had imported from Finland.

"So what can I do for you?" I asked more boldly than I felt. "Do you have more questions about my husband?"

The detectives exchanged a long, meaningful glance. "We're not here to talk about your husband," said Detective Hale.

"We're here to talk about your boyfriend, Karl Wilson," said Detective Grosso, her voice bright with satisfaction.

I stifled a gasp and froze my face into a neutral expression despite the wicked pounding of my heart. I was exquisitely aware of Karl's possible presence in my attic. I wondered if Mann had left a letter or a file somewhere blaming me for his death. And under the terror was a thick foundation of guilt that I had let Karl literally disappear without a backward glance.

"What about Karl?" I asked in a tight, reedy voice.

"He disappeared while he was living with you. Why didn't you ever report it? His family is distraught."

I took a long, deep breath and hewed as closely as I could to the truth. I tried not to think about the maybe-body in the attic. "It was a long time ago. Karl was, um, an interesting character, but he wasn't reliable. It wasn't unusual for him to disappear from time to time.

"When he left, our relationship was winding down. I thought he'd just moved on and stuck me with the rent." I exhaled softly. What I said had been true until the night Mann and Julia died.

Detective Hale cleared his throat. "It's a strange coincidence. One husband allegedly tries to kill you. And you last boyfriend disappears without a trace."

Detective Grosso smiled ruefully, as if she reluctantly sympathized with my predicament. "I'm sorry, but he's right. Bad things happen to men who get involved with you."

I stifled a giggle. Detective Hale was painting me as a femme fatale, luring men to their deaths. I remembered my old self, the woman who enjoyed riding her motorcycle and subtly torturing Karl, the woman Mann had killed for. Was that really me? "Detective Hale is right," I said. "It's a tragic coincidence."

Detective Grosso leaned forward as if she was about to tell me a secret. I could smell her sweet, musky perfume and her stale, sour breath. "Maybe you and Karl were fighting, and he had an accident. Maybe he slipped and hit his head. Or maybe he got violent, and you defended yourself.

"Just tell us the truth what happened. All we want is to give Karl's family some closure. What do you say?"

Detective Grosso's eyes were warm and empathetic, but her mouth curled into a smirk. A sudden chill passed through me. I was still afraid, but I was also remote and resigned to my fate, whatever it may be.

I took a deep breath and said, "I say that I have nothing to tell you. I have no idea where Karl went or what happened to him. And now I'd like you to leave. Or we can all drive to your station and wait for my lawyer."

Miracle of miracles, the two detectives actually left.

***

After the police left, I sat in the empty silence, contemplating my future. As far as the police knew, I was a widow who was going to become obscenely rich after shooting her wildly successful husband. It was only natural they wanted to cast me as the Black Widow.

What happened to Mann went against the natural order of things. Women like me aren't supposed to become billionaires. Instead, we grow flabby and obsolete until we are bullied and replaced. Of course, the police didn't know that Poppy would likely inherit Mann's legacy and eclipse the bad, old wife who didn't know when to lay down and die.

I was reminding myself to call Beatrice in the morning when Poppy slid into view, as if conjured by my thoughts. Her face was greenish and her skin was chalky. She definitely did not glow.

"Helen," she said softly. "The girls are asleep. Is everything OK?"

"Everything's fine," I said curtly.

Poppy nodded. "I'm going to bed. My stomach is a little off."

I nodded back. "Goodnight, Poppy."

"Goodnight, Helen."

Once she handed me the baby monitor, she slumped forward, allowing herself to feel the full weight of her grief for Mann. She padded towards the guest room, her steps slow and deliberate.

I inhaled and exhaled, savoring the silence. With the girls asleep and Poppy off to bed, I was entirely alone. The wine in the kitchen called to me. So did the Ativan on my nightstand. I let their siren calls wash over me. I'd watched enough television shows to be fairly certain that nobody could accuse me of Karl's murder without a body. I had to know: was Karl really in the attic?

I stood slowly and made my way upstairs. I looked in on the children. Their sweet backs rose and fell, an innocent rhythm that made me ache. Had I ever been that soft and unknowing? I passed my office, an endless succession of guest rooms, our neglected yoga studio.

Finally, I found the small door labeled "storage." It opened onto a plain wooden staircase that brought me to a neatly organized space that looked more like an Amazon warehouse than a homely attic. It only took a few moments to find Mann's camping gear, including the massive Yeti cooler.

Huffing and gasping, I dragged the cooler from its niche. I prepared myself for anticlimax. Did my late husband Mann, benevolent titan of Silicon Valley, really keep a corpse in his attic the way other men might save a bowling trophy? Yes, he had killed Julia because she knew too much, and he had wanted to kill me to protect his fortune. But Karl?

I shook my head and put my hands on the lid. I counted silent to three the way Rose did before she stepped into the bath. Three, two, one. The cooler opened, and I nearly died. My heart vibrated in my chest. My lungs screamed for air. A desiccated skull covered in papery flesh lay folded inside the cooler like a trussed deer.

The air around the cooler smelled musty and slightly sweet. I was suddenly conscious I was breathing minute particles of Karl, and I let out a small, strangled scream. I wondered how I was going to get rid of the body. I wanted it out of the house and away from me and my daughters, but I didn't dare part with it. Once it was out in the world, anyone could find it. Anyone could use it.

I was envisioning wild plans involving a late night sailboat ride when I heard a door closing, followed by even, steady footsteps. I wasn't alone. Someone had followed me. I wondered if the Angels of Vengeance—the real ones—had somehow found me. Or maybe the past weeks hadn't been real at all. Maybe Mann and Julia were climbing up those stairs, or a doctor from a psychiatric facility.

I spun around, looking around for a weapon, for some way to defend myself. I was frantically pawing through a cloth drawer filled with cutlery when I heard a familiar voice.

"I'm sorry, Helen. I heard the noise up here, and I thought someone might be breaking in. What is *that?*"

Poppy was standing next to the cooler, pointing at Karl's remains.

***

I surprised myself by telling Poppy everything. After all, who but his other living widow would understand?

I started with Karl and ended with Mann's confession of love for Poppy and his deadly intentions towards me. I wept as I described my terror for my children and the last moments of Mann's life. Poppy sobbed too, but quietly. Tears slid silently down her pale cheeks.

"You're pregnant with Mann's baby, aren't you?" I asked.

Poppy nodded and sniffled, dabbing at her eyes with her sleeve.

"You must miss him. I mean, he was a monster, but I'm sure he loved you."

Poppy's face darkened from chalky white and dusky rose, and her face contorted. "Fuck no. He was a stalker and an asshole. And, apparently, a total psycho. I'm glad he's dead. Thank you, Helen, for killing him."

I blinked. "What? I thought you loved him?"

Poppy sighed. "I only slept with him once. We were working late, drinking wine and talking about my startup. You and Mann had just opened your marriage. We got carried away."

Anger surged through me. I remembered her telling me she had no interest in my boring husband. I was about to ask her what changed her mind when she spoke again.

"After we slept together he changed. He started texting me in the middle of the night, demanding I send him pictures or get on Skype. It was menacing and gross. I should have told him to fuck off, but I didn't. He was my main investor. I didn't want to lose my company," she said.

I sighed and took her puffy hand in mine. "He's gone now. It's just us and the kids." I paused and glanced down at the mummy, which now felt more pathetic than menacing. "Well, it's just us and the kids and Karl here."

It took more than half an hour for us to stop laughing.

EPILOGUE

Micah gave the keynote speech at Mann's funeral. He talked about Mann's glorious business victories and all the technologies his investments made possible. He alluded to his death obliquely, suggesting that his friend had lost an epic battle with mental illness. He didn't mention Julia at all.

The reception after his burial was the networking event of the season. As I wrangled my girls past the buffet tables, old Facebook friends came flocking back. They wrapped me in jasmine-scented hugs. Expressed sympathy for my ordeal. Told me all about their startups and multilevel marketing schemes.

Yes, the news about Mann's had gotten out. Defying expectations, he had died intestate. Perhaps he believed he was immortal. Or maybe he shied away from the void. Either way, I would be his sole beneficiary. I remembered the shock and dismay that flickered across his face when I shot him. I imagined him gnashing his teeth in hell.

Simply grasping the scope of his properties and investments—and his power—became my new career. My Legal Aid lawyer Beatrice joined a big, expensive firm, where her sole job is to look after me and my interests. And

I expect she will be busy soon. Poppy is not the only woman carrying Mann's child.

Two other women—both in their late twenties with raven hair and modest bumps—have come forward. One runs a social slash shopping network for pets. The other is inventing an artificial intelligence to book private jets for wealthy executives. Mann was their primary investor.

They both slept with Mann to protect their companies and their people, just like Poppy. Now all three women are suing Mann's estate. And me. They say I'm complicit, that I should have known what he was doing to them, that I should have made him stop.

"But I did make him stop!" I want to scream. "I shot him dead. What more could I have done?"

Poppy, who is practically a second mother to my girls, still shares my house. But she makes a poor spy. Her conversations with me are stilted and strange. She forgets herself and pores through web pages about DNA testing and inheritance laws when I'm pretending to look away.

I'm going to ask her to leave.

I wonder if she'll tell anyone about Karl. I wonder if she's already told.

Thank goodness Karl doesn't live here anymore. Several weeks after the funeral, Micah and Jessie asked me to spend a weekend on their yacht. It was a pure pity invitation, proffered reluctantly after I got tear stains on Jessie's sheer blouse. To their extreme disappointment, I accepted.

I brought Karl along for our final date, his corpse still in the cooler, hidden under a tarp and bottles of fancy wine. While Micah and Jessie were drinking in the hot tub, I dumped Karl into the sea. Then I scoured the cooler with bleach and left it in the ship's pantry.

If the police search the attic, they will find nothing. Poppy will appear to be a desperate, greedy, jealous woman, and no one will believe her.

Yes, I see the irony.

For now, the police are leaving me alone. The blog posts about Silicon Valley's own Black Widow are beginning to dwindle. I spend my days caring for my children and looking after my health. I take my medication, eat healthy vegan meals, and get regular, restorative exercise. My heart is less flighty and more grounded. It seems that I might live.

In some ways, I have the peaceful, seamless, financially secure life I always wanted.

Briar and Rose, now almost three, are thriving. Bored mothers who want a glimpse of the notorious widow invite them over for play dates.

We're always happy to accept. Briar tries to overcome her shyness. Rose tries not to break anything. I smile politely and promise to download apps and visit websites.

Even my stubbornly soft body has firmed up. I am a regular at a yoga studio, and I can gaze into the mirror at the front of the room with only mild shame. I look ten years younger than I did six months ago. After next month's nip and tuck, I will look younger still.

The other day, I took an Ashtanga class. The instructor was new, young with a wild mop of dark, curly hair. Her quick movements suggested a bird that was about to fly away. She watched me intently. I thought she must recognize me. I was a minor celebrity around town, the tragic and possibly murderous widow.

As I gathered my mat, I felt gentle pressure on my arm. It was the yogini, and her face was equal parts hope and horror. "Julia?" she asked. "Is it you?"

"I'm sorry," I said softly. "I'm not Julia."

As I walked to my car, I felt the warm sun on the back of my neck. My heartbeat was steady and strong. I remembered Julia and felt a hot pulse of pity. Poor Julia had become me. She swallowed my life, and it poisoned her.

I walked past the parking garage towards a dealership full of Harleys and Hondas and Royal Enfields. I realized that, if I wanted a motorcycle, I could just walk in and buy one. Maybe next time, I will. After all, I deserve it. I've done a lot this year. I tried polyamory. Spied on my husband's girlfriend. Killed my traitorous husband in self-defense. Survived my unruly heart. And disposed of my ex-boyfriend's corpse.

No, I'm not Julia or Poppy, and I never will be.

I'm Helen, and perhaps that's good enough.

BEFORE YOU GO

If you enjoyed this story, please consider leaving a review. Even if it's just a line or two, I would love to hear your thoughts.

If you spotted a typo or other "bug" and you'd like to tell me about it, please feel free to email me at lizella.prescott@gmail.com

Thank you!

OTHER WORKS & WEBLINKS

How to connect

ARC giveaways and occasional free books: https://lizellaprescott.com

Short fiction: https://medium.com/@lizellaprescott

Goodreads: https://www.goodreads.com/LizellaPrescott

Other works by Lizella Prescott

Death Chase

The Girl Who Covers Her Hair

The Half Life of Shadows

Milk Teeth

Persephone: The Life and Untimely Death of a Goddess

Made in the USA
Middletown, DE
02 April 2020